Unfathomable

A Novel

by Rose Moon

Flying Javalina Press

Printed in the United States of America.

1 2 3 4 5 6 7 8 9 10

ISBN-13: 978-0692053010

This book is dedicated to

Rik, Jasmine and Jeff

Acknowledgments

This story would never have been told without the encouragement and help from my husband Rik Farrow or the writing instructions from Gary Every and Michael Cosentino. Thanks to my neighbor Rob Allen for advice about police and for he and his partner Jim Padgett for setting an example of a joyful gay couple. Nancy White took the raw manuscript and put it into a format that the publisher would accept. Many thanks to my friend Suzanne Klotz who shoved me into a new reality where I believed I could accomplish greater things. My poetry group, Constance Patrick, Ann Duchaine, Martha Entin, and Liz Hargrove, Mary Scully Whitaker, thanks for your encouragement and help with editing.I had no idea how much work I was going to pile on you. I'm indebted to spiritual teachers Adyashanti and Brad Warner. And Alberto Rios, Arizona Poet Laureate who showed me how my art and writing fit into the genre of Magical Realism.

Many of the paintings described in this book can be found at https://www.rosemoon.net/.

Table of Contents

1: Kidnapped

"We're both going to get fired," Granger said.

He was slumped in the chair on the other side of my desk still wearing his dusty sculpture clothes. It was the end of a long workday and I wasn't in the mood for putting up with his customary rant about the end of the art department. But Granger seemed unusually stressed, so I leaned back in my chair and went along for the ride yet another time.

"So what have you heard now?" I asked, doing my best to look interested.

"While I was in the storage closet looking for some chisels, I overheard the secretary of the dean talking on her cell," he told me. His face looked twisted, almost cubistic, like I could see the many facets of his emotions. Most of all, Granger looked both scared and angry.

"What was she doing in the sculpture lab?"

"She's taking a class from me."

"You're serious?" This brought me forward in my chair. Not because I was concerned, but because I thought it was funny.

"She was upset because she loves my class. She was telling somebody that the art department would be completely dismantled within two years."

"How would she know that?"

"She knows everything. She has big ears and a big mouth to go with them."

I could see that image too. And a big imagination, I thought to myself.

I took the book I'd been studying off my desk, swiveled my chair, and placed it on the shelf behind me. When I turned back, Granger was sitting up straighter and looking at me with his striking blue eyes. I had known Granger since we were children living on the same street, and I knew what that look meant. He needed a reassuring answer which I'd learned to provide over the many years I'd spent hanging out with him.

"If that happens we will start our own school," I assured him.

Then we both laughed. Which seemed to almost jar him out of his dismal mood.

"Sure, when javalina sprout wings and fly," he said.

We sat there silently gazing out of my tiny second floor window. A couple of students were hanging out below us as the sun dropped low in the sky, causing their shadows to extend so long it made their bodies appear dwarfed. Those same students seemed to always meet there at this time of day. It was a mystery to me, and had inspired the painting I was working on in my home studio.

Even though I tried to dismiss Granger's paranoia, I had a gut feeling there were big changes on the horizon. I probably thought if I reacted calmly to his observations something would happen that would make our concerns magically disappear. Somebody at the top would get fired; someone new would come in and set things straight or the state would elect a liberal governor.

No matter what, I had no control over any of this. If there was a big change headed my way, I didn't want to think about it yet. I was far too focused on being the best art teacher I could be, and that didn't allow me to make other plans right now. If the art department got cut, I would deal with it then. But I took into account what my friend was telling me and I was grateful for the warning.

"I'm sorry you had to hear that," I finally said to him as I closed my laptop and began shoving it into it's bag. I told him I would think about what he had said. However, I had a painting waiting for me at my home studio that was occupying my mind and I was in a hurry to leave so I could get back to it.

We said our goodbyes in the hallway and he headed back to his sculpture lab. I walked to my car thinking only about getting home and putting in a couple of hours of painting before dark. There was never enough time to work on my own art.

I got into my car, thinking about how I might try a little metallic auto paint in the sunset behind the students, causing them to appear even darker, almost silhouettes. Auto paint was toxic so I would only use a small amount – maybe work on it outdoors. If I could find an oil paint that could give me that same shiny effect, I would use it, but I didn't know of any.

I drove out of the teachers' parking lot and the five miles to my home on Hohokam Street not remembering that I had planned to stop and shop for dinner. As I headed towards my driveway I thought about the word 'Hohokam' which means the disappearing people. They were a tribe that once lived in the Phoenix area thousands of years ago who vanished from the planet all at once, and no one knows why.

Junipers blocked the view of my house from the street and there was only a small, almost invisible, gravel driveway that led to my garage. I opened the garage door with the remote, drove into it, and vanished from the rest of the world.

2

Inside the front door, I stripped off my uncomfortable dress before I even reached the bedroom. I threw it onto the bed and slipped on my painting clothes. I was relieved to find leftovers in the fridge because that meant I didn't have to turn around and drive back to the store. I ate out of a CorningWare container, shoving leftover lasagna into my mouth as if I were filling a car with gas. It was energy and not something I was spending time savoring. I put the dish into the sink and filled it with water to soak. There were never enough hours in a day to be creative both in the kitchen and in the studio.

Later that night, while I pushed to finish the painting, my phone rang. I wanted to let the call go to voicemail, but I needed a break, so I wiped the paint off of my hands and picked up.

"Are you Ms. Donahue?" a deep male voice asked.

"Yes, I am."

"My name is Gamache. I'm an FBI agent and I'm working on an art theft case. Your number was given to me by Jim Sanders from the Phoenix Art Museum."

"What can I do for you, Mr. Gamache?"

"Would you be interested in helping me on a case? I need somebody who knows art history to give me some advice. I don't know how long I will need you, but I can guarantee that you will be well paid."

I didn't think to ask him why not talk to Jim, the museum director, who knew knew more about art history than I did. But then again, I thought my friend might be out of town or too busy to help the agent. When I thought about it later, I hated to admit that Granger's rumbling about the possible closing of the art department played into my being open to trying something new.

The agent continued, "Would you be willing to meet with me tomorrow morning at 8:00 AM at the museum? I have a lot of questions and I want you to look at some images."

I'm not sure why I didn't just say email them to me, but I didn't have classes the next day and a trip to the museum seemed like a welcome break from my rigid routine. I said I'd be there. Then I thought *Gamache*, where have I heard that name before?

"Great," he said. "The museum won't be open, so park in the back near the loading docks and come in the back door. Our investigation will be taking place in some rooms in the back. We have a lot of things to go over."

"Sure," I said. "In the back."

"See you tomorrow," he said cheerfully.

I don't know why I didn't ask more questions or call Jim to find out what was going on. Instead I called Granger and left a message for him to meet me there too. Perhaps my mind was focused on the painting sitting on my easel. There was something not quite right about it. The painting should have been finished, but it wasn't. The two dark figures in front of a metallic orange sunset needed something, but I wasn't sure what. I played around with it for another couple of hours, cleaned up, set my alarm for 6:00 AM and went to bed. Paintings often told me what they needed after I left them alone for a while. I was sure I'd get back to it after the meeting.

The following morning, I grumbled about having made the commitment to meet with the agent. Because I was going to the museum, I felt the need to find the proper dress, and I was in no mood to wear one. I only wanted to throw on some jeans and get back to work on my painting. I tried on several and selected a soft grey one, which I accented with silver and turquoise jewelry. I ate a quick breakfast, took one last glance at the painting, and feeling somewhat better about it, I left my house looking for adventure.

That day I decided not to take the freeway, driving instead through neighborhoods. I liked looking at the different houses, trying to imagine why all these people chose to live in the Southwest. Some of the neighborhoods were struggling, others were thriving. It seemed to me that no matter what the circumstances, people were living in a precarious place called Planet Earth. And here in the desert, life seemed even more fragile with soaring temperatures, heavy traffic, rattlesnakes, spiders and scorpions.

It was November and the parks and streets were busy with pedestrians: moms or dads pushing strollers, people walking dogs, children playing games, runners passing elderly people strolling. The air was fresh and cool. In Phoenix, local people hibernated in the summer and came out in fall and winter. Snowbirds landed and doubled the population. It was now party time in the desert city.

I reached the area behind the museum through a narrow alley. The backs of windowless buildings turned the employee lot into a canyon. There was only one parked vehicle – a huge white van which I assumed belonged to the agent. I was early for the meeting so I got out of my car and took time to look at the sky between the cliffs of the surrounding buildings. To an untrained eye, the sky would have appeared clear blue. To me it was a layering of many colors: ultramarine blue, cadmium orange and maybe a touch of alizarin crimson. I took out my phone and snapped a few images, knowing that I could never really capture the essence of that sky in a painting by looking at a photo. But I hoped the photo would help me remember the layers

I could see.

I was standing near my car when it happened. I'd sensed nothing prior to it – no footsteps on the pavement. No car door thumps or slams. My abductors were silent, strong and nimble like ninjas. A couple of bodies overpowered mine with martial arts holds – any movement I made caused excruciating pain in my wrists and shoulders. I tried to scream, but before I could get any sound out, someone forced a cloth smelling sharply of ether over my mouth and nose and stifled any noise I might have made. Consciousness faded and my knees folded. Someone had me by the shoulders and arms. Someone else grabbed my legs and caught me before I hit the pavement. In my mind I was putting up a huge fight, but in reality my body went limp.

Before I completely passed out I was aware of being loaded into the van, placed on a mat and held down by two hooded people. Everything had happened suddenly, soundlessly, and as gracefully as a ballet. If there had been a soundtrack it wouldn't be something exciting from a thriller movie – it would have been a lullaby.

As I began to recover from the ether, there was a loud ringing in my ears. I could tell I was in a moving vehicle. Tires were whirring on a highway, sounds of wind rushing and other cars whizzing by. All these familiar noises I had always taken for granted were now screaming in the forefront of my consciousness. As I tried to look around to see who was holding me, I could feel my body vibrating from the bumps in the road. Was I seeing double or were there two figures dressed in black with ski masks and hoods?

Jesus, I'm in a movie! I told myself. I must keep calm, but my body wasn't listening to any advice from my brain. My heart was pounding and I needed to throw up. Whoever these people were, they were prepared. I had been strapped to some kind of padded board which they easily tilted to the side in time to catch my vomit in a container. Someone wiped my mouth and face and gave me water to rinse out my mouth.

I struggled to sit up, but the straps held me to the board. I heard someone telling me to relax, that everything was going to be all right, that I would not be harmed. Then came a prick in my arm and the feeling of pressure beneath the skin—an injection!

Within a few minutes my body was paralyzed. I was sort of out of it but not completely unconscious. I wasn't sure if the sweat I smelled was mine, or if it was the two dark figures sitting on either side of me. I could hear people talking, but I wasn't sure if the sounds were coming from the people in the van or if they were voices in my head. Then there was music. Thank God there was music. It carried me away. What was it? Yo Yo Ma playing Bach?

As the drug took me deeper, I became convinced that the vehicle had turned into a space ship. We left the road and the land far below. We left the state of Arizona, then floated above the earth. I grabbed the edges of the mat, trying to hold on. I felt as though I was being transported up through the clouds and out into the Universe where I could see stars, planets, and galaxies. Everything felt alien and frigid. I knew somehow the nebulas were not real since they looked more like Photoshop-enhanced photos taken by the Hubble Space Telescope. This had to be something happening in my own mind. The music sounded like it had drifted into the far distance and had become the rumbling engine that drove the ship. Yet the music remained a lifeline that connected me to earth.

I started asking myself questions, like why did people want to travel in space? Were they trying by any means to escape taking responsibility for the planet they were not just on, but were actually a part of? I suddenly felt like I'd been trying to escape a life that kept me from questioning the real reason for my existence. Each time these thoughts arose, they quickly scattered into millions of pieces.

A powerful longing for home took over – not a thought but a feeling. Was longing a word on my list of possible human emotions? I'm certain it had to be there on the list, but what I was feeling didn't seem like any emotion I'd ever felt before. I watched that deep longing for earth become an actual threadlike umbilical cord which was unwinding behind me. At a certain point it began tugging me gently back to the planet, like there was some mystical force that would not let me go any further.

I noticed that the powerful longing had morphed into a deep desire for home and the planet from which human beings could never be separated. Yes, that was the illusive feeling – a merging of longing and desire. Wasn't desire a controversial drive that had been deemed evil by most religions? But wasn't it desire that brought humans to earth in the first place? It moved the will, caused conception, and birth.

Thoughts like these kept coming, then floating off into the Universe, and bursting like bubbles until there was nothing to remember, nothing to hold on to.

My mind kept floating away from the actual experience of being strapped to a board in a moving van. My awareness sailed away as if it wasn't at all attached to the body that I knew was filled with terror and anxiety. I could feel my heart pounding, chills running up and down my spine, and tears running down my cheeks. Yet there was also a sense of eternal freedom.

In my mind's eye I watched a slow motion animated version of John

Lennon's drawing of a man passing through a woman. The title of that piece was *Just Passing Through*. That vision jerked my mind once again out of philosophical thinking mode for a while, and I rested in a state of silent being.

Soon I sensed my body softly landing on the surface of the earth. I also knew it wasn't really happening, that I was still in the van. I began feeling that I was lying on desert sand, roots growing from my backside, digging and searching for moisture. Branches sprouted out of my womb, covered with pale green serrated leaves and long sharp thorns. The bush bloomed with tiny white flowers that morphed into small red berries which I generously offered to a litter of coyote pups.

I was soon able to sit up on the desert floor to look at the landscape and at the same time knew I was also still in the van. I could feel the vibration of the road rushing by beneath me and I wondered which direction we were headed. I was definitely in two places at once.

The me that was sitting in the desert began to see a shimmering image of a man standing off in the distance. Behind him, there was a mirage of sparkling water and pale blue mountains looming in the far distance. He started walking towards me and I thought I rubbed my eyes to try and make out who he was. He wasn't coming into focus, but somehow I knew he was Diego Valdez, my favorite author and spiritual teacher, the one who had drawn me to the Southwest, looking for some kind of life beyond what I thought was the mundane world.

In high school and years into college, Granger and I had devoured Valdez's books. While other students were caught up with super heroes, musicians and movie stars, we read and re-read his nine books over and over, imagining that we would one day live our lives like the sorcerers he wrote about.

"Who are you and what are you doing here?" Valdez asked. He sat down beside me on a flat rock. I could clearly see him.

"I'm Laurence, I'm Laurence, I'm Laurence." I wasn't sure why I said it so many times. I felt embarrassed. Was I saying it out loud or was this all in my head? Did it even matter? Was I even really here? I thought I was in a van somewhere.

"It doesn't matter," a voice said. "You don't look like a Laurence."

"My dad gave me a boy's name," I explained. "He thought it would help me be more successful in life." Then for a moment I thought I was riding in a van talking out loud to nobody.

"How has that worked for you?" he asked. I snapped into paying attention to the man.

"I don't know. I have nothing else to compare it with," I told him.

"Fair enough," he said. "So, what do you want from me?"

"What do you want from me?" I asked back.

"Hey, you contacted me, so what is it you want from me?" He seemed grumpy.

"Oh, I didn't know I contacted you, and I'm not sure I want anything you haven't already given me."

"Good answer," he said. "You pass." He held out his hand to offer me a diploma. I reached out to receive it but it dissolved before my hand could touch it. Then I wondered if that had really happened.

"What? Pass what?" I asked. "Is this an exam?"

He laughed. "I think I like you after all," he said solemnly. "This isn't exactly as it seems."

"What isn't exactly as it seems?" I sat up straighter and faced him squarely, making eye contact. He had soft, deer eyes.

"This – all this." He waved his hands as if to indicate absolutely everything.

"Yes, I know." It surprised me that I said that. So what was it that I was professing to know? Again it didn't seem to matter. So what was the matter? Or maybe the real question is what *is* matter?

That's when I felt the molecules dancing in my body. I could hear them too. It was a familiar sound even though I had never actually heard them before. No one had to tell me they were molecules. I just knew.

"That's it," he said. "It's energy. Little molecules doing their dance. You and everything else."

Of course, I knew that, but never had I heard and felt it like this. "It's the sound of the universe," he said. "You recall all those nasty tricks my master used to play on me? Sometimes he was trying to get me to experience this sound, and you're hearing it at full volume right now. Ketamine is a great drug! Too bad you will probably forget all about this tomorrow and be back in ordinary reality again. Sorry. But don't worry, what you experience on a journey like this never completely goes away. The trouble with using drugs is that it only gives you a preview. You'll have to get back here on your own without the drug. Remember, my master told me he only gave me psychedelics because I was so stupid."

He laughed out loud at himself. "I was a twenty year old smart-ass on the way to becoming a professor like you, and I thought I knew everything. I felt I certainly knew more than that dumb Indian who later became my teacher. You are not like me though, you never totally bought that conditioned

8

program like I did. Besides, you read my books when you were a mere child."

"I don't understand," I said

"Of course you do," he said.

"Where am I? What is happening to me? Please tell me." I sounded desperate. I tried to grab hold of his sleeve, but my hand passed through him.

"Well, my dear, those are questions that may never get answered. That's because of the *Unknowable*. Remember, the *Unknowable*? Don't ever forget that and you will always be just where you are." His voice was fading, and then he was gone. He evaporated like all the thoughts I'd been having. A sadness settled in on me like a heavy wool blanket.

"Don't leave me," I begged. Tears ran down my cheeks. "Not now, not when I am...? What? What am I? Wow! Not that 'what am I' question again."

Then I found myself walking alone on the desert among saguaros, the blasting white sun above. I couldn't tell if it was hot or cold. I shivered. One of the cactuses spoke out loud in a deep resonant voice.

"What did you say?" I asked. It didn't answer me. But the tall, stately-looking cactus next to it responded. They were speaking an alien language, but I seemed to get the gist of what they were saying. It went something like, "Get a load of that." The other one said, "Seems harmless to me." They were watching me intently, and so were the birds, insects and tiny mammals who made their homes in these high rise apartments. On rare occasions when I had actually walked in the desert, I never thought that the desert was looking back at me.

"Pardon me," I said to the two giants. "I think I'm being abducted. Do you have a cell phone?" I could suddenly hear traffic whizzing by the van.

They stood still like they normally do, acting like ordinary cactus. There you go, I thought. Ordinary reality.

"Well, if you do, would you mind calling 901 or 191?" I thought I heard another saguaro off in the distance giggle.

I sat down in the sand again, or I thought I did. I remembered a story of the Buddha. So I put my hands on the earth to steady myself like he once did, and somehow I knew nothing could actually go wrong. Yes, there was good and evil, joy and despair, and there was no escaping it, yet all that mattered to me now was the realization of dancing molecules, the sound of them, the smell and look of them, as though I had never bothered to notice them or rather, know them. I wanted so much to share all of this with Granger. "Granger," I said out loud. I knew I said it out loud in the van. No one responded.

9

I could tell when the van actually did leave the highway. I felt it slow down and make a turn, but I couldn't tell whether it went left or right. When it turned I kept spinning for a while after it had straightened out. It moved slower on a bumpy road or maybe off-road. It made a few more turns, and still the spinning happened every time, and I never figured out in which direction I was whirling. Then we went straight for what seemed like hundreds of miles. But I sensed it might be the drug stretching time. I confessed to myself that I really didn't know. Finally, I let go of trying to understand and surrendered to the dreaming which seemed to go on for a very long time. Some of it I would remember bit by bit later on.

Much later, I opened my eyes again and could actually see out of them. I slowly became aware I was no longer in a moving vehicle. I was on a bed in a softly lit room. I was not being raped, tortured or murdered in a filthy warehouse. Maybe that was to come later—I didn't know. It was the *Unknowable* after all. For now I honestly didn't care because I desperately needed to pee! But when I tried to move I thought I was tied to the bed, so I relaxed, thinking I might say something and let someone know my needs. But maybe that wasn't such a good idea. Perhaps not calling attention to myself could save my life.

I tried to move again, but information sent to my extremities from my brain went something like this: "Are you still down there, feet?"

"Yep," they said. "We can hear you and we know what you need."

"Well?"

"Well what?"

"Move already!" I shouted.

"Nope, can't!"

"Damn it!" I was seriously going to wet the bed.

I turned my head and looked around the room. There on the floor beside the bed was a bucket. If only I could make it to that bucket. With great effort I willed myself to sit up and once I had my goal in mind, I began to feel my extremities struggle to do the best they could. They were heavy and awkward. I slowly inched my legs toward the side of the bed and slid over the edge like a melting cartoon figure. I crawled over to the bucket, and maneuvered myself over it, making it just in time. It was the first time I was thankful I had on a dress. The bed seemed too tall to get back on, so I collapsed on the floor beside it gazing up at the ceiling. It had a smooth white surface with exposed beams exactly like my ceiling at home.

I lay there thinking about how often I had wondered about people in TV shows and movies who were tied up for hours or even days without going to the bathroom. This was real life wasn't it? And my captors had provided a bucket.

I closed my eyes and fell back asleep. When I woke up again it was easier to move. I sat up on the floor and climbed back onto the bed, and pushed myself up to the headboard in a sitting position where I could get a better look around the dimly lit room. It was much bigger than I first thought and it seemed to be fully furnished. I could make out a small kitchen and a table with two chairs. In another area there was a couch, and maybe a desk with a computer. And beyond, was that an easel? I saw windows high up near the ceiling. It was dark outside. The clock on the table near the bed that told me it was 1:53 AM and I was still too drugged to get up and walk around. I sank down into the bed, pulled up the soft comforter and gave way to another deep sleep.

In my vivid dreams I was back at the university having coffee with Granger and talking about the Dada period and the work of Max Ernst and Dorothea Tanning and the time these two world renowned artists had lived in Sedona, Arizona. How did these people land in a place so far away from New York and Paris? I floated around in Dorothea's surrealistic images, seeing myself lying on the artist's dream bed surrounded by unexplainable entities. Even in my dreams I was deeply aware things were not going back to normal anytime soon. Then I was standing in a hallway in one of Dorothea's paintings, my own long red hair standing straight up in the air, while some mythical animal with wings sat at my feet. I had crawled into her painting called "Birthday."

2: Granger

Ten minutes late as usual, Granger parked next to Laurence's red Prius in the parking lot behind the art museum where she had told him to park. It was the only car in the lot. He discovered the back door of the museum was locked, so he walked around the building and tried the front door, which was also locked. He wondered why there were no other cars around, since it was supposed to be a meeting.

He listened to her voice mail message again. Damn, I should have called her back, he thought. He returned to the back door and waited for ten minutes, then decided to have breakfast at the Golden Egg down the street. He thought she and the FBI agent must have gone somewhere in the agent's car. He felt guilty for being late and disappointed for missing an interesting meeting about an art theft, and, who knows, a possible opportunity for a new career.

Perhaps the meeting was taking place at the restaurant. Even though it was not a hot day he was sweating. Something just didn't feel right, but he brushed the thought from his mind, walked half a block to the restaurant, ordered eggs, toast and a medley of potatoes. He read the New York Times on his cell phone while he waited for his food. The news was depressing as usual. Nothing was ever favorable for art when Republicans were in office. He actually knew some artists who were Republicans and could never figure that out. But then again weren't Republicans famous for cutting off their noses to spite their faces, notorious for shooting their own feet?

And what about women? There were women Republicans which made even less sense than artist Republicans. At least there were fewer gays.

Were these thoughts making him sad or was it something else? Why did he feel so sad? He put his phone down like he never meant to pick it up again. When his food arrived, he forced himself to smile at the waitress. He could, at least, do that. He made himself stop criticizing himself for judging his least favorite political party. Maybe someday I'll get over that, he thought. Well, maybe not until they stop acting so insane. There I go again!

A little after ten he walked back to the museum to check if Laurence's car was still in the lot. It was there next to his, and now both of their cars were surrounded by others. He tried the back door of the museum again and found it still locked, so he strolled around to the front of the building and went into the main entry to the reception area, where he waited impatiently for visitors to purchase tickets. He fidgeted while they asked endless questions, as though no one else was in line. Finally he spoke to the receptionist. "I'm Granger Sun and I'm here for a meeting about an art theft."

"Really?" She gave him a questioning look and said, "Hold on." She picked up the phone and punched one button.

"Jim, someone is here about an art theft. Granger Sun?" she whispered into the phone not wanting others to hear, then she listened for a few seconds, smiled at Granger and said, "He'll be right out."

Granger kept wondering if he had gotten Laurence's message right. He chastised himself for not returning her call the night before, and blamed his incompetence on the fact that he and George had finally sat down at their dining table and began making a list of people they wanted to invite to their wedding. He had intended to call her after they were finished, but then it was nearly midnight. He wondered if he was feeling off because he was nervous about getting married. He loved George and had no doubts about wanting to spend the rest of his life with him, but weddings were stressful.

He pulled out his cell and tried to call her again. Still no answer. He wasn't surprised. She rarely answered her phone, but always returned calls right away. It had been nearly two hours since he had last tried her number.

When Jim walked in, tall, straight and dressed in an expensive suit, Granger was suddenly aware he was indeed in the museum. He felt self-conscious in his casual khakis and brightly colored short sleeve shirt. He didn't even own a suit.

"Nice to see you, Granger," Jim said, offering a warm handshake. "What's this about a theft?"

"Oh," he stammered thinking for sure he'd made a huge mistake, but remembered her car was in the lot. "Laurence Donahue told me to come here for a meeting with the FBI."

"Seriously? I don't know anything about that, Granger. Let's take a walk and see what we can find out." Several large groups of people had begun to gather in the reception area so Jim led him out of the room and down a quiet hallway, where Granger replayed Laurence's message on his phone's speaker about meeting the FBI agent at the museum. The two men stood staring at the phone as if it might explain itself.

Finally Jim said, "There haven't been any thefts in the ten years that I've worked here. This is really weird. Lets check the back door."

They continued down the hallway, Granger catching sight of paintings flying by in his peripheral vision. They passed the museum restaurant where the air was filled with the smell of cinnamon rolls and coffee, then took a right turn that lead to an enormous garage door. Jim placed the palm of his hand on a screen; locks clicked and the heavy door slowly rolled up. They entered a huge receiving room lined with boxes that most likely once held paintings. Granger was reminded of the antique car show he had once seen at the museum. So that's how they got the cars in, he thought. The place was immaculate. At the back of the room there were two doors, one just for people and a huge garage-like door for art delivery. Everything looked solid and seriously locked. Jim explained the state-of-the-art alarm system on all of the entries.

"No meetings ever occur anywhere near this place. No visitor would be let in through this door, or told to park in back unless they were delivering or picking up artwork or supplies. There is employee-only parking but not even the employees enter or leave through the backdoor." He grabbed the handle to show Granger that nothing moved. "Only myself and one other employee have the codes to unlock the doors. I can assure you nothing has come or gone through these doors today. If you rattle them around much the alarm goes off and we get a call from the security company. Let's go out and check her car."

They didn't exit the building from the back. Instead they walked back through the long hall and reception room, out the front door, and around to where Laurence had parked. Squinting in the bright sunlight, they examined her car. Nothing looked unusual. The only thing they could see inside of it was a straw sun hat on the back seat. Granger didn't mention that he had a key to her car. It didn't seem right at this point to be snooping around inside of it.

"Maybe she's in the museum looking at the exhibits," Jim suggested.

"I think we'd better take a look," said Granger.

The two men thoroughly checked each gallery in the museum and Granger told all of the docents and guards they were looking for a woman with long red hair but couldn't tell them what she was wearing. Jim had his secretary put in calls to all the employees in the museum complex.

After that Jim said, "I don't know what we can do right now, Granger. Maybe she took off with some friends, maybe had breakfast and went shopping. You know how women are."

Granger knew how women were, but he also knew how Lawrence was. She wouldn't be out shopping with friends. Also, there was that message on his

15

phone from her. She would never have changed her mind and not let him know. He was worried and wanted to call the police, but he knew they wouldn't do anything right away. Most likely they would assume the same thing Jim did.

The two men exchanged numbers and agreed to contact one another if anything turned up. Granger watched the tall man's back disappear into an office at the end of a hallway, but he wasn't ready to leave the building. He had coffee in the museum restaurant. He chatted with waitresses and visitors, casually asking anyone he could if they had seen a woman with long red hair. He spent hours staring at art, trying to take his mind off what was happening. He went back outside and stood in the parking lot next to her car, leaned against it, looked under and around it, even searched the bushes behind the lot. He called George, left a message and George called back in a matter of minutes.

"Hey, what's up?" he asked, sounding like he knew already that something was urgent.

"I'm here at the museum and Laurence's car is here, but there was no art theft, no FBI agent, and I don't know where she is. She doesn't pick up when I call."

There was silence on the line while George gathered his thoughts. "Well, that's weird. What do you think happened?"

Granger was relieved to finally talk to somebody who sincerely thought the situation was weird – someone who knew Laurence well. "What do you think I should do?"

Another pause on George's end. "Maybe you should come to the cafe and hang out with me for a while. I know it's scary and you're concerned – as you should be – but I don't think there is anything you can do right now."

He told George that was the same thing Jim had said.

"Well, I think he's right. For now you just have to wait until something turns up." Usually George had a calming affect on him, but Granger felt more worried now than he had before he called. It was one of those times he would have preferred to hear a lie.

Before he left, he checked Lawrence's car over one more time, then talked himself into believing he was over-reacting. He reluctantly got into his car and drove towards Scottsdale.

3: Waking Up

Waking up suddenly from a fitful dream-filled sleep, I pulled the covers over my head to block out sunlight from the small windows near the ceiling; leaving only a tiny slit in the covers where I could peek out. At first I wasn't sure if I was alone. The clock on the bedside table told me it was 10:07 AM. I strained to see or hear my captors, staying under the covers for almost an hour trying to make sense of the surroundings. When I was sure no one else was in the room, I finally stuck out my whole head.

I had to pee again and saw the bucket I had used the night before. But when I finally got the courage to sit all the way up, I saw what I thought might actually be a bathroom. When I tried to move, everything started to spin, and my legs felt so heavy I feared I might stomp a hole in the floor if I tried to walk. I did anyway, and the feeling of my feet hitting the floor made me think I had on metal shoes. I made it to the door that I thought was a bathroom, and indeed it was. Not just a bathroom, but a really nice one. It could have been in a five star hotel. There was a shower, a sink, and a stack of fluffy towels.

I sat on the toilet looking down at my wrinkled dress. The vomit in my hair made me feel nauseated and I nearly threw up again. I badly wanted to strip naked and hop into the shower, but that seemed completely weird under the circumstances.

Before I used the toothbrush lying on the counter, I slung my hair into the sink and tried to rinse out the smell. It helped a little, but nothing short of a good scrubbing was going get me back to some semblance of acceptable hygiene. First, I needed to make sure I was alone.

With a towel around my head I cracked open the bathroom door and tried to see if anyone was there. Still too dizzy to stand up for long, I staggered out of the bathroom, stumbled across the room and collapsed onto a bright blue sofa, then dragged a beautiful woven afghan from the back of it and wrapped myself in it. It was soft and warm, and I hoped it would stop my shivering. I wasn't cold. I was shaking from sheer terror. I was still too dizzy to get up and search for an exit. My head already felt like I might have been hit with something hard, so I didn't want to take any chances of falling. My eyesight was blurry and sometimes I was seeing double, but I felt around on my head and found no bumps or scrapes. All I could do was close my eyes and lay my head back and try to take slow, deep breaths. No matter how many times I told myself to relax, it wasn't going to happen anytime soon.

Later when I opened my eyes again I could see more clearly and was startled to find the spacious room closely resembled my own house, only without doors or accessible windows. So how did they get me in here? I tried to stand, but felt too weak, fell back on the sofa, this time laying my head on the arm, stretching my legs out, and sailing off into dreamland again.

What seemed like hours later I woke up disappointed to still be alone in this strange place. I so much wanted to find myself in my own home discovering that I had had a very bad dream. I stood up, which was easier to do now, and I felt slightly stronger and more awake. The first thing I needed to do was explore the walls for a possible exit. I desperately needed to pull myself together, so I forced myself to move.

The windows were too high to see out of and too small to climb through. But somehow the ninjas had to have gotten me in here. The place was a creepy version of my own house fashioned into a luxury prison. It reminded me of a movie, adapted from a book written by John Fowles, I had been required to watch in college called the *The Collector*. I remembered that particular film because it was so horrifying to me that someone would stalk and kidnap a female artist. The perpetrator had learned everything about her, then captured her and put her into a place he had built just for her, all in the hopes that she would fall in love with him. Remembering that, I held my hand tightly over my mouth to keep from screaming. I didn't want to make any sounds in case someone, perhaps in another room, might hear me. I walked around the whole place with my hand over my mouth taking in as much as I could. Oh my God, it was like the movie! At first glance I could see that this one room house was, indeed, a smaller replica of my own home in Phoenix. I began to expect a crazy man to appear and inform me that I now belonged to him.

Frantically, I tore open the kitchen cabinets and refrigerator and found the same food products I had in my own home. There was clothing in the bathroom closet which brought me only a little relief since they did not match my own wardrobe at home, like how it had been in the movie. I found underwear, hospital scrubs, and a stack of t-shirts of various colors. What the hell? Prison clothes!

I went to the desk where I had seen the iMac exactly like the one I had at home. I started it up and saw that there was a message for me from someone

called Max. I sat down and gave it a lot of thought before I opened it.
It said.

Max: *Hello, Laurence, no doubt you are scared and confused. First of all, you need to know you will not be harmed. Of course, you already have been, and we agree it was quite a jarring experience being yanked from a parking lot, drugged and then dumped into a strange place.*

In time you will understand the meaning of our chosen method. It had to look to the world like you were kidnapped and not appear as if you had taken off on your own. The police and everyone you know will believe that, and actually, it is true. You will, no doubt, have many questions and we will do our best to answer what we can without causing you more confusion than necessary, but for now we will outline some basic guidelines so we can get started on our project.

What project? I said out loud. This is not my project. I was not in on the planning stage of this. I leaned forward in my chair thinking that if looked hard enough at the screen I would be able to see someone in it. All I could do was continue reading.

Max: *The last thing we want to do is do harm to you. We hope your stay here will be pleasant and that you will be able to engage in some of the art projects you've been wanting to do. No doubt you will miss your friends, school, and family. But you will be able to work full time on your own artwork. We will provide you with whatever you need.*

In exchange for food and supplies you will give us your work as it is finished. The paintings will be done on canvases that roll up and fit into tubes. There is a cabinet near the kitchen containing a dumb waiter which will carry them up to the roof where they will be retrieved by drones. You will receive supplies through the same portal.

You don't have to start work immediately. You will no doubt need to settle in and get yourself oriented and come to terms with where you are.

Since you are reading this you have discovered the computer. You will only be able to message us and receive messages from us. You have access to parts of the internet for research and images. You can use Netflix, Audible and iBooks for entertainment.

There is a digital camera, laptop, and an iPad in the desk drawer.

There are cameras in the room, but they will only be on until we know you are all right. We would like you to check in daily, but you can contact us anytime you need or want day or night. For now we will be your only human contact. Don't worry about your friends. They will be missing you but we will let them know in various ways you are alive and well.

I'm sure you are totally disoriented and have lots of feelings. Please know that you can communicate anything at anytime.

I sat back in my chair and stared in disbelief. What the fuck? I reread the message several times then sent a response.

Laurence: *Who are you and why are you doing this?*
Max: *These are not questions you need to have answered right now. In time you will understand the big picture.*

This must be a chatline, not an email, I thought. Someone was right there waiting for my response. I sat still pondering the situation before I wrote back.

Laurence: *How long are you planning on keeping me here?*
Max: *As long as it takes.*
Laurence: *What is that supposed to mean?*
Max: *I understand your concern. This is only your first day and you should be going through your feelings and getting yourself oriented to your environment. There is food for you, and more will be delivered. For now this is your home. No one will bother you, so live in it like you would in your home in Phoenix. Laurence, you can get something out of this, or you can fight it. I suggest you use it to your advantage. It's up to you.*

I wanted to respond FUCK YOU in large capital letters, but I thought it might not be a good idea. It didn't make sense to enrage these people who were obviously insane and in control. For now, I thought, maybe the best thing for me to do is act like I'm going along with everything. Obviously, it's not going to help me if I fight with them. But GOD I'M PISSED! I took a long time to respond. I stood up and pulled at my hair, and let out a really loud scream, but when I finally calmed down enough to answer I tried to sound like a nun.

Laurence: *Yes sir. I will comply.*

As I typed that response I was feeling the opposite. They will never get away with this. They don't know who they have here, but I'm not sure what I need to do. It's going to take some time and planning. First I need to get my bearings; I need to outsmart them. It's the only way.

I searched the desk drawers and found a new Nikon camera, a laptop, and an iPad, just as Max had said. No phone. There was a printer and scanner on the desk. Just like home, I thought. Someone has been in my house; has to be someone I know well or someone who has been breaking in and stalking me for some time. I thought of Granger. He is the only person who knows everything about me, but whoever my captors were, they had money and influence. Granger did not. I had known Granger long enough to know he had no hidden dark side or even a sneaky side. But could he be involved with others who did? Maybe he didn't even know.

Anger gave me strength and determination. I went into the bathroom and stepped into the shower thinking it would be best to get myself together first. I was grateful for the hot water, natural soap and hair products. Everything seemed a blessing after anticipating and accepting certain death – not that death was totally ruled out yet.

The simple clothing felt perfect. It was ninja-like. So in spite of my predicament I felt a sense of relief. I was not dead, raped or tortured. Not yet, anyway. There was even a small washer and dryer, so I threw in the clothes I'd had been wearing, the bed sheets, and the throw from the sofa, then went about exploring.

Needing to see out of the high windows, I carried a chair from the kitchen area and stood on it to look outside. The saguaros let me know that I was still somewhere in the Sonoran desert, but that bit of information wasn't helpful since this desert was huge. I might even be in Mexico, I thought.

I found a salad with shrimp and chicken in the fridge. I was starving. From the tiny table in the kitchen I could see the whole one room house. Rainbows flashed from crystals hanging from the high windows. The sun was setting and now I knew the windows were on the south side of the building. I could hear quail chattering outside, coyotes howling in the distance. Other than that there was a deep silence, and a total stillness like I had never felt before. I pushed my plate back on the table and placed my forehead down on it. Tears dripped and made a puddle. I turned my head looking back into the room and felt the wet salty water on my cheek.

4: The Police

"Am I talking to Granger Sun?" the gruff voice said.

"Yes," he answered, nervously.

"I'm Officer Dan Coe of the police department. I see here you've filed a missing person report on a Mr. Laurence Donahue, am I right?"

"Ms. Laurence Donahue."

"Says here 'Mr'."

"Laurence is a woman, sir."

The man cleared his throat. "Well, we need you to come down to the museum parking lot where we've located the car of the missing...ah, woman."

"Sure. Are you there now?"

"Well, we're gonna have a bit of lunch...can you meet us back here around 1:30?"

"Yes, I'll be there," he said to the officer.

Granger was staring into his coffee, wondering about the officer saying they had located the car when he was the one who had told them exactly where it was. Actually that wasn't so weird. They still had to locate it on their own, even if he told them where it was, but he was feeling cynical and being a smart ass. He knew that wasn't going to be of any help at all.

George, Granger's partner and owner of the Sanctuary Coffee Shop in Scottsdale, set a salad down in front of him and took the other seat at the table. Granger stared at the salad as if it was a plate of grass.

"You need to eat something," coaxed his partner. "Who was that on the phone?"

"It was the police. I'm meeting them in an hour. They don't sound very capable."

"I'm sorry. I was worried about that." George reached across the table, laying a warm hand over the top of Granger's cold, white one that had a death grip on his cell phone. They both sat there looking out the window hoping no one else in the coffee shop had seen their tears.

George knew telling Granger that everything was going to be okay was a possible lie. So he just sat there and felt the pain with him.

"Do you want me to go with you?" He finally asked.

"No. Not this time. I'm not sure what they…," Granger didn't finish the sentence and George knew what he meant.

"I can't believe this is happening. It's like, it just can't be real."

"Yeah, I feel that way too." George really meant that.

Granger ate a few bites of the salad and realized he was hungry.

The food made him feel more grounded so he choked down what he could.

"I think it's best if I go alone this time," said Granger.

"You won't be alone. Just remember that. Okay?"

"Okay."

Granger slid the plate to the edge of the table, wiped his mouth with a cloth napkin, and took a long drink of water. He stared at George. "I never thought I'd have to be brave about anything. I just never thought about being brave."

"That's a good word, Granger. Kind of like being an Indian brave…a warrior. I know you can do this."

"Thanks, I couldn't do it without you." They both sat staring out the window for the next fifteen minutes. There just wasn't anything else to say. Granger wondered how the people passing by could look so happy.

He left the restaurant feeling stronger, but not hopeful.

The drive was slow in the backed up traffic on the 10, and when he arrived, two police officers and Jim from the museum were waiting near Laurence's car. They introduced themselves as officers Dan Coe and Melissa Waits. It was a hot day for November, making everyone wish winter would hurry up.

"We just have a few questions," said Coe, squinting in the sun. "We can't report Mr…Ms. Donahue missing until she has been gone for three days, but we might as well ask a few questions today, since Mr. Sanders here," he pointed a nubby finger at Jim, "is quite adamant that this is not Ms. Donahue's customary behavior. So Granger, how do you know Ms. Donahue?" He scribbled something on his pad and stood prepared to take more notes.

"I'm her assistant at the University," he said. "But we've been friends since we were kids."

The officer scribbled again and asked, "And how long have you worked for her?"

"Seven years," he said.

"So tell me why you think she is missing."

Granger started to say because her car is parked here and she isn't here, but thought better and said. "She has no family and I'm her closest friend." He pulled out his phone and played the message from Laurence about meeting an FBI agent at the museum, and told the officer how he and Jim had searched the building and grounds when she didn't appear.

"So that was the last time your heard from her?"

"Yes, sir." Granger felt like he was in a dream. The glare off the cars in the parking lot began giving him a headache.

Officer Coe kept looking at his watch as if he were late to another crime, while Waits stood silently in the background seeming a little more concerned, but not speaking up. Granger tried to hide his agitation and was holding back tears.

"So how long has she been gone?" said the officer, pen in hand.

"Since yesterday morning."

"And you're telling me this isn't a common occurrence with Ms. Donahue. You don't think she's out with a boyfriend?"

"No, she would have let me know."

"Really?" said the officer. "Does she tell you everything she does?"

"Well, no sir." Granger was bristling. "She and I grew up together. She's like my sister."

The officer looked at Granger in disbelief, like he might have been thinking that Granger was a jealous boyfriend. He scribbled more onto the notepad.

"Look," Granger explained. "She's an extreme introvert. A loner. She doesn't do things like this."

Coe stopped writing when he apparently got to the word introvert.

"A what?" he said.

"Introvert." Granger started to spell the word for Coe, but he held his tongue deciding to let the man struggle through it on his own.

The two officers made a few quick searches around the car, then returned to Granger and Jim. "Look, there isn't much we can do right now. If she doesn't turn up in the next two days give us a call, and we'll put her on a missing persons list." He put his hands on his hips and stared out into the parking lot. "We can't get excited about some little Missy's car left in a parking lot. Do you know how many calls a day we get over things like this?" Coe looked back at Granger, looking bored and helpless, and Waits, who seemed to be the one concerned, remained still. Granger wonder if she was an officer in training.

Finally she spoke up and said, "At least five or six calls a day. Usually it's a husband or boyfriend. Mostly we don't hear anything back. Sometimes it's the woman finding her husband's car parked outside a bar."

"Wait a minute," said Jim. "I don't think you know who you are dealing with. I don't know Laurence as well as Granger, but I can attest she's not the kind of woman who would do that, and what about the phone call to Laurence from the FBI agent about an art theft?"

"We'll be taking that into account," the officer said as though he'd just heard about it for the first time. His face turned red. "Be sure to keep that message on your phone," he said to Granger.

Granger couldn't believe the man didn't ask for his phone, but thought maybe things like that only happened on TV cop shows. He and Jim gave each other a look of dismay.

The two officers said their good-byes and good lucks, got into their vehicle and drove off leaving the two men feeling stunned.

"I'm going over to her house to take a look around," said Granger. "I have keys to both her house and her car, so if she doesn't come home soon I'll drive the car off before they impound it."

Jim said, "I don't know, Granger. It might be a good idea to let them take the car if she doesn't come back. It's evidence. Maybe it's best you don't go into the house for the same reason."

"Jim, I think you are assuming the cops are going to do something, even if she is missing," said Granger. "We've all seen too many cop shows where cases not only get solved, they get solved in less than an hour. I think this might be a lesson about how things work in the real world."

"You've got a point there." The museum director was showing sweat on his forehead and Granger felt concerned for the man's expensive suit.

"Okay, I'll wait another day, but no longer."

Granger was working to keep his voice from cracking. Feeling like he was moving around in a thick soup and wanting to cry he said good-bye to Jim, got into his car and drove out of the parking lot.

He arrived at the university just in time to teach Laurence's class, which was a welcomed distraction. He had no lessons prepared and no notes from Laurence, so he allowed the students to carry on a lively discussion about the artist Joan Miro and how he could have gotten some ideas for his paintings from spilled paint on a floor. He suspected Laurence had shown them some images of historically famous artists' studios where layers of paint covered walls and floors showing patterns that might have had a strange resemblance to their paintings. It was a technique she used to help her students loosen up in their work and allow everything in view to be an inspiration. He said nothing to her students about her disappearance.

After the class, against the museum director's advice, Granger drove to Laurence's house. Why wait, he thought. On the way there his mind was so filled with thoughts he had no awareness of having driven there at all. He let himself in with his key. There was a faint smell of oil paint when he walked in. Everything seemed as usual, neat and tidy except for a few dishes in the sink, an indication she had left in a hurry. He thought it best not to touch anything in case – God forbid – she had been killed and there would be a murder investigation.

He studied the painting on the easel and recognized the two students standing between the two scrawny trees with an awesome sunset behind them. Her paint brushes were clean and standing up in a container, tubes of paint were laid out on the table next to a palette. A new stretched canvas leaned against the wall leaving Granger to believe she must have finished the one on the easel and had been preparing to start another. In her bedroom, the bed was neatly made, but there were some articles of clothing lying on it as though she had tried on a few things before deciding what to wear. Granger wondered if he could figure out what she'd chosen to wear, but after looking through her closet he gave up on the idea.

He walked through the rest of the house trying to spot something that might be a clue to her disappearance. Then he stood at the glass sliding doors that led out to a small landscaped yard where he could imagine her sitting at the table on the patio studying one of the books from her art library. If only her car had broken and she had gotten a ride home and was waiting for the tow-truck. Maybe he should have tried to start her car to see. But she would have been here by now. She would have called. Suddenly he became aware that he could hear birds singing through the double glass. How could they be singing so cheerfully?

He thought about turning on her computer to see if he could check her email so he went to her desk. But he didn't want to touch anything, thinking he needed to be careful about leaving fingerprints. Or was that just fear from watching too many murder mysteries. On the keyboard he saw an envelope with his name on it. He stared at it and looked around the room as if he thought someone was watching. He was afraid to touch it. But with shaking hands, he picked it up, opened it and read:

Granger,
Remember the painting I did called "God Doesn't Make Little Blue Angels"? I left it in the back of my car. Would you retrieve that piece of work from my car and take it to my office. You have the keys. Please do what I ask.
Always,

Laurence

He read the note several times to be sure he understood. He noticed his whole body shaking and his heart was pounding in his chest. He was sure she would not have left this note. Nonetheless, he headed straight out the door and drove toward the museum. He was in a hurry and fretted about how long roads could be when you wanted to get somewhere fast. And how at the times when you needed to hurry, others seemed to be sight-seeing or carrying on long involved conversations on their car phones or with passengers. He imagined teleporting and other exotic means of travel. Why couldn't it be like in a movie where he would suddenly appear in the next scene? When he finally arrived he saw her red Prius sitting among cars in the lot. He didn't remember Laurence ever painting something called "God Doesn't Make Little Blue Angels", but he wasn't sure he had seen all of her work. Or maybe it was something he had seen, but didn't remember the title. Strange, he thought, she never used titles that long.

In the back of her car, he didn't find a painting. What he found was a tiny model airplane – one of the Blue Angels. He put it in his pocket, closed the trunk, then took some tissues he'd brought from his car and wiped off his prints. He resisted a strong desire to get in the car and look around. But the last thing he needed was to become a suspect.

He drove back to the University and carried the little jet up to Laurence's office. Once inside he wasn't sure what he needed to do. He read the note again several times, searching for clues, then sat down and swiveled the chair so he could see the shelves behind her desk. At first he didn't understand why he was there or what he should be looking for, but for some reason he suddenly had a feeling there might be a message in a book. Growing up, he and Laurence had read the same books repeatedly and would leave messages to each other on certain pages, like "what do you think about this?" A paragraph might be highlighted. He ran his hand across the shelf at eye level, and just as he thought, he noticed that one book was standing out about an inch from the others and it was different. It was not an art book. It was an old self-help book that he remembered being in his parents' library. He pulled it out. He was sure it wasn't the exact same book, but another copy of it. The book was called *I'm OK, You're OK*, by Thomas Harris. There was a sticky note on the inside cover. Not in her handwriting but carefully printed. It said, "*She's OK.*"

He sat in Laurence's chair holding the note and the book not knowing what to think. It was a tattered old paperback book, not one of hers, he was sure.

He just sat there for the longest time staring at it, thumbing through it, looking for other messages, but nothing else appeared. She only kept art books in her office. Why this one? He felt the room spin a little as he turned the chair and leaned forward, elbows on the desk and hands on his forehead.

He wondered why it was so hard to accept that something was happening when it was happening. Isn't that what life is like? We wander through life not really knowing what is going on, and not realizing we don't know until something goes completely awry. Then we start asking questions. Up until this point he thought his life had been incredibly mundane. That word mundane jumped out at him the minute he thought it. How had he and Laurence ended up like this when they both had spent so much time reading Diego Valdez books on sorcery and vowing never to grow up and live in a mundane world? But now things seemed far from normal, and he felt devastatingly uncomfortable with the very notion of existence. He wondered why whoever left this book had not left a Valdez book. Then it occurred to him that they had chosen a book that would stand out and yet at the same time have some similar messages.

In her office, he didn't need to worry about leaving fingerprints. His prints were already all over her library so he took this time to search everywhere. But nothing other than the airplane and the book with the note seemed to stand out. Before she disappeared, he always felt safe and reassured in this office. There was something about this place. Here, located in the middle of a hectic, chaotic school, this tiny closet of a room held a certain energy that calmed his nerves. The room was small, but the ceilings were high and the walls lined with dark wooden shelves that were filled with every necessary art book available. Between the books, neatly arranged, were some of his small sculptures. The only other things in the room were the old fashioned wooden desk and two chairs. Not a speck of dust appeared on anything, no papers cluttered the desk, and no sounds seemed to penetrate the walls. It smelled like books and lemon oil. Sitting there alone he felt like he was in a display in a museum. He looked up to check if there were still four walls.

Laurence had let Granger use her office to meet with his students. And, in a way, it was his office too. There were so many things they shared – so many things that were theirs. But they were not officially family. What if she doesn't return, he thought. All of this will be gone and I would have no rights to any of it. The thought slapped him in the face. That couldn't be. She isn't gone. She will come back. He vowed to never stop believing that she was alive and would return.

When he left, he took the airplane and the book with the note and drove back to the Sanctuary Coffee Shop. Granger knew Laurence had not left those notes, but whoever had left them had intended for him to find them. They wanted to let him know she was not dead or being tortured. It didn't make him feel any better. It made him feel like there was little hope that she would show up anytime soon.

At the coffee shop, George was finishing up after the dinner rush and Granger was too distracted to appreciate his long term relationship with the chef. The smell of food, even though it was the best in Scottsdale, made him feel queasy. It was noisy and he was agitated.

George, upon seeing his partner looking pale, turned his chores over to an employee and ushered Granger outside. They walked the two blocks past the fancy stores and art galleries to their apartment, where Granger dropped onto the sofa and through tears told George what his day had been like. He did not mention the airplane and the note. He felt like if he told George about that it would make everything that was happening real and he wasn't ready to accept it yet.

5: Where Am I?

The next morning, waking up still woozy from the drug, I stared at rainbows floating on the walls and ceiling caused by crystals hanging in the high windows. I could hear chattering quail as I lay there remembering my dreams: random things happening in the halls at the university, conversations with Granger about what new classes to add or drop. But there was a darkness to these dreams – something in the background lurking. It slowly sunk in that I was still in this room located somewhere in the Sonoran Desert.

The day before, I had determined the four directions from the light movement inside the building and from standing on a chair looking out at the shadows cast by tall Saguaros. North windows were considered to be the best for good studio light, but I found myself curious about how high windows all around would work. I liked seeing the clear ultramarine blue sky and occasional small white clouds. But I had to stand on a chair to see the ground outside.

I questioned my lack of motivation to find a way to escape, so once again I circled the space looking for exits, trying to determine how the ninjas had gotten me into the room in the first place. My heartbeat was still occasionally irregular, but I wasn't feeling debilitated by the hysteria that I had been feeling the first few days.

It was quieter than my home in Phoenix, where the roar of a distant freeway – however far away – disrupted the stillness. This place was dead quiet except for sounds of quail and other birds I didn't recognize, and they didn't count as noise. I don't think I had ever been in a place so soundless.

In the bathroom mirror, I stared at my image: long hennaed red hair, still tangled, deep circles under my eyes, skin white. My eyes seemed bigger and slightly bulged – evidence of being terrorized. I thought of what my grandmother used say when I made faces. "You keep doing that and your face will get frozen like that forever!" I tried to relax but that did nothing for my eyes.

I quickly determined I would never get the tangles brushed out of my hair. So I grabbed a pair of scissors from the drawer, and cut it short. My hair fell around my feet in great heaps. I don't know why I did that, why I didn't try harder to brush it out. But I felt better afterwards. I hadn't realized how heavy hair could be. With a broom I'd found in the bathroom closet, I swept it up off the floor and dumped it unceremoniously into the trash.

In the tiny kitchen I made a healthy breakfast drink out of carrot, cucumber, coconut milk and protein powder. I stayed away from the vitamins, concerned that they may be laced with drugs.

It was time to check in with Max. There was a message from him.

Max: *I hope you slept well. The mattress is like the one you have on your bed at home and the sheets are very high thread count. Maybe you've had breakfast and I hope it suited you as well.*

Laurence: *Have you been breaking into my house in Phoenix to learn all this about me? I notice you have some very nifty ninjas.*

Max: *Oh yes. They are extremely good, and yes to your question about breaking in. I have a good feeling that in time you will see all this in the light of appreciation, but now I'm not surprised at all by your reactions. I am sure this is quite disturbing. I wish we had other ways of going about it, but this is the best solution we could come up with.*

Laurence: *Going about what? What is it you are going about? I need to know what are you doing and why.*

Max: *Yes, of course, you need to know. But as I have said before, the knowing will come in time. If I tried to explain everything to you now it would only confuse you and make you more uncomfortable. We want you to make yourself at home. Our only aim is to make your life better.*

Laurence: *That sounds a bit co-dependent don't you think? How do you know what is best for me? What makes you think it is your job to do that?*

Max: *We know things you can't possibly know. We hope you will understand that this is bigger than just your life. I can tell you that you are a part of a huge project to make the world a better place for everyone.*

I sat back in my chair staring at the computer and reminding myself that this was like email and that I didn't have to answer right away. I sipped on my breakfast drink and re-read what he had said. I had to give this some careful thought without giving in to an inclination to be sarcastic and snarky.

Laurence: *Wow! I need to think about what you just said. I'll get back to you later.*

Max: *Of course.*

The walls to the east and west underneath the high windows seemed to be made of closets, drawers and shelves filled with a plethora of art supplies and art books. I ran my hands across the backs of the books as if to check to see if they were real. And I wasn't surprised to see the whole set of Diego Valdez books among all the art books. One tall cabinet that looked like a broom closet held very interesting things: a coat, hat, gloves, a pair of boots in my size and even an umbrella.

I kept trying to stay in touch with my feelings, put a name to them and feel them in my body. It was the healthy thing to do. "Disoriented. I'm disoriented," I said out loud and my body swayed a bit as if to thank me for staying connected. I went back to the Valdez books, pulled one from the shelf and opened it at random. I read.

Don't deny death. It is always with us. It is the best adviser a person can have. Whenever you feel that everything is going wrong and you are about to be killed, you can ask your death if that is true.

So that is what I did. I asked my death to let me know and death said, "No, not now."

I said, "Thank-you, ninjas, for not killing me today. Maybe you are not assassins after all."

Then I went back to the computer and wrote:

Laurence: *When will I get to meet you, Max?   Where are you? In some other part of this building?*

Max: *Someday we will meet, but not right away. For now you are alone in the building. Your supplies will be delivered by drones. They will land on the roof and be sent down the dumbwaiter. You'll be hearing the sounds of it and perhaps you may sometimes be able to see it.*

Laurence: *So you're saying I'm home alone.*

Max: *Yes and there is no way you can escape. Even if you did get out of the house, you can't carry enough water to walk out of the desert. And you wouldn't know which direction to go.*

Laurence: *I know better than to ask how long I'll be held here. What have you told people? Where do they think I am?*

Max: *They all think you've gone missing. They suspect kidnapping which is, of course, true.*

Laurence: *What about Granger? I don't care about what the college thinks, but I'm concerned about the feelings of my friends. Granger is like an*

33

adopted brother. I'm close to his whole family.

Max: *Yes, that is a problem. I wish we had been able to come up with a better solution for this, but your friends and family are better off not knowing what has happened to you. We need to keep them safe. They will recover in time.*

When I heard that, I felt rage rising. I'd been concerned about how Granger and George might be feeling and the Sun family and other close people. I couldn't stop feeling their pain in my own body.

Laurence: *Now I'm mad!*

Max: *Yes, of course your are. But I can tell you we left clues for them that let them know that you are safe. I'd suggest not spending time stressing about them unless you can use those emotions to motivate you in your work.*

I wanted to write back "Fuck you!" but I didn't. I was getting good at walking away from the computer, but as I headed off to the studio I heard a ding and noticed another message from Max.

Max: *It's totally okay if you express your true feelings.*

Laurence: *Good then. Fuck you!*

He didn't respond.

In the studio area there were two sturdy easels and two tall work tables. All of the supplies I needed were carefully organized. Everything was of the best quality: rolls of linen canvas, Gamblin paint, walnut oil, and a whole drawer full of bristle and sable brushes. The smells reminded me of the first day of each school year when all the supplies were brand new and clean. There was also a ventilation system, hoods designed to exhaust fumes. I switched it on and off and was amazed at how quiet it was. I was intrigued by the newness of it all. I wanted to grab some brushes and start a painting immediately, but stopped myself. I was too paralyzed by the weirdness of everything. So I sat on the sofa staring into the room, watching the rainbows shimmer on the cabinet doors.

I was fully aware of the conflict in my mind between wanting to fly into the studio, pick up a brush and go for it, and all the thought patterns that were stopping me. This was nothing unusual for me even when events in my life were not so dire as this. I needed to get out of the dreadful thinking mind and keep asking questions like how do I feel right now. I hated that, but it was working. It was a game Ana Sun had taught me when I was going through the loss of my family when I was young. I opened one of the sketch books and wrote at the top of the page: How do I feel?

Stunned

Angry

Disoriented

Fearful

Resistant

There, okay. Where do I feel it in my body?

All over, but mostly in my head. I'm trying to find answers and it's not working. What now?

I cried – not for myself, but for those I loved: Granger, the Sun family, my students. They must be beside themselves with grief. It was painful to think about it.

I lay back on the sofa, pulled the soft throw over me and snuggled under it – head covered – still thinking too much. When am I ever going to grow out of dealing with life like an ostrich? But then, why should I?

The last thought I had before falling asleep was: I don't understand what is happening to me, but so what? How is that really different than how my life was before? The difference was that I had never thought of what others would be going through, finding out I was missing. My parents had barely shown that they cared whether I was alive or dead. Now they were all dead – parents and brother. My grandmother was in a facility for Alzheimer patients. She did not remember me. I had figured out long ago that I had a tendency to miss what I never had anyway. But I did have the Sun family: Granger, Apollo, Ana and Parker. I craved to be in their house right now, lying on their sofa under their blanket where, when I was a child, I would hide when things got unbearable. They would walk by me, tending to their own business, knowing I would be fine in a while. I would come out and they'd be waiting with open arms as though nothing unusual had happened.

I didn't sleep longer than thirty minutes – just the right amount of time to reboot, start over, begin again, accept that I wasn't going to magically wake up back at home anytime soon.

Still, I didn't move off the beautiful cerulean blue couch. It was soft and welcoming and faced out towards the studio area. I sat up and positioned my legs meditation style. I felt as though I was floating in the sky. Rainbows were still painting the walls and cabinets. Usually I couldn't be bothered with anything that might be construed as New Age. But this place was beyond

New Age. It was organic and earthy.

My thoughts turned to painting. Art was what had always driven my life. Obviously, someone wanted me to do nothing but paint. It surprised me to remember how often I had wished for a life where I could immerse myself in nothing but my art work. Granger used to tell me to be careful what I wished for. But this, this was just too weird. I was too tired and traumatized by what had happened to think about painting. I remembered how my landscape gardeners, Carlos and Jesus had shown me how they put B vitamins on plants when they planted them in my yard. But they still drooped and struggled to take root, some of them not making it. Somehow, without knowing why, I knew I would make it. Death was telling me it was not my time.

Finally, I got up off the couch, stood swaying a bit, went into the kitchen and took my vitamins. Then in the studio area, I took out a canvas roll, and placed it on the table, cut off a 32x18 piece, and from a rack of boards I selected one and stapled the canvas to it. I guess that is how they wanted me to work since the paintings had to be rolled and put in a tube for pick up. I placed it on an easel and stared at it. It seemed to stare back at me saying, "I dare you!"

My primary subject matter had always been the figure. What now? There were no people here. Did everything now have to depend totally on my imagination? Possibly I could make up people. I had painted from models for so long the human figure was burned into my brain. I could get images from the computer, but they were limited, stilted, posed. Yet it could be of some help.

I wandered around the room again looking through the drawers and cabinets, searching for something. But what? Just searching. It was a kind of hysterical behavior, mindless and frantic. My heart pounded in my chest, but I caught hold of myself, sat down in a studio chair, and put my head down between my legs – something I'd been taught to do when I was a little girl prone to fainting.

When I felt the blood back in my head, I sat up slowly and saw that I was facing the tall cabinet where I had seen the coat and boots. I opened the door, and that is when I first saw a full length-mirror.

I noticed that all the art furniture was on wheels, the easels and the tables. It made it easy to reposition everything so I was able to sit with the easel in front of the mirror. Okay, I thought, I have a model now!

6: The Library

For a long time I studied the reflection of myself in the mirror, but I didn't move to squeeze paint out of tubes or even make charcoal sketches. The glass palette remained as clean as a freshly washed window. My image in the mirror kept fading in and out, being erratically replaced by flashing images in my mind. For many years I had been absorbed in the phenomena of two different ways of seeing the world: images hitting the retina of my eyes, and different ones conjured from memories and made up from my imagination.

Sometimes I could be absorbed by the outside world, sometimes, the inside, but most often it was an intertwining of both. This is how I learned to paint magical realism. I'd always been fascinated by how we could see in our dreams with our eyes closed. This day the phenomenon seemed more exaggerated and I felt frozen in my tracks.

The inner visions were winning out. I couldn't stop replaying the events of the last few days: teaching my last class at the college, working on my last painting of the two students I had seen from my office window, the long van ride, waking up in this place. I was still having bouts of dizziness and nausea, and as I sat trying to see myself in the mirror and running over thoughts in my head, I suddenly had to run into the bathroom and vomit. Afterwards I sat on the lid of the toilet, and cried. But I got bored with that, so I swished my mouth out with mouthwash and washed my face with a warm cloth. I was still light headed, but at least I was no longer sick to my stomach.

In the kitchen, I made a cup of mint tea, then sat on the sofa letting the tea settle my stomach. Books were calling to me, so I got up and selected a few: John Singer Sargent, Rembrandt, Degas, and one on the living artist, Tina Mion. I set them all beside me on the sofa and took one into my lap. Degas, warm and friendly, who always spoke to me of dynamic composition. I was looking outside my own mind now and viewing another artist's world view; ballet dancers moving off and onto the canvas. He painted the truth about them and their agonizing profession: aching muscles, stiff scratchy costumes, fake smiles hiding the torment.

I had always disliked ballet so that is how I interpreted Degas' paintings. Others – most likely the patrons who bought his paintings – would be mesmerized by the beauty of it all, not seeing those young women destroying their feet and backs. I thought about how many artists were doomed to die slow and torturous deaths due to using up their bodies at an early age – like painters and sculptors having to work with toxic materials. I was suddenly grateful that my captors had installed an exhaust system and provided me with the least toxic paints available. I wondered if that meant they wanted me to live.

Once I read somewhere that Degas had a studio close to the theater. He hired dancers to model for him in his studio where he photographed them, then worked from the photographs to make the dancers look as though they were on stage or in the dance studio. When I first heard about that, I was stunned. Hadn't most of us envisioned Degas hanging out in the audience, or being backstage, or in the dancer's studio with his easel and paint? Neat trick. I did, however, believe he also must have made sketches of the dancers in their common environment. Cameras in his time were not small things inside your cell phone that you could whip out where ever you were. Anyway, he was a genius in my opinion. The paintings were certainly masterpieces no matter how he came about creating them. I thought about the Nikon camera I had found inside the desk drawer. It would be useful.

I often pondered about how non-artists think about art and artists. Putting myself in their place, I could easily understand how artists were often categorized as weird or even insane. Most people think artists are just born with talent and don't have to spend hours practicing to become skilled. Students often came to my classes thinking they were born with talent and needed no training. They thought they were going to sail through college with little effort only to find low grades in classes they thought they would have excelled in. The lucky ones woke up and got busy. The others changed majors or, sadly, dropped out. Success was often driven more by desire than talent. Degas wasn't a magician. He was a technician – a focused and driven perfectionist – as were Singer, Rembrandt and Tina Mion.

Mion is still young and very much alive. The book was a small catalogue, so I went to my desk and looked her up on the computer. She is all about the figure. Her favorite subject matter is mostly death and some politics. I love Mion for her exquisite imagination and her disregard for perfect anatomy. That is a hard one to pull off and she does it with expertise. Her emotionally loaded art work leads viewers to tears and laughter. Mion just makes stuff up. That's what I'm going to have to do here – make stuff up.

I couldn't remember the last time I had just hung out on a sofa and looked at books and computer images. It felt weird. The stillness in that place made me realize that some of the strangeness that I was feeling was a sense of

38

relaxation and that throwing up was me sloughing off the stress I'd been living with for most of my life.

I hadn't thought of Max in a while and I didn't feel like sending a message. Not now. After all he – or someone – could be watching me on a screen and could see I was behaving well. For the first time I felt okay with the cameras, because it meant I didn't have to communicate when I didn't want to.

I noticed I was feeling hungry so I took a break and rummaged through the cabinets and fridge. There was still some prepared food so I didn't have to cook – not yet anyway. I warmed up some lasagna in the microwave, and to my relief my stomach seemed to accept it. It gave me energy and an even greater feeling of peacefulness. I washed my plate and fork and made another cup of tea to take with me to the studio area. Then I put back the books I'd been looking at, and found a new one on portrait painting. Thumbing through it, I found some color charts and decided that would be a good way to get started, so after reading the instructions I selected a small piece of primed canvas and squeezed out equal amounts of Indian Red and Titanium White onto the virgin glass palette. I mixed them together with a brand new palette knife. For the next two hours I mixed three shades of blue, three of red, three of yellow and three of green with the tinted Indian Red, and began painting squares. With each hue I added small amounts of white, creating a gradation of skin colors. I thought of nothing else as I worked. Holding the brush, smelling paint, and making color squares became the most important thing in the world. It brought me fully present with myself as if I had been blasted apart and was now coming back together.

When I finished my project I was happy with my work and what I had learned from the exercises. Colors never stop amazing me. I cleaned my brushes with Ivory soap in the studio sink and placed them back on the table by the easel, then I scraped the excess paint off the pallet and deposited it into the a plastic bag inside a trash basket. I wondered how I was supposed to dispose of it. I would have to ask Max what to do.

It was now late afternoon so I climbed up onto the chair and looked from the narrow windows into the desert. The shadows were long and falling to the left of the saguaros and bushes, small rabbits nibbled on grasses. Quail chattered and pecked the ground. The sky was a clear blue with only one tiny white cloud.

When night came, I felt the need to communicate with Max. Here's how it went.

Laurence: *Max, how am I to dispose of the leftover paint? I made a color chart today, that's all.*

Max: *Excellent! I'm happy you got started. There will be a trash pickup each week. Just put the leftover paint in some small plastic bags and keep them until we let you know when we are coming to pick up.*

Laurence: *Sometimes I save the leftover paint to use for grounds on a new painting. I like to keep it in jars. Will that work?*

Max: *Sure, we will deliver some jars. How are you doing?*

Laurence: *Better. I don't have a lot to say right now. I don't even know what questions to ask.*

Max: *More will be revealed to you as time goes on. I promise you that. I just want you to make yourself at home as best as you can and don't worry about your future. Your health and well being is a major goal in our project. Please let us know what you need anytime day or night. I know you like to listen to audiobooks while you paint so be sure to visit Audible on your computer where you can download any book you like. I know you like to watch movies so you have Netflix. You can also get music from iTunes or Amazon. Also any books you want to read can be downloaded onto your Kindle.*

Laurence: *You seem to know a lot about me.*

Max: *Yes, this is a well thought out program.*

Laurence: *I see. I think I need to sleep now. Good night.*

Max: *Good night, Laurence.*

I changed into some soft night clothes and crawled into the bed with my iPad. It was too early to sleep so I took my mind off of everything by watching a movie. It was "The Story of Luke" which made me both laugh and cry. I felt like I was in my bed at home. I could feel the muscles in my body letting go. For the first time my mind was not on how to get back to my life in Phoenix. When I thought of that, I felt a tinge of guilt.

7: The Detectives

Granger's hands were shaking when he tried to demonstrate a chiseling technique in one of his sculpture classes. He accidentally chipped a huge chunk out of the face of one of his student's marble sculptures. Horrified, he left the room feeling ashamed and distraught. Later, he came back, took the student aside, apologized profusely and promised her an A in the class even though he knew she didn't deserve it.

Earlier that morning, as he had walked to the art building, Laurence's face had stared at him from posters. They hung from kiosks and buildings asking if anyone had seen Professor Donahue. The night before on the local news the Dean of the school had announced, "We are doing all we can to find out what happened Professor Donahue. As our campus security is excellent we are assured this abduction did not take place on the premises. We are glad this wasn't a nasty mass shooting."

Statements like that disturbed Granger. What campus security? There was only one officer left. How does the dean know this isn't as bad as a shooting and doesn't he know she was taken from the museum parking lot?

Later Granger was even more disturbed when he looked up and saw two Phoenix police officers peering into his classroom. He dusted himself off with a whisk broom and met them in the hallway.

It was Coe and Waits again.

"Mr. Sun, we'd like to take you down to the station for questioning," Coe said. Waits was standing to his left and about a foot behind him nodding her head.

"Now? I've got a class? Are you arresting me?"

"No, no, no." said Coe. "The DA just wants us to ask a few questions. Why don't you finish up here and meet us downtown. When is your class over?"

"Another hour." said Granger trying to take the resentment out of his voice and not succeeding. He was wondering why they were wasting time with him instead of going after the criminal, but then he realized they might be after some pertinent information that could be of help. His tone changed.

"Sure," he said more agreeably. "How about I see you at the station around

3:00." Then added, "I want to do everything I can to help find her."

"Of course you do," said the officer sounding more engaged than he had when they first met in the parking lot.

"I'm sorry. I've been so impatient," Granger said.

"We understand. I'm sorry we didn't respond appropriately in the parking lot when we first met. We were burned out over so many missing persons calls. That's no excuse. I hope you will give us another chance to help you out. We'll see you downtown," replied the officer.

When the class was over, Granger washed his hands and face, dusted out his hair, and changed into some clean clothes from his locker. Then he reluctantly drove to the police department.

He was ushered into a sparse room with an oak table and three matching chairs, no two-way mirror like on TV, just a couple of ordinary Southwestern paintings hanging on two of the walls, both well done but boring in his opinion. Just as he started to fidget from the long wait, two people burst into the room – a man and a woman dressed in plain clothes.

"Granger Sun, I'm Detective Joe Lewis and this is Amanda Brown. Can we get you some coffee?"

"No thanks," he said as he stood to greet them. Granger was more afraid of the coffee in a place like this than he was of the two people who seemed relaxed and friendly. He shook both their hands and they all sat down.

Joe Lewis was a man probably in his forties. He was stocky, with a buzz haircut and was good looking in an ordinary way. Amanda Brown was a lovely African American woman with intelligent eyes and an all-about-getting-down-to-business look on her face. She was younger, maybe in her early thirties. They were both dressed in casual business clothes which set Granger at ease. He was glad he wasn't having to talk to police officers dressed in uniforms with guns and other unidentifiable things strapped to their bodies.

Brown pulled her iPhone out of a pocket turned it on and said to it "November 19, 2016 3:15 PM, Brown, Lewis with Granger Sun." She placed the smartphone on the table between them.

"So," said Lewis, "How long have you known Professor Donahue?"

"Since I was five." He sounded a little choked up and felt a bit like he was still five. He looked down at his hands folded on the table in front of him. He had not expected his emotions to spill out first thing.

"That's a long time. Were you close friends?" Lewis's voice sounded compassionate, but Granger could sense it was an act – some kind of a skill he'd learned in a training class – a way to get people to talk.

"Sure. I don't remember much before she came into my life. It's been that long. My mom took care of her after school. She lived a couple of doors down the street. Her mom was sick so she spent most of her time at our house." Granger looked up at the painting on the wall across from him. It was a scene from the Sonoran Desert. He thought for a moment he could see Laurence standing in the shadows of a saguaro. He wanted to get up and take a closer look.

"Mr. Sun, are you okay?" asked Brown.

"Oh, I guess." He shook his head and blinked to clear his eyes and took another look at the painting. She wasn't there.

"Mr. Sun...Granger. It seems you were the last person to see Professor Donahue," she said. "Please tell us everything you know leading up to her disappearance."

"The last time I saw her was in her office at the college. She had just finished teaching a class. I went to tell her I thought we might be losing our teaching jobs since funds are being cut to run the art department." He immediately felt guilty for that having been their last conversation and he wondered if the information was relevant.

"And how did she take that? Was she upset? Was she depressed? Tell us everything you know and what you think might help us locate her." Brown's voice was soft and reminded Granger of a therapist. He wanted her to be a therapist. He thought he could use one. He wanted to put his head down on the table and cry without restraint. He wanted her to put a warm brown hand on his shoulder and tell him his feelings were normal. But that was not why they were here. He had to get a grip. He sat up straighter in his chair, cleared his throat and spoke more clearly.

"Laurence is not one to get depressed. If anything, I was telling her about our possible job loss so she could cheer me up, and she did. She said we would work it out, or something like that. I felt better after I talked to her. I went to my studio for the rest of the day and became absorbed in my sculpture. She called me later that night and left a message telling me to meet her at the museum – something about an art theft. I thought I sent a text, but I don't have any record of it. My mind was on my wedding and I just flaked. But I did show up the next morning at the museum. That's when I found her car parked behind the building. There had been no art theft according to the museum director. He had no idea who had called her and set up the meeting."

"So," said Louis "that was you and Jim Sanders, the museum director."

"Yes sir."

"We need to take your phone. We might find something helpful in it," said

Lewis.

"Sure," Granger fumbled in a pocket to retrieve it and handed it over. "Look, detectives, Laurence and I practically grew up together. I feel like I have always had two sisters, Apollo and Laurence. She became one of us. She's family. I hope you don't think I had anything to do with this. I'm beside myself with grief right now. All I want is to find her and bring her home safely. I'll help you in any way I can." There was a little catch in his voice that didn't go unnoticed by the detectives. They knew he was holding back tears.

Detective Brown said, "You understand, Granger, we have to make everyone a suspect in the beginning. We appreciate your cooperation and we will need you to help us, so don't leave town. Understand?"

"Can you tell us something about your other sister," he looked down at a paper he'd placed on the table. "Apollo?" asked Brown.

"Sure. She's much older than Laurence and me. About the time Laurence showed up, Apollo was already in high school. She left for college when we were just kids. I don't see much of her now. She's a computer scientist and works for Los Alamos National Laboratories. She isn't allowed to talk to us about what she does. Besides we're artists and probably wouldn't understand her very much. We usually see her at Christmas and sometimes a bit in the summer. She's albino and likes to work underground. Laurence and I always thought of her as – well, a prairie dog."

"Do you have contact information?"

"Sure, it's in my phone."

Lewis asked, "Laurence's parents are both dead. Is that true?"

"Yes. Her grandmother is still alive, but she's very old, and I don't think she knows who Laurence is anymore. She's in Sun Valley Retirement Center not too far from Laurence's house. Laurence visits her once a week."

They all became aware he was speaking of Laurence in present tense. She wasn't dead in his mind.

"Tell us more about Laurence's friends. Any boyfriends?" Lewis was leaning back in his chair, arms folded across his chest. Granger realized he was a man at work, just another day at the job. Laurence was just another missing person among many. He began to feel hopeless again.

"There was a guy, but it's been awhile since she's seen him."

"So, tell us about that relationship." Lewis had a strange look on his face that Granger couldn't read. He squirmed in his seat wondering how they might feel about his being gay. Did they even know about George and the coffee shop? He started to be concerned.

"I don't know much. She saw him off and on for about a year, but the relationship didn't seem to be going anywhere. Both of them were very busy, and Tucson isn't next door. I think they just drifted apart. Got too busy to spend time together. There didn't seem to be any animosity. You probably won't have any trouble locating him."

"I see," said Lewis. "What is his name?"

"Manuel Martinez, he's in my phone too."

"Any other friends?"

"Detectives, Laurence Donahue is a very private, very solitary person. She doesn't socialize much at all. Occasionally she comes to dinner at our house, but only if there aren't too many guests. Socializing for her means students, university, her grandmother, me and George. That's it. She's extremely focused on her work.

Amanda Brown glanced over her shoulder at the clock on the wall. "Granger, we need to check out Laurence's house. We would like you to come with us. I understand you have a key and you might be able to give us some important information."

"Sure."

They all stood. "How about we meet there in about two hours," said Lewis reaching out for another handshake. They all stood up and exited the room. The two detectives disappeared down the hallway and Granger breathed a sigh of relief and stepped into the elevator. Outside a cool breeze hit him in the face as he walked down the steps of the Phoenix Police department. At least it wasn't summer and a hundred and ten degrees.

He drove directly to the coffee shop and had a quick lunch with George. Finally he was eating again. He was feeling a surge of energy probably from the fact that some action was finally underway. When they finished eating, George asked "Do you want me to come with you? I'm worried about you."

"I don't think it's a good idea. I'm not sure I trust these people. I want to, because I need their help. Then again I'm afraid they might think I had something to do with it, as there are just too many innocent people in jail these days. I don't know how they feel about us," he swung a pointer finger between himself and George.

"I see," said George. He reached across the table and put his hand on top of Granger's. "You're going to be fine. You didn't have anything to do with this. You have no motive. Besides, this isn't a TV show where they actually work on cases. My guess is they'll pay attention to this for a week or two then move on to something else."

"Well, that's a mixed blessing. I want them to find her alive and bring her back," he said.

"Of course, you do and so do I. But perhaps it will just work itself out. I don't think Laurence is dead. I don't have those feelings I get when something bad has happened to someone. You know how I am," he said.

"I don't think she is dead either." He told George about finding the note on the computer, that led to the little blue jet that led to the book on the shelve with the note saying she was okay. He pulled the toy plane out of his pocket and placed it on the table.

George held the little airplane up close to his eyes, looking at all it's details. "Why didn't you tell me about this before, Granger?"

"I don't know. I put it in my pocket and forgot about it. I was so messed up and didn't want to believe this was actually happening. I thought she would be back by now. That it had all just been a big misunderstanding."

George said, "Wow, that gives me chills and makes sense. I don't want to speculate on what this is about." He held up the plane. "There's magic in the air. Don't you feel it?" He leaned forward in his chair looking into Granger's eyes. "I just know deep inside that she is coming back to us. I just don't know when."

Granger could tell that George was doing everything he could think of to keep him from falling into despair, and he owed it to his partner to do his best to keep it together.

"You're right. I get that same feeling. The world is never what it seems to be. I feel like I shouldn't tell the cops about the note and the book. What do you think?"

"I don't know," said George. "You're going to have to play this one by ear. Feel out the situation. Trust yourself."

"Also, I spoke to Apollo this morning. She concurs. She tells me not to worry and that everything will become clear in time." For a few minutes Granger stared out the window as if he were looking for someone. Then he looked back at George, blinking back tears. "I think she knows something and isn't telling us. I don't know why I think that. But the three of us have always had a psychic connection. It used to drive my parents crazy."

"How are your parents?" George asked.

"They aren't saying much, but at first they were quite disturbed. Laurence is definitely one of their children. Apollo has been talking to them daily and I don't know what she says to them, but they seem calmed and assured that everything will be okay."

"Apollo does have that effect on people," said George.

"I'd better go now," Granger said pushing back from the table. "I'll call you as soon as I can."

"Here take my phone. I'll be waiting to hear. Call me on the restaurant line," said George.

Granger took the smartphone and put it in his pocket realizing he'd forgotten about the detectives taking his phone. "What would I do without you?"

"You would do fine, but you don't have to do without me...ever." George made a face like he was secretly blowing Granger a kiss, having learned that it was safer to act that way in public.

When Granger arrived on time at Laurence's house and found Detective Brown and Louis waiting in the driveway, he felt a sense of doom, and wished he'd brought George along for support. He opened the front door with his key and they all went in.

"We've looked around the property." said Lewis, "There doesn't seem to be a forced entry." Granger stood in the living area and watched the two detectives look thoroughly at everything. They opened drawers and cabinets. Brown spent a long time in Laurence's bedroom and bath.

Granger felt awkward standing there watching them tear through the house. He offered to help, but they told him it was best he didn't interfere. He sat down on the sofa, but did not lean back. He kept staring at Laurence's painting on the easel wondering why the detectives weren't looking for clues in the painting, because it seemed to him there was a message in the image. He had seen those two students standing in that same place more than once. Were they looking up at Laurence's window?

He was relieved when the two detectives joined him in the living area. Joe Lewis looked at his notepad; Amanda Brown had her iPhone. They both compared lists then Brown spoke to Granger. "Does she travel much?" she asked him.

"No, not much at all. Just when she used to go down to Tucson to see Manuel, but that was months ago. She moved her grandmother here from Colorado so she wouldn't have to fly there to visit her."

Joe Lewis said, not looking up from his list, "We're having the Tucson police check out Manuel. Unless she had an already packed travel bag, it looks like all her stuff is still here. She must have had breakfast before she left. There's one plate and one cup in sink and a container of sorts on the drainboard. It doesn't look like anyone was here with her. All her messages have been deleted. We'll take her laptop with us and have our team look it over, and we'll send someone out to check for fingerprints and DNA. We'd like to take your key and have our own copy made. We'll return yours, but you'll need to stay away during the investigation. We'll have our team put up yellow barricade tape. As for now we just have to wait and see what turns up. Oh, we've also impounded her car and turned it over to forensics."

"Is there anything else you can remember that might be of help?" said Brown.

Granger was stunned to hear the word forensics. He thought about telling Brown about the book with the note in it, but he said, "No, not right now."

She handed him both their cards. "Call us if you do."

That was it. They exited the house, got into their cars and drove off in opposite directions.

Granger sensed the detectives were not especially interested in this case. They just seemed bored. Being in Laurence's house had given him a feeling that he had to get on top of things. Somehow he knew she was alive and was being held somewhere. But where?

He pulled over into a parking lot, called Apollo and told her what had happened.

"Do you think you could come home and spend some time with mom and dad?" He asked her.

"If I come home, they might feel like it's worse than I think it is. We've known Laurence ever since she was a child and we know she's quite capable of taking care of herself. She's a survivor. Mom knows that too. For now, I think we best not treat it like we think she died. I'll come later," she told him.

Granger told her about the note in the book.

"That note and the plane says a lot," she said. "I'd suggest looking for more clues like that. Look for things the police might not think is important. Have they searched her office and classroom?"

"No, that's weird. They didn't even ask," he said.

"That means their minds are not on solving this mystery. I don't think you can count on them. They've got too many cases and some of them are much worse than a missing person. You know, serial killers, terrorists, and stuff like that," Apollo said.

"You're right." He dramatically turned his car around and headed back to Laurence's house to check out the painting again. He knew where she kept a key hidden in the yard under a rock.

"Granger," Apollo said trying to get his full attention, as his mind was on driving. "Granger, she is not dead. If she were we would feel it. There are some things you just have to turn over to a higher power. You know, like they say in twelve step meetings. Above all, you gotta' remember that! Promise me you'll remember that, will you?" He thought it was a strange thing for Apollo to say, but it made some sense to him.

When he arrived back at Laurence's house, the police had not yet returned and put up crime-scene tape. The key was right where he thought it would be – the fifth rock in a line that sectioned off a tiny herb garden. He went in the house and turned on the full spectrum lights in the studio to look at the painting. He saw the tops of the heads of the students standing between those two struggling trees, orange sky casting a glow on the edges of the silhouetted figures and trees. He looked at it close up and far away. He put it upside down and sideways and he even turned it around and looked at the back of the canvas, but nothing unusual stood out. Then he did something he knew he shouldn't. He took the painting and left, hoping the police wouldn't miss it. The detectives had not taken photographs. That would probably be the job of the uniformed cops. It was also a great risk. But for some reason he had to have that painting. He also kept the key, not trusting the detectives to return his. As he reached the stop sign at the end of her street, a cop car turned the corner heading to the house.

***

It was around 7 PM in Tucson when Manuel Martinez left the university campus and headed towards the parking lot. A police car pulled up beside him and two officers jumped out, grabbed him and slammed him against their car forcing his hands above him and spreading his legs. They roughly patted him down, read his rights, handcuffed him and pushed him into the backseat of their car. His heart was pounding louder than he'd ever heard and he smelled his own sweat – strong and acrid – the kind the body produces when you're scared to death.

Martinez had never been arrested, didn't have a clue why this was happening to him. At the police station he was fingerprinted, photographed and placed in a small room on a hard chair with a hard metal table in front of him. There was a two-way mirror on the wall across from him like on TV. He tried not to look at it.

He sat there so long his butt hurt and his legs went to sleep, but he was much too frightened to stand up and move around. He didn't even stomp his feet and get some circulation going. He was cold. They must have had the air conditioner on in November.

Just when he felt like he might put his head down on the table and cry, a couple of detectives burst into the room. They didn't introduce themselves.

One of them said. "Do you know this woman?" He shoved a photo of Laurence Donahue onto the table in front of him.

"Yes sir, I do," he heard himself say.

49

"Is she your girlfriend?" Officer number one said.

"She was," he said. "But I haven't seen her in months. I guess we've broken up."

"You guess you've broken up?" said officer number two. "How do you feel about that?"

"I don't really know exactly. I'm pretty shaken up about what's happening to me right now. Where is Laurence? Has something happened to her?"

"You tell us," said one.

"I'm sorry, I don't know what you want from me. You need to provide me with some context. Why am I here? What's happening?"

"We ask the questions around here," said Two. He seemed peeved that Martinez spoke such excellent English. What did he mean by 'context'? "When did you see her last?"

"It was..." Manuel looked up at the ceiling trying to calculate how many months ago it was. Then he remembered it was May, a couple of weeks before finals. "May," he said. "We took a trip together to the Gulf of California. It was our last time together."

"Did you fight?" asked Two.

"No."

"Then why did you break up?"

"I'm not sure. We were too busy. We weren't all that close. We were mostly just friends and we drifted apart. We talk on the phone every now and then, but that's all."

"When did you talk to her last?"

He consulted the ceiling again. "About a month ago, I think. Please tell me if she's okay. What's happened to her?"

The two officers seemed to get the feeling Martinez seriously didn't know.

"She's missing," One said.

"Missing? Since when?" Martinez was getting emotional.

The two cops stared at him.

Then the door opened and a female officer came in with a phone and handed it to Two.

Two put it to his ear and listened.

"Okay," he said and hung up.

He looked at Martinez and said. "Okay, you can go now."

The two officers stood and left the room. A female officer came in and ushered him to the main entryway. He was handed his belongings and told to leave. It was 10:00 PM and he had no idea exactly where he was. He looked for an address on the front of the building...nothing. He tried to get back into the building to ask...locked. He had no coat, so he shivered in the wind and stood under a freshly planted, scraggly mesquite tree. It wasn't even that cold out.

He took out his iPhone which was low on charge and had only a couple of bars, but he managed to reach Juan, his assistant. He shouted into the phone. "Juan, you need to come and get me!"

"What?"

"You need to come get me, man, I'm at the police department."

"Yeah, and where is that?"

"I don't know. Look it up. It's too dark and I can't see the mountains!" To himself he sounded desperate and scared. To Juan he sounded crazy. Then the phone cut out.

Manuel slid down the slender trunk of the tree and watched a police car come from the back of the building and drive out of the parking lot and down the road.

8: The Long Dream

The first time I slept through the whole night in my new location, I woke up from a dream that was so vivid it felt like I was being torn from one reality and shoved into another. I was wondering if this was going to become a common theme in my life now. I snuggled under the comforter and tried to get back to where I had left off in the dream. But I didn't fall back to sleep. I lay there remembering it.

I recalled a stunning vista of flat land with a railroad track in front of me. Next to the track, a museum – of sorts – had a sign on it that said *Free on Weekends*. I entered. Everything felt familiar, yet I don't think I'd ever been in a place like this. In one tiny room elegant fabrics were artfully displayed. A man wearing purple and pink striped pants and a brocade floral shirt spoke to me. I thought he had a British accent, or was it French? He showed me each piece of fabric, telling me all about how they were made. His stories went all the way back in history to the sheep or worms who started the whole process. I tried to retain some of the details, but everything he said was fleeting. It was more like he was not talking at all but was transferring information in some other way.

I found myself attracted to a piece of blue fabric with images of multi-colored cartoon versions of tropical fish printed or painted onto it. I purchased a yard of the fabric and was surprised when I tried to wrap it around my waist. It was way too small. Had I become more than thirty six inches around? No sooner had I thought that, the fabric began to change shapes, stretching out longer or wider depending upon how I held it. Sometimes it morphed into a very full gathered skirt which enticed me to twirl around and giggle like a child – the skirt flaring out all around. But the amusement soon changed into a feeling of regret for buying it. I don't deserve something so magical, I thought. I can't afford this. I wondered why I had to feel this way about purchasing nice things, even in my dreams?

Suddenly I was in another room where a video was being projected onto a wall. The same man was engaged in an exotic acrobatic dance with a woman. Both wore outlandish multi-colored costumes, and they were performing in front of bizarre circus-like sets. Pink, green, blue and purple lights blinked off and on like strobe lights. I found some cushions on the floor and sat down to watch them, but soon fell asleep. How could I have fallen asleep when I was already asleep and dreaming?

After a while, I wandered out of the building. Or was it a large tent? Multi-colored crocheted doilies made from recycled plastic dotted a trail that had mysteriously appeared. Somehow I knew the artist had intended people to walk on them, but no one did. Instead people had made trails in the dirt alongside of them. I studied the intricate mandalas and felt elated by the expertise of the artists.

The trail led to the museum store which was a large room filled with books, jewelry, teapots, umbrellas, prints of fantasy and surreal paintings. I was looking around when it began to rain and since there was no ceiling, large drops fell right into the shop. "Why is there no ceiling?" I asked the store clerk.

In a serious tone she replied, "Don't you know? It never rains here!"

What a weird dream, I thought. Shaking myself out of the memory of it, I got out of bed and went to the bathroom. Standing in front of the mirror, I replayed the dream several times trying to remember more. There was more but where did it go? Then it came to me. In the second part of the dream – I called it the second part, but I'm not sure where this happened in the sequence – I was standing by the railroad tracks with Manuel. We were looking out into a vast expanse of barren land. The sky we stood under was a huge ultramarine blue bowl. "It's out there," he said to me. The memory of the sound of his voice made me tremble.

"What?" I had asked. Our voices sounded like we were in a cave instead of out in the open.

"That place we used to like to go. Remember, we went there many times. I think I can find it again." His voice was soft and seemed to invite me to follow him.

"I think I can remember too," I said.

Then there was a huge hill that rose up and lifted the railroad tracks high above us. We tried to climb the hill in order to cross the tracks to get to the flat land beyond. It was as though that vast flat place was only in our minds, and the hill was all that really existed. It was an impossible hike up the hill, and the more we climbed, the higher it got. It occurred to us that we were never going to reach the top.

The dream memory followed me into the shower and surrounded me, like a rainbow colored fog. Manuel, how had I not thought of him since I arrived here. How could I possibly have forgotten all about him?

I dried off and tried to see myself in the fogged up mirror. And for a moment I thought I could see him standing behind me. I reached out to touch his face in the mirror as though I knew if I turned around it would break the trance and he would disappear. Then I remembered something that had not been a dream. It was something that happened last May.

"Laurence, can you come visit? I want to take you fishing," Manuel said. It was a three day weekend for both of us.

"Fishing? Are you serious? I've never been fishing. You go fishing?" I asked incredulously. "Manuel, fish live in water, in case you don't know. So, where is this water you plan to take me to?"

"It's a short drive down to the Gulf of California. We can stay a few nights. How about it?" I loved it when his Mexican accent came out. How could I say no?

I went with him, and I learned that fishing wasn't what I thought it was. "First we must rent a boat," he said. But when we got onto the boat, to my surprise there wasn't any fishing gear on board, and the boat had a glass bottom for watching fish, not catching them!

"There, see those?" he said, pointing out some yellow and turquoise colored fish. "Those are called Blue Tang Surgeonfish. Those over there are Eyestripe Surgeonfish." He seemed to know all their names. Of course, he could have been making it all up because I knew nothing. But why would he? I asked myself. Why can't I just trust him? The next day we snorkeled, which was another thing I had never done before.

Each night he made a delicious vegetarian dinner. "I know you are not a vegetarian," he said. "Neither am I, but how can we eat a fish after seeing it alive in the ocean? I try not to get to know the animals I consume. At home, you know those chickens that live next door to me? They have names."

I laughed a lot that weekend and loved how we snuggled in bed letting the sound of the ocean sooth our tangled minds and work-strained bodies. After that week-end, we each got consumed by our jobs. It was as though a huge work monster swallowed us. We both lived under a demanding belief that art is long, life is short, and we had to get it all done before we died. It was good that we loved our work, but now I was wondering if it really was more important than human contact. Now I'd been thrown off my work routine long enough to notice I missed him terribly.

I left the bathroom and trudged to the kitchen, feeling like I was carrying a heavy backpack filled with regret. I made a cup of tea to take with me to the couch, where I sat staring into space, remembering Manuel and our time together at his house in Tucson, making love in his bed. It was in a tiny messy room off his equally untidy studio, paintings and color scattered everywhere out of place. But somehow it didn't bother me. He lived inside his own paintings, and I liked that about him. It gave me a sense of freedom – a devil may care attitude. Whenever I returned home from his house I would feel frightened as though letting go and having so much fun was dangerous.

When he came to Phoenix he would leave behind his messy world and appear immaculately dressed and dignified. We attended art receptions, visited museums and spent long quiet evenings at my house. But soon we both started making excuses. "I have to finish three paintings before the end of the month for my gallery; two others need to be completed so I can ship them to California," he would tell me. I would breathe a sigh of relief, because I had an equally demanding schedule.

We talked occasionally on the phone. "Hey," I would say. "How did the reception go at Gallery 67?"

"Great!" he would reply. "I made three sales, and you?"

"Not bad. I sold that big one called *The Slide Fire*. I'm thinking of doing more fire paintings. I finally got the hang of painting pink smoke." We would lie in our separate beds talking long into the night, but taking a week-end off to be together seemed out of the question.

"See you soon," we would promise each other and ourselves. But it never happened. The number of calls dwindled. My life was too full of other things and he had become a thin memory.

Suddenly I realized that something was staring me right in the face! I'd been sitting on the sofa lost in a dream world, thinking of the past. I had not seen what was right in front of me. The wall with tiny windows close to the ceiling was now a whole wall of windows and I found myself looking straight out into the desert toward the south. My heart started thumping in my chest and I jumped from the couch and flew across the room to stand in front of them.

Each window pane was small like the ones at the very top, and were held in place by what seemed like metal bars. I could never fit through them. Even if I could, I still wouldn't know where I was or how far away from civilization I was. The scenery outside was glorious. There were so many more things to see that I had not noticed while standing on the chair peeking through the top windows. There was a vast vista of hills covered in vegetation, and blue and purple mountains in the distance. A covey of quail pecked the ground and chattered, a rabbit sat still looking at me with one eye, a raven shadow passed on the ground. I leaned into the windows, pressing my cheek to a pane, tears finding pathways down my face. I didn't want to spoil the clean window surface so I grabbed a paper towel and quickly wiped up the smudge. I never thought I could feel so grateful for something I usually took for granted.

Laurence to Max: *Thanks for the light.*

Max: *Glad you like it. The windows have an electrostatic film on them controlled via WiFi. You can adjust them, so they are translucent or transparent using an app called iWindows on your iPad. The app icon looks like an old-fashioned window, the type that had little panes framed between wood. Just click on the icon, and slide the window open or closed to adjust the translucence. They are great for passive solar, but when you are painting you'll be able to control the direct sun. They should function more like north light when you need them to.*

Laurence: *Okay, Max, I love the windows but what I'm hearing from you is that I'm not going home soon. I'm worried about my friends. What about Manuel Martinez?*

Max: *Oh yes, Manuel. I assure you we are letting those loved ones close to you know that you are safe and very much alive. Your friends, or should I say, extended family, are very bright people who are paying attention to the clues we are leaving them. They miss you terribly, but all will be well in the end. You will see.*

Laurence: *The end? Max, sometimes I feel terrified and sometimes I don't care what happens to me. I do care about them. You know I will never trust what you say to me. Today I thought of Manuel. We have not seen each other in months, but I'm certain he will be worried. This is all beyond unsettling.*

Max: *Yes, he is worried, but we are doing all we can to let him know you are alive and well. I suggest you keep to your painting and not worry about how they are feeling. I'm sure you miss them too. You might consider yourself a loner, but we know how close you are to the people you let into you life. We are watching out for them as best as we can. And, if all goes as planned, you will be back with them in time.*

Laurence: *I see...if all goes as planned. Does anything ever go as planned?*

Max: *No, actually, it never does, but we can set our intentions and leave it to the Universe to decide what happens.*

Laurence. *Max, are you the Universe?*

Max: *Yes, but so are you and all the other constellations around us.*

Laurence: *Great! Thanks again for the windows. Bye now!*

I was still being more than a little hateful to Max. The windows were great.

The whole place was awesome, and given the choice to spend some quality time here was welcomed. But to be forced to, well, you can imagine my distress!

This day, though, I was too excited by the windows, the dream and the recall of my time with Manuel to stay on the computer talking to Max about anything. I spent the afternoon starting a painting of Manuel from a small photo of him I found on his website. Of course I was blocked from making contact with him online, but I was able to grab the image and make a paper copy. The painting had to include fish. I could have looked up images of fish on the internet, but opted instead to make them up as I went along. I purposely didn't want them to be realistic, but more cartoon-like.

I stapled a piece of canvas to a board and made a sketch with vine charcoal. I made Manuel look serene and confident, but surrounded by wicked looking fish with teeth. Maybe it was my wish that if he were in pain about my being gone, he would not suffer, but continue on with his life as he did before I went missing; like the man – I had to admit – I had fallen in love with. The fish would represent whatever difficulties he was dealing with now. In the painting he would be ignoring them, but not in a way that meant he was not aware of their threat.

I made swatches of skin color doing my best to remember how he really looked which was not at all like the photograph I was working from.

When the face was done I wanted to touch it, to feel the softness of his skin and the rough parts where his beard would have grown, had he not shaved. I wanted to put my hands over his ears and hold his head in my hands while I kissed his lips.

Then there came the shirt, his arms, his hands. I remembered how it all felt and how he smelled but all I could smell now was paint. All I had was a painting. I found myself talking to it anyway. Telling him where I was and how I ended up here. I told him how – that if we ever got together again – I wouldn't let work come between us even if it meant I had to quit my job and move to Tucson. I was surprised by my flood of emotions.

For the rest of the painting I chose beautiful and vibrant colors, Prussian Blue, turquoise, orange, and various bright greens. I painted the fish orange, green and yellow, and they looked startling. I started with acrylic paint because it dries fast. Then I worked over parts of that surface with oil paint. Some artists - the purists - shudder at adding oil over the top of acrylic. My favorite painting teacher Clive Pates would not have recommended it. I wonder about that myself, but for now that was what I was doing because it was convenient. I planned to do some straight oil painting when I had more paintings going on at once and didn't mind the drying time.

The light from the windows gave me great joy. My colors were more vibrant and I could see better in order to make the details stand out. I am not an impressionist painter. I am a realist. A magical realist, and details are important.

The last thing I put in the painting, before I signed it, was the ruby ring he wore on his left hand. It could have been a woman's ring. It was delicate but roughly made. It had belonged to a friend – a struggling artisan who had been mistaken for someone else, and shot dead in the drug wars. The ring was rough because it had never been finished.

I put a lot of time and energy into this image. I didn't know where my paintings were being taken, but maybe it, or word of it, would reach him. I had no idea why I thought that might be a possibility. But it seemed like a strategy I might stick to. Artists have always put secret messages in their work for various reasons. All the time I worked on it I couldn't wait to wake up in the morning to Manuel's face. I wanted to keep the painting for myself. But after it dried for longer than a couple of weeks, I sadly rolled up the canvas and slid it into the cardboard tube and placed it strategically – as I'd been told to do – into the dumb waiter. Then I missed him terribly.

I thought I Was a Fish

9: 1980

"I'm not doing this anymore." Fred leaned forward towards the windshield trying to see though the frozen gravel blowing horizontally across the road. "Damn sleet! Why can't we have snow like they do in civilized places. This stuff's deadly!"

"So is snow, Fred. You need to calm down. We're almost at the hospital. See? The entrance is right up there on the left."

"Grace, we've tried everything with this kid. Look at us...putting our own lives in peril...all because of him. I don't know what else to do. We've read all the books, tried therapy. I've had enough. This is the last time!" He slapped the steering wheel with a gloved hand.

"How can you say that? Raising teenagers isn't easy for anybody. It's not our fault. He'll grow out it. We did...remember?" she reached over and patted him on the thigh.

Her weary voice tugged at his heart – made him feel more like a failure. It was at that moment the car lost traction and began to slide sideways. Careful not to touch the brake he took his foot off the accelerator and adjusted the steering wheel in order to gain traction. His heart pounded in his chest. "Shit!"

Grace relaxed the grip she had on the edges of the seat, stopped talking and let him focus on driving. She too preferred the snow they had back in Colorado. It was white, not this dirty grey stuff. Here in Fort Worth there wasn't any skiing, snowboarding, or sledding. Only ice, and not the good ice like the kind on Mary's Pond, near her childhood home where she and her friends used to skate. She thought Randy would have been happier if he'd learned to ski, or rather, snowboard. That's what the kids were into now. She made a vow to make sure he got to spend more time with his grandmother in the mountains even if he missed school. That kid needed the slopes.

At 1:16 AM the emergency room was surprisingly busy, and they were told to take seats out of the way of a train of gurneys whizzing in from the ambulance entrance. They turned their eyes to avoid seeing what looked like blood soaked sheets. It was so chaotic they feared a worse collision might happen in the hallway.

They had expected Randy to be waiting for them with a bandage on his arm or leg, or worse, maybe a cast. Now they felt stunned and ignored, sitting in what they thought was a dark, quiet corner which only seemed dark to them because in reality they were being assaulted by fluorescent lights, clattering noise, and voices shouting orders. Perhaps only their minds had crawled into a dark cave away from everything. Grace gripped Fred's arm like she might drown if she let go. He occasionally patted her hand to reassure her that he was there.

The waiting room felt unsanitary and smelled like someone had disposed of soiled diapers in the nearby trash. Grace hoped the treatment rooms were sterile and Randy was being cared for by a calm professional. She just wanted to see her son. She sat there thinking about how she had always been closer to Randy than her daughter. Maybe she made a mistake by going along with her husband and giving her a boy's name. Laurence was a smarty pants, a know it all, always correcting everyone with the facts. Laurence made her feel dumb. But Randy accepted her for who she was. She got a lot of hugs from that one. He was sweet, charming, and she had a tendency to let him do whatever he wanted. It never occurred to her that might have been the reason he was so troubled.

The couple waited for an hour and a half before a nurse had them follow her into a cold room with nothing in it but a small table and three uncomfortable metal chairs. They were left there alone to wait another 30 minutes. When the doctor finally came in looking grim, Grace felt Fred stiffen. She wished the doctor had been older, but no matter who it was the news would have been the same.

"I'm so sorry," he said. "We did everything we could."

When he began to explain the gruesome medical details of how their son had died, he seemed to be speaking from the end of a long hallway that kept stretching further into the distance with every sentence.

"Wait a minute." Fred finally aroused himself and in a loud voice interrupted, "What the hell are you saying? Are you telling me my son is dead?" His voice startled his wife, and she started sobbing uncontrollably.

"Yes, Mr. Donahue. He had a massive brain injury. There was nothing we could do." The doctor looked tortured by having to be the bearer of such bad news. "The other boy in the car, Jimmy Dale, was dead on arrival and Billy Smith most likely won't make it through the night. I'm so sorry. It was a nasty head on collision. I'm afraid your son was driving drunk. People in the other car didn't make it either."

The exhausted doctor continued. "He had other injuries as well: internal bleeding, punctured lungs. If the head trauma hadn't taken him, something else would have. I'm so sorry." He realized his words were beginning to fall on deaf ears.

The couple had sunk into complete denial. Whose car was he driving? He didn't even have a license to drive yet. This could not be happening. This was not their Randy.

"Are you sure it was Randy, not someone else?" asked the father.

"I'm sorry," said the doctor. "You can see the body if you like, but I don't advise it. We had his medical records so we checked his blood and the police department had his fingerprints and they were a match. We will be checking the dental records to be sure, but that will take a few days.

A nurse arrived as though she had been waiting outside the door in order to intervene at the just the right moment. She helped Grace up from the chair and led both of them to the chapel office where she introduced them to the hospital priest. He looked like a penguin and acted as though it was his first night on the job. Years ago both parents – with the help of therapy – had let go of their childhood religions so his comforting words and prayers only sent them deeper into despair. All they could do was cry and the priest's words were driving them mad. Grace finally jumped to her feet and slapped the young man across the face and screamed, "Shut the fuck up...asshole!"

So stunned, the young priest put his head down on his desk and cried like a baby. Then they all cried together.

***

The next morning, I wondered why my dad had not awakened me for school. I followed the sounds and cooking smells into the kitchen. But it was not my mother making breakfast. It was Grandma Hattie. She had arrived the day before for Christmas.

"Grandma, where's mom and dad?" I asked.

Grandma didn't turn all the way around to face me, so I was looking at her profile when she spoke. "Oh honey, something bad has happened. Your mom and dad are at the hospital. I have something sad to tell you," she said still gazing out of the window into the barren winter-scape. I could tell by grandma's voice that she had been crying even though I had never before seen her cry and didn't know that grandmothers could cry.

"What?" I suspected it had something to do with Randy. I was used to it by then. It always had something to do with Randy.

"Well," Grandmother said. "It's like this." She didn't look at me. She turned her back to me, facing the stove and tended to the crackling bacon. "It's your brother. I'm afraid he's gone to heaven."

Grandma took two eggs and broke them in a bowl, stirred them rapidly with a fork, then dumped them into the skillet beside the bacon. I watched her carefully, having never seen eggs and bacon cooked together at the same time in the same pan. Something was very wrong with that.

When everything was well done grandma put the food on a plate and set it down in front of me. She then poured a much too large glass of orange juice.

"Here, you need to eat this," she said. "And drink your juice."

I looked at the plate and made a face. That food looked like it was meant for the neighbor's dog.

"Where is heaven?" I asked her. It didn't sound like a very good place to go since my grandmother was crying about it, and my parents were in the hospital.

Grandma gave me a look of surprise, knowing all too well my mom had never taken me to church. She must have been wondering how my parents could have been so irresponsible. Maybe she was blaming what had happened to Randy on the fact that we didn't all go to church. Maybe that was true. I really didn't know for sure. She raised up the bottom of her stained apron and wiped her eyes underneath her grease-spattered glasses.

I had heard about heaven from friends in the neighborhood and school, but no one had been able to tell me where it was. Somewhere in the sky they would say. I looked at the steam coming off the eggs in front of me and felt queasy. Something wasn't right about them. Grandma went back to kitchen chores: washing up the pans and wiping the countertops.

I was staring at my plate wondering what to do when a sudden knock came at the backdoor. I was startled to see the neighbors, Dora and Sam and their Yorkshire terrier named Skip. Having never come around that early in the morning, I felt disturbed when they joined me at the table. Grandma served them coffee. Then as usual the adults started talking in low voices and acting like I wasn't there. I dropped a few pieces of bacon on the floor and Skip snatched them up in a split second. A few more bites of egg would do the trick, but the dog had lost interest. I scooted to the edge of the chair and tried to push the food with my foot farther under the table, hoping it couldn't be seen, but the pieces of egg just smeared on the floor which the dog sniffed, but didn't eat.

Having scattered the rest of the food around on the plate I slipped away from the table unnoticed – a skill I had developed over the years. I walked past the undecorated Christmas tree in the living room thinking everything would be fine. Santa would come soon and life would be back to normal, but I had a vague understanding that heaven was associated with death and that people usually didn't come back. I didn't know for sure. Since Randy was my brother – as opposed to someone else's brother – he would be back, if he had in fact really gone. Didn't he come back that time he ran away?

In my room I took my sketchpad and colored pencils out of my school back pack, climbed back into bed and began drawing. This always took my mind off of stressful situations, but this morning it wasn't working, so I put them away and walked down the hall to Randy's room. I cracked open the door and saw that he was in bed. So what was the problem?

Standing there staring into the quiet, cold darkness, made my pounding heart sound like the bass in Randy's favorite music. I didn't like his room – all those scary looking posters, especially the black light ones that seemed to wiggle. They were just gross! Finally I stepped all the way in, wincing at the pungent odor – a mixture of spoiled food, sweat, and other unidentifiable things. But I needed to know if he had gone to heaven, so I took the risk and tiptoed over shoes, damp towels and musical instruments. I stood by the side of his bed staring at the back of the knit cap he always wore when he slept. I was afraid to touch him. But I knew I had to wake him up to find out what was going on.

"Randy," I said quietly so not to draw the attention of the adults in the house. He didn't move. I said it louder. "Randy...wake up!" Nothing, so I reached over and gave his shoulder a strong shake which caused his head to separate from his neck and roll off the pillow. I jumped back, tripping over a shoe, my butt landing in the middle of a pizza box. I stifled a scream. I was used to his tricks. I had learned to catch myself, stop my screams, so not to give him more reasons to terrorize me. I got up, pulled back the covers, and saw only a rolled up blanket and some pillows. The cap that looked like a head was filled with socks.

"Shit!" I shouted. I put my hand over my mouth because I didn't like it when words came out that I had heard my brother use when he was mad. He must be hiding in the closet, I thought. In a minute he will jump out and try to scare me. I braced myself for it, and stood waiting – shivering. I eyed the closet suspiciously and knew what I had to do. Maybe he didn't know I was in there so I would have the upper hand and scare the wits out of him. So, very slowly, I traversed the uncertain terrain, stepped over mountains and crevasses of my brother's stuff, then flung open the closet door and yelled "Boo!"

But he wasn't in there either – just sloppily hung clothes and an overflowing laundry basket tilted over because of a scrunched shoe I saw sticking out from underneath it.

"Yuck!" I said louder than I meant to.

I wished I'd left the bedroom door open so I could see better in the shadowy room. I tried to hurry, but tripped over a wire and fell, knocking over Randy's electric guitar. It screeched and my hands instantly slapped the sides of my head to cover my ears. He must be in the bathroom, I thought.

But he wasn't there either.

Standing on my stool, I brushed my teeth, washed my face, and ran a brush through my sleep tangled hair. I did the best I could without my mom's help. I stood for a while, looking at myself in the mirror and listening to the adult voices chattering in the kitchen. Back in my room I managed to get myself dressed for school. There was only one more day before Christmas break and there was going to be a party in my first grade classroom. I wasn't going to miss it, so I put on my warmest coat, hat, boots and gloves and slipped out the front door into the biting wind. Walking a mile and a half on slippery sidewalks, through the winding neighborhood streets to school was the hardest thing I'd ever done.

I arrived – lips trembling and fingers aching – only to discover the door to the school was locked. There was a sign on it that said *Closed Due to Weather*. That is when I finally started crying – tears freezing on my blue chapped face.

***

There was a funeral that I was not allowed to attend. Copious amounts of food dropped off by friends and relatives covered the dining table and kitchen counters. My parents moved ghost-like around the house preparing while I mostly hid out in my room, occasionally passing by that sad and dying Christmas tree on the way to the kitchen to nibble on various casseroles and chicken legs. The sleeting had stopped, but the wind had not; outside everything was gray. The ground was cracked and frozen. I'd always been afraid of those cracks – fearing they might grow so big I would fall into one. Was that how people ended up in hell?

The night before, I thought I heard my mom crying, but I was dreaming that the sounds came from a howling wolf that was standing in front of me in a forest. It seemed to be sending a warning. But I couldn't understand what it was. Another time that same night I woke up to the sound of Randy's guitar. But it wasn't his. A neighbor must have been having a late night holiday party and was playing Stevie Ray Vaughn too loud. When I closed my eyes again I dreamed I did fall into one of those cracks outside and I ended up in one of Randy's posters where terrifying images became a parade of neon ghosts. They looked like smoke from the weird cigarettes Randy and his friends used to smoke on the nights my parents went out and left him to baby sit. I'd always liked hanging out with him and his friends for a while, until the atmosphere made me cough and the smell drove me back into my room. Behind my closed door I would lose myself in one of my books of fantasy illustrations. The colors always seemed brighter on those nights. I often wondered how my parents could miss the smell when they got home, but thinking back on it, I'm sure they were drunk.

On the day of the funeral, mom and dad hired a teenage girl from down the street to baby sit. The only thing they knew about her was that she was the same age Randy had been, and probably went to the same school. She arrived on time.

Except for the brightly colored streaks in her cropped white hair she was the whitest person I had ever seen. She was dressed in a short black dress mostly covered up by a black leather jacket. Her legs, pink from the cold, hung down straight and thin, and disappeared into the tops of her boots, which she slipped off in the foyer. No socks. She plopped her leather jacket over the back of the couch and stuck out a long skinny arm, offering a handshake not to my dad, but to me.

"Hi! I'm Apollo, you must be Laurence. Cool name, Laurence...great for a girl," her voice low and strong.

I liked the feel of her slender cold hand, my eyes must have been big and round trying to take in this creature standing in front of me. Apollo looked like one of the fantasy characters I'd been drawing in my sketch books. It made me wonder if things I drew would come true. I had not drawn my brother dead, but I sometimes drew ugly pictures of him when he made me mad. I felt bad. Later I would learn a name for that feeling...guilty, like I had something to do with his dying.

My parents and grandma slipped out the door without goodbyes and Apollo and I stood in silence. She scanned the room while I continued to stare at her. I was awestruck. She spoke first.

"Hey Laurence, what's with the tree? It looks really sad." She walked over to it and touched a branch knocking off some dry needles. Got any decorations?"

"Sure." I led her to the front hall closet and pointed to a couple of boxes on the top shelf.

Apollo had no trouble reaching them. She carried them to the couch, opened each one and got busy; first trying out the lights to see if they worked then, ignoring falling needles, she wrapped them around the dead tree. I helped hang balls and other trinkets. When we were done, we sat side by side on the giant foot stool to admire our work, our faces changing colors as the tree lights blinked on and off.

"Now, that's better," said Apollo getting up to close the empty boxes and replacing them on the shelf in the closet.

"TV work?" the girl asked as she grabbed the remote. "Do you like MTV?"

"Sure," I said, but when we started watching, it made me sad. It was something Randy liked a lot. So after a while, I slid off the couch in my usual way and disappeared. As I eased down the hall to my bedroom I glanced back to look at Apollo. I thought she looked like a baby giraffe all folded up on the couch, her face and hair now blue from the TV.

In my room I closed the door to a bitter winter day and sank into spring. I remembered the time my mom had helped me pick a paint color for the walls – lavender, my favorite. My comforter was a garden of soft peach and purple flowers with pale green leaves. This room was the only tidy room in the house and I was meticulous about it and the things I kept in it. A small stereo and a stack of albums lived on the white lacquered dresser. The desk was always dusted and uncluttered. Clothes hung, color coded in the closet. Everyone knew not to mess with my stuff – even my brother. I could barely stand the rest of the house which wasn't all that bad except for Randy's room. I guess I would let him mess with my stuff now if he would come back, I thought.

***

The mom I knew before the accident never returned from the funeral. When my dad tried to explain what had happened to Randy, I began to think that Randy's ghost had grabbed away parts of my parents to take along with him to heaven. I gave that concept a lot of thought and drew pictures of it in my sketchbook. It made sense he still needed them because, even though he was big, he was still a kid. I was careful not to get angry or feel hurt when my parents ignored me. When he grows up, I thought, I'll have them all to myself.

In spite of my brother's death, Santa did come that year, but left lots of strange things. I would learn years later that if it hadn't been for Grandma, Dora and Sam from next door, and Apollo's family, Santa probably wouldn't have come at all. I was the only one in the living room on Christmas morning opening presents and wondering if Santa had given my gifts to some other little girl and left mine for someone else. I forgave him. After all, the world was too big for one little man in a sled – well, big man – so mistakes were probably made all the time.

That afternoon, Apollo came to take me home with her for Christmas

68

dinner. Grandma was knitting and watching television. She was sniffling and I saw her wipe her eyes a lot. I don't think my parents ever left their bedroom that Christmas day. Probably didn't even know I was gone.

10: Journal Entry

It's been fourteen days and the only sign of human activity are messages from someone called Max. And he could be nothing more than a computer. I've decided I need to keep a journal, of sorts. I'm not one to do something like this, so I doubt I'll be consistent or even good at it. I'm writing in one of the sketch pads by hand, which annoys me to no end, but I dare not type it into the computer. I need some privacy. If the cameras are still on, they can see I'm working in a sketchbook, but I'm not sure they can tell if I'm drawing or writing. I will do a little of both to hopefully throw them off. I sent them the first painting yesterday by rolling it up, putting it into a tube and shoving it into the dumb waiter. I'm not sure if it was picked up or what. There is so much I don't know yet.

Thursday was Thanksgiving and my captors delivered a complete dinner – the usual turkey, stuffing, cranberry sauce, etc. I'm still eating leftovers. The scary thing is I could get used to this. I feel right at home with the solitude and the silence. The windows have added a lot of comfort so now I don't feel so trapped.

While working on my next painting I listened to the audiobook of "The Goldfinch" by Donna Tartt. What a ride! I stayed up painting late every night because I could not stop listening. She won the Pulitzer Prize for this amazing work and I read that some people were not happy about that. They must be insanely jealous. I've downloaded the written book so I can read it as well. I see she has two other books and I can't wait to dive into them later.

Once I get a painting planned and started, there are a lot of tedious details to be handled. A good audio book can keep me from getting distracted. My captors were smart to provide me with that. The painting I sent was the image of Manuel with those fantasy fish swimming all around him. It was fun to do and I completely forgot where I was. I hope it is what they want from me; otherwise it might be "off with my head."

Anyway, back to Donna Tartt and her attention to detail. Along with the elimination of distractions, her writing will certainly influence what I do here. The fact that the Goldfinch was about a painting and the power it held over people made the story more pertinent for me right now. I can only hope

71

that someday I might be able to create a piece of work that emits that kind of energy.

Perhaps I haven't been valuing my own work or I haven't been spending enough time on each piece to see that it reaches the standards of the great masters. I'd like to feel like I can reach for that, even if I fail. I hope my captors don't start telling me what to paint in order for my work to fit into a decorative art gallery. I'll kick and scream over that.

I hope my friends in Phoenix had a great Thanksgiving and are not worrying about me. I've never been much for praying, but I find sending them prayers several times a day makes me feel better. I can't help feeling like it reaches them somehow. Maybe it's taken facing death to get me to think about spirituality. It's not that I've overruled it in the past, it's just that I was so busy working I lost touch. I've always been attracted to Zen Buddhist teachings and of course the writings of Diego Valdez who must have studied Zen.

With all the time I have now I've been meditating each morning. I wonder if I had made time for meditating before it would have made my work days easier. I may never know the answer to that. For a while I attended a Zen Meditation Center, but found it too restrictive. It didn't line up with any of the great Zen books I've read. It was too much like ordinary religion. Like in art I have to find my own way.

It's a bit gray outside today and I wonder if it will rain. It hasn't rained since I've been here. And I haven't checked the weather, because I don't know exactly where I am.

Well...a new day and time to think of the next painting.

11: The Mountains

I had removed the tiny table and the two chairs from the kitchen area and placed them in front of the windowed wall, so I could sit in the mornings and share breakfast time with my friends in the yard. It really isn't a yard. It's a clearing. One morning I noticed the mountains in the distance were covered with a light dusting of snow. And the wildlife had been dwindling in numbers as the temperature dropped.

I don't know why I had moved both chairs. Was I thinking I might have a guest someday? Actually I don't think I thought about it at all. I just didn't know what to do with the extra chair in the kitchen and it looked nice when I glanced at it from across the room.

Looking out, I began to think I was farther north than I'd first thought and probably higher in altitude. I could feel the cold air coming off the windows but I chose to wear a sweater rather than press the command button on my iPad and cover the glass.

These mornings had become a special time for me to connect as much as I could with the outdoors. I'd come to think of the quail, javalina, deer, rabbits, and an occasional coyote as family. There were lots of birds I didn't know by classification. There was a bird book in the library and I kept promising myself I would look them up. To start with I just began naming some of the animals. There was Scraggy Javalina, Mama Cass, Billy Bunny and so on. Once I saw a huge tortoise. All the other animals made way for it's regal march across the clearing in front of my window. It definitely had a demanding – leave me alone I gotta get somewhere – attitude. That's kinda how I was before captivity, I thought.

After breakfast I checked in with Max.

Laurence: *Good morning.*

Max: *Good morning, Laurence. I hope you are warm enough.*

L: *I'm fine. I can see snow on the Mountains. The birds are puffed up. It's funny how they do that when they're cold.*

M: *Yes, cold birds are unlike humans who shrink and hunker down. I guess you didn't see them like that in Phoenix.*

I felt too embarrassed to tell him that I never had time to watch wildlife when I was in Phoenix.

L: *I'm hoping you weren't expecting more than four paintings from me. It's been ninety nine days and I was worried you might be expecting more – or else off with my head. I paint slow – lots of details.*

M: *Take as long as you need. They are well worth waiting for. I'm still studying your paintings and I'm more than pleased with your work. Tell me about the one with the man sitting under water with the fish.*

L: *Oh that one. It's from a memory of a trip I took with a friend. We went to Mexico together. He wanted to take me fishing, but what he really meant wasn't about catching fish, but watching them.*

M: *I see. But these are not typical tropical fish. You made them up.*

L: *Yes, well I don't have much else to do. Making things up keeps me at least a little busy. And speaking of making things up, I have a question. At night I can see a cluster of electric lights below the big mountain. Can you tell me about that?*

M: *What would you like to know?*

L: *Who lives there? What are the people like? Is it a town or a village?*

M: *Actually, I've never been there, so I don't really know. What do you think?*

I paused and slapped my forehead with my right hand. So typical of Max to answer a question with a question. I was getting better at not feeling frustrated. He acts like a therapist, I thought. I kept hoping he might slip and give away some information that would let me know where I was and how long I would be here.

L: *Hmm, what do I think? Well...I think they are a community of sorcerers living in Mexico.*

M: *Really? I'm interested.*

L: *If I tell you, will you go and visit the place and let me know if I'm right.*

M: *Of course, if I can find it.*

I sat back in my chair and closed my eyes and let my imagination take over. I was getting used to the new way my mind was starting to work, since I wasn't having to keep up with lesson plans, scheduling and university politics.

74

L: *I imagine people of all ages, but mostly young adults, all of them beautiful. There is a party of men and party of women living separately. It's kind of like a school, but there is no building. Life is the only subject taught at this school and the teachers live among the students. I'm impressed with the way they are dressed. I'm not interested in fashion, but this is not fashion. These are power clothes.*

M: *Nice, Laurence, can you make some sketches of these people in their "power" clothes?*

L: *Yes, I think I will. In fact I want to capture my ideas before they leave my mind. I'll send some images later.*

M: *Have fun.*

L: *Max, before I go I have a question. Sometimes you use the pronoun we and sometimes I. What can you tell me about that?*

M : *Yes, there is a we and an I. There is only me sitting here with my smartphone conversing with you. But I'm far from the only one involved in this project.*

L: *Are you in charge?*

M: *Hmm, how to answer that...I tend to think God is in charge, but I know that answer won't appease you at all.*

L: *God, Okay...later dude. I've got work to do.*

I couldn't believe I said "Later Dude." What kind of professor am I asked myself? Obviously I was one who had picked up some slang expressions from my students.

I turned to face the window and picked up the sketch pad that I kept on the table for occasions like this when fleeting moments of inspiration came knocking. If I were at home in Phoenix I would be rushing around getting dressed to go to work. But now I could sit here and dress my parade of characters. Funny, I thought, I'm starting with clothing. Sorcerers are meticulous in their dress even if they put on costumes to disguise themselves as peasants. It is, of course all about acting or as Valdez would call it – controlled folly.

I thought about these magical people learning to behave in a world where most people are unaware or untrustworthy. They can't be isolated in their tiny villages. They have to be involved in the rest of the world, so they probably go to Mexico City, Tucson, or even Phoenix for business. Sorcerers are all quite well off and one doesn't get that way without banks and investments.

75

In the cities, these powerful people tap the resources of the leisurely rich in need of their healing services. Their clients need help to curb the suffering that they had brought upon themselves from their addictive indulgences. When sorcerers help their clients they have no expectations in the results. They collect their fees and move on, never looking back. Occasionally they run into a grateful client who has made a miraculous change. Some of these people end up living with the sorcerers because they no longer fit into the world the way they used to.

I sketched these people in their magical clothing all morning, having chosen a 4H hard lead pencil in order to achieve a soft detailed effect. I used acid-free mixed media paper. Occasionally I used the computer or art books for references, but I was surprised to find that my experience teaching live drawing for years had given me skills to draw people fairly well without having to use models or photos. Occasionally I used the computer for references but changed the images extensively, morphing them into the people I saw in my vision.

I drew: clothing, faces, unique-looking men and women, an occasional precocious child or a cat or dog. I even sketched the buildings and floor plans for some of the interesting dwellings where they might live. By lunchtime I had taped 12 quick sketches to the doors of the cabinets and saw that I was creating a whole world from my imagination, triggered by a few lights at the foot of a mountain range miles away, dusted with powdered sugar.

I took a break for lunch, stir fried some vegetables with a bit of chicken picked off the bone of a breast that I had roasted the day before; then took my plate back to the table at the windows and ate while watching a rabbit nibble his or her lunch of desert grasses. It was a rare gray day. Streaks of dark clouds were moving across the sky like they had to be somewhere by nightfall.

By mid-afternoon I had plans for seven more paintings, but for some strange reason I felt exhausted – a kind of heaviness fell over me and I was shivering from cold. Thinking that I might be getting sick, I dragged the comforter off my bed and snuggled on the couch for a nap. It wasn't long before I was dreaming.

In the dream, I was somewhere in a city at a huge shopping center. Shops like Saks Fifth Avenue, Neiman Marcus and other fancy stores lined the street. I passed the shoe department in one of the shops and picked up a strappy high heel sandal. The price was marked down to $1,486. I could smell strong scents of expensive perfume wafting throughout the building and it made me cough, so I left. In the street outside, I saw a man wearing an expensive suit, sitting in a chair in the back of a pickup truck. He was a big man, both in height and width, with a head covered with fluffy blond hair. Turquoise lights seemed to shoot out of his eyes, and his toothy smile made me think of magazine ads.

"Would you like a ride?" he asked me in a booming deep voice.

"Yes," I said, and climbed into the back of the truck and sat down at his feet.

Another man walked by and said, "Good morning Judge Harris, I hope you win the election. You've got my vote."

He said, "I'm ever so grateful. Thank you." He shook the man's hand, then he smiled down at me looking as if he were saying, now you know who I am. A gold cross on a chain dangled from his thick neck.

"Where are you going?" he asked me as he pocketed a wad of cash he'd just been handed.

"To the hotel," I heard myself say as if speaking into a tunnel.

"Which hotel?" he asked from the other end of the tunnel.

I didn't know, so said, "Any hotel will do." I was thinking if I get to any hotel I can find my way back home. I can call a cab and go to the airport.

"Why are you here?" he asked.

"I came with my...my husband," I said. "He's on a business trip and I'm shopping." I was thinking about Manuel, but I didn't say that he was just a boyfriend.

"Good," he said. "I'm here with my wife. She's having lunch with her friends. We can meet up with them and I'll give you a ride." He didn't say to where. He seemed to have a slight Texas accent.

I agreed, thinking a ride to anywhere would be a good choice.

Suddenly I was in a very large heavy grey car with several women and the man who answered to the name *Your Honor*. The car was speeding along a curvy road and I felt my body stiffen. This is too fast, I was thinking when a woman reached out took my hand and held it gently. She whispered into my ear, "It's okay, don't be afraid."

I still didn't relax. The car went faster and faster – too fast for a car to go – faster than a jet. Objects shooting by the window dissolved into gray smoke and they began spiraling way. It was like we were in a vortex, or a worm hole, and in a split second we were in a house.

I was sitting on a chair in a bedroom. Bags and opened boxes of newly purchased clothing and wrinkled tissue paper were scattered around me on the floor. The judge was on the bed with his wife, lying on top of her, making out. Feeling embarrassed to be witnessing such intimate behavior, I left the room and found myself in a large living room where other people were milling around. There were pictures of Jesus and other Christian images and symbols everywhere and the people were chatting softly in Texan, a dialect familiar to me. I expected someone to ask if I was ready to take Christ as my savior, but no one did. A beautiful woman brought me a plate of food: fried chicken, potatoes and gravy. I started to hand the plate back and say, I don't eat this kind of food. But I ate it because I was ravenous and it tasted amazingly delicious.

"You're new here," a woman said sitting down next to me. "Where are you from?'

I had to think about that. "Arizona," I finally told her.

"Well, we're just real happy to have you here. My name is Norma Jean. What's your name?"

"Lorie," I said, wondering if I was being patronizing by not saying Laurence. The name Norma Jean rang a bell. Wasn't that Marilyn Monroe?

"What brings you here to Texas? Arizona's so far away. Did you drive?" I glanced over my shoulder as if looking for answers. I wanted to say, I'm lost. I need to get back home. Can you help me, but I couldn't get the words out.

"Someone else drove," I told the woman.

"Oh...well, I hope you have a nice visit. I like your dress. Did you get it at Neiman's?"

I looked down to see what I was wearing and what I saw on my body were the paint-stained scrubs I'd been wearing in the desert house. Apparently, I was now referring to my current place of residence as "The Desert House."

"No, well...maybe. I can't remember," I finally said.

"Oh, I do that all the time. Sometimes I can't even remember I bought something until I find it in my closet years later with the tags still on. I'm terrible," said the woman.

I looked into Norma Jean's clear blue eyes and saw a kindness that made me want to weep. I kept trying to say, please help me. I've been kidnapped. Can you take me to the airport. But I couldn't form the words with my mouth.

Suddenly I woke up from the dream, feeling drugged or altered in a very strange way. Fortunately I no longer felt cold, or sick. I was hungry. Apparently dream food doesn't stick to your bones. In the fridge I grabbed some leftover tuna salad and took it to the sofa to eat. I kept wishing it was fried chicken and mashed potatoes like my favorite food when I was a child.

The dream had somehow unsettled me. It made me think about people as bizarre, exotic, highly developed animals with instinctual behavior patterns.

Since I arrived here, I had observed: quail taking turns being the lookout person ready to alert the rest of the tribe of danger, while the moms paraded the chicks for all to see, javalina surrounding their babies, marauding young males banished from the herd, and the married raven couple with their housekeeper.

People are animals too with different tribal behaviors: the university culture, the Christian Texans in my dream, the sorcerers living at the base of the mountain. I spent a long time trying to imagine the people who had captured me. Where were they? What did they look like? What were their long term intentions? Why was I having such vivid and memorable dreams? Why was my imagination so enhanced? I came to the conclusion that the world was truly unfathomable.

Inner Child

12: My Dad

Fort Worth was hot and humid in the summer, bleak and dreary in winter. Spring and Summer blew by in a flash. The land in Texas was unbelievably flat, windy, and prone to floods. Hattie Linkletter, my grandma, missed the beautiful mountains in Colorado and her friends. It had become too expensive for her to keep flying to Texas to help pull our home and family out of desperate chaos, so she locked the doors of her charming home in Evergreen and settled into ours for the long haul. She slept on a tiny day-bed in the laundry room. I felt sorry for her sleeping in there, but she insisted on that being her place. It would have made sense to clean out Randy's room, paint it and fix it up for her.

After school, I had become accustomed to finding her knitting in an old chair she had dragged from the back porch into the kitchen. This day was no different.

"Cookies for you." She pointed to the table where a small plate of chocolate chip cookies, warm from the oven, sat with a tall glass of milk.

"Thanks, Grandma," I said grimacing at the milk. "Grandma, you know I can't drink milk. I'm allergic."

"Nonsense," Grandma said sternly. "You need to drink your milk."

I sat at the table staring at the milk and trying to think of someway I could convince her to leave the room, so I could pour it down the drain. I didn't know how many times I'd be able to get away with doing that, but milk gave me a terrible stomach ache. I wished for a big thirsty dog. I missed the sliced apples, peanut butter and juice my mom used to give me.

I sat listening to Grandma's needles clicking and thinking about the conversation I had heard between her and my mom the day before.

With as much compassion as Grandma could muster she said to my mom, "Don't you think it's time to let me or someone else go into that room and clean it out?"

"He doesn't like anyone going into his room," Mom snapped. "When he comes home he'll want to find everything just as it is. No one is touching anything in there. Not even me!"

Grandma didn't pursue it. "Okay dear, you just let me know when you are

81

ready."

"What are you talking about...when I'm ready? I told you he's coming back, didn't I. So leave it alone!"

I hardly recognized my mom's voice. It was deep and gravelly like a smoker. I could barely remember what it had been like to sit by her on the sofa, or hang out with her in the kitchen drawing in my sketchbook. I missed looking up to see her cooking or washing dishes.

But I wanted my mom to be right. I wanted to find out that it had all been a mistake and some other person had died in that car wreck. As far as I knew no one had actually seen a body. Maybe they only thought it was Randy. I too wished everyday he would come back home. So things could get back to normal. Sometimes I thought he had run away and was living with some other family. He had done that before, but this time I feared he might stay gone.

The smell of Randy's room permeated the entire house. It was like a rotten spot on a piece of fruit that I feared would grow until the whole house became a glob of goop like the peaches that fell off the tree in the backyard and laid there covered with bugs and flies. I hadn't opened the door to his room since the time I tried to wake him up, and found only pillows. It was next to impossible to sleep close to that room now. I only slept well every three or four nights when exhaustion took over and knocked me out.

My mom, on the other hand, slept in her bedroom most of the time, except for a small part of the day when she would wander into the living room and turn on the television. Sitting in the reclining chair, she would dare anyone to interrupt the relentless flow of soap operas and loud advertisements for cleaning products and scary drugs.

The doctors had insisted that the medicine she took would help her in the long run, and Grandma and Dad were firm believers in following the doctor's orders. They made sure she took the handful of multi-colored pills right on schedule as prescribed. Everyone believed, in time, she would be herself again, but I wasn't so sure. And I didn't understand how, whenever my dad took her to the doctor, she would somehow rally. She would dress appropriately, sit straight up in the chair, smile and tell the doctor how much better she felt. Then she would thank him for the miracle drugs that were helping her overcome the tragedy that had befallen her. So the doctor would pull out his magic prescription pad and suggest she continue on the same regimen. In the beginning he had often suggested grief counseling, but Mom had assured him she was fine. I know about this because I overheard Dad and Grandma talking about it.

"I've accepted his death," she would announce, "And I'm getting on with my life. I have a wonderful husband and a daughter and no more time to spend mourning."

"Darling," my dad would say. "Maybe we could try a little counseling. We could both go. I can't see how it could hurt."

"Absolutely not," she would say. "I'm far too busy for that. I think these pills are all I need for now."

It had been three years since Randy's death, and I could see her declining. So the day I was trying to figure out the milk problem, I decided to give my mom a little encouragement.

"Mom," I had wrestled a chair over from the dining table and placed it next to the recliner. "Mom...Mom, I got an A on my spelling test today."

She turned her head from the TV screen and stared blankly at me like she didn't have a clue who I was.

"Would you like to see it? I got all the words right. I didn't miss any of them." I pulled the paper out of my book bag and tried to hand it to her but she just kept looking at me as if I were transparent.

She smelled weird too, like beer and cigarettes – a lot like Randy's room. Her dress was dingy and wrinkled and she wasn't wearing shoes or socks. Her feet were pink on the ends of her white unshaved legs, and her face was gray-blue from the light of the TV. It was cold in the room. Anyone else would have worn a sweater or covered themselves with a blanket.

"Mom? Are you alright, Mom?" I reached out touched her arm and gave it a gentle shake. "Mom, I really miss you," I said, as my throat tightened and tears streamed down. I hadn't intended to cry, but the tears came rushing out anyway – lots of them. I hadn't meant to say what I said either, but that's what came out of my mouth. So I sat there in the chair sobbing while Mom turned back to look at the TV screen not even noticing I was still there.

Grandma, busy in the kitchen, didn't come to get me, didn't give me a hug, wipe my tears away and talk to me about my mom's condition. So I just sat there remembering how things used to be and realizing it might never get back to the way it was. I hated my brother for dying and that scared me because I knew that if you hated somebody you could go to hell. That's what Grandma told me.

My dad came home two hours later and saw me sitting there holding the damp wrinkled paper in my lap – still sniffling. He knelt down in front of me, took the paper out of my hand and straightened it out to see what it was. Then he asked "Is this your weekly spelling test?" He held it like he had found a treasure map.

"Good job, Laurence. Let's go see what Grandma has made for dinner." Ignoring his distracted wife he took my hand and led me to the kitchen. He sat down in Grandma's chair, held me on his lap and wiped my nose and cheeks with his handkerchief. I blew my nose into it, then noticed he smelled fresh like the outdoor wind. I loved the feel of his neck and cheek – a bit scratchy and cold but it was turning warmer by the minute. His plaid shirt felt soft on my chapped cheek.

We sat warming each other while Grandma put food on the table, and with some coaxing she managed to get my mom to join us for dinner. The four of us ate in silence. No one shared anything about their day; there was no eye contact, no one asked for seconds. Even the meatloaf and gravy seemed cold. Later that night my dad sat with me on the side of my bed and read a story to me like mom once did, then tucked the covers around me and kissed me on the forehead.

"I love you," he said.

"I love you too, Daddy."

The next thing I knew it was morning.

On Monday before I left for school, my dad sat down in a chair in front of me and said: "I've arranged for you to go to the Sun's house after school. So from now on I want you to go to their house and I'll come by and pick you up when I get off work. Can you remember to go there instead of here?"

"Sure," I said. "I like it there."

"Of course you do. And they are excited to have you. Ana said she will help you with your homework. Then you can play with Granger. I know I don't have to tell you to be a good girl." He gave me a hug and a kiss on the cheek. "Do you still have my work number in you bag?" He had me check to see if I did, even though I knew I did.

"I think it's best if you call me if you need anything. Don't bother your Grandma. She's busy taking care of Mom. If you need to come home and get something out of your room have Granger or Apollo come with you. Okay?"

"Okay," I said cheerfully.

When he drove me to school I chattered all the way there, telling him lively stories about things that had happened at school. He could tell I'd been saving it all up. I could feel his eyes on me when I skipped up the sidewalk to the front door of the school. I turned and waved goodbye. His face looked different – maybe a little happy.

13: Journal Entry

I've smeared a little paint onto some pages in my sketchbook so I can write on top of color, but it makes it hard for the ball point pen to work, so a pencil will have to do. It's fun getting creative in a journal.

I've been knocking out lots of paintings. But I'm not sending all of them out because I'm into experimenting and some of them just don't work. I'll let those dry and paint over them again and again. I spend time staring out the window for sources of images, but it seems I'm mostly interested in dreams. Marc Chagall comes to mind, but my paintings are very different in style from his. I like to call his style messy. He is a messy painter and I am tidy. I just made that up. However, I started out being one of those kids who always colored within the lines.

It's this dream thing that has me captured. I'm still having vivid dreams. I wake up in the night sometimes and make sketches. But in the morning making sense of them is a challenge. So I'm learning to make paintings that don't make sense. I can just imagine being at an art opening and having people ask questions like, what were you thinking when you painted that or what does that mean?

What I really like is when they tell me what they think it means to them. I'm fascinated by what people see in my work. Each person is absolutely right and they help me to appreciate my work more. Which, of course, that is not what is happening right now. I'm left to my own devices. Oh well. Max says I can email images and he will comment if I want. So maybe I'll try that from time to time.

The Powers That Be seem to be happy if I send only one or two paintings a week. There are a number of paintings started that are unfinished because I'm not sure what they need. I'll get around to them later. By the way, I am now calling my captors *The Powers That Be* rather than *Ninjas* because I've come to realize there are way more of them than just a handful of agile men dressed in black.

One recurring dream image is a woman flying over a village. Her arms are stretched out in front of her somewhat like Superman, but she is holding something with both hands. Each time she appears she is holding something different: a piece of fruit, a kitten, a paint brush or garment of some kind and my favorite, a bird. But the village below remains the same. I can tell though, from the placement of the houses that she is flying in different directions. I thought she might be an angel, but she doesn't have wings. That makes it seem much more dream-like. It's usually night or sunset or sunrise. Never full daylight.

I've made a lot of small studies of this image, but I'm coming to the conclusion that the finished painting should be big – at least 3 or 4 feet wide and maybe 2 feet tall. She would be wearing a white dress and surrounded by lots of swirling colors in an atmosphere almost like the aurora borealis, but not that exactly. She might have a name, but I'm not sure yet if she does or if I need to let people know it. She could just be *Woman Dreaming.* I can't honestly call my paintings fantasy even if people see them that way, because dreams are real. People dream, they see things in their dreams and they aren't like what they see when they are awake. People fly in dreams.

I think I used to draw this woman when I was a child. Since I didn't take to the Christian religion, I never believed in angels. And I'm sure she isn't an angel – no wings. By the way, I think the Old Masters were probably the ones who made up what Christian angels look like – the devil too. When Hindus painted spiritual beings, they didn't call them angels. They were definitely meant to be on another plane of existence or, as I was saying, appear in dreams. These figures represented both the light and the dark sides – not so different than Christians. I'm quite sure wings on humans were merely the artists using symbolism. There is no doubt in my mind people did and still do believe they may wake up after death and find they have wings to fly with. I don't know. Maybe they will.

I guess I'm focusing here on religions because so much of it is revealed in ancient paintings. I was told in college the reason for that was because lots of people could not read so the church paid artists to tell the stories in images. I remember so clearly being a kid and not being able to read. My dad bought me comic books and I looked at the pictures and made up my own stories. I imagine various churches wanted everyone to see the same story, but I know that would never have worked. It's rare when two or more people interpret images the same way.

The old masters must have strived hard to get jobs from the churches. Now we have the advertising of products, movies and all sorts of other ways art is used our the culture. There is so much of it, most people don't even see it anymore, most of it eye-sores. Here's thanks to street artists who give us something other than advertisements.

Nevertheless, I'm sure there are way too many paintings in the world. Yet, here I am making more. I hope at least some of them are appreciated. And it's probably better for the planet than making more people. I made it past that stage, I guess. No babies for me...just paintings.

Well, I guess it's time to wash my hands and cook some food. I'm feeling like a wilted flower.

Woman Dreaming

14: Alice

A project is described as something that takes more than one action. I usually had two or three paintings going at a time – several projects – in various stages of development, with the planning stage often taking more time than the actual painting. I collected images, made sketches and sometimes made small painted studies for a piece before starting the real work. I had time to do all of that. I had all the time I needed and I still felt like it wasn't enough. I had no idea that I'd been suppressing all this creative energy. No wonder I'd been so neurotic in Phoenix!

I also didn't feel lonely. I'd always loved having alone time and often imagined I had a sword that I could use to slash away distractions that stood in the way of my doing art. But with a job, I could never cut away enough. Even though I liked my job, I felt divided. There were meetings, classes to teach, homework to grade, lesson plans and going to the market for food. But now all of that was gone from my life and I only missed it a tiny bit. Here in the desert there were only minor chores like preparing food, washing a few clothes and sweeping up.

However, by at the end of the day I began to think of having coffee with Granger, or lying in bed in the evening chatting with Manuel – well, more than just chatting. But emails with Max was all I got.

However that was to change. Later, I would wonder if *The Powers That Be* knew I needed something more. Because someone did eventually show up.

At first I started seeing glimpses of Alice out of my peripheral vision. I would get a feeling that someone was in the room with me. She zipped by so fast there would only be a vague memory left behind. Sometimes I thought I heard someone talking to me and when I turned toward the voice, I could see a figure shimmering in the light. I could smell her too. Sometimes she smelled like roses or a flower I couldn't name. And sometimes it was the scent of damp leaves that alerted me to her presence.

Finally, one day I surprised myself by saying to her, "Enough of this! Show yourself!" She snapped into view and we looked at each other for a while before she spoke, "Hello, Laurence."

Everything in the room and out the window seemed to disappear as I held my gaze on her beautiful face.

"I don't know what to say," I said, finally hearing my voice speak to someone other than the animals I'd been talking to through the window.

"Don't be scared," she said.

"I don't think I am. But this is weird. Where did you come from?"

"That is a difficult question to answer. But I will get around to it," she said in a voice that seemed to fade in and out as if she was talking to me from a cell phone.

I noticed she was wearing a dress made of flowers. Not a dress with flowers printed on it, but flowers growing from vines that climbed around her tall movie star body. Her hair was red, but not like mine. Hers was bright cadmium red. It made her head look like a bloom.

She followed my gaze looking down at her dress. "Oh, I'm sorry," she said. "I just came from a costume party. I must have fallen asleep in the hammock. It was such a nice day and my friends were all sitting on the grass talking. We are always happy to be together in one spot for a change. Sometimes months go by and we don't get together in awakened life. You see, I'm dreaming you now, while napping. I won't be here for long since someone is sure to interrupt." She rustled across the room and sat down in the other chair at my table.

"Do you mind?" she asked.

I sat down across from her and noticed a tiny white chihuahua sitting in her lap.

"This is Bonita," she said.

The dog seemed to know she was being introduced. She appeared to be smiling. I shook my head as if I were asleep, dreaming and trying to wake myself up.

"You are really seeing me," she said. "You're not asleep."

I looked around the room and saw that everything looked solid and real. She on the other hand was slightly transparent.

"Remember, you asked me to show myself. I assumed you were ready for this. But I can see you are in a slight state of shock. Shall I come back another time?"

I felt my head nodding yes.

"How about tomorrow for breakfast? Here at your table. I like tea, but I don't eat."

I nodded again. And she and the dog slowly faded away.

I don't know how long I sat there staring out the window and glancing back again and again at the chair across from me. I didn't feel scared, just mystified and curious. I remembered Valdez's stories of people and their dream bodies, but I'd never thought I would ever actually have an experience like I'd just had. In fact, I was not so sure I believed that all things in his books were actually true. Even though he claimed they were.

Outside it was growing warmer every day. The snow had melted on the peaks of the distant mountains, and more animals gathered in the clearing. I enjoyed a fierce orange sunset – trying to let it whisk away thoughts about what had happened earlier. Feeling weird, I went to bed early and slept fitfully. I had finally adjusted to being here alone, lost in making paintings. My research on solitary confinement convinced me that this day's experience was a symptom. I decided to wait a while before telling Max.

Alice came the next morning as promised. We sat at the table looking out the great windows watching quail foraging and rabbits shuffling around ignoring us. She was wearing a stylish, rose-colored dress that accentuated her tall frame. She must have been about 5'11' – a model's height.

At first I sat staring at her in dismay. She had actually appeared out of thin air. Needless to say I was startled and she, being fully aware of my discomfort, said to me, "Don't be frightened. In order for us to be together you must abandon belief systems that keep you locked into limited realities. I can explain how this is happening. Yes, you are right to consider that you might be having hallucinations, but from my point of view I am dreaming you."

Bonita leaped from her lap and began eating crumbs from under the table. Alice said, "The dog doesn't belong to me. She is a roommate who moved in several years ago. She's a sorceress like the rest of us who live in my house. We take care of her, but no one has ever trained her." When the dog was finished with her morning chore she sat looking at her friend until Alice swooped her up into her lap again. She stroked the tiny animal's head and Bonita seemed to smile from the attention.

"She is her own person," Alice explained.

"Does she ever bark?" I asked thinking it was uncharacteristic of a dog of that breed to be so calm and quiet. Also it was a kind of mundane thing to say in a very bizarre situation.

Alice looked at the dog and said to her. "Bonita, do you bark?"

Bonita barked. One short, sharp yip.

I laughed.

"I would like to tell you a little bit about me, if you don't mind."

I nodded and she continued.

"Having been born with a natural talent, I mastered the art of dreaming

91

when I was a little girl. My parents didn't know what to do with me. First they put me in a very strict school where students would get their hands whacked with a ruler if they were caught day-dreaming." A shadow fell over Alice's face right on cue as she looked down at her delicate hands: one with a finger through the handle of a teacup, the other hand, decorated with turquoise and silver rings that lay flat on the table. The fingers were slender and white with perfect nails painted pink to match her dress; I shuddered to think of them being hit with a wooden stick.

"When my parents saw the bruises on my fingers they took me out of that school."

"At least they did that," I told her. I couldn't imagine my own parents even noticing if I came home from school with black and blue fingers. I felt envious of her loving childhood home.

Then she said, "Finally they heard about a new school. Actually it wasn't new. It had been around for centuries, but it was...well, sort of hidden."

Before continuing her story, Alice hooked a tendril of curly red hair behind an ear that was dripping in turquoise and silver jewelry that matched her rings.

"It wasn't a building, like other schools. It was a community of people who lived together and offered apprenticeships to children who didn't fit into ordinary public schools. We met in small groups and went from house to house to learn whatever the residents were teaching that day. They made sure we learned the basic school subjects, but they offered much more. They called it *The Castle School of Magical Realism*. They let us choose the subjects we found most interesting, and I was drawn to dreaming."

We both sipped tea, me from my paint stained mug, and Alice from a dainty antique tea cup that I would later learn only appeared when she was here.

"I want to know everything about your school," I said. "Before I came here, I was a teacher."

"Yes, I know you were a teacher. Teachers make the best students." I wondered if Alice was implying that I might now be her student. It thrilled me to think it could be true, but I had no idea why I thought that.

"Instead of punishing us for dreaming, they encouraged it. They taught us to know the difference between sleep dreaming and awake dreaming. Right now you and I are now awake dreaming."

Somehow I knew what she was saying was true, but I didn't know how I knew it.

She continued. "We realized that the kids we met in the school were kids

92

we had been meeting in our dreams for years. We talked about our experiences in small groups, and were allowed to go as far as we needed to in order to understand ourselves. We began to discover that we were not unique. We learned that every human had dreaming capabilities, but most had been taught to distrust that part of themselves."

I was fascinated by what she was saying about dreaming being a school subject. "Please," I said. "tell me more."

She took a couple of sips of tea and continued. "Humans still form societies that strive to fit everyone into molds, causing them to behave in ways that are considered normal for their culture. They tell children dreams are not real. But that is not altogether true. Our brain is real and the subconscious mind where dreams live is real. We may not remember our dreams, but we also don't remember much of what happened yesterday when we were fully awake. But remembering isn't what is important. It is about being present with whatever is happening, whether we are awake or asleep."

She looked into my eyes as if she was trying to see if I was open to hearing more. I looked down at her hands, then back into her eyes, not knowing what to say.

"If we aren't careful, our minds start playing tape loops. This repetitive thinking keeps us from experiencing what is right in front of us. There is a part of our brain that thinks it has to solve every problem it has encountered. So it will go over and over something trying to come up with some solution, any solution. But it fails most of the time. I'm not saying there aren't solutions to some problems and that we don't need our brains to help us solve them. But most of the time that's not the case. The brain...well, for lack of a better way to put it, has a mind of it's own and can go off on fruitless journeys that are a complete waste of time. It's silly, isn't it?" she laughed.

"Trauma can exaggerate this kind of thinking and believe me most people have experienced a lot of trauma. Some without fully realizing it," she said.

"So how can they stop that kind of thinking?" I asked, knowing I was certainly guilty of excessive and repetitive thinking sometimes.

"Some people believe they can hand the problem over to a power greater than themselves. And that is often an effective method of letting the problem-solving mind rest. Geniuses have said that taking a walk and stopping thinking sometimes produces the solutions they are striving for. To be honest, stopping the inner dialogue isn't an easy task."

"Does meditation help with that?" I asked. I wanted to know because I had been meditating every morning, and it had helped calm my mind. But it had not come close to stopping it.

"Yes. Meditation and yoga can work very well for softening the internal dialogue. But you have to understand that the mind thinks and that is its job. Like the heart pumps blood, the stomach digests, the lungs breathe. We can't stop the thinking. But we can stop believing it. When we believe it, we are going down a path away from the truth of who we are. And we will act that out if we aren't careful. That is pretty much why the world is in such a mess. Don't you agree?"

"Sure, I can see that," I said

"In so called *normal* schools that have been invented by thinking minds and people with lots of limited belief systems, children are programed to fit into what adults think is normal behavior. In our school, no one was trying to make us fit into anything. However, our school didn't throw the baby out with the bath water. We learned the usual skills that people need to survive, but we were encouraged to go further than that. We were taught to pay attention to more than what most people realize exists. In other words, things that are not perceived by our five senses. That makes it seem like there is a difference between an ordinary world and a magical one."

"So what do you mean by ordinary world?" I asked.

"Well, there really isn't any separation from the magical world and the ordinary world. It's all magical. We use the word ordinary to describe people who are locked into their old belief systems that cause their world to appear extremely limited, which can cause a boring or suffering existence. Becoming aware and letting those beliefs go brings about freedom which can feel very much like magic at first. That is only because the majority of people aren't used to it."

"For instance, some people take every story found in religious books to be literal where others might experience these stories as metaphors. You can take that even further. The stories themselves are tools that religions use to tell people what God is, instead of guiding people to find God for themselves. No matter what, everyone has a different understanding of God. So a collection of stories that try to fit God into a box is crazy-making. It can only work for the few whose personal viewpoint is aligned with what they are being told. Most people just go along with the beliefs out of fear of being rejected even though it doesn't really make sense."

"Some people buy into all these beliefs about reality and therefore the world appears to be the way they believe it to be. Since they are delusional, truth will often whack them over the head from time to time. Only occasionally does it wake someone up."

She was quiet long enough for my imagination to come up with some interesting visuals of people getting whacked over the head with the truth. I wanted to say something, but didn't.

"Others," she said, "know they are living lies, but they go along with it anyway. They go through the motions of acting the way they are told to act because they are terrified to not go along with what everyone else is doing or thinking. People will say *I am a Christian, or I am a Buddhist or I am a Muslim or a Republican or a Democrat. My god is called God, not Allah, so your god is not the real god.* That's what they are told to believe. However, they were not born that way. Nobody is born a Jew or a Christian or a whatever. They are hypnotized into thinking what they have been told is true, and they become terrified of the real truth."

"They become like that because they were told by others that these belief systems are the truth. Truth can be nebulous, even when backed by facts, but facts are, in fact, only closer to the truth. Learning that they are something different from what they thought they were people begin to feel like they are waking up from a dream. And they are. They are snapping out of a hypnagogic state. Not many can actually accomplish that act because when they get close, they get scared and pull back into what seems normal to them. They get rewarded by family and peers for returning home, and for a while they may find contentment, but it doesn't last. They become restless and sad."

Alice looked at me and smiled as if she were checking out if I was open to hearing more. "I'm only telling you this," she said, "because you were already waking up before I came."

I was quickly getting hooked on what she had to say. I wanted more. It felt to me like no one had ever said anything like this to me in this way before. Nor had I read it anywhere. I was starved for this information. As a college professor, I must have fallen into thinking that I knew everything I needed to know. I had not been looking for more. Or perhaps I had known this before from Valdez's books, but had forgotten.

"People don't like to stand out or feel different," I said.

"It comes from tribal days when being ostracized from the tribe could mean death. So humans tend to go along with what everyone else around them is doing whether or not it is the best for them and the group," she explained. "Or for the whole world, for that matter."

"But there is more," she went on. "Some others may completely rebel against what everyone else is doing, causing harm to themselves and others. Doing the opposite is usually not a healthy option either. We refer to that as pushing off. Then they just go find others who engage in the same destructive behaviors. Mostly it involves addiction to drugs, alcohol, food, sex or other people and things. Or just bad choices. They entirely miss the middle road which is powerful, creative and healthy."

I squirmed in my chair. I was thinking how I had been so addicted to work. Even though she had not added that to her list of addictions, I knew I fit into that scenario. I began to hope she was here to help me find that middle road.

"We can't really get rid of all beliefs. Nor should we. We need some as guidelines. Like the belief that it's best to be kind to others. It's a good one to keep, however it's just a belief. It's not true, but as long as you know it's not true you don't feel so disappointed when people are mean. People are not always kind to each other...that is truth. We are always picking up beliefs from living in the world around other people. But it doesn't hurt to try to clean our brains, like cleaning up the desktop on our computer, and throwing out data we don't need anymore. For instance, a belief that most children have is that they need to hold the hand of an adult when crossing the street. That is a necessary belief for a child. We can hang onto beliefs like that way into adulthood. I'm not kidding. They burrow deep into the subconscious mind making change of any kind seem difficult!"

"That makes sense," I said.

"It's good to remember that beliefs and truth are not the same thing. You don't have to believe that you have a hand on the end of your arm. You know it's there. And truth goes even further than that, like into molecules and whatever else that eventually leads us to the fact that we are all a part of the one universe."

I remembered the trip here to the desert and the drug that caused me to realize that everything, including myself, was just a collection of molecules. "Can you give me an example? What are my limiting beliefs?" I asked.

"You could start with the belief that you have limiting beliefs but that might be too far of a leap." She laughed out loud and her laugh had a kind of funny-sinister tone to it. It made me laugh at her laugh.

Sunlight streamed through the window causing dust particles to look like fairy dust. The rainbows on the walls seemed to be stronger and for a moment I was lost in a fantasy of how I might paint the twinkling atmosphere and when I looked back, Alice was gone, along with the tea cup and the dog. I wondered if she left because I got distracted. I wondered if I got distracted because what she was telling me was in some way overwhelming. I'd heard about limiting beliefs before, but not in the way she had explained it. There was a time when some of my students were into changing beliefs in order to change their reality, but they were only changing negative beliefs into positive ones. What that did was create another set of belief systems that seemed to fall apart over time and didn't keep out the bad stuff. It wasn't at all about getting to the truth. But the idea of letting go of most limiting beliefs got my attention.

I picked up the sketchbook, and while I drew Alice and Bonita from memory, I thought more about the concept of limited beliefs and how hanging on to them might cause a person to get stuck in certain situations. For instance, if you believed God was a punishing dictator, you would surely live in fear. You probably would not like yourself very much, because all people screw up from time to time. It's a part of being human. Beliefs can keep people stuck in following some very antiquated rules. Can you imagine believing that if you mess up you could be punished by God and made to suffer in hell for all of eternity? In our modern times it is considered child abuse to speak of hell and the devil.

I thought about myself in my current situation. In so many ways I had been freed from a very stressful and limiting life, but now I was a prisoner in another way. I began to ask myself what beliefs would I need to change to be totally free. Or did I really want to be free? I would have to think about that for a while.

After finishing my sketch, I went to the kitchen, made a salad, and returned to the table. What on earth had just happened? I asked myself as I slowly crunched away at the veggies. There was the sketch and the memories of what she had said to me, but I didn't know what to believe. Did it happen or not? In a trance, I finished my lunch remembering how it felt when I first woke up in this room. I was having some of those same feelings of disbelief and wonder.

Alice

15: Outdoors

It was the day after Alice's first visit that I remembered I had missed checking in with Max. It was now afternoon and I'd spent the morning trying to capture the likeness of Alice and Bonita in a painting. It wasn't as easy as I thought it would be. I was used to having a model sit for me or a photograph to work from. So in frustration I took a break and contacted Max.

Laurence: *Max, I can't remember how the earth smells. I can barely hear the birds through the window.*

Max: *You haven't mentioned this before. I can understand how you must feel cut off from nature. Would you like to go out?*

L: *Why do you have to ask that? Of course, who wouldn't want to go out?*

M: *Sorry, I can see that being indoors so long is making you a bit grumpy.*

L: *I'm grumpy?*

M: *Well...it's understandable...this is not a judgement. You've just never before mentioned that you might like to go out.*

L: *Can I go out?*

I wanted to add daddy to that sentence. But held myself back.

M: *Of course. Hold on, I need to install an app on your iPad.*

L: *You've got to be kidding.*

M: *No, I'm not. Okay, See the icon that looks like a door?*

L: *Yes.*

M: *Press it.*

I did what he said, and the west wall between the cabinets and the north wall began to hum, then rise. It sounded like a quiet elevator. Behind the wall were glass sliding doors.

L: *Are you kidding me? That's been there all along? Now the mystery of how I got in here is solved.*

M: *Never thought you were wondering about that.*

I left the computer and slowly walked towards the doors where I could see out into a courtyard. I stood there for several minutes in disbelief, then reached out and touched the glass with my hand. I began to shake with excitement realizing how, before I came here, I had taken so much for granted.

I backed away and looked at the metal lever, fearing if I tried it I might be disappointed. What if I were only dreaming? But, like everything else in this house, the doors felt sturdy. I turned the lever, heard the click, and slid the door open. I could feel the dry outside air on my face and hands. Desert smells bombarded me– dust and creosote. With bare feet I stepped out onto a flagstone patio and looked straight up into the ultramarine sky. As if on cue a red tail hawk swooped by and screeched a piercing welcome. That would happen in the movies, I thought.

I found myself in a large square enclosure with high adobe walls. A decorative iron gate on the south side was the first thing I checked out. It was locked. The walls were too tall to scale. Turning back to face the north I could see raised garden beds and a door on the west wall. I went to the door and opened it. It was a closet that contained garden tools, shelves with jars of seeds and everything else I needed for growing a garden.

Passing by a hammock, a chair and a chaise lounge, I went to the first of several garden beds. I wasn't sure what to think. I'd never grown a garden. I sat down on the edge of the bed and stuck my hands into the dirt. Underneath the top layer that had been warmed by the sun, the earth was cool. I sat there for a long time feeling, smelling and trying to deal with intense emotions that came in waves. After the joy of feeling the sun and smelling the earth I realized this meant I would not be going home anytime soon. I didn't know exactly what that meant to me or how I felt about it. But after having the bizarre experience of a phantom visitor I knew I needed to put my hands into the earth.

Well, I guess I'll need sunscreen, I thought. I quickly let go of any feelings and thoughts of disappointment that I might be staying longer. Somehow the memories of living in a huge city had faded into the distance.

16: Max

Laurence: *Do you think I can really grow something here in this desert?*

Max: *Sure. Just follow the instructions in the "Desert Garden" book. Don't worry. We will still be sending food. We have no intentions of making you grow all of your own food. We thought you might need something else to do besides paint.*

L: *Max, I think of you as the "God" voice in here.*

M: *That's funny, Laurence. I can see how it would seem like that to you. How would you feel if I told you I'm just a person like you and this happens to be my job.*

L: *Glad to hear you are person. You could after all be a computer.*

M: *I have feelings, Laurence...Computers do not.*

L: *Then tell me about your feelings. Do you love someone? Do you have kids? Who exactly are you?*

M: *This is my job and that means there are rules and the rules include that I am not to share my personal information with you. This is a private chat. But, as you know, nothing is private on the internet. I wish that were not true. Sometimes I feel like unloading on you.*

L: *Are you serious?*

M: *Yes, I'm serious. Haven't you noticed I'm always at your beck and call. That means I don't have much time for other relationships and this one is limited. Lots of things are off limits according to the job description.*

L: *I bet. But I tend to think of you as the boss, the one who makes the rules, not someone who follows them. You are the "all knowing" in this universe.*

M. *That's part of the truth, but as you know by the "we" statements that I'm not the only one here.*

L: *So tell me more about yourself. How do you qualify for this job?*

M. *Well, okay...it's like this. Perhaps you can think of me as a psychologist of sorts and understand that I've studied a lot about solitary confinement. You might say I have a PhD.*

L: *Is that true? If so, I guess that explains it. I'd be your test subject and you are studying me. I'm not the only one, am I?*

M: *I don't know. I'm just hired to be here for you. I don't know a lot about what else goes on. Well, I know some, but I don't think it would be helpful for you to know everything.*

That made me squirm. I rolled my chair back and placed my forehead on the table in front of my keyboard. I hated the question "why me?" But "why me?" was a question I most wanted answered.

Did Max know that Alice visited me? I don't think he had a way of seeing her. It made me think again that she might be some sort of hologram that they cast into the room with technology. I've seen artists do this kind of work. But she said no. She said she was dreaming me. But then again, Max was an expert on people in solitary confinement, so he might conclude I had had a visitation. And there were paintings of her with the dog sitting at the table talking to me. But no photographs.

L: *Max, sometimes I feel life is so simple. I go about my day dealing with one thing at a time. There aren't other people here, no job stress, no complicated love relationships and so on. Then, at times like this, I'm just totally overwhelmed with how exactly complex it all is. Even thinking of how a tiny seed sprouts and grows into an edible plant is mind boggling. Telling me something like you've just told me blows away every illusion that anything is ever simple.*

M: *I love it when you talk to me like that.*

L: *MAX!*

M: *Sorry, I really am a human being. Not a computer. I have deep feelings for you and I'd like to ask you to trust me. But I know it's way too much to ask. I can only promise you that someday you will understand all of this.*

L: *You keep saying that, Max!*

M: *I do?*

L: *Yes, you keep telling me that someday I'll understand what is happening to me. So how could it be a bad thing if you just told me now?*

M: *I don't know the answer to that, but it's an interesting thought.*

L: *And why don't we do something like FaceTime where I can see you?*

M: *Whoever put this whole operation together felt it was better if you couldn't see me. What if I got fired or maybe I wanted to quit my job? They would hire a new Max and hope you wouldn't be able to tell. Honestly, I don't know.*

I stared at the screen as though I thought if I looked hard and long enough I'd be able to make out the features of his face hiding somewhere behind the words. Then I thought, maybe he was a her.

L: *Max. I don't want to give you a hard time. It's not to my advantage to do that. As you can tell, I have a sarcastic side. It's a fault.*

M: *Laurence, my dear, I'm well aware of the stresses of your current situation. My aim is to make you as comfortable as possible. I sort of like your sarcasm. I like you a lot. Just the way you are.*

L: *Good grief! I like you too, Max. Being here like this, just makes me see the insanity that has always been with me. It's just a mixed bag of agony and ecstasy. I can't believe I just said that. One moment I hate being here and all I can think about is getting back home and the next minute I feel blessed to have this time to myself to create. Sometimes I hate you and sometimes I'm grateful to have somebody who seems almost real.*

M: *I understand...I really do.*

L: *Max, I wish I knew more about you.*

M: *Who knows? Maybe someday, you will.*

I had a feeling I never would, but I was grateful that Max appeared to be more human than he ever had before. All I've had from him are word messages on a screen. Maybe I really do miss humans and all their messiness. I don't know yet.

Whatever. It was time for me to get back to work. Having a patio and outdoor time was awesome. But I soon became obsessed with making art again.

I began to notice that there were two different subjects that interested me most: surrealistic landscapes with or without the human figure, and portraits and clothing influenced by the village at the foot of those distant mountains. I worked mostly in acrylic and oil. But occasionally I would pull out the watercolors and pencils and work on paper. It was refreshing to switch back and forth with subject matter and media.

I began working on a floating figure wearing a dress made mostly of organic found objects. From outside I brought in a few sticks, stems, and leaves from the back deck and garden to use as reference. I integrated them into the design of the dress: flowers, birds, butterflies, sticks, roots, rocks and other natural objects.

I worked on this sketch using graphite, watercolor colored pencils, watercolor paint and gesso. It was lovely being able to drop watercolor paint into a wet background and let the sky make itself. It was so different from the last two paintings I'd done with oil paint where I had to paint in every little detail of the clouds and sky.

Also, I will never get over my love affair with paper. I'd been given a huge selection. Three hundred pound cold press and hot press Arches watercolor paper and something that was new to me, a mixed media paper which I found to be delightful.

I had started with a very detailed drawing using a 4H pencil. Then, I sprayed the drawing with a workable fixative. Over that I applied watercolor and colored pencil. It turned out to be lovely, and I later did an oil version of this same image.

I began to challenge myself by learning how to paint better portraits. I didn't want to do ordinary portraits, so I became creative with costumes, backgrounds, and such. I painted a knight in shining armer with a chihuahua like Bonita.

Because I did not forget about my stressful life at the University, I appreciated the luxury of all of the uninterrupted time that I had to paint. I only took breaks to eat, work in the garden and rest in the hammock in the late afternoon. Oh, and I did take time to learn more yoga from a video. But painting was what I loved the most, and I often worked late into the night. I just kept thinking that the more paintings I sent out, the sooner my captors would let me go. But it also occurred to me that the opposite might be true. Somedays I just felt, so what if I'm here the rest of my life. It was true that it wasn't so bad, but I eventually discovered that solitary confinement had a mind of it's own.

17: Journal Entry

Even though I haven't been showing you all of my journal entries, I've been writing in my sketchbook almost every day. Without my journal to help me remember what happened I wouldn't be telling you this story now. Because when I write I tend to wander around and often not make sense, I will only be showing you a few entries throughout my telling of this story. So here we go...

After spending months inside one room I can't get enough of the sun and the smells of the earth. Sunscreen came with food delivery today and I'm glad for it because it didn't take long for my ghost-like skin to turn pink on the first day out. With the tall walls, there is always some shade, but this is the desert so you can get blasted anywhere. I love the hammock and the chaise lounge. I can see that I'll be spending hours outdoors just laying around and reading books on my Kindle. What luxury. I think it's the first day I've actually taken off from my work to rest. Maybe I thought that if I gave them a lot of paintings they would let me out early. Well, I don't know what their plans are, but I see I may be here for a while. So I might as well back off of the customary way I have of driving myself. Besides, I feel like I can't get enough of natural light.

Last night I spent time on the internet learning everything I could about gardening. Also, there's a desert garden book in the library. I always wondered why it was here. I thought it was references for paintings or maybe it was a joke. Glad to find out differently.

I've learned that I'll need to be careful where I plant certain things. I found out that in the desert it is not a good idea for vegetable plants to get full sun. Most of the beds are in the center of the patio so some of the plants will get morning shade and others will get afternoon shade. It's not spring yet, but it's warm enough to plant some things like broccoli, Brussel sprouts, kale and turnips. It looks like someone already planted some garlic and onions. One of the beds has a plexiglass cover over it and inside are small pots for starting seeds. From what I have read I can start some seeds now. Max has promised some baby tomato and chili plants when it gets a warmer.

I found an outdoor easel in the patio closet so I can paint outdoors without having to drag out the heavy one in the studio. I've never been much of a plein air painter, but I've got time now to try it. Believe it or not, I was starting to get bogged down in painting. I never thought I'd ever reach a place where I'd get tired of doing it. Maybe that was why I was having to struggle so much with that painting of Alice and Bonita. The garden is a welcome relief and my head feels clearer now.

It was a dark winter and I thought I was losing my mind. I hope Alice comes back. Or should I say whatever happened with her, I hope it happens again. Even if it's just me being insane.

Artists do need their imaginations, but it's the other people in our lives that keep us grounded in the real world. I mean the other real live people, not phantoms. I wonder if without live people, visitations from an imaginary friend could become much too believable.

It's strange, I seem to have stopped missing the people I left behind. Well, maybe I do miss Manuel late at night. My body misses his. By the way, I didn't mention there was a vibrator in the drawer next to the bed. Gosh, they thought of everything. Unfortunately it does not replace Manuel. It doesn't hug me.

Lately I haven't been thinking much about Granger and George. I have a feeling they are doing fine without me. Probably married now. I wonder if Granger is still working for the University. Yes, these thoughts cross my mind every now and then, but I don't worry about them. I'm much more interested in what I'm painting.

It's strange how Alice gave me so much information. If I imagined her, how could I alone have made up what she told me if I didn't already know it? Do I know it? Some part of me feels like I've always known. But I'm not sure how. Perhaps it has to do with truth. When she talked to me, everything she said made sense, causing me to realize that when I was in the world back in Phoenix, I kept myself distracted from the absurdities that were going on all around me. It was my way of preserving my own sanity while living in an insane world. With my new – perhaps imaginary – friend, I hope that there are ways to co-exist with the craziness of the world and actually use it as an advantage. But she isn't real, is she? I'm the one making all of this up, right? Maybe she's a hologram. Could it be that she is being projected into the room by some device? I can tell by what I'm writing that there probably isn't any way of escaping insanity no matter where you are. All of this is pretty crazy, right?

You know, the truth is, I don't really care one way or the other. Life really is just one day at a time or one moment at a time. It's all absurd. We never know what's coming down the pipeline. I thought I was totally in charge of my life. HA! Truth is, I'm not unhappy. I'm not depressed, I'm not angry about what has happened to me. Of course, I'm still not sure if *The Powers That Be* are feeding me some kind of happy drugs. I haven't noticed any side effects if they are.

Guess I'd better check in with Max before I hit the sack. Wow, I haven't thought about "hit the sack" since I was a kid. My dad used to say that. Dear old dad...I'll talk about him later. Right now I need to contact Max.

Journey to Ixtlan

18: Alice Speaks

Alice sat at my table with tiny Bonita on her lap. I was excited that my imaginary friend had returned because I had a lot of questions for her about some of the things she told me the last time she visited. Both she and the dog looked at me with expectant eyes.

This time she was dressed in traditional Mexican clothes, much like those worn by Frida Kahlo – a pink embroidered blouse and a green gathered skirt. Her hair was piled on top of her head and embellished with roses and daisies. The whole room smelled like a flower garden.

"I'm not really an artist like Frida," she told me, "but I thought you could use some inspiration." The little dog in her lap seemed to be smiling at me with her dark round eyes.

"I'm amused," I said, stirring a dash of stevia into my tea. "I'm glad you are here."

"I'm happy to hear that."

"I'm not convinced that you are real. I've found lots of information on what happens to people in solitary confinement and it's not uncommon for them to start hallucinating. Can you tell me more about yourself?" At that moment I was totally skeptical.

She took a sip from her dainty tea cup and smiled. "You are a scientist as well as an artist, and that is a good thing," she said with a mischievous smile on her face. "However, there are things unexplained by science. It has yet to catch up with everything that is happening in the world. Science is still in its infant stages and many people say they don't believe in it at all. And there are people who don't know anything about it because they lack education. Also, you can't totally trust education either. Often the information given is falsified on purpose in order help maintain ignorance. For instance, the lie that perpetuates the belief that Christopher Columbus discovered America. Children are trained early to believe things that just aren't true. Plus most schools are run by the government and some people in politics understand that ignorant people are much easier to control. I don't know who thinks they are controlling who, but nonetheless those agreements are in place."

"What do you mean, agreements?"

"Subconscious agreements. In order for people to be manipulated or made to believe something that is not true – except for children – on some level they have to agree to being fooled," she said. "It's how things work. On the other hand children are just innocent victims of lies told to them by adults."

I wanted to argue with her about that, but I didn't know where to begin. I would have to give that concept more thought.

"Anyway," she continued. "The study of true science has fallen into the hands of only a small part of our population. However, I think that may be changing rapidly thanks to the internet, movies and TV. People need to understand that they don't have to give up God in order to understand science. In a sense science is the true study of God. Or fully understanding God has to include science. God simply means *all that is.*"

She paused ever so slightly and added. "Well, they might have to give up religion. Or at least change it a great deal. It's too bad religion got a hold of God like it did. It confuses people to no end."

I don't know why, but the thought crossed my mind that Alice was too beautiful to be so smart. It shocked me to discover that such a belief had floated up from my subconscious, proving to me that even I had been given false information during my formative years about pretty women and intelligence. I found that I didn't have to say something or ask a question about belief systems because I suddenly understood what they were.

She went on with her explanation. "In your lifetime I'm sure you are aware of how things suddenly get labeled, and only after that, become real. Before things were named there was nothing except a kind of disturbance. People would sense that something was happening, like a particular type of disease. Perhaps someone died, but nobody knew why. Now, because of scientific research, they can tell the difference between the plague and pneumonia. And they now know without a doubt that the earth circles the sun. Historically, people were executed for making those claims."

She continued in her mesmerizing voice. "Remember when Post Traumatic Stress Disorder had no name? It didn't seem solid, and of course it still isn't solid, but it now exists as an explanation of a certain psychological condition, and gives practitioners something to work with. It's no longer the mystery that it once was, because it has a label and a description. Physicians can begin to come up with treatments, and perhaps bring comfort to those suffering from that specific ailment. It's all so simple and unimaginably complex at the same time. People used to call it 'shell shock' and only soldiers – having been in war – were said to have it. All other people suffering from the same disorder – usually women – may have been labeled

110

mentally ill. New studies show that more women suffer from this PTSD than men. So no longer was the cause of it attributed only to war."

"Are you a scientist or a magician?" I asked impatiently.

"In a way I am both. On the other hand there are other descriptions like sorcerer, shaman, alchemist, but none of those words actually describe exactly what I am, because I'm really just a human being who happens to be focused on studying everything I can about what being a human being really means. Well, not what it means, but what it actually is. People have very little understanding of what they actually are."

"Yes, I suppose you are right," I said, "I don't think I ever really gave it much thought. I never asked the question 'what am I?' You make me realize how busy I get in order to avoid such inquiry."

I was starting to squirm in my chair, and I felt terribly uncomfortable saying what I said. I've always loved hanging out with smart people, but this woman was beyond smart. I felt afraid I might say the wrong thing.

"My dear," she smiled. "You are far from the only one avoiding knowing what you are. And you are right, most people ask 'who am I?' instead of 'what'."

"Am I still wanting to hide from that question even though I'm here all alone?" I asked. "You would think I'd be driving myself nuts trying to figure out the answer." I grimaced.

"You would never figure it out by trying, so I'd say you don't need to worry about it."

I suddenly began to feel over-stimulated to the point I wanted to stop all the talking and visuals going on in my head. I closed my eyes and for some time no thoughts came. I had a strong sense that Alice and I were only energy. It was so peaceful sitting there with her, not thinking about anything. I thought I could feel our molecules bouncing around like I did on the drug they had given me when I was kidnapped. I'm not sure how long it was before I opened my eyes and noticed the dog staring at me. I'd never been around a dog so alert.

Alice spoke again in a very soft voice. "I have other things I would like to tell you. Would you like me to tell you some stories that may prepare you for understanding how I manage to get here?"

"Of course," I said. I pretended to be eager to hear anything she had to share with me. I wanted to hear, but at the same time I felt frightened by her words. I calmly poured more tea into both our cups wondering where the tea actually went when I poured it into her cup.

"In our school early teachers once tried to give different definitions to the

111

ordinary and magical worlds. They talked about ordinary people and magical people. They taught that ordinary people could learn to step over into one world from another or create another world totally by integrating better thoughts. They called it transformation. Part of the problem with that was they were changing the beliefs from limited to expanded or negative to positive. They thought that once the beliefs were changed, reality would change. It was true that the world would appear to them, for a while, like a special magical place – a better place. The problem with that theory was the 'real' world would soon crash in and smack them in the face."

"Having discovered that, the new teachers learned that most people imprisoned themselves by believing that the limiting thoughts in their minds were true. So they began to have the students just notice they were having thoughts in their minds. Then they needed to remind themselves that they were only thoughts...nothing more, whether positive or negative. They had students practice looking at objects and noticing thoughts in their minds about the object, but they were told not to believe them. That meant any associations with the object and all judgments about it were only to be observed. Over time the students began to accept reality just as it is or was in the past."

"Teachers began to notice that there was no separation between everyday reality and a magical reality. The world was just plain unfathomable and the unknowable had a more powerful effect on the world and people than anyone had ever imagined."

"They began to practice putting down their microscopes and picking up mirrors. They had to stop looking out and judging and start looking within. They needed to quit trying to change things outside themselves to make a better world. This began to give them the kind of freedom they had been searching for. It stopped them from projecting their belief systems in an effort to make a better world outside themselves. I hate to use the word ego, but what the old teachers had been doing was developing a more expanded ego. That was not a bad thing. It just wasn't the enlightened state they were after."

"They used to think they created their own reality, but that became a major limiting belief as well. That was when they truly began to be able to know the world as it is. It didn't mean they had to like it, but they stopped trying to change it or make it different from exactly what it was. It was enough just to be able to do that. They stopped labeling things as good or evil, positive or negative. It became clear to them that it was just what it was."

"It also meant they had to give up their own power and tap into a power greater than themselves. They found some people needed to hang onto their old belief systems because it was imperative for them to go through certain processes that brought them to awakening. Some very ancient teachers had already said the way to enlightenment was through Samsara. Samsara, meaning ordinary, everyday life lived without awareness."

"Of course, if someone wanted to be involved in catching their limiting beliefs and changing them, that wasn't a bad thing to do. It could be uplifting and that might be a step some people needed to take to bring them out of unconscious behavior. It might alleviate debilitating depression. But it wasn't ever going to bring them all the way to enlightenment. The new teachers had to admit they didn't know what was best for other people. They had to learn to leave the students alone and let them have their own experiences even if they were sleepwalking."

Alice stopped explaining and began petting the dog's head. While I waited for her to continue I tried to absorb what she had said. Then she went on.

"Of course there were pitfalls along the way. It became easy for some students to fall into beliefs about enlightenment being a state of ecstasy. They could easily become addicted to those states of consciousness which only led them into a spiritual cul-de-sac. Our group decided to hand it all over to spirit, which is the ineffable. Only then did most of the problems we couldn't solve or change dissolve without anyone doing anything. We discovered that in the past we had been interfering and making things worse, or causing things to take longer to heal than if we had just left them alone. So we stopped. That is how we discovered true freedom."

As the sun moved in the sky across the windows, Alice's hair glittered. I was beginning to feel more relaxed even though I was still struggling to decipher her concepts.

She continued. "We began to realize that each of us had a different relationship with our higher powers. I experienced it as a kind of nothingness. In other words, the less I got involved in trying to create my own reality, fix other people, or get addicted to spiritual highs, the better life became for me and everyone else around me. So my sense of a higher power is that it isn't anything at all – just life moving along like a river – sometimes peaceful, sometimes turbulent."

"It was important for each of us, not only to allow our differences, but to view them as essential. There was no reason to be judging each other because spirit flows through each person in a different way."

Alice paused and looked out the window. I was relieved that she had stopped looking at me so intensely.

She then turned her gaze on me again and said, "Some of the sorcerers still maintained a relationship with a personal God. If that was the way they saw it, so what? Many of them remained involved in their childhood religions but were able to grasp the source of that particular teaching and bring it up to date. But they could plainly see that the many religious beliefs were the cause of most of the suffering people brought upon themselves. They were astounded to see that people were willing to die defending their beliefs. It's a form of mental illness to choose to die for something that actually stands in the way of the very freedom one is seeking. So teachers and students came to the conclusion that no matter how hard and scary it was to let go of limiting conditioning, it was necessary in order to be the humans they were born to be. They spent years experimenting with ways to do this. Some of those ways failed."

"But how can we just let things happen?" I asked. "Don't you think we should all be trying to change the world into a better place? How can we be expected to accept someone if we know for a fact that person is dangerous? How can we just ignore people's suffering? How can we just think only of our own personal freedom?" I was fidgeting in my seat again and feeling embarrassed that I had rather forcefully blurted out a barrage of questions.

She patiently continued. "Learning to accept the world as it is doesn't mean we have to hang out with a bunch of assholes, murderers or rapists. Nor do we have to avoid working to make the world a better place. Accepting the world as it is was a way to understand each situation better and to see it clearly before taking action. It doesn't mean that we don't take measures to put people away or even kill them, if necessary, to stop massive carnage and destruction of the planet. We also need to make sure that everyone gets their needs met. If we want to work on a worldly cause we do it. It only means that in each moment we are accepting the world as it is, then and only then can we move in ways that make a difference. It prevents us from running around in a tizzy screaming out crazy things like *revolution*!"

"Most of the time people hold on to ideas of how things should be, so they make choices out of ignorance instead of wisdom. If we turn our lives over to a God of our understanding, God will guide each of us in the moment. That might mean we need to stay out of something we think we should fix, or do the opposite and play a part in helping things work out for the best. Sometimes we leave people to their suffering because that might be what is best for them. And, of course, we have to admit that we don't have answers for everything. Or anything, really."

My head was beginning to spin, so I told her, "My grandmother used to make me go to church with her, but it didn't make a lot of sense to me at the time. The preacher kept talking about getting saved and I could never understand what I was supposed to be saved from. When I asked my grandmother she just told me we needed to be saved from evil. But I wasn't sure exactly what that was. And she didn't offer any clear explanations. Because it was so confusing I rejected church, God and all religions. I just thought it was something weird my Grandmother did and it was okay for her, but not for me."

Alice gazed at me as if she were trying to figure out how to say the next thing, then carefully proceeded. "Many of my friends began accepting parts of themselves they had rejected, like past religious beliefs. They re-visited the scriptures and understood them in a different light. They also understood attempts some people had made in the past to manipulate spiritual messages in order to control the masses. With new understandings of ancient writings from enlightened beings like Jesus, Buddha, Dogen and many more, these teachings suddenly became comprehensible for those of us living in modern times. But above all, the new mystics discovered a higher power and saw that they no longer needed to claim power for themselves. Nor did they let anything or anybody become their higher power. Enlightenment was there all along for every living being. I think scientific explanations for all of this can be found in the social sciences like anthropology, sociology and psychology, all studies of human behavior."

Alice continued stroking Bonita's head and was silent. I hoped I would be able to let all this sink in because when Alice spoke I seemed to go into a kind of trance. Or maybe it was a heightened awareness like what Valdez talked about in his books. I tried to hang on to the words and the feelings.

"Don't try to hang on to any of this," she finally said as if reading my thoughts. "If you do, you will struggle with it. Also, don't believe any of it either. They are only words and no words can possibly ever be true. It's like if I describe a cup of tea to you in words," she held up her cup of tea then took a sip, "you will never know what it really is until you feel the weight of the cup in your hand, taste the sweet tea in your mouth, and feel the warm liquid flowing down your throat."

Then she said softly, "I must go now. You have a full day ahead of you. I will see you again in a few days." She began to fade from view, and soon the chair across from me was empty. I remembered the day I had moved the table, and the two chairs from the kitchen area over to the windows. At the time I thought it was odd that I moved both chairs. Who had I thought would come to visit? I laughed, then picked up the sketch pad and drew Alice dressed like Frida Kahlo.

Later I wrote to Max.

Laurence: *Max, I've been meaning to tell you this for a long time now and haven't but now I will because maybe I need some help.*

Max: *Hello Laurence, I hope you feel safe enough to tell me anything, but I will understand if you don't.*

L: *Max, I think I'm having visions, but I'm not sure if it isn't some strange hologram that is being projected into my space. Can you tell me what is happening? I've looked up effects of solitary confinement, and I'm well aware that I could be hallucinating.*

M: *So what is it that you are seeing?*

L: *A woman named Alice.*

M: *Interesting, can you tell me more? Are you afraid of her?*

L: *No, I'm not afraid of her – not anymore. In fact I really like her, and look forward to her visits. I've been making some paintings of her. She tells me things I could not have thought of myself and she looks like no one I've ever seen before.*

M: *That sounds fascinating. You must let me know more and certainly you need to tell me if you are afraid.*

L: *At first I was. Well, actually I have a lot of mixed feelings. Sometimes I think I'm going crazy, but I don't mind if I am. It's not an unpleasant feeling. In fact I feel disturbed by her and comforted by her at the same time. Alice talks to me about philosophy and spirituality.*

M: *Cool!*

L: *She inspires subject matter for my paintings, but it's weird stuff – disturbing and comforting at the same time.*

M: *Laurence, I'm glad you shared this with me. You can tell me whatever you want to about these visitations. You know there is a lot of magical energy in the desert.*

L: *Max, I've never been into magic or spiritual energy. I've done yoga and meditation, but that was more about stretching my body and relaxing my mind. I still do that everyday. This is something different. Alice tells me things and it all makes sense when she is talking, but after she's gone I can't quite remember what she said. It's like I go into a trance when I hear her voice. I'm somewhat reminded of things I read in Valdez's books. I see that I have all of his books here on my shelves. Maybe I need to read them again?*

M: *That might give you some insights. If it isn't making you feel uncomfortable and afraid, I'd say just go with it. Keep me posted.*

116

L: *Thanks. I made a sketch of her this morning so I think I'll paint now while it's fresh in my mind. Maybe some of the things she said will come back to me.*

M: *I find this extremely interesting too. Let me know when she visits you again.*

L: *I will...more later.*

I took my sketch to the studio area and placed a fresh canvas on the easel. I began putting down a dark red wash in acrylic paint, let it dry. Then, consulting the sketch I had made of Alice, I made a quick charcoal drawing of her face with her hair on top of her head, decorated with flowers. I got the book of Frida's paintings off the shelf and began to copy her style. I wanted to learn how she painted. It wasn't long before I gained a deep respect for Frieda's technical ability as a painter. I'd always loved her art, but I'd never paid much attention to her painting technique. Maybe that was due to the commercialization of her images. I can be a snob sometimes.

When the painting was finished, I had a red-headed Frida portrait. It was not a work I would want to claim as mine due to the 'copy' part, but it was well worth the time I spent.

19: Granger and George

A blazing orange sunset lit up the living room walls in Laurence's Phoenix home, giving the room a pink glow. Granger and George sat holding hands on her sofa.

"I don't know if we did the right thing moving in here," Granger said. He was crying again.

"Do you remember why we made this decision?" asked George, "Somebody has to hold onto her property and her things. With the investigation closed there is no telling what could happen to this place."

That's what he said to his distraught partner. But at the same time he was thinking about money. He knew they needed his business mind to hold things together. It was tough times. Granger had lost his job at the university and now worked at the cafe. Even though it was a concern, George would never diminish his partner's emotions over the loss of his closest friend.

"I know," said Granger. "There are times when I can't stand her being gone. And it's worse not knowing what happened to her."

"What did Apollo have to say last night?" George recalled she had come by the cafe and the two siblings had gone out for a walk. Seeing Apollo in Scottsdale was rare because of her albino skin. When she was in town she would only come out at night.

"We didn't talk about the fact that it was her idea that we move in here. She said she still doesn't think Laurence is gone forever. She says it's just a gut feeling, but I'm picking up something different. I think she knows something and she isn't telling me. She's not one to show emotions, but...I don't know. I can't put my finger on it."

"Well, with a secret government job like hers, she's well trained at...well... keeping secrets."

"Yeah, but this seems different. It's like she knows something about Laurence, but won't say it. We never had secrets until she got that job. And why isn't she as upset as the rest of us? She just keeps reassuring me that everything is going to work out fine. Don't you think that's just a little too weird?"

Granger gripped a sodden tissue and laid his head on the back of the couch and let out one last sob. George didn't say anything – just leaned over and put his palm on Granger's cheek and kissed him on his forehead. It always came to this – a realization that talk wasn't going to bring her back, and that Granger had to somehow find a way to move on. George was patient with his distraught partner and tried to understand family closeness which was not something he'd ever known first hand for himself. He was still shy and standoffish around the Sun family.

"I guess it's dinner time," Granger finally said. "Thanks, George. I'm sorry I'm so emotional. You are so patient with me."

"Why wouldn't I be?" he asked.

"Let's go see what we have in the fridge." Granger eased off the sofa and headed towards the kitchen. His puffy face and red eyes indicated he had just gone through yet another intense emotional upheaval. The cause of it had been a call from the detective saying they had closed the case. George could tell Granger was making a huge effort to lighten up for his benefit.

"I know I bought some chicken breasts and we have a selection of fresh veggies from the farmer's market," Granger claimed while rummaging through the refrigerator.

They did however, always come to the fact that there was nothing they could do about Laurence, and the best medicine for the pain was to try to act as normal as possible. They prepared food together as usual. But there was only the sound of chopping and smells of fresh basil and oregano. Granger remembered times in the near past when they made jokes and laughed together a lot. That would come back again someday he knew, but he couldn't force it. He still felt that moving into Laurence's house had been a setback for him.

"I know what," Granger said. "Let's go out tonight."

George looked at him and smiled. He had thought of mentioning that to Granger, but had held back not wanting to push things.

"Where would you like to go?" he said.

"Let's go to the poetry slam at Ronson's. We'd be in an audience and not have to socialize much. I need something that will take my mind off this for a while. A movie would be way too much drama and why go to a movie when we could just watch it here? A bar is out of the question. Too noisy."

"Good idea," said George who would have gone along with anything Granger suggested, just to help him through this emotional crisis. He began to listen to his own thoughts. It wasn't that he didn't mourn the loss of Laurence, he just didn't have the history with her that Granger did. So he felt he had to be the strong one in this situation. He didn't mind that. He also didn't want to let anyone know he thought she was dead. No one had called about a ransom. She wasn't from a rich family so he suspected foul play. He was sure the police thought the same thing. Therefore, they closed the case.

In the kitchen Granger turned to George and said, "George, I'm going to be okay." Dramatically he grabbed his partner's shoulders in both of his hands and stared straight into his face. "I love you so much and I'm sorry I'm putting you through all this. I just wanted us to be married by now and living happily ever after in our own place with Laurence as my closest sister. I worry that I've dragged you into something and I might lose you if I don't snap out of it."

"You haven't dragged me into anything, Granger. I'm not going to leave you. And there is no happily-ever-after. Life goes on with all it's terrible ups and downs. It's not like you are some drama queen. You've lost a sister, someone you love very deeply, and I miss her too. The last thing you need is to worry about losing me." They stood there for a long time hugging as if they had a death grip on each other.

George whispered into Granger's ear. "Maybe we should get married."

Granger backed up and stared at his partner.

George continued, "We don't have to have a big wedding like we thought we did. We could have a small gathering. We could do it here out on the back deck underneath the big blue sky. At least that way you would know I'm here with you through it all. Will you marry me?"

Granger was genuinely surprised by the sudden proposal. For the first time in months he suddenly stopped thinking about Laurence. He could feel his brain shifting in his head. "Yes, yes, of course, I want to marry you. That's a great idea. Can we keep the wedding down to family and a few friends?"

"Of course. We can do it any way you want."

The mood in the kitchen shifted from a slow sad dance to something more like a polka. "Laurence would want us to do this," Granger finally said. He felt uplifted thinking he would be doing something that she would want him to do. Wasn't that how it had always been. She had been his teacher, then his employer. He did what she wanted him to do. He did it because he trusted her. He trusted her because she had always had his best interests at heart.

"Yes, Granger I'm sure she would want this,"

"Yeah, I know. She is like my mom. Come to think of it over time, my mom became her mom. So she must have learned to how treat me from my mom. I'm so grateful for the women in my life! Even though Apollo left when I was a teenager, those three were the best ever. They insisted I always do what I liked to do best. I was always making things and they loved it. Dad too. I didn't realize I had it so good until I grew up and found out about other families. I have to say it was quite a shock to hear about how other people grew up."

He stopped and turned to his partner. "George, I'm sorry. I hope I'm not making you feel bad."

"No, please, I'm fine. My situation is probably more typical. I know more people with families like mine than like yours, so I have lots of support."

Even though that was true, Granger could see a slight shadow fall over George. He hadn't spoken to his family in years.

They decided to stay home. Laurence's home, after all, was their home now. Except for a few things they kept in the guest room – hoping she would show up someday – they had stored most of her belongings in a climate-controlled storage unit in Scottsdale. Granger's art hung on the walls and sat on the easel in the studio side of the living room. His sculptures sat on pedestals indoors and a few larger ones occupied the backyard. The only painting of hers was the one that he had grabbed from her house the day he'd come by before the police turned it into a crime scene. It hung in the guest room and he still felt there was some kind of clue in it that he just wasn't seeing. The two men referred to the guest room as Laurence's room where he often found himself sitting on the bed examining that painting from corner to corner; occasionally removing it from the wall to search the backside. He always came to a dead end.

George proposed a toast. "To the beginning of something new," he said, holding up his wine glass filled only with fizzy water.

"To the beginning of something new," said Granger.

It was then that Granger's phone rang. He cursed that he hadn't turned it off. It was lying on the dining table beside his plate, so he finally gave in and picked it up to see who it was. Manuel.

He answered, "Manuel, hello!"

"Granger, I have something important to tell you."

Granger put the phone on speaker so George could hear.

"I don't know how to say this," his Hispanic accent taking over. "How to begin. Well...I have a student who sent me an image of a painting she saw in some town in Europe. It's a painting of me! I think it was painted by Laurence! I never saw that painting before and I never modeled for her. And there are all these fish!"

"Slow down, Manuel. What fish? What town?"

"My student, she texted me from Hungary. She saw the painting in Budapest. I swear it was me. Did you ever see a painting she did of me?"

"No, but I can't say I've seen everything she painted."

"It was in a gallery, but my student was pretty looped and doesn't remember the name of it. She left that city the next day. I'll text you the image. Man, I know it's me! Laurence and I went to Mexico to look at fish. These fish, man, only Laurence would paint fish like these fish. They weren't like the real fish we saw!" Manuel was talking fast.

"Did she say who the artist was?"

"Yeah, she said it was signed 'Donahue'. You can't see the signature on the photo. Also you can't see the ring. She told me my ring was in the painting too, but it is too small to show up in the photo."

"I can't believe she didn't get the gallery name or the street or anything, just Budapest. I'm surprised she remembered that. When she get's back I'm going to wring her neck. I tried to get a list of all the galleries in that city, but there is a lot. I think I have to go there."

Granger was surprised that Manuel was so hyper. He didn't know him well, but he had always thought of him as a quiet man. But Manuel's excitement was contagious and he suddenly began to feel even more alive. Granger looked over at George thinking this call might be ruining the mood of the night, but George's eyes were as open and bright as he imagined Manuel's were.

"Hey Manuel, slow down and text me the image."

"Okay," the voice on the phone said, and in a matter of seconds. Granger had the photo.

The man in the painting was definitely Manuel. The style of painting was hers because nobody else in the world could copy Laurence's quirky imagination. Who else would paint a bunch of made up fish with faces and teeth?

"You're right Manuel, that's you and that painting has to be hers. No, I've never seen this one and I think it's one she would have shown me if she had done it before she left."

"I'm sad to say," said Manuel. "I didn't see any of her work for at least six months before she disappeared, but don't you think she would have sent me an image of this one? And how in the hell did it get to Hungary?"

"I think we need to give this some serious thought," said Granger. "Hungary is on the other side of the world. Lets try to do some research and see if we can find out anything."

"I'm telling you, man. I will go to Hungary to try and find her. I will go to Mars if I have to! But I cannot leave the university right away. I'm the only one I know of who still has a job. But, I don't know, maybe I don't care."

"Well, don't jump on a plane right away. I'll check around and get back to you, okay? Let me look into this. Don't do anything until I call you back." He didn't want to be disappointed again but it did sound promising.

After cleaning up the kitchen, Granger and George searched the web for galleries and artists in Budapest. Most of the websites had lists of artists they represented in their gallery. But no one had a Laurence Donahue. There had to be galleries that didn't have a website or who didn't keep their websites updated. Sometimes galleries would not show an artist's work who they didn't consider to be one of their regular artists, therefore, not posting their work online. Maybe the student wasn't in Budapest. Perhaps she was in a small town near the city. These days cities are clumps of small towns that have grown together.

The next morning Granger wanted to call Apollo and tell her the news, but he kept getting distracted. Later, he decided to keep the information to himself so his family and friends would not get their hopes up again. Now he was keeping secrets too. In the meantime, his spirits were high.

He didn't want to let George down so he decided to make the wedding plans a priority. After all, he now had Manuel who seemed to be as committed to finding Laurence as he was. All he needed to do was stay in touch with the man.

The next day he read over the potential wedding guest list and began making phone calls. First to family to see if the date they had picked would work for them. It would be a spring wedding, May, a perfect time. It would give them months to prepare. He finally called Apollo but he didn't say anything about Budapest. She said she could come to the wedding. He decided not to invite Manuel, but he would make a trip to Tucson to visit with him in a few days. He thought it might be best if he and Manuel became closer friends with a common goal: find Laurence! He would let everyone else think he was moving on.

20: Everything Is Energy

I didn't have the great outdoors. But I had the great out-patio. Fresh air, sunshine, the ultramarine blue sky above, and a ground level view through the metal gate of a vast desert with pale purple mountains far beyond.

Carlos and Jesus, my two lawn men back in Phoenix, would be proud of me for the garden I planted. I was grateful for the times they enthusiastically talked to me about plants. My little sprouts were turning into toddlers. I guess plants don't toddle, but you know what I mean. Beets, radishes, green beans, and all sorts of herbs were flourishing. I never thought I'd like doing this, but there I was, spade in hand, and something other than paint under my nails.

Plus – in spite of all the sunscreen – I was toasty brown. I'd noticed earlier in the bathroom mirror that there was about three inches of my natural light brown hair color showing. That, and the scraggly hair cut made me look exactly like what I had become, a wild woman living alone in the wilderness. I could have used the red henna they had given me, but it seemed like a waste of time since nobody would see me.

I also began to exercise more. I'd found one of those small trampolines in the shed. I'd always considered my work and the long walks on campus to be aerobic enough for me. Now living in such close quarters I was finding that I had a build up of energy in my body that needed to be worked out. So that's where that word "workout" came from. I'd never given it much thought, but now I was recalling how much of the time I used to spend living in my head and not paying much attention to what dangled below my neck.

Even though I was still doing all of my painting indoors, being out in the sunlight had changed my choice of paint colors. I had finished two paintings using lots of ultramarine blue for sky and shades of green mixed from combinations of yellow and blue and yellow and black. Browns became richer, like the garden dirt, and I could see loamy black clots of compost crawling with pink earthworms, and lots of green things appearing in various passages of my work.

The temperature was rapidly rising, so I got up early and spent a couple of hours in the garden each morning. I was beginning to feel more sane. I often thought about Alice and wondered if she had been an hallucination caused by my isolation. Were the words she shared with me merely the rantings of my own mind? I thought I was just making her up, but if that was the case how could I have already known the things she was telling me?

I began to think a lot about what she told me about limited beliefs. The last time she came we talked a lot about my beliefs in victimhood. Once I began to take responsibility for everything that had happened to me I found that there was no one to blame – not even myself. I was getting better at letting myself feel the feelings that arose when I remembered my painful childhood. At first I would feel miserable, but then, if I gave these feelings my undivided attention, they would soon dissipate. I wasn't sure how this process was going to affect me in the long run but it helped with everyday living in captivity.

In the middle of the day when it was too hot to go outdoors I spent time painting in the studio. Later in the day when the patio was mostly in shadow I liked to lie in the hammock and read. If it looked like there would be a stunning sunset I would climb a ladder and sit on top of the shed and absorb the colorful view. It was obvious that I could have dragged the ladder up onto the roof and put it down on the other side of the wall and be in the desert, but what then? Where would I go? So I didn't bother, but I was happy to feel like I had some way of escaping – if that ever felt like a viable option. I was sure Max knew I had figured this out, but we never discussed it.

After spending some time in the garden, I made sure that I was sitting at my table near the windows every morning. Other things that Alice had told me had also been percolating in my mind and seemed to be changing my outside behavior. I was now understanding about perceiving reality in different ways. By releasing limited beliefs from my thinking mind, I began to make different choices in how I lived my life and how I made art. Noticing that I had spent most of my time judging everything instead of accepting things as they are brought me to the realization that I could make choices moment by moment, unencumbered by thoughts about how I thought it should be. In other words if I noticed things and let them be as they were I would soon have a better idea of how to improve something if it needed my help. Many times things would be transformed in their own time without my interference.

It was good that I had been given a simple lifestyle in which to practice my new behaviors. My conversations with Max became more fruitful. My eating habits and exercise sessions improved. But where it mattered most was in my painting. I soon found that I could spend longer periods of time just letting the paint flow from my brush without my over-thinking it. I began to let paintings sit around a lot longer so I could observe them as they were. Often I found they were indeed finished. And if they weren't I would know what to do.

I soon understood what Alice meant about all things being energy. Making changes in my behavior took a massive amount of energy. I actually had to save it up in order to make the shift. Imagine the energy it takes to turn a huge ship around in the ocean. That is what this was like.

The next time Alice visited me at the table she was dressed in a T-shirt and jeans, but still appearing like she had walked out of a fashion magazine. Bonita also wore a tiny T-shirt with the words *Big Dog* on the front of it. I laughed and the dog acted exactly like she understood why.

"It's my day off. We are going hiking in the mountains," Alice explained.

"You guys look great!" I said.

"We don't have long," she said. "I wanted to check in with you to see how you are doing. The garden looks great! And I see you have some color in your cheeks."

"Yes. I'm enjoying the outdoors."

"That is something new for you isn't it?" she asked.

"I guess. I'm embarrassed to admit it."

"Don't be. You've been a busy person."

"More like driven," I explained.

"Well, being driven is probably how you got chosen to be here; however, it is good that you are paying more attention to your health. You will live longer and produce more quality work if you don't run yourself into the ground."

"That's some common sense that I must have lost somewhere along the way."

"No worries, you are fine."

"Alice, I've given a lot of thought to what you said about subconscious agreements and being a victim. I can't decide if I really am the victim here. Obviously kidnapping is a federal crime. But I only panicked for a few days, then I just settled down and started working. Sometimes I do feel angry and want to take it out on Max. I guess you know about Max."

The look on her face told me she didn't know.

"Max is the guy on the computer. Well, I think it's a guy, for all I know it could be a group of people or just an artificial intelligence."

"An AI, really?"

"I don't know," I confessed.

"Well, let's get back to your inquiry. Before you were kidnapped you were a victim of your job, the university administration, your past. How do you feel now after you have accepted that you were a victim for so long?"

I starred at her for a moment, then said. "Let me see. When I tap into the energy of victimhood I try to feel it as much as I can in my body. Then after a minute or two it dissolves and I feel like it doesn't matter at all. I think I used to pretend I couldn't feel it, but it was there. Paying attention to it seems to make it dissipate rather quickly. I didn't realize I was carrying so much anger in my body. I guess I thought it was all in my head."

"That means you have not only changed the agreement with your captors you've let go of a bunch of stored pain."

"I know. Now it kind of feels like I always wanted to be here," I admitted.

"What about the far past? Have you thought much about that?"

"No. Not yet."

"You will."

I looked at her with a questioning expression.

"Think about it all as energy. Everything is energy. Objects seem solid like this table, but we both know it is made of molecules that are bouncing around. Since we see things as solid we tend to try to make everything solid. Like people and even situations. Then we get locked into agreements both bad and good. We want to hold everything in place, make it black and white."

"If we think of everything as energy, we know it will change either with or without our participation. Or just dissipate like you said. Someday this table will be something else. Someday you will be something else. Agreements with others should be the easiest to change, but they aren't because we have been programmed to believe they won't. That's why in the world we have war and all kinds of uncomfortable situations that people get stuck in. Many people spend lifetimes in bad relationships, be it a job or marriage or family. Their minds tell them that is how it is and it can never change. Or they suffer from something that happened in the past that they just can't let go of."

"I see," I said. "There was a big change when my brother died."

"I'm sure there was," she said. "Next time we will spend more time talking about that. Now, my little friend and I need to materialize in those mountains over there." She pointed out the window.

"Thanks, Alice. I will see you soon. Bye Bonita."

They faded slowly away.

I shook my head in disbelief. I was no longer concerned about how Alice got here. It didn't matter if she was a hologram, ghost or hallucination. I needed her. She made my life rich and meaningful like no one ever had before.

She referred to herself as a sorceress, but she had carefully explained to me that it didn't mean the kind that appeared in the world or in children's books or fantasy novels. The use of supernatural powers, or the calling of spirits through charms, spells or rituals had nothing to do with what she was. She told me it was all about understanding energy.

However, she did indeed seem to be right out of the Valdez books that Granger and I had read in high school. But there was a huge difference between reading words in a book and being in the presence of an actual sorcerer. Those books had introduced Granger and I into altered states, but being with Alice took me into new realms of reality. Not made up magical realms outside of the real world. She was helping me to see how magical the everyday natural real world actually is.

Granger and I thought there was a mundane world and a magical one existing side by side. And we wanted to leave the mundane one and join the magical one. The truth is there is only one world and we just needed to clear away what stood in the way of our recognizing it. I hope I will get a chance to share all of this with him. Or was he already somewhere else learning all the same things I was learning by living here in the desert?

21: Romero

I kept forgetting to ask Alice if there were others like her. It scared me to think the desert might be crawling with los brujos. I wasn't sure I could handle more than one. When she wasn't around I could still feel her essence in my studio. But never outside. I often thought I felt a male energy near the garden. Maybe it was because I sometimes wished for the guidance of my Phoenix gardeners, Carlos and Jesus. But one day I was sure I caught a glimpse in my peripheral vision of a man zipping by, then vanishing, much like when Alice appeared. He too left a scent – a woody smell. He smelled like...well, trees.

Romero appeared when I was lying in the hammock rereading "The Tribe" by Valdez. There was no doubt that he was not a live flesh and blood man, because I looked up and there he sat in a chair looking at me. He had made no sound arriving. The gate didn't open and I had not heard footsteps or rustling sounds of a person sitting down in a chair.

His brown sinewy body did not cast a shadow. The contrast between his skin and his brilliant white T-shirt made his shimmering appearance seem more concrete. He was staring straight at me and when I looked up at him I could see through him and the vividly colored tattoos on his arms.

"My name is Romero and I've come to tell you a story," he said. "Do you mind?" Something about his soothing voice made me think he must have been a singer or an actor.

I had to have been in an altered state because how else could I have avoided reacting fearfully; I wasn't screaming from the sudden appearance of another human being in my courtyard. After having Alice in my life, his sudden appearance seemed natural. That's why I said out loud to him, "Why am I not surprised?"

"I get that," he said. "I am not like Alice though. I am a storyteller."

"So, Storyteller, I suppose you come from the same place as Alice?"

"You could say that."

"How did you find me? Did she tell you?"

"That is a question not so easily answered," he said.

"How many of you plan to show up here?"

"Don't worry, there are only a handful of us with the abilities to move around like Alice and me. There are more with different abilities," he said with a mischievous smile.

Rather than be offended by that, I was soothed. I always listened to books when I worked in my studio and I was curious as to what it would be like to have a real person tell me a story. Or was he real?

"What does it matter?" he said as if he were reading my mind.

I suddenly felt like I wanted to hide. Mind readers made me most uncomfortable. But I quickly overcame it and tried to act more matter-of-fact. "What kind of story are you going to tell me?" I could see him more clearly now and noticed he had interesting hair – very short in the back and sides and long on the top so locks of hair fell over one side and part of his face. There were three hoop earrings with turquoise beads in the ear that showed. He was too handsome to be an ordinary person. It was kind of like having Johnny Depp sitting across from me, which made me self conscious with capital letters. I was never a great beauty, but now I felt just plain ratty with my wild hair and dirty fingernails.

"I like your art," he said distracting me from my thoughts.

"Thank you," I said, thinking that I hoped he wasn't an artist too and a much better one than me. I needed something to put me on an even footing with him.

"You are a genius with the brush and you don't paint anything that has been done before. Nothing mundane about your work."

"Funny you should say that," I said.

"Yes, and why is that?" he asked.

"I'm not sure I have the words to explain it," I said.

"Well maybe it will come to you and you can let me know. I would love to hear you talk about your artwork. I have questions, like how do you decide what to paint?"

"A lot of people ask that."

"I'm sure they do."

"Sometimes I like to talk about my work. It sort of clarifies it in my own mind. But it is infinitely more interesting to hear what other people see in it."

"Your paintings tell me that you are not satisfied to show only what people see in front of them on a daily basis."

"I would get bored with that."

"So you search your imagination and project it outwards, integrating it with everyday reality."

"You could say that."

"You are right, it isn't boring."

"You said you came here to tell a story."

"I did say that. And I need to let you know, I don't make stories up."

"If you don't make them up, where do they come from?"

"They come to me from a parallel universe. And I intuitively know what story a person needs to hear. In other words I really don't know what is going to come out of my mouth until it comes. It's a strange talent, I know. It started when…"

Then Romero just blipped out.

Well that was weird, I thought. I was disappointed that he left so suddenly. I was hot to hear that story.

I stayed there in the hammock for an hour or so thinking about what had just happened, leading me to believe I must have fallen asleep and had a dream. Meetings with Alice often left me feeling exhausted and this event with Romero was no different. I concluded it took a lot of energy to operate on a magical plane. But then again I questioned myself as to whether this was real or just my imagination going wild. Or were both of these visitors being projected into my space by some advance technology?

At least I wasn't bored.

22: The Queen

It wasn't until I stopped thinking about Romero, that he finally showed up again. If it hadn't been for the different clothes he was wearing, I would have thought this encounter was a seamless continuation of his last visit. He had on a yellow shirt printed with tiny rocket ships. The sleeves were rolled up as were his jeans. On his feet he wore what looked like patent leather loafers which made me think of vintage post cards featuring Latin lovers. It made me giggle.

Again he smelled like a tree, but not just any tree, a blooming tree, like the peach tree I remembered from my childhood backyard.

"Would you like me to begin our story?" he asked.

"Sure, why not?" I said.

"It's about the Queen of Arizona," he said in his musical voice. I sank into that voice, letting it carry me along, like a raft on a lazy river.

He began, "As I said before, this story takes place in a parallel reality. One that runs alongside this reality that we appear to be in now."

"Yes, I get that," I said very close to a whisper. I wasn't sure I really did.

I was trying to act like nothing was out of the ordinary. But I was feeling extremely disoriented not knowing for sure whether I was awake or dreaming.

He moved his chair into the shade and closer to me. He spoke softly like he was telling a secret. "Do you know that Arizona once had a queen?"

I shook my head. No.

"Well, I will tell you about her. Her name was Ellie, short for Elizabeth. Ellie's birth had been televised, and the birth video played repeatedly every night on local stations right after the Late Night Talk shows. During her whole life as queen Ellie's mother, Queen Rose was mortified by that. Throughout history, all royal births had to be observed by as many people as could fit in the room in order to have proof that the child was authentic – whatever that means. In modern times TV cameras sufficed. And when they agreed to it, Queen Rose and King Ralf had not once thought the footage would be available to the public. It was so disturbing that Rose became a recluse, never to be seen in public again. And that was unacceptable behavior for a queen. She became a victim of the press and the local people."

"When the daughter grew up, to save the queen from more embarrassment, and with young Ellie's blessing, the king and queen faked their own deaths and disappeared. They staged a nasty car crash which was, of course, videotaped. It quickly replaced the birth video. Bodies dragged from the wreckage were corpses from the morgue. And I won't go into the details of how they made that happen. The authorities did not put a lot of time and energy into investigating the deaths because everyone was overjoyed to have a new video to replace the old birth one."

"Where did the king and queen go?" I asked raising my head to look at Romero.

"Well," he said. "The happy couple retired in Palm Springs, California, on a horse ranch with a large swimming pool. Finally they began to truly live like normal people. They were freed from all expectations. No public appearances and no castle to maintain. Ellie didn't mind taking over the job. She had grown up as a princess and had always expected one day to be queen. She was thrilled that her mom and dad didn't have to die first, for real."

"Since her parents had been ambivalent about their roles as royalty, Ellie was never trained to be a Queen. But along the way she had invented some intensely strong ideas about what a queen should be. She was a stubborn, independent woman and shocked everyone by letting them know right off the bat that she did not intend to get married. It was modern times after all."

"But did she ever see her parents again?" I interrupted impatiently.

Romero pushed the long locks of hair off his forehead, leaned back in his chair and smiled. "Yes she did, and often. Of course, they were never able to visit the castle again. And just to be safe they had been totally made-over to look nothing like their former selves. They used to look like hippies, but they both cut their hair and wore ordinary clothes."

"Ellie would visit them often in Palm Springs. And the press thought she was hanging out with her aunt and uncle. The family went on long trips together to Europe and South America. Begrudgingly, Rose would help Ellie choose elegant clothes from Paris for her public appearances. Mostly they visited art museums and cathedrals like everybody else."

"That's a relief," I said.

"Well, it's probably every famous person's dream – to be incognito. The family became well adept at the game. But at first, it wasn't going all that well in Arizona," Romero said, looking grim.

"Ellie was newsworthy," he went on. "Every tabloid and trashy magazine had their way with her. Some very skilled graphic designers manipulated photos of Ellie and her court. And, believe me, there are always hordes of people who believe what they see and read in those publications."

"Ellie was gorgeous, long shiny red hair and fair skin and she was tall – probably around 5'10". Everyone wanted to know her, to possess her, to be seen with her. But Ellie, like her mom, was an introvert. She could entertain herself for hours on end and preferred not to be told what she was supposed to do."

Like me, I thought. Only she must have looked like Alice. I wondered, what is it with all this red hair?

"Her servants became her closest friends. Often it was hard to tell they were servants. They all lived together in the castle. But Ellie was just as much a part of the work team as any of them. She mucked out stables, fed the many animals, cooked and cleaned like everyone else. It didn't make sense to her that she should be excused from any task needing to be done. She wanted the servants to think of her as one of them. They had, actually, all grown up together."

"Ellie didn't pay attention to the publicity, nor did anyone else in the castle. They had the latest technologies: flat screens in many rooms, a movie theater and all kinds of computers and devices. But Ellie told them it was out of bounds to read gossip publications, watch them on TV or even to look at images on the fronts of magazines in the grocery stores. The servants complied without a fuss. In fact they were relieved. They had all seen what it did to Queen Rose and they were extremely protective of Ellie."

"Occasionally a low flying helicopter would video tape the top of Ellie's red cowgirl hat as she rode her favorite horse Maggie – short for Magdalena. But all the other photographs and videos were probably models and actors looking for work. Not many people knew what Queen Ellie actually looked like, so the public was easily fooled."

Romero became quiet for a moment or two then again leaned forward and asked. "Do you believe that Arizona had a Queen?"

"Sure why not," I said. I thought I could believe anything now. Besides, I was enjoying the story. Why not go along for the ride?

Raising up on my elbow I looked at Romero. "It's fun to think of a Queen being so young and playful. Also, her parents seem like fairy tale parents. Well, not exactly fairy tale because fairy tales are usually gruesome and have ugly step mothers and such."

Romero looked pleased that I was engaged. I felt like a little girl.

"You are so right," he said. "Ellie didn't have a terrible childhood. She was well adjusted and happy. And that is how she was able to change how the world viewed her. She managed to accomplish more good than any other queen."

"Did she have magical powers?" I asked.

"Sort of. Yes, I guess you could call it magical, but it was more like natural. She had natural powers. The world responded to her because she never thought she was separate from it."

"I'm not sure what you mean by that."

"She was never at odds with anything. She accepted everything as it was and everyone as they were. She felt that she had to be coming from that place in order to understand how to improve things. She even accepted the tabloids and made peace with the reporters. By doing that she stopped them from harassing her by making it advantageous for them to support her and her projects," he said.

"Were you sent here to tell me this so I'll accept my fate of being here alone in the desert against my will?" My voice sounded bitter and I had no idea why I blurted that out. I could feel anger rising.

He looked at me with his kind eyes and slowly began to shimmer away. I blinked and he was gone.

I sat up. "No – no, don't go! Please come back." I reached over with my hands as if I might be able to grab hold of him, but there was nothing there.

Damn it! I should have kept quiet, but I had not trusted him. I didn't trust myself. I didn't trust anything. I am not like that queen who lived in harmony with everything. Who does that? Certainly not anyone real. My face must have been twisted in rage. I was angry about a lot of things, but right then I was angry with myself for being sarcastic and ruining a perfect moment. I forgot that these visitations never lasted long. They always ended before I was ready for them to end. I suddenly felt like I missed real people – ones that didn't just disappear into thin air.

I went in the house and sat down in front of the computer and wondered if I should tell Max about Romero. I worried if I told him he might think I was going crazy. But I wasn't sure that I wasn't going crazy because I wasn't convinced that I'd ever been really sane. What if I do go insane and they kill me because I'd be of no use to them. But maybe they would just let me go. Up until this point I'd remained strong, in hopes that if I complied with my captors' desires I would have a better chance of surviving. But perhaps the opposite was true.

I didn't like the feeling of not knowing. But then again if I looked honestly at life no one had any way of knowing. People could only think they knew what was in store for them. Somehow I knew I had to keep understanding that not knowing was a state of mind that I had to accept one hundred percent. The only thing I could truly know was that I existed and someday I would surely die. But I couldn't know when!

It was a sobering thought when I realized my thinking was what was making me crazy. I went to my easel and picked up where I left off on a painting. I guess the next image after this one will be Romero, if he ever comes back, I thought. I promised myself I would be on my best behavior if he did.

I began to think of the Queen of Arizona. I made a promise to myself that, as soon as I finished painting, I would spend some time on the internet finding out about queens.

23: Alias

The next morning while I was pulling a few weeds and watering I heard a drone arrive. Back when I was confined to the house, I used to hear them. But at the time, I wasn't sure what I was hearing. I thought it might be house noises – maybe a water pump. Outside I could not only hear, but see them arrive and take off. They sounded like gigantic bees, flashed red and blue lights, and went about their business of dropping off supplies and picking up paintings and garbage. Seeing new technology still makes me feel like I've been hurled into the future, causing me to suffer from the world's longest jet lag.

After it left, I went in to check the dumb waiter to see what had been left. Before I opened the cabinet door I heard the distinct sound of what I thought was a cat meowing. I stood looking at the door, listening, and wondering – what the hell?

Finally I slowly opened the door to find a squealing box with holes in it. "What the hell?" I said out loud this time. I placed the box on a work table, opened it and out jumped an obviously traumatized animal. I jumped back and screamed as it flew past me and landed on the floor zipping out of sight in a matter of seconds. My heart was pounding.

"Holy Cow! What the hell?" I kept repeating that out loud while I quickly closed the door to the outside patio and started looking around for what I thought was a cat. I had no idea where it was hiding. I made a thorough search of the place to no avail. I looked again in the dumb waiter and found a bag of cat food, took it out, opened it and put a little of the food in a bowl which I placed on the floor along with a bowl of water.

Even though I knew nothing about having a pet, common sense told me that food and water might be a good place to start. I was right. This animal turned out to not be shy at all. And it wasn't long before it hesitantly creeped out from under my bed and went for the food. It only ate a few bites then started trotting around the room searching every nook and cranny. I sat quietly on the sofa watching, every now and then saying, "Here kitty kitty."

After the animal checked out every inch of the house it suddenly jumped into my lap, frightening me half out of my wits. We both shrieked at the same time. I jumped up off the sofa and it flew halfway across the room again.

Breathlessly, I sat back down and folded my legs under me Indian style. I thought it might return. So I prepared myself to remain calm. And that is what happened. This time the animal was a lot more cautious. It first leapt onto the couch, walked around as if investigating every crack or bit of dust, occasionally butting its head against the cushions. Finally, it crawled into my lap. I petted it's head and it purred loudly and started mashing my legs with it's front paws. Then it curled up in my lap and stayed for only a few minutes before it leaped off to check out the food dish again. I watched it crunch, dropping a few pieces on the floor. It checked out the water, but didn't drink.

"What the hell?" I said.

Laurence: *Max, what the hell?*

Max: *I thought you needed a friend.*

L: *It's adorable.*

M: *He's about 6 months old. You complained about mice. He comes from a fine line of mousers.*

L: *He? Okay, he's not shy. Seems happy to be here.*

M: *I'm sure. It was a long journey for someone who isn't fond of travel.*

L: *Thanks, Max. I've never had a pet. I never wanted one, but I can see already how great it is to have a live being around. He purrs a lot. I hope he doesn't bother the birds.*

M: *Contrary to popular belief, most house cats prefer rodents.*

L: *That I will welcome. I've heard stories about the Hantavirus.*

Hantavirus is a serious disease passed on through the leavings of desert mice.

M: *Be sure to wear your garden gloves.*

L: *I do. What would you do if I got sick?*

M: *I certainly hope you don't.*

L: *You didn't answer my question.*

M: *You know you can tell me right away if you get sick. You know that don't you?*

L: *Max, there are things I don't tell you, but I'd surely whine loud and clear if I got hurt or sick.*

M: *Good*

L: *I think I will name him Alias from that old movie about Billy the Kid*

142

where Bob Dylan played a minor role. His name was Alias.
  M: *Oh yes, I remember that one.*

Alias jumped up onto my desk and batted around a pen until it landed on the floor. He followed it down and knocked it around until it disappeared under the sofa. Then he took off looking for more trouble.

L : *I'll talk more later, Max. I feel the need to make some cat toys. I'll research how to care for a cat. I put some dirt into the box that he arrived in so he can do his business. Can I let him outdoors?*

  M: *At first I'd only let him out for a short period of time when you can be outside with him. There are predators. But in time he will adapt since he's a Bengal. His lineage is wild, so he should do well in the desert.*

  L: *Okay, but first, I need to make him some toys.*

  M: *Send me some photos.*

Watching Alias made me feel joyful. But every time *The Powers That Be* sent me a treat I had to come to terms with the fact that I would not be leaving soon. At first I would try to tamp down the anger and sadness, but the last thing I wanted to do was fall into a depression. So I'd learned to be with whatever I was feeling until it dissipated. I cried a little while watching the cat tear up a piece of wadded up paper I'd formed into a ball. But the crying didn't last. Alias was just too silly.

24: The Queen's Court

It was amazing to me how abruptly the weather changed from chilly to sweltering hot. Plants in the garden were saved only by lots of water and partial shade. I wasn't sure where the water was coming from, but there was plenty of it. I'd grown to love puttering in the garden. But it became so hot outdoors that I could only be out in the early mornings and late afternoons. Indoors, the house remained a perfect temperature, and I spent most of my time painting.

Alias was adjusting to his new home and was adding a whole new dimension to my life. In the late afternoon when it began to cool down, I took him outside to play. At first he was suspicious of everything, jumping at every sound, but it didn't take long for him to fall in love with the garden and start chasing insects and finding imaginary friends. After a while he got tired, leaped onto the hammock and settled in on my belly.

Romero came back while I was sipping cold water and petting my cat. He appeared suddenly, as before. I looked up and there he was, like he'd been sitting there for a long time without my noticing. Alias did not appear to see him.

He was staring at me, not talking, which made me feel very uncomfortable. So I spoke first. "Tell me about your tattoos."

"What would you like to know?"

"Well...I'm not going to ask you if getting them hurt," I told him

He began rubbing his left arm with his right hand. "It's not too bad. It depends on the artist."

"I like them. They are quite amazing." I sat up, and Alias jumped off and went back to his cat-only world. Romero watched him go and gave me a thumbs up letting me know he was aware of the new arrival. I was trying to get a closer look at the tattoos, but Romero was transparent. So the tats were faint.

"Keep still," I said squinting. "If I tried to put a permanent drawing on someone's skin I would be terrified. Surely I would screw up then, feel guilty forever."

"You're not that kind of an artist," he said, rescuing me. "But I'm sure you could do it if you had to. Artists who do this kind of work are doing it because it pays the bills. Some of them don't have any other skills. Some of them do paintings on the side or street art." He laughed a little.

"I never thought of it that way," I said.

"Most people don't," he added. "Laurence, you don't need to blame yourself if I vanish like I did. I'm here in my dream body and sometimes I can only maintain that for a short while. It isn't possible for me to warn you that I'm leaving. Something or someone might wake me up."

I considered what he said. Then replied, "Thanks for letting me know. Being here has made me think about how snippy I've been with people. It's made me think about a lot of things. But mainly the way I behave with others. If I ever get out I hope I'll be more aware of other people. It's not at all about being a nicer person. I guess what I'm saying is that I want to be a healthier person. I want to have healthy relationships. I want to always be aware that other people have complicated lives and emotions. I've just been too busy to actually connect with others. I hope someday, I get another chance."

I noticed how strange it was hearing my own voice speaking to another person. It was particularly weird that I went on so long talking to someone I didn't know and who probably wasn't even real.

"Don't worry," he said. "I like it that you have this sarcastic side to you. But I can see how standing back and taking a good look at yourself could cause you to want to make some changes. Not many people get to have that chance. I'm amazed at how well you have adjusted to your situation. I'm not even sure exactly where you are, because you come to me in my dreams. I'm a dreamer and that is my job."

"So, you're not one of the people who brought me here?"

"Not at all. Like I said, I'm not sure exactly where you are or how you got here. I see the same things you do: desert, animals, your dwelling. From my point of view you've got an awesome set up here. The only problem I see is the isolation. I know you are a reclusive kind of person, but this is extreme. I can only assume you are not here by your own choosing. However, that might be debatable."

I struggled with what he was saying. I fought the notion that he could be a hologram – some fancy technology that made him appear ghostlike in my vision. It had to be that or I was hallucinating. I had a hard time buying the fact that I was in his dreams.

"Do you know Alice?" I asked.

"Yes, actually, I do. We've known each other since we were kids in school.

We are both dreamers. We learned to dream together when we were young. We decided not to visit you together because we both wanted alone time with you to share our individual stories."

"Do you live over there below the mountains?" I pointed west through the patio wall.

"Yes, we do. You've been watching us. That's how we knew about you. We became aware that you were here and that you were, let's say, open to our visits."

"But you said you don't know where I am."

"I know you are in this desert somewhere, but I'm not sure of your exact location. I could not drive here in a car or even fly here in a helicopter."

I noticed that sometimes Romero looked like a teenager, other times he appeared to be much older, maybe in his forties. It made me think about dreams and how you could be any age in a dream.

"What about the Queen of Arizona?" I asked trying to distract him from looking at me.

"Sure, I'll tell you more of her story." He sat back in his chair, ran his hands though the longs strands of hair on the very top of his head. Then he smiled, and of course, it was a dazzling smile. I laughed a little for imagining a flashing gleam coming from his teeth, like in a silly tooth paste ad. He must have picked up on my thoughts because he laughed too. Alias settled in again on my belly and fell asleep. He quickly became so limp it was like having a warm towel folded on top of me. It made me feel to warm, but I wasn't going to interrupt what was happening to make myself more comfortable.

Romero started where he left off in his story.

"Ellie, the queen, was a unique person," he said. "Her parents had been heavily influenced by the hippie movement. Since they had few duties to perform, they had a lot of time on their hands. Along with their daughter and their servants they watched every hippie movie ever made, and read everything they could get their hands on about the 1960's and 70's. It was no surprise that they began to dress and act like hippies. That included making things – even their own clothes, eating natural foods, and, of course, smoking lots of pot. And by the looks of the paintings hanging on their walls, it was clear LSD might have had an influence in their thinking."

"They also began treating the servants more or less as equals. They still remained servants but were called by their first names and were told to address the queen as Rose and the king as Ralf. Rose and Ralf knew all of the servants' kids by name too, and made sure they all went to school. And that included college. Ellie played with these kids everyday, because everyone lived on the castle grounds.

"After her parents were gone, Queen Ellie had a hard time at first. It took her about a year to get a handle on being queen. She wanted to make something out of her royalty and not just be some figurehead cutting ribbons at celebrations and riding on floats in parades. She continued to stand her ground about not getting married just so the country could have a king. This sent a lot of fear around the kingdom, because they had never before had a queen without a king. In fact it was almost always a king, with a wife – a queen."

I was fascinated by Romero's story and fearful he would disappear in mid-sentence. I looked at his face and saw that his eyes were closed as if he were recalling a memory.

He continued. "Ellie started out by having weekly meetings on Sunday mornings. She needed to convince the servants to accept her, not as a boss, but a leader. She wanted them to take up roles as team players. At first the servants were standoffish. They had grown up watching their parents, dressed in brightly colored hippie clothes, but still serving the royal family in pretty much a traditional way."

"In the beginning Ellie's meetings were a disaster. Everyone would sit at the round table in the meeting room that her parents had named *The Situation Room* and let her do all the talking. So she came up with a plan."

"The next meeting was held in the ballroom. There were no chairs – just an amazing woven carpet and some brightly colored fluffy pillows. The rest of the room was completely empty except for a sound system. Crystals hanging in the huge windows were casting rainbows all over the room."

"That sounds familiar," I said.

Romero looked at me as if he wasn't understanding why I would say that. As far as I know he had not been inside my house to see the rainbows caused by crystals hanging in windows. For some reason I was reminded that the hippie movement had morphed into the New Age movement which brought about the crystal craze.

"Is there something I should know?" he asked.

"No, sorry. Go on."

So he did. "Queen Ellie had them all stand in a circle. Then she clicked the remote and started playing soft, flowing music. She asked them to close their eyes and sway to the sounds, then to open their eyes and start walking around making eye contact with each other. Before the music was over she had them all dancing wildly to loud drum rhythms. It seemed as though they were cracking out of shells that had formed around their bodies. This went on until they were breathless and tired. Then she told them to sit down on the soft pillows. Their faces were flushed, they were smiling, and they all looked a lot less shy of her and each other."

"'Now,' she said. 'I know you all know each other and I know you too. For God's sake we've been playing together since we were born, but we've been away at school for quite some time and look what happened. We all grew up and now I'm the Queen. Voila!'"

I was happy Romero was able to stay longer. I kept still and quiet hoping that if I didn't interrupt he would have more energy to keep talking.

He went on. "She told them, 'I want each of you to introduce yourselves to me and each other. I want to know what you majored in at college and what do you want to do with your lives. I know for sure there is not one of you here who is totally happy about the thought of spending your lives serving a forgotten Queen, cooking food, polishing silverware, and mucking out the stables. I know you don't mind doing that, but who the hell wants that to be all you do. If that's all you want, I want you to raise your hand right now.'"

"Nobody did. They were still grinning from the oxygen boost they had gotten from the wild dancing."

"'Okay now, is that understood? Who wants to start?'"

"A tiny mouse-like girl in the front of the room shyly raised her hand."

"'Good, Cecilia, you go first.' Everyone burst into song.'"

"'Cecilia, you're breaking my heart.'" They all laughed at the old worn out joke. They had been singing that song to her since she was a tiny baby."

"Ellie's heart soared. She had not seen them act this happy since they got back to the castle."

"'I'm Cecilia Bankhart. I went to Yale. I have a degree in law and accounting.'"

"'Get serious,' said Neil."

"'Hey, no interrupting,' ordered the queen. 'So tell us more. What exactly are your wildest dreams, Cecilia?'"

"The young woman looked down at her hands in her lap and started talking. 'That's hard to say because I always wanted to come back here and work at the castle. It's home to me. I don't mind the grunt work. It's physical and I like that. I think I need to think about this for a while. Right now I can say, if you need me I might be handy interpreting the Arizona laws. I passed the bar in this state. And I'm good at keeping up with money.'"

"'Great Cecilia, thank you, that's what I want to hear.'"

"'Jesus Perez here,' said the thin young man sitting next to her. 'I majored in graphic design – Art.' He had a long black ponytail and was wearing a shirt and a pair of pants splattered in paint. 'I have a master's from The Design School in Pasadena. I like to paint. I have a studio behind the barn. Of course, you all know that already. I'm also not sure what my long term dreams are. I've always wanted to come back here and do whatever it took to stay. Esta es mi casa.'"

"'Good,' said Ellie. 'Who's next?'"

"'I'm Juan Flores,' said a tall muscular man. 'I didn't go to college. I have a black belt in Tai chi and Aikido. I study spiritual stuff and practice meditation. I'm also a farrier. I take care of the horses. I guess I wouldn't mind teaching some classes. I like to teach.'"

"'I'm Atsa Begay. I graduated from Arizona State University with a major in English. I like to write, mostly poetry. I like slam poetry. I guess my life's dream is to write and publish books. I have some stories to tell. I never really left here because I commuted to school everyday. Don't know where else I'd go.' He was a soft spoken guy with stunning black eyes and very light skin for a Native American. He looked like a poet.'"

"'I'm Kai Begay, Atsa's sister. I'm the IT person here at the castle. I maintain all the computers. I also graduated from Arizona State. I stayed here too and managed the computers for Ralf and Rose.' She blushed a little, probably from referring to the King and Queen by first names. She had a kind of geek look which included Harry Potter glasses.'"

"Queen Ellie was recording all they said so she wouldn't appear to be taking notes and not paying attention."

"'Well,' she said when it was her turn. 'I'm Ellie. I went to Queen school.' They all laughed. 'Just kidding. I wish I had. I might have a better idea of how to go about queening. Seriously, I went to UC Berkeley and majored in psychology and philosophy. Closest you can get to queening, I guess. Great! Anybody else have anything to add to this?'"

"A shy hand went up from Cecilia. 'You know we have a band. We all play musical instruments and some of us sing.'"

"'Yes, how could I not know that. I hear you practicing everyday, and I think it might be one of the most important things you all do. You know why?'"

"They all shook there heads."

"'It shows how well you all work together. Plus music, the arts in general are some of the most important things to have. Mind if I join your band? I'm not that great at singing along, but you could teach me.'"

"To say the least, Ellie was stunned at the wealth of talent and intelligence of her staff. She breathed a big sigh of relief, thanked them profusely and told them they would now begin to have meetings daily for awhile. None of them groaned at that. In fact Ellie could see them all coming alive like little tadpoles suddenly turning into frogs. Well, with the idea that they would all soon be princes and princesses."

I could see Romero fade this time, and before he could speak another word he blipped out like someone had turned off a TV.

This time I felt no disappointment – only gratefulness for having been entertained for awhile. The sun was setting and the sky had become peach colored. Outside the iron fence quail gathered and chattered to each other as if they were sharing about their day's adventures. Then all at once in a mad flurry they all flew into a nearby mesquite tree to roost for the night. I could hear their bedtime stories die out as the sun slipped over the horizon allowing the stars to become visible, first one at a time, then millions at a time.

I carried Alias inside and we both slept well that night. It was good for me to have conversations even if it was with phantoms. I kept imagining what it might look like if the cameras were still on me and someone was watching me talking out loud to myself. Max told me the cameras were off now, but it was easier to believe that Arizona once had a queen.

25: Journal Entry

Alias sleeps next to me every night. I'm kind of mad at Max for not having him here from the beginning. But maybe I wouldn't have appreciated him so much. He is so funny. I don't think I've ever heard myself laugh out loud so much. He has made himself right at home and now thinks he's the boss. It's hard to convince him otherwise. I had to make a place for him on my work table, and fence off my palette in such a way that he can't jump into the paint. I quickly learned what happens without the blockades. It took me a while to clean up the crimson paw prints on the floor. Thank God he didn't jump on the sofa. I'm certain at his age he can't be trained not to fly through the air and land wherever he sees fit, so I always need to have my line of defenses in place.

I've made him lots of toys. Paper pom-poms that hang off the furniture and wadded paper balls he can bat around on the floor. He loves the garden and often goes out there on his own. Max told me about the cat door that was hidden behind some books on a high bookshelf. According to Max, putting it up high will discourage him from bringing me gifts such as mice, lizards and snakes – dead or alive. He has to leap up pretty far to get in and I guess that would be too hard to do that with a mouth full of the day's catch. So far he hasn't had much success hunting, but he isn't full grown yet. I have hopes for the future as the mice and rat problems are scary. I hope he isn't interested in lizards and birds. I need to have a talk with him about that.

He likes to lie on my lap when I'm working on the computer or when I'm watching a movie. He smells like the outdoors. Max says he is a Bengal, although he doesn't have the exotic markings. Often in litters there will be one or two who come out looking like an ordinary tabby. The breeders give them away because they don't bring the high prices like their fancy marked siblings. These cats make great hunters and survive well in a hostile territory, like around here where there are lots of coyotes and bobcats. I hope he's going to be okay because I'm already attached.

He sleeps a lot. I put a towel on my art table for him to lie on and watch me paint. When he gets bored he falls over asleep. What a hoot! I mean, literally falls over...plop. I don't recognize myself. I'm like a new mom or grand mom. I want to send pictures to my friends and talk about him endlessly. Well, I have Max and he likes seeing the photos. Alias has been here a week and I have not seen Alice. I'm wondering how it will work with Bonita. There I go talking like these people are real. How will I know if Alias will even see Bonita and Alice. I don't even know if they will come back.

On the internet, I read about symptoms of solitary confinement and I've found it is not unusual for one to have hallucinations. Actually it's quite predictable. I can understand how I can make up people, but I can't understand how I've made up their personalities. Plus, I don't think I would ever have thought of a dress made of flowers or all those interesting tattoos on Romero's arms. And no way could I come up with the things they tell me. But then again I've never been in solitary confinement before so I have nothing to compare my experiences to.

I don't care if I'm hallucinating or not. I find them infinitely interesting. I honestly have to say that lately I have had no desire to leave here. Maybe that will change in time, but for now I've never felt so content. Life was messier when I lived around lots of people. The closest I ever came to really feeling comfortable with another person was with Granger and George, and a little with Manuel. But I have to say, at this time I'm not missing them. Who knows, that will probably change five minutes after I quit writing this. But that is just how it is right now.

26: Therapist

Rain in the desert smells delicious, like an exotic salad crafted by a renowned chef. It can actually make you hungry. I stood in the doorway looking out at my garden thinking, if plants could move they would all be dancing. When I lived in Phoenix, I would simply go to work as usual paying little attention to the weather. But now I didn't have to go anywhere and have no pressing deadlines. I have plenty of time to paint, tend to the garden and watch it rain.

I made a simple breakfast and some hot tea and took my seat at the table in front of the windows where I watched rivulets of water on the ground in the clearing. Thunder rumbling in the distance and flashes of lightning made for an exciting morning. Quail and rabbits were nowhere to be seen, probably hunkering down somewhere like I was. The distant mountains were out of sight for the day.

I had a long daydream about how I might paint a rainy desert landscape. I tried to remember other paintings of rain and only came up with a few impressionist ones, mostly cityscapes. I couldn't remember seeing a recent one. When I looked back into the room I was surprised to see Alice sitting across from me again.

She was dressed in a lime green business suit that looked expensive and was based on styles from the 1940's. She even wore a hat; an open umbrella appeared to be dripping water onto the floor behind her. A yellow raincoat hung on the back of her chair.

"You never cease to amaze me with your attire," I said.

"Is that a compliment?" she asked.

"Absolutely," I said.

I poured her some tea which she sipped. I could tell by the look on her face she loved it. "The tea is delicious. Is it from your garden?"

"Some of it. The rose part actually came from a tea bag, but the mint is fresh."

"I think I dreamed about this tea last night," she said. "It's like making love lying on rose petals and soft green leaves."

I flashed in my mind a vision of Alice naked, lying on rose petals. It caused me to pause for a second before I said. "I'm glad you like it. Where is Bonita?"

"I'm on my way to the city today so she stayed behind with friends. Like most dogs she is not happy when it thunders."

"What do you do in the city?" I asked.

"I'm a psychotherapist. I have an office. But I only work there three days a week. I think that is enough time spent working. Don't you?'"

"Well, I don't know. I work everyday, but I don't have to get dressed and go to the city anymore. It all happens right here." I swooped my arm around towards the easel.

"Most people think artists are just playing all the time. They resent people who have fun and get paid for it. How do you feel about that?" she asked me.

"Actually, it isn't all fun like they think it is. It's just a job that I happen to like. Of course, that attitude promotes the notion that art isn't important and that it's probably why when funds are cut, the universities always try to eliminate the art department. Do you know what finally happened at my university?" I asked her.

"No, I don't. I don't go to Phoenix."

"So, you are not involved with the people who put me here," I said fishing for some answers.

"Not at all," she said emphatically.

"Do you like your job in the city?"

"Do you mind?" she said as she took off her hat and laid it on the table. Her curly red hair tumbled down onto her shoulders. She shook her head and ran her fingers through it. I was sure I'd seen that flirtatious act in an old movie. It usually happened in front of a very handsome man. Flashing lightning caused her face to blink off and on a few times which made me realize it was quite dark in the room. I was used to having so much light from the windows I hadn't bothered to turn on the electric ones.

"Of course I do. I even love going to the city." Alice sipped her tea, eyes smiling over the rim of the cup.

The thought occurred to me how different Alice was from me.

"I didn't come just because of the tea," she said

"Oh? So what would you like to talk about?" I asked.

Alice paused and looked down into her cup as though she were studying her reflection in it or maybe reading tea leaves. "I don't want to spring this on you too suddenly, but I need to know something about your mother. I'm working on a case with a client today and I think you could help me shed

156

some light on this young woman's situation. You see, I think you and she have similar stories. Could you tell me more about you and your mom?"

I was surprised by the direction of the conversation. However, it suddenly felt right to talk to Alice about my mom. "She died from an overdose of pharmaceutical drugs. She never recovered from the death of my older brother and was seriously depressed." It was a line I had memorized so I could answer in situations that called for a quick explanation of why my mom died at such an early age. I used it when I couldn't get passed just saying she died when I was a teenager.

"What was she like before your brother died?"

I noticed my eyes glancing upward as if searching for memories of my mom prior to the accident that killed my brother. Her depression was always what came to mind when I thought of her.

"Well, before the accident she was pretty much like any mom, I guess. She ran the household, was tidy and organized, cooked up a storm."

"What was she like with you? What was your relationship like?"

It suddenly became evident to me how deeply I had suppressed memories of how it had been with my mom before the tragedy. I looked out the window at the rain hoping I would find an answer, but nothing appeared. Then I began to notice a heavy feeling in my chest and a queasiness in my stomach.

Alice sat watching me as I squirmed. I thought again about getting up to turn on some lights, but I was glued to the chair.

Then words spilled out. No matter how hard I tried I could not stop them. "I can remember sitting next to my mom on the sofa with her arm around me. She smelled a lot like the tea we are drinking. Like the garden. She had a beautiful garden with flowers and vegetables. I remember eating sliced fruit and pieces of cheese and me telling her all about my school day. She always wanted to know how I was doing in school. Not just about my studies, but about everything. She wanted to know if I was happy. If I had friends and if teachers were nice."

Alice looked interested in what I was sharing so I continued. "On Saturdays she would take me shopping and sometimes to art museums. We always had lunch at the museum cafeteria. I would get a chicken salad sandwich with potato chips. She had soup. We would talk a lot about art. She wasn't an artist, but she loved it and could talk endlessly about her favorite artists. I think she might have read a lot of books about it. I don't know where else she could have learned so much."

And then, I began to cry. At first I tried to wipe the tears away without

Alice noticing, but they seemed to be coming from the pit of my stomach and there was no stopping or hiding them. Outside the thunder and lightning had subsided, but the rain was coming down hard.

Alice looked at me with soft eyes and I stopped feeling self-conscious and let the tears flow. I finally stood up and snatched a paper towel from my art table and blew my nose. I had the feeling I was only at the beginning of releasing a barrel of sadness.

"I'm sorry," I said when I caught my breath and sat back down. "I've never let myself think about how it was before the accident."

I continued to sob into the towel for quite a while. Alice sat patiently and Alias, who had been hiding under the bed, jumped into my lap, laid down, and started purring. His weight and warmth comforted me.

"It's okay," Alice finally said. I think she would have put her arm around me had she been able to, but I could feel her empathy and I welcomed it like desert plants soaking up rain.

"I have this affect on people," she finally said. "I know you are not a client, in my office, but this seems to happen whenever I spend private time with people. I guess I kind of tricked you, although I wasn't lying about my client who has similar issues. I do hope this will help you feel better too. I could tell that you had a very special mom. She was there for you in the most formative years of your life and it shows."

I stroked Alias and wiped a few remaining tears. "I guess I should be grateful then," I sobbed.

"I have something else to tell you before I leave. Is that okay?"

I nodded. The heavy rain subsided and it became much quieter in the room. Everything seemed to slow down.

"You still have a lot of guilt around not having been able to help your brother and your mom." Alice's voice was calm and I began to feel nervous about her staying so long. I didn't want her to suddenly disappear in the middle of all this so I sat very still and paid close attention, careful not to interrupt.

She continued. "You could not have helped your family. No one could have helped them. You thought you should know what to do and what to say and if you could only find the answers you would have been able to change the outcome. You carry a lot of guilt for not being able to learn what to do about it."

"Let me explain. There are things we don't know called the unknown and things we can't know called the unknowable. Those two things are very different. The unknown are things we don't know but can find out and learn."

"Here is how I explain the unknowable. Imagine you want to play Monopoly with Alias. You put out the board and all the pieces to the game, but Alias can only bat around the pieces. You can both have a good time playing like that, but a cat will never be able to play the game of Monopoly because his cat brain can only understand what it understands and that does not include how to play the game your way. His game is a different game."

"We as humans in the Universe are like the cat. We can only bat around pieces of the game, but we cannot understand the Universe well enough to play the game at a greater level. There are things that you and I will never understand, so we fail to participate in the game at the fullest. If the game is simple enough, sometimes we can determine an outcome, but most of the time we cannot. Most humans never forgive themselves for their failure to be able to understand the game. They continue to strive to win a game they don't know how to play. It's frustrating and stressful and it's the cat who wins because he doesn't care. He only knows how to accept the world according to his understanding. He doesn't even know that he isn't playing the game properly according to your knowledge of it. He's just happily having fun."

"I know the game at your home was far from fun, but it was still a game you couldn't possibly know how to play. No one did. And by the way, I am sure there are cats in the world having to play painful games also. Your cat is a lucky fellow."

Alice paused and watched me try to wrap my mind around her words. She spoke in a way that kept me in a feeling state. I had to give up understanding and just be with the sound of her voice, the energy moving in my body and outside in the world. It was both uncomfortable and freeing at the same time.

"Well then, you can say that I can't catch a mouse with my claws and teeth," I added on a lighter note.

"You are right. You would not go about catching and killing a mouse in the way a cat does. Our brains don't work the same way. Just imagine all the dissimilar brains operating in the entire Universe. We'd be arrogant to think we could grasp it all. But we do grasp it all in some ways, because we are not separate from any of it. In time, you will learn that Alias does understand more than you think, and you do too. But it's not possible to put all that into our limited vocabularies."

"Okay, back to your family. You may have really wanted your brother to stop drinking. You may have thought he should stop so he could be a better or happier person. But truth be told you wanted him to stop so you could be happier. You wanted him sober so your mother would be happier and that would have made everything okay for you. You thought everything depended on him changing his ways. You wanted your mom to shift out of her depression so you could have her back the way she was. Then you could be okay again. You thought they both had to change so your life could be normal. But what you were not understanding was that maybe your brother was as happy as a lark when drunk, and your mom was pleased as pie to be depressed and irresponsible. They could have been in love with their misery. And they were playing their part in the greater universe. Who gives you the right to change it, even if you could, which you cannot. We humans seem to think that we know what is best for another person when in truth we are only trying to serve ourselves. Even if changing things seem logical and right, it may not be what is needed in the greater scheme of things."

I could feel waves of something that felt like acceptance. That's the only way I could describe it. My shoulders must have dropped two inches.

She continued. "You were fortunate that the Sun family took you in and you found love, and your basic needs were taken care of. But in the back of your mind you were waiting for your mother to get better so you could find what you thought was real happiness. When she died, you believed you would never find what you wanted. You thought you didn't deserve to find it because you had not solved the problem in time. You and everyone else could only bat around the pieces of the game. But it's a game that only God, a Higher Power, or some ineffable something, knows how to play. Alias doesn't condemn himself for having a cat brain, nor should you for being human."

I was overcome by a sense of truth with compassion coming from Alice. To me she was an unexplainable alien who had graced my life by offering me the gift of freedom from the pain of my past. I just wasn't sure I would be able to accept it over the long term. But I was willing to give it a chance.

All I could say was, "You are an excellent therapist." I knew I'd been nailed, but I felt past agitation melt away and cloud lift from over my head.

"It doesn't make sense to beat yourself up for wanting something you couldn't have. You were not a selfish person for wanting what you had lost. I suggest that you bring this past into the present and talk to your mom now so you can clear it all up."

"But she's dead. How can she hear me?"

"Don't worry about that. Understanding our relationships with people who have passed on really isn't something we can completely grasp, but I promise you something will change in you if you talk to her. I'm not sure about your brother. It might be best to wait on that one. But you were close to your mom before the tragedy and I think you can reach that place with her again, if only in spirit."

"What should I do? Just pretend she is sitting here at the table with me?"

"That would be up to you. I suggest that you lie in a comfortable place, close your eyes and image she is with you. You don't have to do it now. Just let it happen naturally. You might be amazed. I have to go now. You have helped me a lot with that client I am seeing today. Let me know how it works out for you."

She smiled at me as she slowly evaporated with her hat, raincoat and umbrella. There were no drips left on the floor.

I sat at the table staring out the window visualizing Alice getting on a train headed for the city, her umbrella dripping on the floor near her feet. I picked up the snotty paper towel and tossed it into the wastebasket. I felt my burning eyes and knew that this experience had been real whether Alice had been real or not. "What am I to do with this information?" I asked Alias who purred louder at the sound of my voice and the touch of my hand on his head.

"I know," I told him. "Let's get to work." But wasn't that what I always did – get to work. Anything to avoid feeling things. I didn't want to linger in the sorrow either. I moved in my chair and Alias leaped from my lap and headed for the kitchen to nibble. I stayed, thinking about the storm that had blown through me like the one outside. I pushed my tea cup out of the way and laid my head in my arms on the table and cried some more. In fact, I cried most of the morning. Even after I got up and began painting, I continued crying. Outside the rain came in spurts. I checked the garden often thinking the plants might get beaten down, but they seemed to stand stronger than ever.

In the afternoon, I suddenly felt exhausted. I lay down on the sofa, wrapped myself in the throw and dozed off. Soon, my mom appeared in a dream. She and I were sitting on the couch together in our home in Fort Worth. We held hands. She looked like she did before the accident, but there was a new feeling of serenity about her when she spoke to me.

"I am so proud of you," she said. "You became the artist I always wanted to be. When you and your brother were born, I let that dream go. Nobody should ever give up their dreams. There was no excuse for me to not paint even though I was a mom. But times were different back then. Maybe if I had pursued my desire to be an artist I would have had something to return to after Randy died. Or maybe my happiness would have prevented his death. But I can assure you I am happy now that you are living out your dream no matter what circumstances brought you to this place."

161

"Mom, it's okay," I tried to reassure her.

"Yes, it is all okay, my sweet daughter. None of this is your fault and I only want to say I'm sorry I abandoned you. When I was alive and you were little I didn't know what I know now. I had no control over what happened. You see, nobody was to blame. We all did our best in a very challenging situation. I'm glad that I made that phone call to Apollo that day to come and babysit. It led you to the place you needed to be. I could never have given to you what the Suns were able to offer. Someday you will understand what is happening now and you will be grateful. Trust me."

Neither of us spoke after that. There was only a feeling of love and forgiveness. When I woke up, I had been asleep for over an hour and I could feel that other things had happened in the dream, but I couldn't remember what. I could tell I was a changed person and there were no words to describe it.

After the dream I stopped crying and became completely absorbed in painting. But as I worked I found myself singing along to some music I was playing from my iTunes list. I only knew a few of the words, but it reminded me of when Granger and I would spend weeks learning songs so we could sing them for Apollo when she visited from college. We even made costumes. We must have been adorable. I laughed out loud thinking about it. Alias stood at the edge of the room staring at me as if he didn't know whether to stay or run away. He had never heard me sing before.

27: Death

I didn't expect Alice to show up the next day, but there she was. She might have been taking advantage of the rain which was keeping me out of the garden and sitting at the table. "It's a female rain," she explained. "The male rains arrive in the afternoon growling and rattling on our roofs, then moving on quickly. Female rains are gentle and can last for days. True, it's rare for this time of year. But it's awesome. Don't you think?" She took a sip from her dainty tea cup.

"Yes," I said. "You're right, it softens everything. I grew up in Fort Worth where it could rain for weeks. It didn't bother me but I know it caused a lot of depression for others. I have to admit I'm loving this break from the relentless sun. Have you seen the garden?"

"Yes, your plants are celebrating. It's a relief and a release. You had quite a release yourself yesterday. How do you feel today?"

"The best way I can describe it is...I feel softened."

"That's good," she said. "I'm curious. Do you mind if I ask more about your early life? How did things change when you began to hang out at the Sun's house?"

I looked at her suspiciously, thinking that she knew things about me that I hadn't told her. I couldn't remember exactly what all I had told her. I started to ask her about that, but I held back. There were too many things in my life happening now that made no sense. And I was doing my best to stop asking for explanations for everything. I'm sure she could tell what I was thinking by the look I must have had on my face.

I was grimacing, letting her know I didn't like talking about my past. It was gone and there was nothing I could do about it. But I found myself acquiescing anyway.

I cleared my throat and began. "At first it was strange, being in someone else's house so much of the time. But I loved being with Granger. He was homeschooled, and Ana Sun gave me an allowance in exchange for my helping him with his studies. He was two years younger than me, but he was sharp, creative and loads of fun. We became best friends right away. Our gender differences were never an issue. In school, boys and girls were mostly kept separate. Boys in one line, girls in another. I never had any boys for friends at school."

"Granger always greeted me after school – happy as a little puppy. Everyone was happy in the Sun family and it had never been like that in my house. I mean, we weren't miserable until after the accident, but there was always tension between my parents. Also, my brother was contrary and a bit mean."

"So how much time did you spend at the Sun's house?"

I noticed I was glancing up to the ceiling again looking for memories. I didn't like it when I did that. It made me feel like I was fitting myself into some kind of psychological behavior pattern. And that made me want to rebel. But I was also tired of rebelling. It wasn't working for me. I slumped in my chair feeling deflated. It was a good feeling, like I was waving a white flag and surrendering.

I continued. "After a while I didn't feel like a guest in the Sun house. I didn't want to go home to my own room and sleep at night. I had terrible nightmares in that house. So Ana, Mrs. Sun, put a little bed in Apollo's room for me to sleep and a small dresser where I could put some of my things. Apollo was only there for a year before she took off for college so after that I basically took over her room."

When she visited from college we were roommates. I worshipped her like little kids do with older ones. I lapped up the attention from her, and she was forthcoming with that. She seemed to enjoy both Granger and me. She liked to play board games and cards. But the most fun were the plays we put on for Ana and Parker. Apollo loved to write what she called ten minute plays and she was really good at it. Also, she would come up with some of the strangest costumes. Granger and I would make backdrops out of cardboard. We had a paint station in the garage. It always became a huge project. His parents stood by observing our creativity, never once being concerned about the messes we were making."

"That's amazing!" Alice said, pushing her curls behind her ears. "I've never heard of such a creative family. You were most fortunate."

"I still spent time with my dad. Mostly on Sunday. He would take me out somewhere. Often Granger came along. We went to movies, ate out and did lots of fun things together. The Sun's also invited Dad and Grandma over for dinner and the ten minute plays. They came when they could. It was a great arrangement. When my mom died, my grandmother moved back to Colorado and only visited at Christmas. Then it was just Dad and me, so I felt obligated to spend more time at my real home."

That day Alice was casually dressed and her hair was loose and curly from the humidity. Even so, I knew she had her therapist hat on and she was heading me straight into emotion city. For a brief instance I froze, but I realized there was no turning back, so I said, "You're going to ask me about my mom's death, aren't you."

"I don't think I have too," she said.

It felt like I was on a train going over the cliff. But this was something that happened when I was a child and now I only had to remember it, and speak the words. I'd gone through a lot of feelings at the time, but I'd never talked to anyone about them after I became an adult. Right on cue, Alias jumped into my lap and settled down in his usual position, purring. That morning he had woken up early and spent a long time tearing from one end of the room to the other batting around his toys and ripping up several paper balls I'd set out for him. It was his nap time now. His warmth and weight in my lap helped me understand the human need for pets.

I took a deep breath and when I exhaled, my breath was jagged. I reluctantly started my story. "One day I came home from school and there was an ambulance in the driveway of my parent's house; my dad's car was parked in the street. I saw this from the front porch of the Sun's house. I went in, laid my books down and told Ana and Granger I was going to check on it. She said to wait a minute while she gathered coats and hats for them so they could come along."

"It had been over a week since I had seen my mom. The last day I saw her she actually seemed happy. She asked if she could read a story to me. I was taken aback because I was in high school by then. But I sat next to her on the sofa. Her body was bone thin and she smelled like an old rug, but I was thrilled to be getting some attention from her so I just went along. She must have searched my closet where I had stored some keepsakes, because she had one of my favorite childhood books. It was *The Little Engine that Could*."

She read it to me in that same voice she used when she occasionally read to me when I was little. That day I listened and snuggled in beside her. It felt so weird to notice how small she had become and how big I was. I could tell how much she wanted to be a mom to me, so when she finished the story I let her put her arms around me and hug me for a very long time. I could feel her breath on my neck and her bony body under her clothes."

"I had to pull myself away from her embrace. I really didn't know what to say. So I just said thank you and got up and left like any other teenager would have done. As I was leaving I heard her say I love you. I stopped and I turned around and said. 'I love you too, mom.' Then I just walked out thinking how weird she was."

"Somehow I knew that she was dead when Ana, Granger and I arrived at the house that day. Dad met me at the door and told my escorts that he needed to be alone with me. Then he guided me to the sofa and we sat in the same place where mom had read to me. We cried together. Grandma was sitting in the kitchen in her usual chair, knitting and crying too. We sat there as the paramedics wheeled the gurney out of the front door. I turned my head so I wouldn't have to look at it."

"'What happened,' I asked him."

"'She had been saving prescription pills and finally took all of them,' he said. 'It must have been last night. She didn't come out of her room this morning and Grandma didn't go in and check on her. I think she was afraid of what she might find. When she didn't come out by the afternoon, Grandma called me to come home and take a look,' he explained. His face was drooping and his eyes were watery and red. He appeared older than I'd ever seen him. I wanted to make it all up to him and I think he was thinking the same about me."

"'I stopped checking on her in the mornings a long time ago,' he continued. 'I guess I'd just become complacent. But I'm sure she passed sometime in the night.' I could tell he needed to believe that so I didn't say anything.

"'Oh Dad,' I said. I threw my arms around him and held him. He relaxed in my arms like he was the child. I was beginning to feel a huge sense of relief. It wasn't the way I expected to feel. Believe me, I had imagined this moment time after time. I thought I'd be crying my eyes out, but it wasn't sadness or grief that got to me. The feelings were more about guilt."

I only wiped away a few tears while telling this story to Alice. It was the first time I realized that my mom's death had brought with it a tangle of conflicting emotions. In a way, she had died when Randy died and we had been grieving that loss for years and now there was a possibility that all of this tension might end.

"Most of your childhood was about dealing with loss," Alice said in her low therapeutic voice. "What interests me is how much joy and love came your way through all of it. Your dad, your grandma, the Suns. Did your mom leave a note?"

"Yes. I think she left a note because she didn't want anyone to think somebody else might have killed her. You know a mercy killing. Believe me, I think we all thought about it from time to time. The note didn't say much, but when the authorities came to investigate the death they were in no way suspicious when they read it."

"What did it say?"

No one had ever asked me that before. I was a little taken aback that a complete stranger, perhaps even a ghost, would be the one I shared that information with. I could still visualize the note in my mind's eye like it had been burned into my brain. "It was addressed to me. She didn't mention my dad or grandma, and that felt very strange to me. It said:

Laurence,
In spite of how it must have looked, you were always my favorite child. I know you and everyone else will be better off with me gone. Just remember, you can do whatever you want to, if you think you can.
Love and Goodbye,
Mom."

"I know all of this seems so primary. But as messed up as she was I was amazed at how she managed to do what she had done. She found the book, she read it to me and she left a note. That was huge for her. It was like she had to wake up from a trance to take that kind of action. I wish things could have been different. Looking back on it, I can easily get angry at the doctors who kept giving her all those medications. But none of us knew any better back then. And who's to say that if we had known it would have made any difference."

Alice looked at me with her kind eyes and said, "There is a reason you and the Sun family were thrown together like that. Without this family you may not have achieved all that you have. I can't help thinking your mom played a big part in making sure you had a place to go. Wasn't she the one who called Apollo that day when she came to babysit?"

"She would have been the one to find a sitter, but I don't think she did it consciously. I'm sure she didn't have any idea it would turn out to be a good thing for me. It was more like magic."

"Wow, thank you so much for sharing your story," she said. "It will help me with my client tomorrow."

I eyed her suspiciously.

"No, I'm serious," she said. "We are all connected. I must go now so you can have a fruitful day." With that she faded out and I was again alone with my cat.

I sat there petting him and staring out into the gray day. I had never talked so much about myself to anyone. It wasn't like I thought I had something to be ashamed of. My problem had to do with the fear that if I let myself have my feelings I might end up drowning in them like my mom did. However, maybe my mom's problem had to do with the fact that the drugs – without the help of therapy – kept her from actually feeling her emotions. She always seemed numb and in denial about the whole thing.

In the Sun family, feelings got felt and shared in the moment. When I was there, even though I was free to share my emotions, I continued to ignore them a lot. I had to be the strong one. I could see how that led to me becoming an overachiever. But it wasn't a bad thing. Nothing that had happened in my life was a bad thing. It was what it was. And my life, in this crazy situation in the desert, was just what it was. I don't understand it, but I also didn't understand my life before I got here. It actually seems much easier to be here than at the university. The politics drove me crazy. The administration always made the worst choices in order to benefit themselves while the teachers struggled to make things work best for the students. I really didn't miss it.

Unceremoniously I stood up, dumping the cat off my lap. I walked over to my easel in the middle of my studio and stood looking at the blank canvas that was waiting for me. It was like an invitation to a blind date; I had no idea what to paint and I was frightened I might start something I didn't want to finish. I sort of like blank canvases just the way they are – all clean and white.

As I sat there staring at the canvas I began to remember cleaning out both my mom's and brother's rooms after my mom died. My grandma, dad, Apollo, Granger and Ana all pitched in. There was no way my dad and I could have done it without them. There were only a few things in the rooms worth saving. So most of the stuff just went into the garbage. I gave Randy's guitar, amp and all his stereo equipment to Granger.

Afterwards we painted the rooms white, like the canvas in front of me. We tried to convince my Grandma to move into my brother's room, but she wanted to go back to Colorado to live close to her friends. She came on holidays like before and still tried to get me to drink my milk. I began to use his room as an art studio. My dad bought me an easel and some tables to work on. I set up my own stereo. I still spent lots of time with the Sun family, but my dad and I lived comfortably in that house until I completed four years at a local college.

I still remember those white walls. I'm positive no other color would have cleansed those rooms the way white did. Randy had insisted on heavy dark curtains that he could use to keep out the light and I was surprised how huge those windows were once exposed. Light flooded in. I had my dad buy some white sheets and Ana Sun helped me sew them into curtains for days when I wanted to control the light coming in. It was my first studio and it was a good one. So many years had passed since Randy's death and I never felt disturbed in that room. Sometimes I imagined that he could see me in there and know I was recovering. I had a sense that he too was getting well. And that he and my mom were somewhere together. Even if it was only a belief, it was one I needed. But then who knows what was real.

The Fallen

28: Manuel's Journey

Hot wind assaulted Manuel's face as he walked across the parking lot at Sky Harbor Airport in Phoenix. Except for visits to Mexico, he had never been out of the country, and knew nothing about Europe. He boarded the Skytrain carrying only a backpack.

He was still thinking about projects he had left behind: a painting on the easel, gallery openings he should be attending, and students still clamoring for his attention – even though the semester had ended. After takeoff, he closed his eyes, put his head back on the seat, and tried to let everything drop away. He wanted to be free to focus on his mission. He imagined flying back with Laurence – her head on his shoulder.

Even though months had passed, Manuel seemed to ache from head to toe with residual emotional pain. No matter how many times he'd been told by friends and family that it wasn't his fault – that it could have happened anyway – he wasn't able to convince himself that they were telling the truth. But it wasn't just the guilt that drove him to rob his savings account in order to acquire airfare, hotel rooms, food and such. He thought it was better to take a generous amount of money out of the bank in case of a crises. He was convinced he would come back with some solid information that would lead to the rescue of the woman he loved. He had not bought a return ticket.

The plane was crowded. He tried to stretch out his legs, but his backpack was stuffed under the seat in front of him. Too late he realized he should have brought a smaller bag to keep at his seat so he could store the larger backpack in an overhead compartment. He noticed other people had brought food. Didn't they serve food on airplanes anymore? It could be worse, he thought, I could be on a boat.

He was grateful for the window seat. A friend had given him a few Xanax tabs, so he took one and soon melted away. He slept the whole way with his head against the window. When he got off the plane in Iceland, he was feeling stiff, but rested and hungry. When he found out his flight to Budapest had been canceled, he found a hotel room. He wished they had landed in London where there would be something more interesting to do.

Disappointment vanished when he smelled the island. He discovered the intoxicating rare flower scent that wafted on the wind came from the geothermal water. For two days he walked the main streets of Reykjavik, visited the art museum, and ate at charming restaurants. But best of all he soaked in the hot mineral water pools. He rented a car and drove around the island, stopping to pet Icelandic ponies and watch sheep. He hiked around volcanic rocks and stood next to an erupting geyser. But mostly he sat on beaches and questioned his sanity.

He was rested and peaceful when he finally got on the plane to Hungary. He promised himself he would go back to Iceland someday to ride ponies and walk on glaciers. He would bring Laurence. They would stay in the same nice hotel, and soak together in the neck deep tub filled with water that smelled like flowers, then make love at night with the sun still up.

As soon as he checked into the hotel in Budapest, he studied the map where he had marked all the galleries listed on the internet. But instead of starting out looking for them he went directly to the National Museum, which was near the hotel. It would be where he and Laurence would have gone had they come here together. What if he ran into her at the museum?

He played that fantasy in his mind several times. He would be looking for her, then see her standing in front of an amazing painting. He would walk up beside her and subtly ask a question about the artist. She would turn and see that it was him. He would take her into his arms and they would tremble from happiness. He could remember the feel of her body, slender and strong. They would sit close together on a bench and she would tell him her story about running away to a foreign country in order to live out her dream of becoming a successful artist, showing her work in galleries and museums. She would tell him that she had thought he no longer cared. He would convince her that was never true and would talk her into coming to live with him. He would build her the studio of her dreams. He would move to Europe if she wanted to stay.

That fantasy made him feel great, but he knew that couldn't be true. She never would have left her loved ones, Granger, George, and the Suns. Yet he refused to believe that she was not somewhere painting.

It was a weekday and he was early, so there were few people in the museum. He did not see a lot of inspiring paintings. Instead he saw a visual account of the history of Hungary which was all about brutal invasions and occupations. Though masterfully done, the paintings were grim and violent. For a while he was caught up studying the techniques of the highly skilled artists, but he soon began to feel sickened from seeing so many slashed throats, stab wounds and tortuous forms of killing and death. Needing to escape he tried to flee, but he couldn't find his way out. He hastened through one gallery room after another, looking for a hallway or staircase. He didn't know the word for exit in Hungarian. So he finally sat on a bench in a dark room filled with bloody pictures, and with his head in his hands, he cried.

He cried for Mexico, his native country and how – in spite of all the violence – the Mexican people still painted with bright celebratory colors. He pondered how they energetically danced and sang loudly, how they celebrated death and rebirth, and how they painted the buildings with bright colors so the towns looked intensely cheerful. He cried for the violence still happening there, the drug wars, deportations, poverty. He cried for all the world and all tragedies – especially ones that could be avoided. He cried for his own lost love.

Then he felt guilty again. Why was I so lucky? he asked himself. His grandparents had become citizens of the US before it became too complicated and expensive. He remembered how hard they had worked to send his dad to school and college. His parents, who had met at the university, were fortunate because college was affordable then. He was lucky they had saved money for him. But now he was crying for those who had been left behind.

He kept his head down, but out of his peripheral vision he saw a man enter through a door he had not seen before. He stood up and walked to the end of the room and went through that door, finding himself on a mezzanine looking down on some extremely huge, brightly-colored watercolor paintings. He recognized the flower paintings as ones painted by German artist Emil Nolde. He'd only seen them in art history books where they appeared a few inches in size. These paintings were huge. Not inches but yards. And they were stunningly beautiful. He descended the stairs and stood close to each one. He felt his eyes and heart healing from the assault of the other dark paintings in the museum. He thought about how art told the truth when words failed us.

He left the museum feeling a renewed commitment to his quest. He had purposefully bought a bigger cell phone so the image of the painting he thought was Laurence's could easily be seen when he showed it to gallery owners. But as he scratched names off his list after visiting one gallery after another, he was beginning to wonder if he'd made a mistake traveling so far. He rode buses, streetcars, taxis, and walked miles. He spoke to no one except gallery owners and managers. He didn't mind being alone. He didn't want distractions.

In two days he had marked off all the galleries on the map with no success.

No one was forthcoming with information about an artist named Laurence Donahue. He found an outdoor coffee shop and sat watching people, trying to take his mind of off his obsession. His feet hurt from walking so much on pavement and cobbled streets, and he was still exhausted from jet lag. Maybe Laurence would just walk by. But no. The world seemed to swirl around him. The smells were weird reminding him that he had never been so far away from home. He was staring blankly at his map when a woman walked up to his table.

"Pardon me," she said. "Yesterday you stopped into the gallery where I work and I was wondering if you found what you were looking for."

"Are you American?" he asked.

"From San Francisco. I'm Rochelle." She stuck out a slender hand.

He stood and gently shook her hand. "Please sit down," he invited. "I'm Manuel. What are you doing here in Budapest?"

"Oh, it's a long story, but I work for 3D Galleria. You came in when I was busy with a customer, so I didn't get to talk with you. I'm amazed to see you here today. It must be magic. There are a lot of people in the city now."

"I've noticed," he said, feeling how awesome it was to hear English spoken without a strong accent.

"I can tell that you have been having some trouble communicating with the locals. Most people around here don't speak English very well." A waiter appeared at the table and she order a cup of coffee and chatted a bit with the him in what sounded to Manuel like perfect Hungarian.

"Wow!" he said, impressed.

"My mother," she said. "She and my dad divorced when I was young and I've been coming here every summer since. I guess the habit stuck, so here I am. She owns the gallery...my mother. She's Hungarian."

"Really?"

"When I saw you here I thought I might be able to help you." She smiled at him with a determined look in her blue eyes. "Can I look at your map?"

He handed it to her.

"Oh, I see. There are some galleries not on this map. Let me think. Can I see the painting you were looking for?"

"Sure." He handed her his cell phone with the image.

"It will help if I know what kind of gallery might show this style of work. Is that a portrait of you?"

"I think so," he said.

"You mean you didn't sit for this."

"No." He knew then he would have to tell her more of the story. So he did.

A warm breeze blew strands of her blond hair across her face, which she kept tucking behind an ear as she listened.

"That is amazing," she said. "So are you the only one who thinks she is still alive?"

"No, I'm not the only one. And I don't think it is just wishful thinking."

"I believe you. I can see that you love her very much, and I don't think you are the kind of man who would make a trip halfway around the world looking for a woman if you believed she was dead. I also don't think you would hold on to someone if they wanted to leave you."

"I'm not sure how you can tell so much about me," he said. "I am not so sure I even know myself that well. I could be bat-shit crazy," he said laughing. He hadn't laughed much lately and it felt strange, like he had been believing that some dark presence was requiring him to be grim all the time. The laughter made him touch base with sanity – if only for a moment. He was aware that he could actually feel the difference, like the sun coming out after a dark stormy time.

"Don't worry so much," she said placing her hand over his. He wasn't sure whether or not if she was coming on to him. He felt concerned. He had heard stories about European women. But she was the closest thing to a lead so far. So he thought it best to ignore the gesture.

"You know what? I will help you, not just for you, but for her. She is a woman and it sounds like she only has men looking for her. I want to help her. It's too late now to check out the gallery that I have in mind. We'll need to wait until tomorrow. Would you join me for dinner with some of my friends? Where are you staying? I'll pick you up."

He said yes, even though his heart was pounding and he was starting to sweat. "I'm at the Grand Hotel," he told her, not understanding why he was so frightened. Maybe it was from all the scary paintings he had seen at the museum. He needed to take this chance and he decided he could feel stupid later if he found out he'd been tricked. He had to do this.

"Good," she said. "You won't be disappointed. Let me drop you off at your hotel and I'll come back at seven."

He followed her to her car.

At seven he was pacing in the lobby. She came right on time smiling and appearing self-assured. He thought if she was up to something she might show some nervousness, but nothing like that was evident. He was happy to see she was dressed in jeans, black leather jacket and boots, and not the expensive work clothes she had been wearing earlier. All he had brought were jeans, a couple of shirts and a hoodie. He hadn't counted on socializing.

Earlier he had considered shopping for a nice shirt. Now he was glad he hadn't.

They drove about 10 miles, ending up at a house on the outskirts of town. He had yet to go inside of anyone's house in Europe. Having watched a lot of foreign films with Laurence, Manuel felt deja vu upon entering Rochelle's house. They walked down a long hallway towards an exciting conversation in a language he didn't understand. He wanted to freeze, to turn around and go back out the door, but he quietly followed her into a simple Scandinavian designed interior littered with stacks of papers and books. Of course, true to the movies, the walls were lined with original paintings. Five people were sitting at a long plank table drinking wine and snacking on cheese, bread and an assortment of olives. No one stood up when Rochelle introduced him, and he was grateful for the lack of formality. Several people pointed to an empty chair.

He took a seat and they switched to English for his benefit and he tried to get the context of the conversation. Needing more historical background, he lacked information about the local political climate. It was an emotionally charged discussion. He gathered that, but they all seemed to be on the same side and in agreement.

Occasionally a man named Iggy spoke directly to him in Spanish, trying to fill him in. He could barely understand him, but it was fun conversing with someone in Castilian-accented Spanish. Occasionally Manuel asked what he thought might be an intelligent question, feeling embarrassed for having not done more reading about the place before he'd hopped on a plane.

Rochelle had informed her friends of his story, and they soon focused their attention on him acting intrigued by his quest by asking lots of questions. A women named Beata said in a strong Hungarian accent, "I've heard of things like this happening. It can be a kind of underground business where they capture artists and make them paint. Then they sell the paintings in countries far away. Usually the artists are so distraught they wouldn't think of painting portraits of people they know, like someone who might try to find them. Usually they are told to copy styles of other artists and the dealers sell them for cheaper prices. But that painting you showed us is not something that would sell cheap. It is an original painting of museum quality. I don't think this is the way it happens with the other artists."

"You mean like the Chinese painters who work in painting sweatshops?" Manuel asked.

"Something like that," she said. "Only these people I'm talking about have actually been, how you say, kidnapped. Not like the Chinese who hire

176

painters to work in painting factories."

"Do they ever get away and come back?" Manuel's heart was pounding. He did and didn't want to know the answer.

"My cousin's friend disappeared about eight years ago and reappeared about four years later. She had this story about being kidnapped and made to paint, but no one believed her. That was because before she left she was a little crazy and told a lot of lies. When she came back we just thought she was worse, but she also had a substantial sum of money. No one knew where the money came from, and she never said much about it. I don't know what happened to her after that. I can ask my cousin."

"I would like to talk to your cousin, if you can share her contact information." Manuel handed Beata a card with his information. The cards were Granger's idea. He had sent them to Manuel in the mail and suggested he leave them with all the galleries.

"I will try to find out what I can," said the woman.

Iggy said, "I think it happens a lot more than we know about. There are a lot of creative people who live alone, and don't have a family. People who you might think just moved away for a while and then came back. We are all so busy with our lives and there are so many people on the planet now that we have trouble keeping up with each other."

Manuel gave that some thought. He knew there were a lot of missing persons in America, because he had spent time looking into it by reading online and questioning authorities on the subject. Most of the time people didn't come back, but he wasn't sure about Europe or the rest of the world. Tucson was a relatively small city, and he had known friends who moved away for several years, then returned. Maybe he hadn't learned about their leaving in the first place so it just seemed that he hadn't run into them in a while. But that didn't seem relevant to what had happened with Laurence.

After a while, the conversation veered off into more talk about politics, and how weird the world was in general. As he grew more accustomed to their accents, Manuel became captivated by their interesting stories, especially ones about the last occupation of Hungary by the Communists. Most of these people had been out of the country during that time. But they were all still affected by those dark times. They all had family members who had stayed.

It grew late into the evening before finally Manuel was served a huge bowl of Hungarian goulash, which he reluctantly tasted. He was always suspicious of new foods, but he was much too hungry to turn it down. "Wow, this is amazing! It looks like a rather ordinary soup, but has a powerful flavor."

"It's the Hungarian paprika," Rochelle told him. He had two servings and would have had more if he hadn't feared it would be impolite. He asked the group if they had ever eaten Mexican food and found that most of them had traveled to Mexico, leaving him feeling unworldly.

For a while he stopped thinking of Laurence and just enjoyed the stimulating conversation with some very interesting people. He was amazed at how knowledgeable they were in the arts, philosophy and politics. It seemed to him that in America, only artists knew about art and even that could be debatable. He made a promise to himself to travel more and invite visitors to his own home. He imagined these people visiting his house in Tucson.

Later, Rochelle drove him back to the hotel keeping up a slightly intoxicated chatter as though she had forgotten all about his mission. He was glad when they reached the hotel and she assured him she would pick him up at eleven the next day. He had to get some sleep, calm down, get back on track.

Back in his room, he thought that even if he didn't find Laurence, this travel was going to change him for the better. He felt bad for having the thought that he could be happy or in any way be better off without Laurence. He was of two minds, one was genuine grief for the loss of someone he loved. The other thought was that he wanted to move on and live life as though losing Laurence had never happened. Vacillation between these two emotional states seemed to be at the root of his discomfort. He imagined that root looking like an elongated beet. But not red. It had to be dark brown. He would put one in his next painting and maybe call the painting *The Root of Suffering*.

29: Dreaming Alice

Alice and I are walking on the desert together. There is no trail, so we are skirting around lots of prickly-pears pointing angry spines at us. While giant saguaros watch suspiciously, cottontails scurry to hide, but stop in their tracks, freeze, then stare at us with one eye. Numerous lizards streak by.

I ask her, "Can you see the future?"

She looks at me strangely as if I'd said something shocking. "No," she answers, "But I think logically and that makes me skilled at understanding what the natural consequences might be when people make certain choices. I'm not always right."

"So you can't tell me how long I will be here?"

"No, I can't. Can you tell me why you are here?"

I'm surprised by her question. I wonder if she is asking it to avoid elaborating on her answer to me about understanding the future.

"I don't know," I say. "To paint, I guess. I'm not here by choice."

"So you don't know who put you here?"

"No, I don't. I thought it might be you."

She laughed. "You seem to be making the best of it. Am I right?"

"What else can I do?"

"I don't know. I would do the same thing you are doing if I were in your place. But now you know that you can dream your way out of your cell, because here we are walking on this awesome desert. Isn't the sky beautiful today?"

I look up into it's blueness at the huge billowing white thunderheads scattered across the sky. Indeed, it is stunning. When I look back at the earth we are standing before something shockingly strange. It's a bed high above the ground mounted on what looks like up-rooted trees. It reminds me of an Indian burial stand, but it is a bed with white sheets and pillows. There are prayer flags and other objects hanging from the branches of the nearly leafless tree trunks. Instead of roots at the bottoms of the trees, there are animal claws gripping the earth.

Mouth open, I stand before it in awe.

"Don't be surprised," she says. "This is a dream."

"Right," I say. We walk under the bed and sit down in the shade. There is a cool breeze and the ground beneath us is sandy and soft. A little ground squirrel happens upon us. Surprised by our presence, it shrieks loudly, turns and runs. We laugh.

She begins to communicate with me again and I become aware that she is not talking but transferring information to me from her mind to mine.

She continues. "I can't see the future, but sometimes it seems that I do. I am not like other people. Most humans don't think through the choices they make because they are acting out of fear, or they're drunk. Or perhaps they are hypnotized, or just plain stupid. When they are stunned by the consequences of their actions, they look for someone else to blame. But there is more to it than that. It has to do with their feeble intent to control everything around them."

"I don't like to use the word ego, but for lack of a better word we can call it that for now. There really isn't anything called an ego. If you think there is an ego, show me where it is. Ego is a process, not a thing. The ego process only wants to avoid suffering at all costs. But by trying so hard to do that, it causes more pain and chaos. The control that the ego seeks is an illusion. Only an ego would think it can control things. But it never really does. People are generally idealistic, not pragmatic. They think they are the center of the Universe so they can demand perfection. And they want it now!"

I can feel my forehead crunching up as I try to decipher what she is saying. I'm wondering if she means I could have prevented being abducted and brought here.

She stops and looks at me and sees that I am staring at her with this concentrated look. Then she laughs.

"You are beautiful," she says through giggles. "Not only your outward appearance, but inside too. I've never met anyone who has received her destiny as gracefully as you have. Most people would be angry and climbing the walls trying to get away, but you are making the choice to co-operate with the inevitable. You take advantage of your situation rather than fight against it. That is why I am so interested in you."

"I never thought of it that way," I say. "But are you telling me I could have prevented being brought here in the first place?"

"It's possible. Tell me what led to your being captured."

In a matter of seconds she had the story without me uttering a word.

"Possibly you could have made some different decisions on that day, like calling the director of the museum at his home before you went. You could have done any number of other things to change that event. But to be honest,

I think you would have only put off the inevitable. There really aren't many things we can control. We can choose how we accept what is happening. I'm not saying we have to like it, but it is what it is. Fighting to change something usually leads to more distress."

"It's complicated, because we can do things to improve our lives, but we first have to realize what is happening. Most people don't realize what is happening, but decide they don't like something based on their unique way of viewing things colored by their beliefs. Then they act extravagantly to make changes without understanding what it is they are changing."

"That's crazy. Strong belief systems are rarely effected by facts. Almost everyone in the world relies on their belief systems, even super intelligent people. You are different because you didn't waste time trying to change your situation. You started off by gathering facts about where you were. You haven't spent a lot of time asking why. You just got busy living life right where you found yourself to be. I can't say it enough: when people think their belief systems are true they perceive a very limited world."

"The people who brought you here must have done a lot of research in order to pick just the right person for their plan."

"What plan is that?" I ask.

"I don't know. I can tell you that I don't believe they mean you any harm. I can't say why I think that. It's just a hunch. I think you will be released and there will be great things in store for you after this."

"What makes you think that?" I ask.

"I guess I am arrogant enough to say I only encounter people who are on magnificent journeys. People whose destiny it is to contribute great things that benefit the world and it's inhabitants. The paintings you send out of here touch people in unique ways. The messages are embedded in the images. But it's not just the images. It's also the way you paint them."

"Seriously?" I respond. "I'm only a teacher. Not a master painter."

"Oh stop that!" she snaps. "Do you think Leonardo Da Vinci thought he was a master painter? If he did he would have painted more. What about Van Gogh? He died being rejected by everyone. In fact, he died from a self-inflicted wound. I don't think he thought very highly of himself. Humans are conditioned to believe that thinking highly of oneself is a sin, while at the same time believing they are made in the image of a god. It's crazy-making!"

"Okay. What am I supposed to get out of this discussion?"

"Nothing, absolutely nothing at all." She stares at me, her green eyes are shining and she's smiling like she might laugh out loud any minute now.

Suddenly I wake up from the dream and find myself lying on the blue sofa in the desert studio. Was I dreaming with Alice? I look at the rainbows on the walls, and they are beautiful. The whole space is beautiful. Alias comes bounding in from the cat door and leaps on top of me, purring loudly. He mashes on my body with his front paws. I can see that his life is a miracle. That all life is. But even being a miracle, our lives are never protected from suffering. It can be lessened, but that is about all.

I don't know if Alice is right about the possibility that I might be let free. I think that I've learned to accept that there is a chance I will never leave here. Never go back to my former life. That something terrible could go wrong with this whole operation. But what I've come to understand is that this has always been true about life on this planet. So I don't see any reason to ruminate over my present conditions.

After Alias and I have breakfast, I start sketches for a painting of a bed raised up to the sky. A name came to me right away. I will call it *A Place to Dream Up a Storm*. I only make one study, then start painting in oils. I find an image on the internet of a huge thunderhead in an ultramarine blue sky and choose that for a reference. All the rest I make up as I go along. I work on the sky, thinking that if I don't get this right I'll start over before I dive into doing the detail work of the bed and trees. I end up working on it for three days before I'm pleased with the clouds. While I allow the oil paint to dry and before adding the next layers, I spend time lying on my back on the top of the tool shed looking at the spectacular Southwestern sky and the billowing thunderheads. I love monsoon season.

The painting goes faster than I thought it would. It's the first time in a long time that I've done a whole painting in oils. I didn't feel the need to work out the composition in fast drying acrylics, even though I'm somewhat disturbed by the toxicity of oil paint. But this studio has an amazing ventilation system, and *The Powers That Be* have provided me with Gamblin paint which is less toxic than other brands. I use Ivory hand soap to clean my brushes.

As soon as the painting is finished I place it outdoors to dry and store the tubes of oil paint in an airtight plastic container.

I've given myself a lot of time to think about what Alice shared with me in the dream. She was right that I haven't put a lot of energy into trying to escape. I've thought things through and know I'd be wasting time and energy trying. I'm not sure what has made me act this way. At first I thought they were giving me happy pills, but I'm now positive I am not being drugged – no common side effects. So maybe I'm content to be here because it is a peaceful place.

Plus, in so many ways I am enjoying myself because of the time I have to work on art. With the garden and Alias, the visitations from Alice and Romero, and of course, Max, I know I'm settled in for the long haul. My desire is to take full advantage of the opportunity and paint furiously like a mad woman, only taking breaks to deal with the plethora of weeds in the garden that the rains have brought. Where do they all come from?

30: The Castle School

"Hello," Romero said, greeting me with his big Hollywood smile. "Did you enjoy the rain?" he asked.

"Who wouldn't? I feel plumper – more like a grape than a raisin." I sat up so I could see him better.

"Have you ever thought of writing a book?" he asked me out of the blue.

"No. I'm not a writer," I answered, surprised by his question.

"You're focused on painting now, but perhaps you will give it some thought for the future," he said.

"Words have never been the best way for me to express myself. I struggled with writing in school. My mind thinks in pictures, making it hard for me to access the word producing side of the brain."

"Really?" he said. He looked skeptical. "Can you describe in words the process you use to make a painting?"

"I've had to write artist's statements and comments about my work. But, I make them as short as possible. When I was in graduate school, I had to do a lot of writing about art, but I resented every minute of it. I resented time taken away from painting. Since I didn't like taking the time to do it, as soon as I could avoid it, I did. I knew a lot of other students who took great pride in writing about art. I thought they might be considering a career in writing for art magazines or books. Since I rarely agree with what is said about art in publications, I didn't want to go there."

I thought to myself that I wanted him to hurry up and get on with his story about Ellie, the queen, but I didn't want to seem rude. I felt like a little kid in a classroom squirming in the spotlight, and waiting for the teacher to turn her attention elsewhere and if I were lucky get on with something more interesting.

I must have had an eager look on my face because he said, "I suppose the reason you are on the edge of your seat is because you are waiting to hear what happened with the queen and her court."

"Sure." I tried to sound nonchalant, but was failing miserably. I certainly was a bad actress.

He slouched back in his chair for a few seconds and appeared to change into an old man smoking one of those Sherlock Holmes-style pipes. I blinked a few times and he was back into being young and handsome Romero. I shook my head and tried to pretend that it hadn't happened.

"I haven't seen you in quite awhile. I try to come out into the garden everyday so it will be easier for you to find me. However, with the rains and all." I sounded like I'd regressed to a Texas drawl.

Alias was charging around the garden going nuts with his version of an imaginary friend. We both turned to look at him and laugh.

"Well..." Romero said. "Shall we get on with the story?"

"Of course."

"Ellie was most pleased with what she had learned about her staff. They were more than competent for what she had in mind. The meetings began in the ballroom the very next day. Again they went through the dancing routine. But unlike the day before, instead of sitting on cushions in the ballroom, they adjourned to *The Situation Room*. In other words they seated themselves at a round table like knights."

"'We need to have focus, some goals, some purpose that we all agree upon to carry out,' she said. 'We need strategy and tactics.' They decided to brainstorm, so while Kai typed up their suggestions which were projected on a screen on the wall, they randomly shouted out their ideas. The list was long and some things were ridiculous, like turning the castle into a tourist resort and hiring actors to play comic roles of royalty. They had a good laugh as they fleshed out this idea. But Ellie trusted they would come up with something more noble. And they did."

Romero said, "I won't go into all the stuff they talked about because their discussion went on for almost a week. But I will tell you what they decided in the end."

I sort of wanted to hear the entire discussion, because I thought I had all the time in the world. Romero did not. He would vanish before we got through all those meetings. I tried not to look disappointed.

"Here is a quick synopsis of what they came up with. They decided the Queen's focus needed to be on education. They supported almost all education. The exceptions were people who chose homeschooling for the purpose of conditioning their children to become Christians by ignoring science. Ellie considered that to be serious abuse. All the educational methods would be carefully vetted, making sure they were legitimate."

"They would raise money for schools by having several music festivals each year. Ellie would give speeches all over the state about the importance of education and The Castle Band – that was it's name – would play and sell their albums, proceeds going to the cause. But the biggest of all was this: they would start their own alternative school. It would be on the castle grounds and would be tuition-free."

"The staff worked for months to develop the concept by which the school would be run. Their plan was to start small. And they would all be teachers until they could afford to hire others."

"Ellie said to them, 'We are qualified to run a top notch school. I researched alternative schools and came up with a lot of great ideas. So I want us to find out everything we can about how those schools work. If need be we will send a representative to each school and observe. Also, we will be supporting many other schools unlike ours. I know we can't change every school in the state nor would be want to, but we can check them out and see how we can learn from them and support them. At the same time we will create a model school and invite visitors. In fact we will hound them to come often. So let's talk about how to start.'"

"'We need a building!' someone shouted out."

"Then Juan said. 'We need to examine the buildings we have and see what repairs are required. Then we can determine if we need to build more. There are a lot of spaces in the compound that have been closed up for many years. Who knows what we will find?'"

"'Great idea,' said Ellie. 'Who wants to work with Juan on this?' Everyone raised their hands. 'Okay then, tomorrow we will all meet in the courtyard and start opening up some of those rooms. I think we don't need to discuss anything else right now. Let's all take notes tomorrow and we can talk about this once we've explored the grounds.'"

"The next day Juan, carrying a huge assortment of keys, lead the way. They were astounded to find that there were rooms filled with valuable antiques left behind from Kings and Queens dating back as far as the 17th century. "Holy Cow," said Ellie, 'We are rich!'"

"They all rushed to examine the contents. There were trunks and boxes full of lamps, kitchen supplies, including silverware and crystal goblets, weapons, and many other things they could not identify. The biggest treasure of all were trunks full of carefully stored Navajo rugs, Indian jewelry from many tribes, kachina dolls and paintings. These things must have been gifts to Ellie's mom and dad. The rugs were packed with moth balls, and the smell wafted around the room and drove them all out into the courtyard coughing."

"When she caught her breath Ellie asked. 'Cecilia, do you know how to set up auctions?'"

"'No, but I can find out.'"

"'Who wants to work with Cecilia on this?'"

"'I will,' said Kai. 'You are going to need a computer person to create a database for all this stuff. We need to have it appraised.'"

"'I had no idea we had all this,' Ellie said. 'I don't remember ever seeing these things before.'"

"'Not a problem,' said Cecilia. 'We can hire an estate company. Someone who knows what to do. In the meantime we can organize all these things into one or two rooms and start renovating the empty ones.'"

"'Do we need to hire a contractor who will know how to turn this place into classrooms?' Ellie asked."

"'Maybe not,' said Jesus. 'We don't know if the rooms are in bad shape or if they are just full of stuff.'"

"Good point,' said Ellie."

"'The first thing I'm going to do his hire a cook and someone to keep the castle clean. As of today you are all now officially fired from your jobs as servants. Anybody know a good chef looking for a job? We are all going to be too busy working on this project to tend to minor details. There are lots of people out there needing jobs. Let's find them.'"

"And that is how it all got started," said Romero. They all rolled up their sleeves and got busy. And within about four months they had everything ready, including plenty of money to open a small school.

"Romero, where is this castle and where did the students come from?" I interrupted.

"Good question. You may wonder how people found it. The castle and the school could only be found by people who were right for attending. Word of mouth was the only way anyone heard about it and because the students and their families were very protective of what they had, they were careful not to reveal much about it. Children were accepted only after they turned seven years of age because the school felt that all children needed to spend more years in close contact with family before spending hours away from their homes. However, the families interested in the school could bring their younger ones to the school as long as they stayed with them."

"The school didn't have grades. Kids would progress at their own speed. They also were not expected to attend everyday if they didn't want to. They wanted the kids to decide that they wanted to go to school because it was fun. Some students were picked up by busses and dropped off in the evening, but they could also stay overnight if they wanted to or if the parents went out of town. The only requirements to attend the school was if the kid was happy there, and if the parents were willing to participate in their child's education.

188

They never forced anything on any child. And they spent a lot of time finding out who the students were and what they were interested in."

"Many times the parents would hang out all day and help out, even doing kitchen duties. In other words, the Queen and her staff attracted a lot of like-minded people. The parents and grandparents came in droves and brought with them professional skills and a willingness to contribute time and energy. And some of them had a lot of money and were willing to contribute to the daily operation of the school."

"It sounds a lot like the hippie schools in the 1970's," I said.

"It was. But by the time Ellie started the Castle School there was a lot more information available since the hippie days about alternative education. And they also had a lot more money than the hippies."

"Wow! What a gift Ellie brought to the state of Arizona."

"Not just the state, but the whole world. In time her school became famous in certain circles and people who were in the know came from all over to observe. Many of them went back to their own states or countries and built their own schools modeled after The Castle School. As the school grew in popularity they hired more teachers and opened more classrooms. Families bought land nearby and built new houses just so they could live closer."

"Did other private and public schools start to teach more like this school?"

"Many of them did. But truth be told not all children learn in the same way, so other schools began to focus on other alternative ways in order to accommodate different individuals. In fact, Ellie didn't accept all special ed students, but instead financed other schools in other places all over the state to make sure nobody got left out. Later she helped start alternative special ed schools and participated in hiring the right people to teach. They began to have events like the Special Olympics with other schools helping to put on the event. Occasionally some special ed students were allowed in if it seemed to benefit them and the other students. This created a situation where all the kids got to participate with each other."

"So where did the rest of the money come from?"

"People donated it. Also Ellie became famous and traveled the world. By the time she was in her forties she had written five books on education. She was paid enormous amounts of money for her speeches."

"Did she ever get married? Was there ever a King?" I asked.

"Oh, my dear," said Romero. "You are jumping ahead. There are many stories about the Queen of Arizona and her court. The story of the King is best left for another day. But I can give you a hint. He was an astronaut. There is a lot more to tell about the school, too."

"Seriously, I can't wait."

"Seriously," he smiled. "It's time for me to go. So I will leave you on that note."

He and Alice always left so quickly. I was accustomed to humans and all their drawn out greetings and goodbyes, so it always felt abrupt and awkward. He left me sitting upright in my hammock. So I lay back down and stared up at the fading light in the sky and thought about Ellie and the school. I remembered the schools I attended as a child and how I would get so bored tears would roll down my cheeks.

I thought how strange it was that there was so much new information about how people learn. Yet most schools seemed to ignore it. Not that there aren't some good public schools and certainly there are a lot of great teachers. But over time everything seems to have slid backwards.

Many really great teachers quit teaching because they were being told to go against what they knew to be effective. Kids need a lot of physical activity, play and fun. Too much studying and trying to teach kids how to pass tests was sending education back to the dark ages. Well, not exactly back to the Dark Ages. Education was more like a crazy train speeding forward along a track and heading to a cliff where the tracks ended.

"Is that because schools are run by the government?" I wanted to ask Romero. I thought about myself as a college art teacher. My biggest obstacle was young adults who showed up with little or no training. They should have been learning to draw at the age of eleven. But the government had closed down the art departments, fired the art teachers and turned art instruction over to regular teachers who probably only took one or two art classes in college, if that. And those classes were all about playing around with art supplies.

That is not a bad thing, but totally misses the students who are serious about growing up to be real artists. Which, by the way, was most American parent's biggest fear. So it became the will of the government and the parents that shaped the system. There were strong social belief systems in place about starving artists. In Europe art and artists are celebrated. Everyone hangs original art in their homes. And artists are more than encouraged.

With a powerful leap, Alias jumped on me, rocking the hammock and causing me to grab for my iPad before it dropped to the ground. He settled down in a hot dusty heap on top of me purring, and demanded I pet him. I wished he had licked himself clean first, but wondered which was worse: the dirt or the cat spit.

I thought about Queen Ellie and how she wanted to research the most successful schools in the world. She learned a lot from schools in Finland. I had heard about Finland's schools before and had done a little research myself. I'd found out that their schools were protected from government and corporate intervention. They were run by educators and no one else was allowed to make decisions for them. This told me the adults in charge were geniuses.

I know how impossible it is to influence the government, but I had often dreamed of ways to skirt around it. That is exactly what the hippies did in the 1970's and what many homeschool families still do. They just start a non-profit organization to deal with the legality of keeping children out of the school system. It's that simple.

I'm all for public schools for kids who like it, and kids who have no other option. But I love the idea that people can make other choices if that's what they want. However, I agree with Queen Ellie about the religious abuse. It's a serious problem in our country. Children are being homeschooled in order for parents to condition their children to accept religious belief systems. They often remove the study of science from their children's educations, forcing them to accept beliefs instead of being taught to search for the truth. And they are often made to ignore proven facts. It's hard to break down those walls of ignorance once they are in place.

It felt strange to be thinking about teaching. I realized I had not been missing my old job. It was a relief to be working only on my paintings. Romero's story was reminding me that I was missing the teaching part of my job. But teaching had become only a small part of my work. Most of my time was spent dealing with meetings and bureaucratic red tape. I did not miss the politics and the constant fear of losing my job. I did not miss the feeling of having a guillotine blade hanging over my head just waiting for me to utter something that disagreed with the system.

When night fell, I wrote to Max.

Laurence: *I was hoping you could tell me what happened at the university with the art department.*

Max: *Nice to hear from you, Laurence.*

L: *Oh sorry. Hi Max. How are you?*

M: *I'm fine, thank you.*

L: *So you need time to think over your answer to my question?.*

M: *I don't know exactly what happened at the university. But if you give me some time I will see what I can find out. You know schools are very secretive if you are an outsider.*

L: *So you are not an insider.*

M: *Not at all. But I know some people who work there.*

L: *You would really do that for me?*

M: *Of course.*

L: *Thanks. Let me know when you hear something.*

M: *You know this is a slippery slope.*

L: *What do you mean?*

M: *I think it is best for you not to think too much about what is going on the rest of the world right now.*

L: *Seriously?*

M: *Are you happy getting all the artwork done? Do you like your garden? How is Alias?*

L: *God! How quickly you can turn me around!*

M: *It's my job.*

L: *So be it. But if you do find out anything I'd like to know. You know I am still aware there is a greater world going on outside my compound.*

M: *Of course, I do. I just don't want you to slip out of your reverie. You are creating so many wonderful masterpieces. It would be sad if you lost your focus.*

L: *I do get your point, Max. It's true the university drama used to drive me mad. I do think it affected my painting. Sometimes I got home after a rough day and only wanted to lie in bed and read a book. I was often kept awake at night trying to figure out ways to survive rather than coming up with good ideas for art work. I'm beginning to think I had things backwards. I should have spent more time creating art.*

M: *Maybe so. Tell me. Are you sleeping well now?*

L: *Perfectly.*

M: *Well?*

L: *Okay, you win! Sometimes, I love you, Max.*

M: *How sweet of you to say so, Laurence.*

L: *Okay, nuff of this. Over and out.*

I didn't believe that I was painting masterpieces. But I do have to admit that I was not suffering here in the way I did when I was teaching and not having time to paint. I didn't know why Romero was telling me a story about schools. But I found it a worthwhile thing to think about. I didn't like the current U.S. school system. I often thought about how to make it better, but didn't take much action. I was more into skirting around the problems. I know I was a good teacher because I had waiting lists for my classes. The school expected me to follow my syllabus, but once I learned who my students were, I would make changes on the fly. I was always concerned about the administration finding out. I can tell you, they would not budge from their stance, even though it was evident that the way I was teaching was getting results.

31: Manuel's Discovery

"Sorry, I'm late." Rochelle said. "There was an accident on the road."

"No problem. I'm enjoying the coffee," Manuel lied. He held up his to-go cup, and then felt awkward because he'd been pacing back and forth in the hotel lobby worried she would not show up. He didn't like being dishonest out of politeness. He always thought people could tell when he was lying.

She noticed his nervousness, but tried not to let him know. "I'm so happy to have met an American," she said, quickly moving on. "It's fun traveling back and forth, but it always takes me a while to adjust to the language. And then there are all the many accents that come into the gallery I have to deal with. It's hard to relax. I don't know anybody who speaks Hungarian in the states so the language sort of slips away and I have to struggle a little each time I come back."

"That must be a challenge."

"It's not only the language, it's the customs too."

"Do you speak any other languages?" he asked.

"No, I can read a little French, but I have a hard time understanding it, and my pronunciation is pitiful. Well, let's go. My car is right by the door. I can't promise I will be able to help, but I have some ideas. There are some very old galleries who don't need to advertise because they only deal with certain collectors. I think it's like a secret European club or something like that. In fact we might have to make a phone call to get someone to open the doors. But I think it's worth the time to find them. I don't think they get many walk-ins though, so they could be closed."

"It sounds mysterious."

"Oh, it is. I really don't know much about these galleries that function in the shadows. I've been curious about them for years."

They crossed the river and drove to a neighborhood where the streets seemed more like alleyways; many of them were walking-only streets. Ancient buildings butted right up to the pavement and looked more like entrances to dwellings instead of businesses. They walked down two streets and checked out several galleries with no luck before they stopped in front of a heavy wooden door that almost disappeared behind vegetation. A small sign on it said Danube Galleria. Rochelle pushed the door open and a tiny bell rang as they entered. Inside, the walls were covered in what looked and smelled like old master's paintings and Manuel thought how could Laurence's work be in here? They were staring at the paintings when an old man came from the back room, and appeared as though he'd been torn from his morning breakfast table.

In Hungarian he must have said something like, "Can I help you?"

Rochelle answered then, in English asked Manuel for his cell phone with the image of the painting. The man stared at the photo for what seemed like a long time, then said something in Hungarian. The two of them began a conversation, so Manuel studied the paintings hoping to avoid appearing desperate. He saw another open door and went through it into another room containing surrealistic paintings. He recognized them as the works of Salvador Dali, Dorothea Tanning, Leonora Carrington and Max Ernst. There were others he didn't know, probably Hungarian artists. He got goose bumps on his arms. He could definitely see Laurence's paintings in this room even though her work was still much more colorful, probably due to the fact that the chemistry of modern paint was different. On top of that he thought the paintings in this gallery might have been fakes because he was sure the originals would go for millions of dollars at auctions.

"Manuel, come here please," demanded Rochelle from the other room.

He saw a look of hope in her eyes. "This is Mr. Kiss. He says he used to have this painting in that room you were in, but it sold a few months ago."

Manuel's heart began to beat wildly. "Do you know where the artist is? Does he know who bought it?" He asked Rochelle.

"I can speak English," said Mr. Kiss with a strong accent. "I could not be in this business without knowing English."

"I'm sorry," both of them said at the same time.

"Mr. Donahue is no longer alive. He died about six years ago. We buy paintings from his estate. Whenever we make a sale some months later somebody from the estate shows up with another painting and we give him a check for the sold one."

Manuel started talking fast in a strong Mexican accent. He said, "Mr Donahue? Actually Laurence Donahue is a woman, and she is very much alive somewhere. And she is my girlfriend, and I am trying to find her because somebody has kidnapped her. And they are making her paint. Can't you see, that's me in the picture?" He handed the cell phone back to the Mr. Kiss.

Rochelle put her hand on his arm trying to calm him down.

"I'm sorry," he said. "I will slow down." He told the story again at a slower pace, but he could definitely tell that Mr. Kiss was not able to accept the truth in his rantings, or maybe he didn't understand Manuel's English. And the story did sound quite preposterous.

Rochelle began talking to the man in Hungarian and he seemed a little more convinced, but not totally.

"So what is it you want from me?" Mr. Kiss asked.

"I need to know where these paintings are coming from," said Manuel in a less frantic voice. "In fact, any kind of information you can give me will be helpful. I need to find my girlfriend."

"I can't tell you that, because every time a new painting is delivered it is a different person who drops it off. I don't ask their names. I make the check payable to...let me see, I forget. I will check. With shaky hands he reached inside a drawer behind the desk, pulled out a box, and began to slowly thumb through the papers inside. It took all the effort Manuel could muster to restrain himself from grabbing the box and looking for it faster, even though he didn't know the name of the estate or the painting.

It seemed like hours passed. And finally Mr. Kiss said, "Ah, yes. Here it is." He handed a folded receipt to Manuel. On it were the words *Solo Estate, Munich, Germany, artist Laurence Donahue, "I Thought I Was A Fish" sold 2017, 4,944,910.00 Euro.*

Manuel gasped, paused and did some calculations in his head, then said, "That would be about $6 million in American money! But, there is no address!"

"No, they pick up the checks and deliver the paintings. We don't need to have an address. Plus most of the time these painting go to auction and we don't handle the sales."

Deflated Manuel asked, "Do you have any pictures of the paintings that have sold?"

"Why would I have that?"

Manuel and Rochelle stared at him with incredulous looks on their faces. Then turned and looked at each other in disbelief. There didn't appear to be a computer in the gallery, so maybe no digital camera or even a cell phone. They had been transported back to a different era.

Manuel did not want to leave, but Rochelle said "Thank you" to Mr. Kiss and grabbed hold of Manuel's arm, forcefully turning him around and guiding him out the door.

"What was that all about? What can we do now? We can't just walk away." Manuel was trying to tug away from her.

"Calm down. Come with me," she said in a low voice, leading him to a cafe, where they ordered coffee, and sat outside in the almost warm sun.

"Manuel, if you can stay in Hungary for a while, you can come back here, and over time maybe another painting will show up. If you make a scene, they won't let you back in.

"I can't stay."

"Then, if you have to leave, I can come back here for you, to check if another piece gets delivered. Maybe that would be better since my mom owns a gallery. He will know I'm in the business." She was thinking to herself, not that kind of business. Manuel noticed that she looked pale.

"I can't ask you to do that."

"I don't mind. I just hope your outburst didn't make him suspicious. Because if he knows more than he is letting on, he may not show her work here again. I'm not sure, but there must be a reason these galleries are so secretive. It's got to have something to do with the Dark Market. Don't you think?

"Oh God. I really screwed up, didn't I?"

"I don't know. Beating yourself up isn't going to help. Besides it's my fault too. I should have suggested we have a plan. We could have pretended we wanted to buy one of Laurence Donahue's paintings." She said that to him knowing that nobody just walked off the streets and spent that kind of money.

"Well, goes to show, we don't know how to play games like that."

"Not at all. Reading detective and spy novels doesn't prepare you for real life." She looked over her shoulder back towards the gallery then back at Manuel. "I'm sorry."

They both sat staring into their coffee drinks, trying deal with their guilt. "Do you think we might be in danger?" Manuel asked.

"I have no idea." She shrugged her shoulders. "Look, I know you have to go back to America. I can check back by here. I can keep my eyes open, and maybe ask around. Talk to people I know I can trust."

"You would do that?

"Of course. I get bored here. I need a project. Besides I want to save Laurence too. I can't imagine what I would do if something like that happened to me." She stared off into space as if she were imagining what it would be like to be kidnapped.

"We were so close...so close. I just can't wrap my mind around this at all," he exclaimed. He fidgeted in his seat. The urge to act was overwhelming, but he didn't know exactly what could be done.

"Look," she said staring into his eyes. "There is no more that we can do right now. It's going to take more time. I'll gather my friends again at my house tonight and we will all try figure out how we can help you. Hopefully the gallery doesn't disappear." That is what she said, but what she was thinking was it probably would.

Manuel wasn't used to people having so much time that they could just meet whenever, and hang out however long they wanted to in order the help a stranger. Who were these people? Were things that different in Europe? He remembered stories of European artists hanging out every night in cafes eating and drinking, long into the night. Was it still like that in Europe? In America, you had to spend every minute of your waking life working, just to scrape by.

"Don't you think we should call the police?" he asked. "Maybe I can hire a detective? There has to be something. How do people deal with things like this in this country?" He could hear the desperation in his own voice. That's what he would do if Rochelle weren't here trying to calm him down. He would go to the police.

"They would deal with it here pretty much like they dealt with it in America. Think about it, Manuel. How do you think your story would sound to the police? Unless there are a lot of artists that suddenly go missing, they aren't going to know what to do either. Besides she is American, and they would expect the American police to handle it."

"What about the American Consulate?" he asked

"Well, it's not like in the movies where you run into the building and they protect you from the bad guys. In this case, the rich guys. There are procedures. And there isn't much proof that your story is true. All you have is a photo on your cell phone of a painting that looks a bit like you. But don't let me discourage you if you think that might work," she said.

He stared back in the direction of the Gallery and felt himself calm down. "You're right," he said "I didn't think about how long this could take. Nor was I prepared to deal with all these obstacles."

"You imagined that you would come here and find Laurence in a few days. But this isn't a two hour movie. However, I think we can come up with a plan. Come back to my house tonight and we can talk it over with the others. It's going to take more than just the two of us. I'll take you back to your hotel now and pick you up later." She reached across the table and put her hand on top of his in the same way she had on the day they had first met. She had a way of soothing him.

He stood up like a robot, turned and forced one heavy foot in front of the other shuffling towards her car. They walked past the gallery again and he saw there was no sign on the door. There were no windows, so he could not see in. It was as if the whole thing had vanished and this was just another door to somebody's dwelling. The sun went behind the clouds and he began to shiver.

"That's weird. I could swear there was a sign on the door. Wasn't it called Danube Gallery?" she said.

When he looked at her he could see that she too was shaken. They turned back to take another look. No sign. "Maybe it only hangs there when the gallery is open, and that might be when someone has an appointment. Then they take the sign down after the client arrives," he said.

"I did tell you it was one of those unique galleries that only sell to a certain clientele, probably by appointment only. You are right maybe it was open to the public for a while, or perhaps he was waiting for a buyer, or for a new painting to arrive," she said.

All the way back to the car Manuel kept stopping and looking back as if he thought he might see someone coming or going. He also tried to memorize the street. Later he would regret having been so distracted that he'd failed to snap photos of the place and the area.

They drove across the river in silence where she dropped him off with a promise to return at seven.

He wanted to sleep the rest of the day in order to shut all of this out of his mind, but he only slept an hour. He paced the room thinking over what had happened at the gallery. He kept running the whole event over and over in his mind until he forced himself stop.

He grabbed a robe and went down to soak in the hot mineral baths adjoining the hotel. The baths were separated by gender, and he entered into a vast, echoing space. There were lockers and benches along the balcony, and looking out, he could see a beautiful room with a vaulted ceiling covered in skylights, held up by ornate pillars. The baths themselves were pale green and smelled lightly of minerals. The only other men there were old Hungarians hunkered in a group on steps leading into one end of the bath. They were talking in low voices and looked like the saddest people he had ever seen. He thought about himself and how sad he had been since Laurence disappeared. He felt like he fit right in with them.

Why had he been so convinced that he could find her here? His desire had been so strong to rescue her that he had fallen into fantasy. He had made up an outcome that wasn't realistic. He wasn't a superhero like in the movies. In fact he wasn't even a very powerful man. He was a humble artist, a scholar, a quiet loner. Not someone who fought bad guys. He never even suspected the gallery owner could have been a criminal, or a dangerous person. Besides there could be a Mr. Donahue who created a painting that strangely looked like him. But why would he think that? He knew it wasn't just a coincidence, and that made him feel crazy. It scared him that feeling crazy was starting to be the new normal.

He sank into the hot water and started repeating the serenity prayer from his days in twelve step programs. He'd gone to Al Anon when he had realized his first wife was an alcoholic. "What were the steps?" he said out loud to himself. He looked around to see if anyone had heard him, then he tried to remember. Step one: discover you are powerless. Step two: believe in a higher power. Step three: turn your will over to that higher power. Changing the way he was thinking made him feel a little better. He knew the only thing he could do was turn it all over to something that he understood was not himself. Something that, perhaps, could actually do something about his situation, because there was nothing he could do. Did it take a trip halfway around the world to come back to this? Well, so what if it did?

He soaked until his fingers wrinkled, then went back to his room, showered and went out for a walk. He was determined not to be sad and disturbed when Rochelle picked him up. If she and her friends could help, he would accept the fact that a higher power had sent them and would simply receive it. Maybe nothing would happen at all and he would have to accept that too. But nothing now could take away the fact that he had given it his all.

This time she took him to another house which was, somewhat surprisingly, a modern mansion. There were huge windows that overlooked the city and the river. "It's my mom's house," she explained. "She left for Paris this morning. I thought you might enjoy the view."

The food, even though it was a simple menu, looked as though it had been prepared by a gourmet chef. There was a huge salad, a roasted duck and a chicken surrounded by potatoes and carrots and various dishes of other vegetables. Everyone seemed cheerful while they ate. But after dinner when the food was cleared away, they turned down the lights and Manuel and Rochelle shared the story of their adventure at the gallery.

Beata said, "Whoa, this is getting very strange. You say the name disappeared off the door of the gallery? Are you sure there was one on it in the first place."

"How would we have known what door to enter if it didn't have a name?" said Rochelle.

Manuel was trying to stay out of the conversation as much as possible, hoping these people would come up with a viable plan. He certainly didn't have one.

"What can we do?" asked Iggy.

Rochelle spoke, "Since Manuel has to leave soon. I think we should keep going by that place to see if the sign is back. We could each act like we are there to buy a painting. Only one of us should ask Mr. Kiss if he has any more paintings by Laurence Donahue. I don't think we should rush the place. We need to be casual and subtle and dress in our best clothes. Maybe we should make a few phone calls too. We could ask about other artists as well, so we don't seem overly interested in Donahue."

Everyone agreed that plan seemed like the best tactic.

Manuel wanted to be excited that these people offered to help find Laurence. But he couldn't believe they would bother after he left. He was feeling a strong pull to go home to his studio and put this trip behind him, and finally, get on with his life. He realized that coming to Hungary was what he needed in order to finally let go. No matter how many times Granger had told him to move on, his desire to be a hero had taken charge. He was slowly and sadly coming to realize how impossible that task could be. Real life was different from novels and movies, or maybe he just wasn't the hero who would rescue her.

Later that night when her friends left, Rochelle insisted he sleep in the guest room. The bed was a huge improvement over the narrow twin he had in the hotel. And it had two sheets like in America and a soft comforter. He felt like it was the first real sleep he had gotten since he left home.

When he woke in the morning Rochelle served him breakfast. There were croissants, a selection of cheeses and espresso. While he stared out the huge windows overlooking the Danube, she chatted about her love of art, artists and her commitment to finding Laurence. He wanted to believe her but he felt distant and suspicious like he was in a movie he wanted to get out of.

When she drove him back to the hotel he worried she was getting wind of the fact that he didn't trust her or her friends. Hoping that didn't put her off if they were actually being sincere and intended to follow through he kept telling himself to hand it all over to a higher power. It was the only thing that kept him calm and prevented him from confronting her.

At the hotel he said, "I'm going to leave now. I'm flying stand-by back to the states. Thank you and your friends so much for your help."

"Can I give you a ride to the airport?"

"No, I'll take a taxi. I hope we don't lose touch."

"Don't worry about that. We can text and call anytime. And when you want to come back, plan on staying at my house. We do that in Europe," she said.

"Thank you," he said. They hugged goodbye and he got out of her car.

He watched the black Mercedes turn the corner and vanish out of sight. He strongly suspected they would never see each other again.

He had given thought to staying another night so he could walk by the gallery again, but he wasn't sure he could find it in the maze of streets in Budapest. And if he did happen to find it, would the business have disappeared? Maybe he just didn't want to know. All of this had turned out to be a much bigger deal than he had ever imagined. He suspected that Rochelle and her friends were actually working for the people who had taken Laurence. But he didn't let go of the sliver of hope that they were sincere.

Even with all of his suspicions, he was glad he had traveled to Europe. He had met some interesting people, and this was something he probably wouldn't have done, had he not had a cause. He prayed for Laurence on the way to the airport. He tried to imagine her living in a beautiful house painting anything she wanted to, free from all university struggles. He prayed for Granger, George, and the Suns. He prayed for himself to gain strength to move on.

The airport was not crowded, and he got on a plane right away. He flew straight to Seattle, then Phoenix, took a shuttle to Tucson, found his car in the lot and drove hime. He fell into his bed and slept for thirteen hours.

When he woke up he felt as though he had been having a long nightmare. It would have been easy for him to accept it was just a dream if it hadn't been for his depleted bank account. He told himself it was worth it, if only because he now knew and could accept that she was gone and that he might never see her again. His heart felt heavy. But there was a sense of relief in knowing he had tried and found out that all possibilities of him finding her were off the table. But he was sure she was still alive somewhere.

He sat on a stool in the middle of his studio looking around at some of his paintings. The painting on the easel caught his attention. He had left it unfinished and he was glad because it beckoned to him like a siren. It was the first time since Laurence's disappearance that a painting had become a stronger pull than the desire to find her. For an instant he felt guilty. But they both had always valued their individual lives. He knew he could trust her to take care of herself. She was capable of that. It was better to imagine her doing that. He needed to forget about the Dark Market. Now he would go to the cafe and have a giant breakfast, then come back and paint all day. Was it day? He would have to open the curtains to find out.

For the next few weeks Manuel got texts from Rochelle telling him how she and her friends had discovered the Danube gallery was actually no longer there. She promised to keep looking for it and the painting. She asked him to send more images of Laurence's work. And after a few months he stopped getting texts. He kept her contact information in his phone hoping that someday he might return to Hungary, and spend a few evenings engaging in conversation with her friends and sleeping in that soft bed in her mother's mansion. He would bring Laurence with him.

32: Journal Entry

After Romero asked me about writing I started to spend more time writing in my journal. I didn't like taking the time to do it, but I realized that it was important for me to document what was happening to me. Maybe someone would find it if I died here, or if I escaped it would help me remember my days spent here. I stopped worrying about whether or not it was well written or grammatically correct. I just scribbled things down. Here are some of the things I wrote:

I've now been here in the desert for one year. Max actually sent a cupcake. He also sent one on my birthday last February. I didn't eat either one, but images of the last one showed up in several paintings. Alias licked the top of one, but didn't take a bite. I've heard that chocolate is bad for dogs, but I don't know about cats. I don't think he liked it much. He's underfoot since it's grown colder outdoors. He sleeps next to my legs at night so I have to maneuver carefully when I turn over. If he can manage to get between my lower legs he's in heaven. He's a hoot!

The days are shorter and the garden has little to offer. I've pulled up the dead plants and worked in some compost. Who knows what will sprout from the seeds that made it though my digging. Max says I can plant some winter greens, so I'm reading up on that. I don't have jars for canning or freezer space, but plan to try some drying. That is if I'm still here next growing season.

I'm totally dependent on what comes by drone or what grows. So far they have supplied me with everything I need. All healthy stuff too. I have no idea what would become of me if something happened to my captors. I try not to think about it, but I also think of ways I could survive if something like that becomes reality. Next growing season I'll be more prepared to store food for the winter just in case.

It's hard to believe I've been here a whole year. I've painted 12 major pieces, one for each month. However, it wasn't a linear process. Most times I had several going at once. I've got stacks of drawings and studies, but *The Powers That Be* have not asked me to send anything on paper. I may have to have a bonfire at some point.

Alice and Romero keep coming. Alice's wise guidance keeps me sane and Romero's endless stories about the Queen of Arizona keep me entertained. I've reread all of Valdez's books. I'm convinced that Alice and Romero have stepped right out of those sorcery stories. When Granger and I read his books as teenagers, the line between fantasy and reality was thin. Reading them again and living here with visitors from the dream world has made me realize he was never writing fantasy stories. It was all about magical realism. I know that what goes on in my mind is not the truth. And dreams are nothing but the subconscious mind processing. Even words cannot convey truth. So the best I can come up with is that there are a lot of things I don't understand. Possibly, because so much is not understandable by the human brain. I realize that most people don't want to know that.

Anyway, so be it.

I'm not thinking much about home in Phoenix anymore. Somehow, I feel like I've always been here. Occasionally I do think about Granger and, of course Manuel, but I do hope they've moved on and are living happy lives. I have absolutely no idea how long I will be here, or if I will ever get back to my loved ones. I'm learning how little control I have and I'm starting to like the feeling of flowing with whatever. I remember when that "whatever" thing became a thing. I loved it. I know it was slang used by the millennials, but it made so much sense.

A few days ago when I was sitting by the window looking out, I thought I saw a man walking among the cactus. For November, it was an unusually warm day and I would swear he was naked. He looked something like an Aboriginal: tangled hair, long beard, carrying a spear or bow and arrow. I'm wondering if he will become another visitor. He didn't look up as he walked by as though this house didn't exist. I gave him the name of Coyote Man. I tried to sketch what I remember seeing, but maybe I'm just making him up.

It's much colder today, and to be honest, I'm looking forward to winter. I have made sketches for numerous paintings. You might say, I'm on a roll. Because of Alice and Romero's influence I've gone deep into the art genre of Magical Realism. It's close to Surrealism, but a bit more upbeat. More humor and beauty. I think the Surrealists painted mostly nightmares, but my paintings are more like adventure dreams. The colors are brighter, and the subject matter has a touch of humor. I feel like I could paint these things for eternity and never get bored.

I have to stop writing now. Alias needs some attention. I think I'll make him a new toy. Something that hangs off the edge of my table and makes noise when he bats it around. I have loads of paper scraps, some sticks from the garden and a few feathers.

So bye now, dear journal. I'll write more later.

A Date with Art

33: Journal Entry

It's my birthday again, February 18, and Max sent a whole miniature cake. He knows I don't eat cake, but would love to have it for subject matter. He also sent party favors which are fun things to use as images in paintings. Alias doesn't know what to think about the party blowers. You know the things that you blow into and cause an air-filled paper tube to roll out and whistle. He runs out of the room every time I blow it, then tiptoes back in the room glaring at me like he doesn't know what to expect next. He can't make up his mind if he likes it or not.

It's cold outside today. The mountains are dusted with snow and it seems like it could actually snow down here. You might think I would be depressed here in the desert alone on my birthday. But I actually like being alone on birthdays and holidays. Maybe I'm weird, but I'd rather socialize on days other than holidays or birthdays.

When I was a child, birthdays were always the hardest, because I didn't like being the center of attention. I think many artists like to hide behind their work. Look what I did, don't look at me. Art openings were always a struggle. It wasn't so bad once I was there, but a few days before and especially the day of the event, I would be filled with ambivalence. It took a huge push just to get dressed and out the door for the event.

Glad I don't have to worry about that anymore. Today will be an ordinary work day. I'll put on an audiobook, and spend the day solving problems with composition and color. I can't think of a better way to celebrate.

I try not to think of Granger and the Suns, knowing they will think of me today and feel sad. I hope that keeping myself happy and sending them good thoughts will help make them believe that I'm truly okay. Who knows? Maybe next year I will be free and be glad to spend my birthday with them.

Anyway, I'm ready to start a new painting, and I've arrived at several ideas, but I haven't landed on one yet. I seem to be settling on an idea of combining a still life and a landscape. I've painted a couple of beds outdoors so why not a dinner table, or a birthday dinner table? Now I have some great props. Question is: do I want to add people or not. I don't have people in the bed scenes so maybe it's best to keep it that way for the table scene. Viewers can wonder what happened to the people or they may feel invited to come into the painting and sit at the table. What do you think? Yes, you, the person reading this.

What do you think? Sounds like a good title. In my mind's eye I keep seeing a sort of dark and ominous scene, but I'm arguing with that because it reminds me too much of Tina Mion's work. Don't get me wrong. I love, love, love her work. But I don't want to copy it. I couldn't anyway. My painting style is different and I use brighter colors, maybe have a little more cheer, but not so much as to leave out the truth about birthdays.

Have you ever noticed at a child's birthday party the poor kid will eventually have an emotional breakdown? That doesn't change much as we grow older. We only get better at hiding it.

Maybe all this party stuff is really about distracting us from existential dread. You know, the feeling that time is flying by and there is absolutely nothing you can do about it. I've come to realize that the only real truth we can count on is one day we will die. If that sounds depressing, well even more reason to understand that all the things we do for fun are to prevent us from getting depressed about that one inevitable thing.

Most religions promise an afterlife because immortality sells. How else could these organizations continue if they didn't promise something people really wanted more that anything else? Most people cannot fathom living without the promise that they will continue somewhere after they die. Isn't it strange that churches and bars are just flip sides of the same coin? The difference is the alcoholics believe they will continue after death in hell and the church goers will be walking on streets of gold. If that were true, shouldn't that also be true while we are alive? I don't see that happening.

Wow, I'm rattling on here, still sitting at the table looking out at tiny flakes of snow hitting the ground and melting. They are snowflakes and then they are not. We are people and then we are not. There is something that continues throughout eternity, but I don't know what that is.

Valdez says that God, or the Ineffable, gives us death so we won't waste the precious time we have being alive. Unfortunately, it doesn't seem to work for most people. But then again what do I know? Or what does anybody know?

On that note I will make some sketches for my next painting.

Oh heavens! Alias just walked in with the end of the toilet paper in his mouth unrolling it from the roll in the bathroom. I never know what is coming next with him? He is so adorable. I don't think I've ever loved like this before. Guess I'd better get him something else to play with. Later.

34: Journal Entry

First, I arranged a still life using the birthday cake and party favors that Max sent. Then made sketches adding in a human skeleton and a skull wearing a party hat. These were the main things that made me think of life and death. I added a bouquet of red roses and some wrapped gifts, plastic plates, forks, paper cups and Alice's fancy tea cup. Of course there were two chairs at the table. I later painted out some items that no longer fit. The skull with the party hat and deer antlers were removed. I changed the positions of the chairs and added a piñata hanging to the right of the table, a donkey, of course. The table was located on the desert, under one of the few trees – I think is a piñon pine – and behind some yucca plants.

I started the painting on a five by five foot canvas tacked to the doors of the cabinets on the wall. I could easily remove it from the wall and drape it over my large table in order to paint in the small details.

My plan was to make the background, which consisted of sky, distant mountains and desert floor very bright and light. The table shaded by the tree would be dark. I'd snatched the idea from N.C. Wyeth. I was using a lot of white paint and had to order more from Max.

After blocking in the composition, I took a break, let it hang to dry while I worked on some small illustration-like drawings.

Making a painting is like forming a relationship with someone. Sometimes it starts out easy then turns into something difficult. Sometimes it's a struggle from the start and stays that way all the way though. Often it can be the very last stroke that brings it all together. Those magical times when everything just all falls into place from beginning to end are rare, like an easy relationship with a person. This painting and I argued a lot.

There are many things that need to be worked through. It's a battle between the artist and the image. This was one of those battles. I painted things in and painted things out, changed the colors in huge sections of the work. That painting and I spent days not speaking or looking at each other. Fortunately I had a number of one night stands with other smaller works.

I was wrestling with my own thoughts and fears of life and death or was it a struggle with technique and composition that gave me so much grief? I don't recall being particularly emotional over the subject matter. Maybe that was the problem. I thought about my potential audience and I wasn't sure anyone would want to look at a painting dealing with life and death. People want pretty things. To counteract the seriousness of the subject I needed to make the composition extremely strong and the colors alluring and I had trouble making that happen.

35: Journal Entry

It's early Spring now and quite warm and I'm enjoying the fresh air. Something very strange happened today. I think I mentioned before that I thought I saw a man walking among the cactus. I was out in the garden and I glimpsed him again through the iron fence. He was totally naked. I'm wondering if there is some crazy hermit living out here in the desert or is he just somebody walking around in a dream body?

I asked Alice about him and she said she didn't know anything about him and she wasn't sure whether or not he was a dreamer. There could possibly be others like us, she told me. Of course, I'm still not sure that Alice and Romero are actually what they say they are, or if I'm hallucinating. This man could also be an hallucination. I feel safe in the compound even not knowing whether or not he could scale the wall outside the patio. I don't know why, but I just don't feel frightened.

Anyway I plan to watch out for him from now on.

The garden is ready for planting and Alias is having a blast chasing real and imaginary things out on the patio. Romero and I have resumed our meetings outside. Spring and fall are just the best, not too hot, not too cold.

I set up the outdoor easel and brought out a canvas, but it's just sitting there blank. I've never been into painting outdoors, so I feel a bit intimidated. It's the light that bothers me. In my studio, I can control the light. Outside it moves, shadows move, colors change, wind blows and insects fly into the canvas and stick in the wet paint. I have a great appreciation for artists who have mastered the art of painting outdoors.

Romero told me a great story yesterday about Queen Ellie meeting an alien. Not an alien from another country, but from another planet. It was nine feet tall, kind of a grey blue and had an interesting face. The weird thing was that he had landed on planet earth to learn how to dance, and Ellie agreed to teach him belly dancing which was the only kind of dance she knew. I had all these visual experiences while Romero was telling the story. I know he didn't expect me to believe that there was really an alien and that he knows I understand that he is telling me a story full of metaphors. Now I must do a painting of Queen Ellie dancing with an alien. Fantasy is just another part of human nature.

I am so excited about the images that pop into my head from the stories the two phantoms tell me. I'm calling them phantoms due to the fact that I really don't know how else to refer to them. I hope that if I ever leave here I don't lose contact with Alice and Romero. They fill my life with joy, color and celebration.

I'm not spending much time writing today because I'm just too excited to get the brushes out.   Later...

Queen of Arizona Dances with Alien

36: The Gateless Gate

Laurence: *Max, the gate that leads out to the desert is open!*

Max: *Yes, I am aware of that.*

L: *So, what is this all about?*

M: *Remember when we gave you the window, then we gave you the patio. Now we give you the desert.*

L: *Get serious, really?*

M: *Don't try to escape. You could die out there. It's too far to walk out. But I do hope you find exciting things to feed your creative mind. Perhaps you could study the plants and integrate more of them into your paintings? There is a book on desert plants on the shelves that can help you identify them. Take your camera. Oh yes, when you go out be sure to close and latch the gate in order to keep out varmints. The number for the lock is 0007. Easy to remember.*

L: *Max!*

M: *Sorry if we have disturbed you.*

L: *No, I mean...I just don't know what to say yet.*

M: *We have never been worried about you escaping. We only had the gate locked so you would feel safe. You don't have to go out into the desert if it scares you. We just thought we would give you a bit more freedom to explore if that was something you wanted to do.*

L: *Wow, I'll get back to you later. At least I want to see what the outside of this place looks like. See you later.*

I checked to see if the lock worked before I walked out of the gate for the first time. It had been eighteen months living inside the compound. My head was spinning and I could feel my heart pounding as I gingerly walked a little ways from the house. Then I returned to check again to make sure I could open the gate. It worked. I locked it again and walked around the outside of the house discovering for the first time the house was not part of a larger building. There were solar panels on the ground behind the house, a windmill and some kind of a pump which I assumed had to do with a well. I wondered how they had been doing maintenance on all these things.

There was a dirt driveway next to the house or simply a place where a road ended. I began walking down the road away from the building noticing there were no recent tire marks. I estimated that I walked for about a mile before I came upon a fork. Oh boy, that does it. Which way? Who knows? I turned around and came back to the house, went through the gate, carefully closing it and making sure it was locked, then back into the house where I sat for a long time pondering my new situation. I felt disturbed, maybe because I never thought this would happen. It did feel awesome to walk so far. Why did I feel so upset by it? Was change, even for the better, so difficult to accept? But, was it for the better?

L: *Max, what do I do about this? I'm afraid of the desert.*

M: *Don't do anything you don't want to. You don't have to. It's only an option.*

L: *Am I crazy? You would think I'd be excited, but I'm not. I feel dizzy and disturbed.*

M: *Sorry to ruin you day, Laurence.*

L: *Ruin my day? Now I'm laughing.*

M: *I trust that you know to be careful out there. The drone will be delivering a device that you can use if you get lost or hurt. Always wear it in the desert so you can be located. If you get lost a drone will come and guide you back. However, I suggest at first you use the girl scout method and mark your trail.*

L: *Roger Wilco.*

M: *Good. Any more questions?*

L: *No. I'm choosing to ignore this for now. I need to get some painting done.*

I focused on work for the rest of the day, with a lot of deep thoughts on my mind about the new open gate policy. There is no hurry, I told myself. I need to think this through. I thought about Zen and The Gateless Gate. I always thought I didn't understand the meaning of that statement. It suddenly seemed so clear having now become an actual prisoner.

I'd spent a lot of time thinking about how good I had become at building my own prison. I guess I could have called my job at the university a kind of prison. But I'd kept myself locked up in many other ways too. I'd had high expectations of myself to uphold the norm even though I didn't agree with it. At that time I was terrified of freedom. Yet being locked up on the desert made me feel more free than I had ever felt before, and many of my fears had dissolved. The Gateless Gate from Zen teachings is about imagining there is a gate that really isn't there at all. Well, it is there, but not in the way people pretend it is.

For instance, one is seeking enlightenment and in the seeking we imagine we have to pass through a gate to get to some other place. And in a way we do, but the only way through the gate is learning that we are already through and always have been. It's kind of like the feet walking around looking for the feet. It's the thinking that enlightenment is something one has to achieve. But as long as we try to achieve it, we will think we haven't. That's a hard one really because it is too simple. There is no where to go, nothing to discover, nothing to do. Until you know that as long as you continue seeking, the seeking stands in the way of enlightenment. People can drop dead from exhaustion seeking something they were never without.

I used to know people who spent thousands of dollars going to India, risking their lives and health to try to get enlightenment from spiritual teachers. Many people made huge spiritual shifts from doing this. It changed their lives for the better. For me it only looked like a huge tourist business that would be a waste of my time. Anything away from art always seems like a waste of time for me. Not for others though. Isn't that how it is? We all have the God of our understanding. It seems like the trend to go to India is now dying off since technology has become a better way for India to thrive. I guess it's a kind of natural evolution.

I suppose some people did get enlightened on their visits, whatever that means, and it certainly expanded the Beatle's music and made a lot of us aware that there was something other than the religion we were raised to think of as the only one. For the most part, it might have been the biggest march that ever happened: feet walking around looking for feet; in this case, traveling long distances, sleeping in strange places and eating weird or even contaminated food. Some of my students told me it was worth the sacrifices. Some regretted it and would have given anything to rid themselves of the persistent parasites and diseases ravaging their health. They were often struggling with a heavy, enlightened ego. Which meant that they had only reached a spiritual cul-de-sac and had to turn around and head back. I can't say their time was wasted. They were changed. The path to enlightenment is by way of samsara, so I've been told.

Looking at my own life and search for greater awareness, I guess I took the easy way. The only sacrifice I had made was spending time with students who were not at all dangerous. However, art is definitely a spiritual path. When Granger and I read Andrew Wyeth's autobiography, we decided that

217

God was art, and Wyeth was its prophet. We came up with that idea from the way he was able to walk through people's lives and not judge or try to change them. There were some things he vehemently didn't like about the people he painted, but he accepted them as they were and recorded their lives with the excellence of a true master.

Before I came here, what seemed to be my biggest block was an ego that was all about trying to be the best art teacher on the planet. And that took a lot of time away from mastering my own craft. How could I be the best teacher when I wasn't setting a perfect example? Don't get me wrong, I wouldn't change a thing. I have nothing to defend or reject.

The next morning I took a red t-shirt from my drawer and cut it up into strips long enough to tie around a branch or hang from cactus thorns. I put the strips in my pocket and headed out into the desert. There were no visible trails so I walked between bushes and cactus leaving strips of cloth in plain sight. I didn't get very far because paranoia caused me to put the strips too close together. So I went back and started over again. This time walking ahead until I could barely see the last red marker. Even though I traveled a lot further this time, I was paying more attention to marking the trail than I was to the terrain.

The next time I went out I took a compass from my desk drawer. I had long wondered about why I had a compass. I still used the red markers and occasionally stopped to stack some rocks. Soon I had my own trail that went about half mile then circled back to the house. After a few days I could walk that trail and enjoy the views and vegetation. After a few weeks I had two more trails going different directions from the house. I decided I didn't need any more trails for now.

I walked every day, mostly in the evenings so I could catch the colorful sunsets. It's amazing how only a little walking exercise can make a body feel more alive. Until now I'd relied on yoga and a small trampoline to keep myself fit.

I began to recognize landmarks in each of the trails that my footsteps had worn down. Also, I now had, I guess you would call it, a tracking device that I wore on my wrist. So *The Powers That Be* could know where I was. I cleaned up the red markers, but left the rock stacks. I found lovely spots along the way where I could sit on large rocks. The animals didn't act afraid of me. Rabbits hopped close enough for me to touch them had I wanted to. A couple of ravens seemed to find me interesting, and often sat on top of saguaros carrying on raucous conversations.

It was interesting to see the outside of the house I'd been living in for so

218

long. It was exceptionally beautiful and blended in with the environment perfectly. It appeared to be made of rock, glass, metal, and wood; very much like the house I'd owned in Phoenix, only smaller.

I still wasn't sure where the water was coming from, but it was clear, sweet and cold. There was a garden hose outside the gate, so I could easily put water in three artistically designed bird baths that I could see from the windows. They had been carefully blended into the terrain so I had not been able to recognize them before.

Now that they were full of water, I spent lots of time in the mornings watching all kinds of birds splash in the pools. I finally brought the bird book to the table so I could name them. Thrashers, Gilded flickers, Phainopepla, Pyrrhuloxia, Road Runners and many more. Noticing my interest in birds, Max had them send me a hummingbird feeder which I hung in the garden area.

Alias could not figure out a way to get out to the desert from the patio beyond the closed gate. He had, however, learned to climb some vines that grew on the walls, so he could sit on the roof and watch me come and go. I think he whined some about that. I would love to have taken him on a walk with me, but I'd seen too many coyotes and bobcats around the compound to feel safe about letting him wander with me.

Max was right. I did need to integrate more desert plants in my paintings and the ones around the house were stunning. There were Big Sage Brush, Rabbitbush, and Apache-plume – only to mention a few. The cactuses ruled though: Saguaro, Cholla, Prickly pear, Barrel and many more. I took all kinds of reference photos, paying close attention to how the light played on the plants. It amazed me to think how many years I'd lived in this very same desert and had never really seen it. I was always driving a car, thinking about something else, or talking to somebody in my head. Somebody who wasn't there. Go figure. I was dizzy with excitement about my new found world. I had no idea how my life would change because of it. But I knew it was going to be huge.

The first thing I noticed was how expansive my paintings had become. They had had distance and perspective before, but there was something more airy about them now. I think the walks helped me become even more absorbed in my work.

Weeks passed and I realized that Alice and Romero had not shown up. I hadn't given it much thought. I guess I felt like they would show up sooner or later and I was – like I said – painting a lot and getting used to a big change in my life.

37: The Feather

One morning, after breakfast, I opened the gate to go on a walk and noticed a black raven feather lying on the ground just outside the gate. My first thought was that it had been left there on purpose, probably by my black feathered friends, who, I imagined wanted to leave me a gift to add to my collection of desert treasures. I bent down to pick it up. But as soon as I touched it I jumped back as if I'd touched a snake. The feather had several beads attached to the base of it. I stood there staring, and could see the beads were handmade, and painted in bright colors. Had some person put it there? Or had the mischievous ravens stolen it from a village and brought it here?

When I reached again to pick it up I noticed footprints in the sandy soil. They must have been left by a barefoot man, or a large woman. I froze and looked around and saw nothing else unusual. I took the feather, quickly stepped back on the patio and shut the gate, frantically fumbling with the lock until it finally clicked. Once inside the house I stood by the edge of the windows peeking out into the desert trying to see something. Was it the naked man? I was trembling all over. I can't remember ever feeling this energized and it wasn't because he was naked. I aborted my desert walk for the day. Instead I turned my easel around and moved some tables so that I might see out the window when I looked up from my work. It would also be harder for someone to see me inside.

The next day I looked through the gate and saw a leather bag, decorated with beads and rabbit fur, lying on the ground. It took a while for me to work up the courage to open the gate and snatch it. Inside the bag I found a couple of my red cloth strips. Trembling I went back inside. I don't know how long I sat at my table holding the bag, studying it and thinking about who might have left it. I had to shake myself out of a trance in order to get back to painting. It was impossible to stop thinking about it. I often noticed my painting hand was trembling.

After a few hours of work, I picked up the bag and saw that it was hand sewn. There was an intricate design stitched on the front. The back was rabbit fur. The beads were handmade from dried juniper berries and seeds. It smelled like the desert. It was more than just beautiful, it had an energy about it that felt peaceful. It was a peace offering of some kind, I decided.

I didn't mention this to Max. Maybe I thought *The Powers That Be* would get rid of the man, and I wasn't sure I wanted that to happen. He could be dangerous though, I thought, but what if he wasn't? For a couple of weeks I stayed inside the house, or on the patio. Nothing else showed up at the gate.

Then I went out again, walking cautiously, carrying a knife from the kitchen. How silly of me, as if I would know how to use it on a human. I saw no traces of a person, no footprints or things he might have dropped. Yes, I was scared, but I was also curious as hell. What if I'd found a way to get home? Romero and Alice had not been around for a while, so I had no one to ask about all this. Like I said before, I was not going to mention it to Max in case this might be a way back home. Wow, how confusing. At this point I didn't know if I wanted to go back home or not.

Weeks whizzed by and I'd given up on seeing the naked man again. I relaxed on my walks and life resumed as usual. And, of course, that is when I saw him again. He was walking in the distance and I yelled. "Hey" as loud as I could. It was the naked man. He turned and looked at me then, sprinted off as fast as he could. His hair and beard were long and scraggly. He was coated in dust, and caked with mud.

I'm not exactly sure why I sat down on a rock and cried. Maybe because it had been almost two years since I'd seen a real human. Then it occurred to me that he might be afraid of me too. I had spent almost no time primping in the mirror. My hair was scraggly and two-toned from having ignored the henna they had given me. My clothes were not the cleanest. Isn't it funny to be thinking of these things just because I saw another human being?

I was scared too, but I felt like I was safe if I stayed in my house. So I remained indoors until I couldn't stand it anymore. Then I ventured out again, knowing I was taking a huge risk. But I was determined to meet this person.

I went looking for him, and there he was, sitting on one of my favorite rocks at the end of the south trail. He didn't run. He watched me walk up without moving. He was wearing tattered blue jean shorts and a t-shirt. He had shaved off his beard.

"I didn't want to scare you," he said. "I'm sorry if I did."

He didn't sound scary, but I stood still, observing him, waiting for him to say something else. My heart was pounding and I began to sweat.

"I know how long you've been here," he asked.

I took a few steps backwards and tears came.

"It's okay. I'm not going to hurt you." He sounded like he was talking to a wild animal.

I wanted to run up to him and grab him, but I was afraid I would scare him away, or that I might find out he was just another phantom, or he might be a very dangerous person. I was frozen about 10 feet in front of him.

"I... I've been here alone," I said.

"I know."

"And you've been here all this time?" I asked.

"I watched them build the house."

"Why didn't you help me?" I said accusingly.

"I didn't know you needed help. I thought you were living here alone because you wanted to be away from civilization. I wasn't going to bother you. That's why I live here."

What I did next surprised both of us. I sat down on the ground and started crying out loud. He didn't move. Just sat there.

When I could finally speak I said, "No, no, no. I was kidnapped and brought here."

"Seriously?" he said.

"Yes. I haven't seen anyone for almost three years."

"You're kidding?"

"So why are you here? Where do you live?" I asked him.

"About three miles from here. My brother brought me here."

"He brought you here and just left you?

"Sure."

Ravens squawked above and quail scuttled in the bushes. It was early fall, but the sun was merciless. I was feeling hot and faint and the tears on my face had turned into caked mud.

"Let's sit over here in the shade," he held out a hand to help me up, but I didn't want to touch him, so I got up on my own. He pointed to a spot under a scraggly box elder tree where we sat down. He offered me water from a canteen and I drank.

"What's your name?"

"Leonardo. And yours?"

"I'm Laurence. I still can't believe this is happening."

"Yeah. I haven't seen anybody in years either. I mean I got glimpses of you through the fence. Nobody kidnapped me. I was a bad boy, so in the middle of the night my brother brought me out here and dropped me off. He comes back sometimes in the night and drops off supplies. I don't have fancy drones like you do. He never tells me when he is coming, and I never see him."

"You were a bad boy?" I didn't want to hear that.

"Drinking, but I haven't had a drink for the last four years."

"You've been here for four years?"

"Close to that, I think. I haven't wanted to leave."

"Oh," I said.

We sat like that for a long time while the quail and ravens kept up their conversations, and the breeze rattled the leaves of the tree we were under. A giant lizard came close and stared for a few minutes, then scurried off. Rabbits wandered by.

After a while, he stood up, offered his hand to help me up. This time I accepted his offer. "I'll come back," he said.

I didn't want him to go and I didn't want him to stay. I didn't know what I wanted. I was too emotional to think.

"I don't want my captors to see you," I finally said. "I don't know what they would do. I'll walk here everyday. We can meet here. Is that okay? You will come back, won't you. At this time?" I pointed to the sun indicating what time we might meet.

"Sure," he said and slowly walked away. Before he was out of sight he turned and gave me a reassuring wave.

I wanted to run after him, grab him and beg him to stay, or take me with him. But I couldn't move. Was this Stockholm syndrome, my loyalty to Max and *The Powers That Be*? I certainly felt torn. So I just sat back down on the ground in a state of shock.

Walking back later, I felt like a half inflated balloon being blown around on the desert, hoping to avoid cactus spines. I could hear Alias meowing on the roof, and I hoped a giant eagle wouldn't fly down and grab him. I didn't even know if there were any eagles around, but I decided it wasn't a good idea to leave him outside when I was gone. Inside I noticed how messy I'd let the house become. I walked past the clutter and went to the shower to wash off the dust and muddy tears. I felt the warm water run over my body and realized how I'd been neglecting personal hygiene. In the mirror I saw my face looking wild and brown. My hair had grown down to my shoulders and was ragged. Half of it remaining a reddish color from the henna, the other half was light brown, my natural color. I had a box of henna in the closet, but I decided I kind of liked the wild look, so I left it alone. I put some moisturizer on my dry skin and it felt good.

I spent the rest of the day doing laundry and cleaning the house. Was I planning on having a guest? I wondered why I'd let things go. Was it the behavior of a depressed person or a workaholic artist? Probably some of both. While I cleaned, I thought of how much the people in my life had meant to me. I'd been a loner, an introvert, and I hadn't needed an army of friends, but those close to me gave me a reason to keep myself together. How I missed them. I thought of Manuel and how much we laughed together, how we had encouraged each other in our careers, how we snuggled in bed. It had been a while since I'd let myself think of him and the other ones I was close to. Now I was flooded with memories and emotions.

By nightfall everything seemed in order, and I once again felt like an adult. Deep feelings seem to come and go like storms; in between I was calm. I went out on the patio and climbed the ladder and lay on the roof looking at the Universe, or at least a little part of it. Alias was purring beside me. "How can I think my life matters so much when I see all of these stars," I said to the cat. It wasn't the first time I'd watched planes fly by and imagined all the people on their way from somewhere to somewhere else. There they were, not seeing me at all. A satellite slowly and silently crossed the heavens. I thought about screaming for someone to stop.

"I know everything matters," I said to the cat. "But I have no way of knowing how. This certainly is the unknowable that Alice talks about. What do you think, Alias?"

38: Leonardo

It was mid-morning the next day when Leonardo showed up. I was waiting on the rock. He was so silent the quail and rabbits didn't notice his arrival. I moved to sit under the box elder tree and he joined me there. Sitting beside him I could see his feet and I noticed he was wearing perfectly crafted handmade moccasins.

"Thanks for the beautiful bag. I see you must have made your shoes too."

"My Nikes fell apart after the first year. My brother brought me a new pair but they never felt right. Since no one was around, I forgot about clothes. But sometimes you need shoes in the desert. The ground gets a little cold in the winter and there are always rocks and stickers," he told me.

I looked down at my ratty Vans which had been a part of my prison wardrobe when I first arrived. "I know what you mean. I've grown sloppy out here. It's been a welcome relief not to think about what I need to wear."

I offered him some cold peach tea I'd brought in a water bottle and he drank half of it.

"Wow, that's good stuff."

"Do you have a refrigerator?" I asked.

"Yes, it runs on solar, but it's tiny and I don't have fancy tea. Just what I find in the desert."

I knew that we had long stories to tell each other and I was impatient as usual to get on with it.

"So you live three miles from here?"

"About two miles that way, three from your house," he pointed southwest.

"I can't believe you are so close and have been here all this time."

"Are you mad that I didn't rescue you?"

"I'm not sure. At first I was, but then I thought about it and understand how you must have thought I wanted to be here. And the weird thing is I'm not sure. Maybe I did want to be here and didn't know it. It's all so confusing. It's hard to sort it all out," I told him sounding like Alice in Wonderland.

"Well, I came here to get away from people so I was a bit angry when you arrived. But I soon discovered that you kept to yourself. For a long time I had

227

no way of knowing that you couldn't get out. Then one day I considered the idea that you may be locked in, but I didn't know what to do." He kept his eyes on the ground. "I guess I was afraid I would cause trouble. I had zero self-esteem and most of the time I was a mess. You said you were kidnapped?"

"Yes, from a parking lot in Phoenix. I woke up in this house and I only have a slim idea of where I am. I know it's the Sonoran desert because of the Saguaros. That's about it."

"Do you want to leave?"

"That's a good question. I've been thinking about it almost continually since yesterday, but I honestly don't know. I'm busy with some engaging projects. I guess I'm concerned about my friends who don't know where I am."

"I'm not sure I could help you escape. My brother comes and goes in the night. Maybe I could send out a letter from you with my bags. I never see him. He is pretty mad at me, but I'm the one who doesn't want to leave."

"Wow, that's interesting."

"Also, my brother doesn't want me to come back and start drinking again. I'm not even sure if it's him who drops off supplies. He could be hiring somebody else to do that. He's a busy man. "

"Is it true that it's too far to walk out?"

"I wouldn't recommend it. I've walked far and wide around here and I'm telling you there is nothing but desert."

"You must have been truly annoyed by my invading your space when they built the house."

"Well, watching it go up was entertainment for me. After I discovered you never came out, I wasn't bothered by you. It was kind of nice knowing somebody was near."

"But it's been close to three years!"

"Yes, but two years can go by plenty fast when you have lots to do to survive. I have chickens to take care of, a garden, and I hunt a lot of the time. There is maintenance on the wind mill and solar panels, plus I make crafts that get picked up by whoever drops off supplies."

"Who takes care of my solar panels and windmill? Have you seen anybody."

"No. I think they come in the night. If you haven't heard anything they must be very quiet. Or maybe they are aliens."

"Aliens, are you serious?"

"Sure. Why not, there are stranger things than that on this desert."

I thought about Alice and Romero, but I didn't say anything to him about the visitations. We talked like that for well over two hours until I felt the urge to return to painting.

"I have to go back to work," I told him.

"Work? What do you do?" he asked.

"I paint. They take my paintings in exchange for supplies."

"Are you serious?" he asked.

"We have a lot more to talk about," I told him.

"Indeed, we do," he said.

We pulled ourselves up from the dusty ground under the tree and said our goodbyes for the day with a promise to meet at the same place the next day.

Walking back, I could tell that my walk was different. There was excitement in my steps. This could be good, I thought, having a neighbor. He seems like a kind person.

I painted the rest of the afternoon occasionally thinking of Leonardo and how one person could change everything for me. It was a huge change but change could have both positive and negative affects and I wasn't sure which way this one would go. He didn't seem to be needy. He let me go back to work. He was used to being alone like me; obviously he was choosing it.

The next day he was at the meeting rock before I was. He handed me a small handmade basket with four chicken eggs.

"I have too many," he said.

"Thanks, I love fresh eggs." Then I handed him a small painting – a study of a Banana Yucca.

"Wow! You did this? You are a serious painter!" he said. "I don't have any pictures on my walls. This will be perfect. I make things, but I don't paint or draw. I might draw but I forget to ask Alberto to bring a sketch pad."

"I can give you one. That is one thing I have plenty of," I told him. In fact, I seemed to have been given everything I need, I thought to myself, except a flesh and blood friend. But that seems to be changing. I couldn't help but wonder if *The Powers That Be* had sent him. However, I'd long ago ceased questioning what came along and where it came from.

I said to him. "I would like to invite you to come to my house, but there are cameras. They told me they were no longer on, but I don't trust them."

"Would you like to walk with me to my house?" he asked.

I hesitated.

"You don't have too. You don't know me. I could be a serial killer hiding out here." He smiled so sweetly I felt a sudden wave of terror. Then he laughed. "I am not a killer or a rapist. Just an alcoholic who hasn't had a drink in four years."

"Yes, let's walk to your house," I heard myself say. I wanted to be brave, take a chance.

"You sure?" he asked.

I stood up and picked up the basket of eggs and began following him. But when we stepped off my known trail I hesitated again.

"Don't worry, I will walk you back whenever you are ready. I would never try to keep you. I have work to do and I have no need of another person who would be nothing but trouble if I kept her away from her work."

"That makes sense," I said. The terrain was much the same as what surrounded my house. Cactus, rocks, sparse small trees and lots of sandy soil. Of course, I knew he could be luring me to torture and death. A psychopath would know just the right words to say. But I followed him anyway.

I didn't think about the fact that I would be walking six miles in a day when I followed him the two miles from our meeting place. It was warm, but not sweltering hot like it can get on the desert. I could see his windmill long before we walked over a hill where green vegetation and a tiny building came into view. As we neared the dwelling I could hear chickens screeching. Leonardo shouted, "Coyote!" Then handed me the little painting and took off running towards the chicken coop. I heard him yell, "Get out. Get!"

By the time I arrived the chickens were beginning to settle down and Leonardo, breathing hard, said, "They're fine. There is no way a coyote can get to them, but they still come snooping around and get the ladies all up in arms. The rooster is the one that hides." Leonardo showed me his very well made coop. Sure enough, the rooster was inside.

"The house is over there." He pointed to something that looked more like a shed than a house. As we neared it I noticed animal skins tacked to the outside walls.

Inside was a tidy room that had a narrow bed along one wall and a rug on the floor. A small handmade table and one chair, also handmade, stood under one of the two windows. It was a work table cluttered with tools and scraps of fur and leather. Hanging on the walls were the bags and moccasins he had made from animal skins and found objects. One end of the room was designated as the kitchen area.

I was looking at his work table.

"I have to have something to do other than take care of chickens and garden."

"Indeed," I said, reaching out to touch one of his creations, than pulling my hand back like a child being scolded in a store.

"It's okay," he reached over me and took down one of the bags hanging on the wall and held it out to me. Like the one he had given me, it was exquisite. I carefully examined it, noticing that everything on it was natural, even the threads he had used to sew it.

"My brother or whoever comes out here takes them into town. I leave them in a box outside." He paused. "Sorry, I only have one chair," he said sitting down on the rug on the floor. I joined him there.

"So we have stories to tell each other. You want to go first?" I asked.

He was sitting Indian style, hands folded in his lap. He was a handsome Hispanic man, dark skin made even darker by years spent in the sun. His hair had obviously not been cut for the four years he'd lived here. It was scraggly, but clean. He looked down and some of the hair fell over his face. I could see shame in his expression.

"I'm sorry. You don't have to tell me anything. I'm too abrupt sometimes. Please forget that I asked." I wanted to reach out and touch his arm to reassure him, but I wasn't certain how he would take being touched. This strong hunter and craftsman who I'd assumed was rugged and tough suddenly looked fragile.

"No, it's okay," he said looking up and making eye contact. "I haven't told anybody my story. No one has been here to talk to. I'm just not sure if I can get through it without breaking down."

"I'm so sorry," I apologized again. "I'm a total stranger. How presumptuous of me to think you would want to tell me right off the bat. You never have to tell me anything about how you got here if you don't want too."

He closed his eyes as if he were asking himself the question, do I want to or not? Then he spoke. "I was a high school teacher in Tucson. I taught Mexican-American Studies, a program that the Arizona legislature banned. They thought we were teaching the kids to overthrow the government. Well, I think they knew we weren't. But that's what they wanted people to think. They were just racists. Anyway, the kids were doing great – performing better in their other classes and on standardized tests. We mostly worked on self esteem by teaching them to feel proud of themselves as Mexican Americans."

"I remember that program, Leonardo. I was outraged when it got canceled. It's hard to accept that government officials can be so stupid and have so much power. Don't get me started!" I had raised my voice and I could feel the rage rising up my spine.

"I lost my job because I was helping with the protests."

I groaned and slapped my forehead with the palm of my hand.

"But that's not all," he went on. "There was a girl in my class named Angela. She was smart and beautiful. Everyone loved her. Then she didn't show up at school for a while so I went looking for her. I went to her house and it was empty. I asked the neighbors and they told me her parents had been deported and she and her little brother had been taken into foster care because, unlike their parents, they were citizens. They separated the two siblings because of their age difference. I tracked Angela down and she was in a foster home where she was being abused. Not only was I fighting to save the school program, I was fighting with child protective services too. I told them I would take both of the kids, but they were concerned about my protesting."

He suddenly got very quiet and tears began to slide down his face. "I had a wife and a daughter. Abril and Sophia," he said almost in a whisper. Then he was quiet again until he found control of his voice. I looked around for a tissue. Old habits.

He wiped his eyes on his tattered shirt tail. "No matter how hard I tried, I could not find a new job and Abril, who was working on getting her degree, had to quit school and start cleaning houses. Sophia was four at the time so I stayed with her."

"Everything would have worked out, but I started drinking. In the evening when my wife came home from work I would take off for the bar. It was crazy! I never drank before and I don't know why I was doing it then. Especially at a time when I needed to be focused on getting our family out of crises. I'd convinced myself I would meet somebody at the bar who would give me the job of my dreams and I would make so much money I wouldn't have any more worries. Then I would quit drinking. But that never happened. I just got more drunk." He looked up and stared out of his tiny window as if looking for more courage to carry on.

"Wow," he continued. "I haven't spoken to another human being in so long I keep having to remind myself that this is really happening. Chickens are different. I guess if I had not talked to them and the other animals that come around I would have lost my voice."

"I can certainly relate to that." I said.

He turned and looked at me and went on with his story. "You probably wonder where I got money to buy liquor. Abril gave me money for groceries and I would buy food, but I would also shoplift from the supermarket so I could save enough money for the bar. Also, people felt sorry for me so they would buy me drinks. Some people think a strong drink will cure anything that ails you. Others call that *stinkin' thinkin'*."

"One night at the bar a man told me that he knew what happened to Angela. He said she had died of an overdose of drugs. He didn't know what happened to her little brother. Hearing that made me even more depressed and I started leaving Sophia with a neighbor so I could go to the bar in the afternoon."

"Now that I think about it, I'm not sure that man was telling the truth. I never tried to find out. I guess I was using what he said as more justification for my drinking."

"That drove Abril to take Sophia and move in with her mom and I was left alone. Soon I had to move out of the house and I had no money to rent another place. I was homeless. That is when I went to my brother and asked for help. He brought me here and he gave me this book." He reached behind him under the bed and brought out the *AA Alcoholics Anonymous* book, the one I knew was called *The Big Book*.

"It's the only book I have," he said. "I don't need another book."

"Wow, Leonardo. So you have been here for four years! And you are sober now. Have you heard anything about your wife and child."

"Yes, after about two years she married another man. My brother, Alberto, left me a note saying he is a good man and he takes good care of her and my daughter. When I heard that, I thought I might kill myself. I couldn't stand the thought of my wife sleeping with another man or my little daughter sitting on his lap while he read her a book. Alberto said I should come back and at least be her real dad, but I was too angry. I was afraid of what I might do. I think I would have killed myself, but I didn't know how. So I decided I had to stay here at least two more years or until I could get a handle on it. I just kept reading my book, hunting and making my bags and moccasins. Alberto sells them to shops. I have no plans to leave because I've found peace here. Truthfully, I'm terrified of leaving. I'm happy that my bags and moccasins bring joy to others and pay for my supplies. It's all so simple here."

"I know what you mean," I said and I really meant it. "Does Sophia know where you are? Do you think she misses you?"

"I don't think my brother has told them where I am, but I'm not sure. I would love to be a dad to Sophia, but I don't want to be a drunk one. I would do more harm than good. I guess someday I will just know it's time to go back. Until then I think she is better off without me."

"That's sad. But I understand." I said. "It's like you're not being selfish if you are putting her well-being above your own desires."

"I think of both of them everyday, and I say prayers for them. It helps me to think that what I am doing is for them too."

We sat in silence for a while. You could tell that we were both used to silence. It felt strange for me to think I wanted to give him a hug. I'd never been a hugging kind of person. But I was touched by his story and impressed by his willingness to go to such extremes to get sober and make a better life for himself and his family even if he couldn't be with them.

I could hear the sound of chickens and quail, a raven squawked, then came the hoofs and grunts of javalina. We were both used to these sounds.

Finally he said, "I think we should cook those eggs."

I realized I was hungry. I stood up and grabbed the basket I'd left near the door.

"Do you like boiled eggs?" he asked.

"Sure."

He put them in a pan of water and placed it on a burner on his tiny propane stove.

"I baked some bread yesterday. How about we make some egg salad and have sandwiches?"

"That sounds great. How did you bake the bread?"

"Outside, in the oven I built."

He had his back to me slicing bread when he asked me. "What about you? Why are you here?"

"I don't have much to tell. Other than I was kidnapped in a parking lot at the Phoenix Art Museum and woke up here. A lot has happened since I've been here and I can tell you all about that, but maybe we can wait until we see each other again," I said. "I feel like I need to be with your story for now, before I talk about me. Thank you. I'm touched that you felt safe enough to tell me."

"I'm surprised I told you too," he said. "I'm sorry if I've just dumped my stuff in your lap."

"Well," I said. "It didn't feel like that to me. Imagine how it would be if you hadn't told me."

We ate the sandwiches in silence. I relished the fresh baked bread and he gave me some to take home.

We were silent walking back to my trail and when we reached it I turned and bowed like a Zen monk. He did the same with his hands over his heart. We agreed to meet again in a few days and I watched him turn and disappear behind some bushes. I walked the last mile back alone.

39: A Big Change

Back in my studio, I opened the cabinet door where the full length mirror hung and stood studying my reflection. Underneath the shabby clothing, I looked thin. My skin was much darker too. I'd always had that white nerdy look. Now I looked more outdoorsy and athletic. I tried to remember what I had looked like when I worked as a professor at the University. Somehow I couldn't imagine myself wearing those clothes and feeling and acting the way I did then. This was a different person I was looking at now.

The impact of having met someone here on the desert was profound. In Phoenix, meeting a new person could be an everyday occurrence, and it wasn't something I usually spent time thinking about later. But here in my current situation I could not get Leonardo out of my mind. Back home many people filled my life, but here, there was only one. It was amazing how a real person could take up so much space. Alice and Romero had been wispy-like. They came and they went leaving hardly a trace behind. Leonardo filled space and lingered in my mind. I would never have imagined a world where there was only me and one other person.

Because he had believed I moved here wanting to be a hermit, he had not made his presence known for nearly three whole years. I suspected that he wasn't going to bother me now. He had not wanted anyone in his life, so why wouldn't he have thought that about me too. He seemed respectful, kind and honest.

We were living quite differently. Leonardo told me he was good with a bow and he hunted for most of his meat. He said he had never killed a javalina, because it would be too much meat at once and he was unsure about curing it. But if we wanted to share one he would be up for trying it. I was a bit shocked over that suggestion. But I tried to act like it wasn't a big deal. He didn't know that *The Powers That Be* were regularly sending me fresh chicken and fish packed in iced boxes. I also had cans of tuna, salmon, sardines and oysters. I noticed he only had a few store bought items that I knew had been delivered – mostly canned beans and chiles, along with a bag of flour and some lard. I could gift him some mayonnaise and pickles. Since I had started my garden and ate a lot of fresh vegetables, I had not been eating the canned goods and other packaged products that drones dropped off. I was sure Leonardo would savor them.

For a Mexican he was quite tall and sinewy. He told me his ancestors were from a tribe of tall Indians from South America. But I thought he could use a bit of fun food which might put more meat on his bones.

I could not, however, stop wondering if he had been put here by *The Powers That Be*. Maybe they wanted someone close by to keep an eye on me. It could all be a part of the plan and his story could be something made up. If so, he was a good actor. Or maybe his brother was in on all of this. Maybe there were a lot more artists and artisans in captivity out in remote places cranking out products for someone to sell. But art was very hard to sell. If they wanted to make money off of someone, wouldn't they have chosen something other than art?

When I got stuck thinking like this I always came back to the same answer. What does it matter? Who cares if Leonardo was planted here or if his story was real or not? What I knew to be true was that in many ways I was excited about having a friend – a real live person, a neighbor. At least that's how I felt most of the time, but there were other thoughts too – disturbing ones. What if he turned out to be an asshole? Or worse, dangerous. What if I found out I just didn't want anyone else around and couldn't get rid of him?

As my thoughts whirled around in my head I slid down on the floor and sat Indian style in front of the mirror, a perfect invitation for Alias to curl up on my lap, purring loudly and demanding his daily petting.

In many ways life had become fuller having Alias, a living being. And it seemed that way now having a human friend. But the human friend was like some huge presence that broke through a well-organized system and shattered all my sense of order. Our meeting was like two universes crashing into each other. And part of me longed to go back to the way it was with just me, Alias, Alice, Romero and Max. I could refuse to see Leonardo, but I knew I would not be doing that. The merging had begun.

"I'm thinking too much," I said to the cat.

"What do you mean?" he asked me.

"Thinking...you know...thinking?"

"No, not really, I don't know what you are talking about." He looked up at me with a huge smile.

"Are you laughing at me?" I asked.

"Not really. Please can you scratch that place under my chin. Oh yes! Right there! You got it. More, more please."

"Alias, am I insane?"

236

"I have no idea. I just know you feed me and talk to me and pet me."

"You're right, Mr. Cat. Life doesn't have to be so complicated does it?"

"Mostly not. But you can't avoid complications if they come your way now and then. It all has to do with how well you keep your cool," the cat said.

"Well, Mr. Sweetness, you are the king of cool. Do you think you can teach me that?"

"Now about that food. I'm out of the crunchy stuff," he said jumping up and heading to the kitchen. I got up and followed, admitting he had made me his slave.

"Hey kid, how about we share some tuna?" I opened a can and poured the water off the fish into his dish. Tuna juice was one of his favorite things. Then I made tuna salad with apple, sweet pickles and mayonnaise. I couldn't help thinking of Leonardo and how he lived without all the luxuries I had. He did, however, bake some awesome bread. I looked forward to doing some trading.

The rest of the afternoon I painted while listening to podcasts. But I wasn't as lost in my work as I'd been. The presence of another human being was definitely invading my space. I told myself not to fight with it. I was sure that within time I would get used to having Leonardo being a part of my life and I would return to my normal level of concentration. I'd heard his story and I rationalized he too needed lots of alone time. Here I was in my own space with plenty of time to work. It was just my mind that was stuck in a place of questioning everything.

I was painting better than before. In fact my brush strokes had become somewhat chaotic in nature and it wasn't an inferior look at all. It was actually playful, less structured and it did not interrupt the overall composition.

Later I cleaned my brushes, washed my hands and wrote to Max, careful not to mention my new found friend. I wanted to see if he in anyway would hint at knowing what was going on. I sometimes imagined he knew everything that happened here and other times I was convinced he didn't.

Our conversation went like this:

Laurence: *Max, I'm working on a new painting. It's a table outdoors in the desert with a birthday cake, presents and party favors and all sorts of other strange things. Thanks for providing me with the desert plant book. I like knowing the names of the plants I'm finding on my walks.*

Max: *Great, Laurence. I can't wait to see the work. If it feels okay perhaps you could send a photo.*

L: *Maybe in a day or so. I have some corrections to make.*

M: *Great, no hurry. I'm just being impatient.*

L: *I understand impatience. I'm spending more time out on the desert. The weather is cooler and it's easier to be outdoors. I'm using more green in my painting. I like it outdoors here when it's not boiling hot. But it has in some ways distracted me from my work.*

M: *It is wise to stay out of the heat. And don't worry about the distractions. Summer will be here soon and you will want to spend more time indoors.*

L: *This is true. Being here has changed me into an outdoors kind of person. But I will be careful of the heat.*

M: *Do you consider it a good change?*

L: *I suppose. I was always surrounded by lots of people at the university. It was hard to find any time to paint. Now it's just me and the desert. Well, there is Alias, of course.*

M: *Is that okay?*

L: *For now.*

M: *You will let me know when "for now" is no longer true for you?*

L: *Seriously? Are you giving me a choice?*

M: *Do you want a choice?*

L: *I don't know.*

M: *You sound good.*

L: *I'm okay.*

M: *Good.*

L: *Goodnight, Max.*

M: *Goodnight, Laurence.*

No hint of his knowing about Leonardo. No indication that he is pushing me into telling him about my meeting someone. I walked around the room looking at the cameras that I knew about. I saw no indication they were on, but I could not be sure, nor was I sure I knew where they all were. I was thinking about covering them with something to see if I got a response from Max. I will do that tomorrow. It would be great if I could invite Leonardo to my house. Maybe they don't even care if he comes as long as I keep producing the paintings.

It amazes me how my mind can entertain conflicting thoughts. Am I scared they will keep me here forever or am I afraid they will send me away? Honestly, I do love my life here on the desert, and I feel less and less sad for those I left behind. I mean, it's not that I don't care that they may be in pain. It's just that I don't feel that pain anymore and I don't think about it as much as I used to. But who knows? Maybe they've gotten over me and moved on and are having wonderful lives. There are so many things I just can't know and I guess I can let go of making stuff up. I do know that my days here are filled with things I love: my garden, my studio, my alone time, my cat, my desert trails and now a possible friend. I do not miss working at a job where I am unappreciated and continually on the verge of being fired. And people, people, people all the time, too many of them who I've found I can happily live without. Only sometimes do I think I miss teaching and my students.

When I do think of people I miss Granger, George, Manuel and the Sun family. In some ways I'm more clear now on what I want and don't want in my life. Looking back, I realize I always had more options, but I never got time enough to stand back and see the big picture. I guess I thought I just had to put up with a lot of insanity.

I'm uncertain right now about Leonardo, but the truth is, I've met him and I can't change that now. I will accept that and see where it takes me next.

I finally identified my weird feelings as stress. Jesus, there was a time when I felt like this all the time. Now it feels weird? I was tired so I wound down my day and climbed into bed. I tried reading some tales from books. I think I only made it though a few pages, but the words stuck with me. Valdez's teacher Juanita was telling him that he worked too hard trying to achieve freedom and that was the very thing that stood in his way.

He writes:

"Lie here on this flat rock with your head facing east," she told me. When I did she covered my body with branches and leaves and sprinkled them with herb infused water. It smelled strong and medicinal and it sent me into a trancelike state. I tried to say something to her. I wanted to ask what she wanted me to do, but I could not speak. I was just muttering something so I gave up. She laughed and said, "There is nothing you can do."

I was terrified. I thought I should be able to move my arms and legs and push the branches away and get up off the ground, but I couldn't.

"Stop running from the terror," she said. "You have made terror your enemy and the only thing you can do is turn around and face it."

I finally surrendered to the feeling. When I gave it all my attention it felt like what I imagined it would be: like being tasered. Electrical currents rushed through my body from head to toe. There was a loud buzzing sound in my ears, and it felt like all the hair on my body was standing on end. Thank

God it didn't last long. I suddenly felt relaxed. It was as though I was lying on a warm sunny beach with the sounds of ocean waves breaking, lulling me. I went from struggling to move and speak to just lying there peacefully. It was so comforting that I wanted to be there forever in the stillness and silence. I had nothing to do and nothing to say.

Then she said to me, "You constantly think that you can fix things with your words and your thoughts. Not only do you think you can. You think you must and that has become your whole view of the world. You see yourself as a hero. You can't stand knowing that you are just like any other man. Powerless. That is what stands in the way of your freedom. In comic books, superheroes are never finished. As soon as they vanquish one enemy another comes, and another, and another. People look upon them as saviors. But the question is, are they?"

I wasn't a superhero like in the comics. I had no super powers nor a Hollywood body. But I had been convinced that my ideas would somehow save the world. As I lay there under the branches and leaves feeling like a puddle of warm water, I was able to see the world without my quest to save it. I knew then that I wasn't needed and I was completely surprised that I felt fine with that.

I laid the book on my chest and had one last thought before falling asleep. It was about how Leonardo did not try to find out if I needed help. If he had made his appearance before now I would not have had the past two and a half years alone focused on my work. I relaxed much like Valdez had when he surrendered. I was sure that my new found friend would be an asset not a bother. He wasn't going to be a hero and apparently I had not wanted to be saved.

40: My Story

Days passed before I saw Leonardo again. He was standing at the edge of the clearing. Not knowing how long he had been there, I opened the gate and motioned for him to come in. He did.

I felt the need to explain things to him. So I said. "I've covered the cameras. At least the ones I know about. I don't know if the place is bugged. But, honestly, I don't care."

He wasn't looking at me because he was more interested in the patio. He wanted to see everything in the raised beds. He looked at my garden tools and examined the watering system. I found myself thinking, this is a man thing to do.

"Nice set up," he finally said.

"I didn't do it. It was all here. I replace drip-heads when they stop working, but that's about it."

"Maybe you have ninjas that scale your wall and fix things when they break."

"Funny, you should call them ninjas,"

"What?"

"Never mind. Come inside. I have some of that peach tea."

We we walked inside and he stopped and gasped. "Holy Moses, this is nice!"

"I cleaned it before you came," I said, trying to sound humble. "Compared to your tiny cabin, it must seem like a mansion."

"Maybe that's it. It's been a long time since I've been inside a real house."

I knew not to ask him to sit down because like a cat he started investigating everything floor to ceiling focusing on the construction.

He said, "I watched them build this house, but the people who worked on it stayed here in trailers so I never got close. After they left, I tried to look inside the windows but they were covered."

"When I first got here I didn't know about the lower windows. Then one day the I learned how to reveal the windows." I got my iPad and showed him how I could make the windows opaque. I showed him how everything worked. He must have thought he had entered a different universe.

241

I was taking him towards the bathroom when Alias jumped in through the cat door. Both he and Leonardo stood stunned.

"This is Alias." The cat stalked around the edge of the wall then zipped across the room and hid under the bed.

Leonardo laughed. "I didn't know you had a cat."

"Well, they sent him to me about a year ago after I complained about rodents. He's been my best friend ever since."

"I want to show you the bathroom since I know you don't have one." Leonardo had an outhouse and outdoor shower with only cold water.

"Anytime you like you can have a hot shower." When I said that I was hoping he didn't come everyday.

"That's very generous of you." His eyes told me he was marveling about the luxuriousness of it.

"No problem. I don't pay the utility bills."

We sat on the sofa with our tea.

"It's your turn," he said.

"My turn?"

"Yes, you have a story to tell me."

"I suppose I do. I don't know who my captors are. I call them several names: *The Powers That Be, The Ninjas, Max.* Like I said, they kidnapped me from the parking lot of the Phoenix Art Museum. They used drugs and I woke up here."

"That's terrible!"

"This house and studio is a small version of the one I have or had in Phoenix. I don't know how long they plan on keeping me or if they might someday just kill me."

His eyes grew wide when I said that.

"Sorry, I've grown detached from the situation. I just paint and drones pick up the paintings and deliver supplies. I sent one off yesterday and I haven't started another yet. The only one I have here is that big one over there." I pointed. "It's too big for the drones to carry so it just stays right there. I have communication via chat to a person or persons called Max. I tell him, her or it, what I need.

"You're serious!"

"It's been two and a half years. I have photos of all the paintings. I'd have to look them up and count them. I've forgotten how many I've done."

"Why aren't you angry?"

"I don't know. At first I was. I was livid, but I got used to being here. It was quiet. Nobody bothered me. Before I got here I was totally stressed out from my job as a professor. I was on the verge of getting fired. You know, they were closing the department. I think I was about to lose everything. So I guess I just settled in and started painting here. I've never had so much time to focus on my work. I was locked inside this house for almost a year, and didn't even know there was a courtyard. Then the door to the courtyard was revealed. The gate to the desert opened only a few months ago."

"Until I saw you walking on the trails I didn't even know how many people were here. In fact, even after I saw you, I still didn't know. I'm not a peeping Tom."

"I guess not."

"So we were both brought here by someone else. And we both stayed because we sort of like it. And we both make art that gets picked up and sold."

"Do you think there may be others like us living on the desert?"

"Not close. I've walked for miles. It's amazing how big this desert is."

"One hundred thousand square miles."

"Really?"

"The internet."

"You have internet?"

"Well, it's limited, but I have Wikipedia and a few other things."

"So there is no way you could have used it to escape?"

"No. I've tried. There is only a chat line and I can talk to someone called Max."

"Max. I see. I'm sorry, but this is the strangest thing I've ever heard. I don't know what to say."

"You think it is too weird for you to understand. Well, I gave up a long time ago. I don't want to stay here forever, but I never would have gotten so much work done living in a city and having a job. So I've never tried to escape."

"Like me."

"Like you."

We sat there in silence for some time.

I left him on the sofa and went into the kitchen area and made us both chicken salad sandwiches. "I know this is not your fabulous homemade bread, but it's the best I can do."

"You are kind."

We ate at the tiny table by the windows.

"This is where I first saw you. I thought you were a phantom."

"A phantom?"

"Yes, I was already being visited by two other phantoms so I wasn't surprised to see another. It wasn't until I saw your foot prints that I knew you were a real person."

"Are you talking about the dreamers?"

I stared at him not knowing how to respond. I was sure I had misspoken and the last thing I wanted was to scare him away by making him think I was a crazy woman.

Then he said, "There are witches on this desert. They live over there below the mountains."

"You say that as if it's common knowledge. Have you seen them?"

"I have some stories."

"I thought I was hallucinating from the isolation."

"No. They exist. I've heard they have a school in that village."

"Have you ever been there?"

"No, It is too far to walk. But there is a train that runs through that place. I think someday I might try to go there."

"I'm curious too."

"So tell me, what have you seen?"

I told him about Alice and Romero. I showed him on my iPad pictures I had painted of them.

"I can't believe I'm talking to you about this." I was both unsure and relieved.

Then he told me, "There is a man called Hernandes. He became my sponsor in AA. But I never attended meetings before I came here. Sometimes I dream I am at a meeting somewhere in a town. He takes me there in the dream state. But mostly we sit together on the floor in my cabin and talk. He comes at least once a week. Often we walk together in the desert. I can tell him anything. He says he used to drink a lot, and like me his wife left him. He was picked up off the streets by one of the sorcerers and they took him to the school where they taught him how to be a dreamer. Now he is a sponsor, not only to me but to several other people who are unable to get to meetings. You are right, he leaves no footprints."

"Were you scared when you first saw him?"

"No, I just thought I was drunk and seeing things."

"I know what you mean. Well, I've never been a drinker, but my brother was. When I first saw Alice I was sure I was imagining things. At the time I didn't care if she was real or imagined because I needed her. She said she was a psychologist and that describes our relationship."

"I think they become whatever you need them to be."

244

"I haven't seen her or Romero in weeks."

"I haven't seen Hernandez either."

We looked at each other as if we were trying to come up with an explanation about what had happened to our dreamer friends. But neither of us had answers, so nothing more was said.

"Maybe I should go," he finally said. "You must want to get started on your next painting and I have some rabbits to turn into bags."

"Do you eat the rabbits?"

"No. They might be diseased. I feed them to the ravens and other animals. It doesn't bother them. Hernandez tells me those rabbits know they are put here on earth to feed others. They are all martyrs."

"I'm glad you don't use a gun. Too noisy."

"You don't condemn me for being a rabbit killer?"

"As long as I don't have to. And you are making art out of them. Alias likes mice and rats. I don't suppose you could use some tails?"

"Maybe. Does he bring home ground squirrel tails?"

"I'll save you some. I'm so glad you came by."

"Me too. I should go now."

We stood and I walked him to the gate. "Please come whenever you want. Maybe Alias will be friendlier next time."

"When is your work time?"

"Late morning and all afternoon. I like to stop before sundown."

"I will be back."

"I'm happy to hear that."

When he was gone I sat down on the sofa where I was joined by a purring cat. I didn't sense anything dangerous about Leonardo. And I didn't think he would be a bother. But I've been very wrong about people before. I couldn't possible know what was in store for my future. But I convinced myself that it was to my advantage to have a friend. Since he was the only human around, I couldn't be choosy.

The rest of the day was very much like all others. I started a new painting. I wrote to Max and he said nothing about my visitor or the cameras being covered. I knew I could settle into things being different. But I was amazed at how quickly I'd become relaxed with another person. Thinking back on my life in Phoenix, I could understand why I wasn't painting to the best of my ability. Back then, my whole body must have vibrated with the raucous music of chaos. Some artists capture that frantic energy in their paintings and make it work for them. Apparently, I'm not like that.

I thought of Manuel and how his paintings were wild dances of color and

245

movement: cars racing, wind and rain blowing and people in motion. It suited his temperament. Had we tried to live together we would have definitely needed separate studios. My paintings were still, quiet and thoughtful. We had been good for each other because we never competed, and we held a great respect for each other's talent. Where was he now? What was he doing?

There was a stillness about me now and I sensed that too in Leonardo. We were a couple of monks living in caves. I wondered what it would feel like if we left the desert and found ourselves suddenly in a chaotic city. Would we walk through it calmly like that kung fu guy on that TV show that Granger used to love? Maybe someday we would both have an answer to that question.

41: Settling In

Leonardo came, once or twice a week. He loved my library. I tried to loan him books, but he refused to take them, saying he only had room for one book in his cabin – *The Big Book*.

"It's because it's so big," he said.

He came often when I was working and sat on my sofa reading or looking at images in art books. When we became more comfortable with each other he asked to use my computer. Then he became lost in research. I'm not sure what he was studying, but he made sketches and took notes. I never asked him what he was doing and I never looked at the history of his searches. I thought if he wanted me to know he would tell me.

Above all he was quiet and kept to himself. I often forgot he was in the room. Alias came to like him too and often curled up next to him. I think both of them were drawn here for the tiny air conditioner that kept the whole place comfortable, even on days when the temperature rose into triple digits. When the sun vanished Leonardo would say goodnight and slip away.

Whenever he came he was clean and shaven. One day he asked me to make one long braid of his hair down the middle of his back. It was black and silky. He said he'd washed it with aloe vera roots and that he would share some with me. He asked if he could use my washing machine. He took the tattered clothes home wet to hang on a line. He often brought food: bread he had made in his outdoor oven, a squirrel or a few quail he would fry in a skillet, and vegetables from his garden that were different from what I grew. He had yellow squash. I had zucchini. I was right, he loved it when I sent him home with canned tuna, oysters, and sardines.

One evening as he was leaving, he asked if I would join him on a hike to a cave. He said we would need to leave early in the morning before it got too hot, and we would be gone all day. It was perfect timing because I needed to leave a painting to dry. It was hard for me to stop messing with paintings when I needed to walk away for a while.

Slathered in sunscreen and wearing a hat and a backpack with my camera, water and food, I was ready and waiting when he came. For two hours we walked, and just as the heat was starting to ruin the day we came upon a crack in the side of a low cliff. It was big enough for a human to easily fit through. I started to tremble, but I didn't want him to know how scary it was for me so I followed him without protesting.

We both had head lamps and he also carried a huge, very bright, flashlight. As we tunneled down a rocky pathway I noticed the cave smelled like rock and moss. Just as I began to feel intense fear of going so far in, we came upon a spacious opening filled with stalactites and stalagmites. There was a pool of blue green water and I guessed the cool damp air was about 68 degrees. The beauty of it stole the words right out of my mouth. I felt like we were in God's cathedral. We found a place to sit and rest and absorb the wonders of it.

Finally he said, "I don't know much about caves. I think it's limestone. Perhaps we can look it up on Wikipedia."

"It's okay. I really don't need to know." We sat next to each other using our headlamps to look around. There was something about the cool wetness of the place that fed our desert-weathered bodies. It was a refuge from the punishing sun. I could feel my skin soaking up moisture and my eyes relaxing in the dim light. And when we became more comfortable Leonardo and I turned off the headlamps so we were sitting in the dark listening to subtle sounds of dripping water. The cave felt vast enough to quell my fear, and also at the same time enclosed and protective.

We couldn't see anything, which prompted us to automatically move closer so our bodies were touching. It made me think about how blind people like to hang on to another person's arm. Without sight and sitting quietly, I had absolutely no sense of time. So I'm not sure how long we had been there when I felt prompted to say something.

I don't know why I wanted to talk about my childhood. But this is what I said. "When I was a kid growing up in Fort Worth, Texas, I felt like I was a visitor in that place. My mom and dad were from Colorado and my dad got a job in Texas so that is why we were living there. But everyone else we knew except my closest friend Granger had been born in Texas. He became like a brother after my own brother died, and his mother became my mom when mine passed away. We weren't like the other people in our neighborhood who were born in Texas. We were transplants. We didn't look or act like them."

I could sense Leonardo listening so I continued. "My grandmother used to make me go to church with her on Sundays. And I never understood anything the preacher was talking about. As a child, I thought one day when I grew up I would understand what was being said, and I would know what the Bible

248

meant. I assumed that when I became an adult and could understand, then I would be led to my salvation. I didn't even know what salvation meant. But I thought it must have been something super important because everyone talked about it like it was the most critical thing to attain. The truth was, the older I got the more confusing the Bible became, and while the preacher talked I daydreamed. When I was in bible classes I was told that I asked too many questions. I was told I had to just believe. When I grew up I began to realize none of the adults had ever understood it either. Perhaps it wasn't understandable."

"When I asked questions they would stutter around and quote passages from the Bible, repeating paragraphs from stories they had heard. I realized they had memorized the verses and stories, and then pretended they knew something that everyone else in the whole world needed to know. It began to become apparent that each person worried that somebody might find out that they didn't really know what they were talking about. So they pretended more and more that they did, until they actually believed it. It was like they memorized the words and became actors in a play with costumes and settings that backed up their convictions. I began to see the whole thing as a really silly play. But then at times, I would become terrified and not be able to sleep at night because I feared I might die and go to hell."

I could feel Leonardo's body tensing. I thought I should stop talking but I couldn't. I went on. "When my mom died and my grandmother went back to Colorado, I stopped going to church and didn't think much about it until I was in college and took a comparative religion class. Then I began to give religion a lot of thought. There was something about studying the different kinds of religions of the world that gave me distance from all of them.

"Looking back at my own religious experience I began to see there was a split. People who went to church and believed everything they were told were labeled good people. And the ones who hung out in bars or honkytonks – as they were called back then – were bad people. But actually they were flip sides of the same coin. They were one thing that had two sides. I began to wonder if they could ever be separated. What would happen if you could get rid of one? Would the other disappear?"

Leonardo's body shifted slightly. "Are you okay with me talking about this?" I asked.

"Yes, please go on. Growing up Catholic, I definitely relate to your confusion," he said.

I took a deep breath as if I were preparing to walk up a big hill.

"Granger and I didn't fit into either one of those categories. We ended up making art our God and that quickly became our salvation. Finally I knew the meaning of that word. For Granger and me salvation was some kind of a basket that we landed in that kept us safe from all the bad stuff in the world. Or maybe Granger had always been in that basket and he and his family made a place for me.

"I was two years older than him, so I went to college before he did. As I surrounded myself with other students like me I forgot about my days of confusion. I became absorbed in painting and stopped thinking about religion. In the art department, nobody worried about going to heaven when we died. We were already in heaven tending to our crafts."

Leonardo turned his body so he was facing me. Our knees were touching. "I'm sorry. I don't know why I said all that," I told him, as I reached out and put my hand on his knee. There again was that strong need to touch in the dark. He put his hand over mine. I suddenly felt merged with this other human being and it wasn't at all scary or unpleasant.

"It's okay. This is a very sacred place. Every time I come here something happens. Your story moves me," he said.

I hoped he would say more and he did. "I was a good man. I went to parochial schools my whole life. I could have become a priest, but I fell in love and got married. I went to church with my wife. I dedicated my life to making the world a better place and when I failed I went to the bars. You are telling me that those two things are two sides of the same coin?"

"Yes, that's what I said, but I don't have an explanation of what that means exactly. It just feels true to me."

"You and your friend jumped out of that dichotomy probably because Granger's family gave you another way of perceiving the world. It's like the two of you found God inside yourself. And it had to do with your talents and how you express yourselves. This retreat you are on here in the desert is a long sabbatical for you to go deeper into the God of your understanding."

I could feel his body relax as he spoke.

"Your story helps me to see that I thought God betrayed me when I got fired. Because I was helping those high school students I must have thought I was priest-like and priests didn't fail. And they don't get fired. I thought God would protect me. After I was fired, I no longer wanted to go to church because I was mad at God and at the same time I felt shameful that I had failed Him. It was confusing."

"I went to the bars where I could find companionship with other failures like me. But I could not escape the wrath of God with alcohol. It would only numb my pain for a little while and then the pain would come back even worse. There is an old country song called *The Night the Bottle Let Me Down*. It's funny they used to play that song on the Juke boxes in the bars."

"Abril kept trying to make me go back to church with her, but I wouldn't because of my anger. But you've just shown me there is another way. There is a way to jump off of the coin. We don't have to be a part of a coin with two sides."

"I see now that it wasn't God that caused me to lose my job. It was some very ignorant people. I know now that I thought I understood my religion, but I didn't. I was only pretending that I did. This whole thing that happened to me was actually the real God forcing me to open my eyes and stop believing in lies. Knowing God is not the same as believing in God or following the rules of some religion."

"Your story helps me to see that Abril and I would never see eye to eye on this matter. She too believes that I had done something wrong and God was punishing me. She thought if I just said enough Hail Mary's I would get my job back. She didn't understand that I would never be hired to teach in Arizona again after the protests. I know that Abril will never accept me if I don't go to church. She is not in a place in her life where she would understand my leaving our religion. I think she was attracted to me in the first place because I was considering the priesthood. So when I left the church, she would have still left me, even if I had not become a drunk. Now she has found a devout man who loves her, and I need to understand that and be happy for her."

"Here in this desert, I too found my art God. I am nowhere near ready to go back and face the world, but I think I am taking my first step which is to realize that I am powerless over what happened. I didn't cause it. My anger at those crazy politicians has only made me suffer. And God doesn't care if I'm angry or not. He, or It, remains constant like the sun. I can let go of being angry now because the governor will never in her lifetime understand where she failed the children. Brown children will never matter to our conservative government in Arizona. I can't make them see the error of their ways. But I don't need to let them stand in my way of doing good work."

He stopped talking and for a while we listened to water dripping from the ceiling. Every now and then a drop landed on my head and I could feel it running down through my hair. The drops were like cool tears from the earth.

Then he said, "Looking back, I could have taken any job that came my way. Then I would have been able to help Angela and her little brother and I could have kept my wife and child. But God had another plan for me and for them. All of that story is in my past now. Some lessons are harsh, but we can only learn if we are willing to accept our failures and move on to the next and hopefully better thing."

I was touched to hear Leonardo speak his mind. I had no idea why I told him my story. Maybe it was the magic of the cave that made us both open up to each other the way we did on that day. But I will never forget the lightness that came upon both of us sitting there in pitch darkness.

"Thank you," I told him. We both moved so we could hug. We held each other for long time. We were savoring human touch. A thing we had both been missing.

"Thank you, Laurence," he whispered quietly into my ear.

We sat there side by side for a long time, then we lay back on the rocks and fell asleep. When I woke up and opened my eyes I couldn't tell if they were open, it was so dark. But I was smelling the food in my pack and wanted to eat. I felt him move beside me. We turned on our headlamps, and started to laugh and joke around as we fumbled for our sandwiches in our bags. We ate and talked. Leonardo told funny stories about his students. And I told him all about the plays that Apollo wrote for Granger and I to be performed for the Suns. I told him about Granger and George, Manuel and my job teaching art at the University.

When we exited the cave our eyes were shocked by the light. The sun was preparing to slide into the Pacific Ocean, and I thought we needed to hustle before it got too dark.

But he said to me, "No need to hurry, I know the way." And I knew he did.

We hurried only because he had hungry chickens and I was sure Alias was waiting for me. When my house came into view my friend said good night and disappeared into the night.

Having slept during the day I stayed up late. There were new feelings of peacefulness that came over me. It was like an old war that had been raging inside had come to an end. It was time to sweep up the dead soldiers from the battle field and plant flowers. The field I imagined was empty and fertile. As I sat on the sofa and absentmindedly made drawings in my sketchbook I noticed I was designing gardens.

42: Missing a Moon

I began painting desert gardens with rocks, cactus, vines and shrubs. By adding furniture and other household things to the image, I married the outdoors with the indoors. Sometimes portals would appear that would take the viewer into different realities as though they could travel from one room to another and not be able to tell if they were indoors or outdoors. I tried to think of an image that would describe my experience with Leonardo in the cave, but all I could come up with were cliffs with cracks that led into darkness.

The thing about magical realism is that magic is always in motion, not easy to capture in a still painting. It doesn't move across a plain like a car or a train. It moves between worlds. It permeates dreams and thins the walls between being asleep and being awake. One becomes aware that there is no separation. Everything is molecular and dancing around, even the heaviest rocks and the lightest of air.

Leonardo and I moved around each other like we were performing a fine ballet. We were never in each other's way because it felt as though we could move through one another if need be. We enhanced each other's lives. He came and he went like a breeze. Sometimes I walked with him to his place and made sketches of his cabin, and the things he had outside including his chickens and goats. When it was cold I went inside and made drawings of his tiny space with all it's magical creations. Sometimes I helped him by sewing handmade beads onto his bags and moccasins. I loved that he stored his supplies in baskets woven out of strips of leather thongs and interesting natural strings and threads. He even decorated them with dried berries. He had extra sharp needles for sewing leather and an assortment of tools his brother had provided.

One day, while I was sewing berries onto a handbag, I casually asked him about *The Big Book*. He wasn't inclined to talk about it.

He reached under his narrow bed and retrieved it. "I'll read something," he said.

"Step one: We admitted we were powerless over alcohol – that our lives had become unmanageable. Step two: Came to believe that a power greater than ourselves could restore us to sanity. Step three: Made a decision to turn our will and our lives over to the care of God as we understood God."

He stopped there and said to me. "When I first read those steps I was incensed. Here I was in this cabin with nothing but a bed, a table and a dresser. I was so sick I could barely move and I still could not admit I was powerless. I had a lot of fight in me. How could God want me to give up my power?"

Even though my parents had college educations, and were school teachers, I grew up in a Mexican neighborhood where showing any weakness could get you killed. But here in this cabin nobody was around to kill me. So who was I fighting with? I felt so bad – so broken the only thing I could do was to lie here, read this book and fight with God about who was in charge."

"You are a brave man," I said. "And it must have been very hard for your brother to leave you here."

"Alberto was so mad at me he probably put me here to keep himself from killing me. Fortunately, he made sure I had food and supplies. At first I hated him for what he had done to me, but now I know he saved my life.

"For the whole first year the only thing I did was bitch and complain. I blamed everybody under the sun. It took that whole year for me to even begin to get what this book was telling me. One day I got so mad at it I threw it into the wood stove. Fortunately I was so crazy and out of control I forgot to start the fire. I found that book sitting there on top of the wood the next day unharmed and, like it was staring me in the face, daring me to pick it up again."

As he talked he was also focused on attaching a shoulder strap to a lady's hand bag. I marveled at how elegant it was even though every piece of it came straight from nature – no plastic or processed metal parts.

I didn't interrupt him and he went on with his story.

"It began to make sense to me a small piece at a time," he said. "Then Hernandes showed up. He said he had been here watching me for a long time. At first I thought he was a real person. Well, I mean, he is a real person, but I thought he was here in his body. I wondered where on earth he had come from. But he asked me what price would I pay to feel serene. That word serene was not a part of my vocabulary. Somehow the way he said it caught my attention. Before then I didn't think I could just choose to work towards something like serenity. At first I made fun of the idea."

"Wow, you are the most serene person I've ever met!" I told him.

"Well, you know, I wasn't even aware of how much I had changed until I met you. You're helping me to see my new self," he said suddenly flashing a huge toothy smile. He was always so serious it made me laugh.

"You know, I'm glad you said that because I guess that's true for me too. What do you think? Do you think we will both be able to handle the real world better when we get back to it?"

"I don't know and I don't feel ready to try."

"I don't either."

We finished the day's work without any more talk. It was a day of serenity.

The next day Leonardo helped me roll my canvases and pack them into tubes and send them up the chute. Then we worked together outside in the garden hoping to get a glimpse of the drone. We heard its giant bee sound long before we saw it. It had no trouble picking up the tube and flying off with it. A few minutes later another drone arrived and dropped off a container holding supplies.

I was mildly interested in the process, but Leonardo was totally engrossed in what was happening. I found myself again thinking it was because he was a man. I would have been more interested in how his shirt was constructed than how the drones worked. I'm glad many of the lines drawn between men and women have blurred over the years, but there is something alluring about what seems to remain different. Leonardo and I were two different types of engineers.

We wove in and out of each other's lives like that throughout the fall and winter. You probably think we would have become lovers, but neither of us were drawn to that. I was sure he had only two females on his mind and those were his ex-wife and his daughter. No matter what had come between them I knew I was observing a man with intent. He wanted to win them back and I supported his choice. As for me, feeding off of Leonardo's love for his family, I found myself thinking more and more of Manuel.

In all my memories of being on the desert these were the best. There were never any thoughts of going home because everything here became home. It was as though the past had mostly faded away.

Winter passed and spring was bringing warm days and one morning when I was home alone having tea at my table, staring at out of the window at the huge sky, Alice appeared again.

"You are so beautiful," she said.

"Really?"

"Yes, you have become the desert."

"I'm not sure how I look, but you are describing how I feel."

She was wearing a cactus colored dress with small brown finches printed on it. Silver bird earrings hung from her ears and feather's dangled from her hair. It was another one of her camouflage outfits.

"It's been a long time, Alice." That is what I said, but I really wanted to know where she had been.

"Oh, I've been around. You've just not seen me, but I will never leave you. We don't always have to meet like this. Did you notice that you never missed me? The reason is because I never really left."

"Hmmm. You are right. Somehow I always feel you are around."

"It's amazing how much work you have done. Your garden is lovely and your paintings sing."

"Thank you. It doesn't seem like work to me. I've never had so much fun. It's been nice having a neighbor too.

"I'm sure it's helped you with your loneliness," she said.

"Yes, I didn't realize it was a problem until it wasn't. Did you know he was here all along?"

"Yes, I have a friend who visits him."

"Hernandes?"

"Yes."

"Where is Romero?"

"He's around somewhere. He told me to tell you that you will be needing him for a project down the road. But you are doing fine without his help for now. He said to remind you of The Castle School.

I laughed. "Queen Ellie, and The Castle School. How could I forget?"

She suddenly seemed distracted and said, "There is somewhere else I need to be, now. But you must know that I will always be in your dreams."

"Of course. Thank you for coming again!" I didn't want her to go. It felt like there was something final about her visit. When she disappeared there was a brown feather floating in the air. Alias jumped into her chair and batted it around.

I went back to my canvas and painted, but found that I was struggling to stay awake. It was true I had stayed up late the night before working. It was one of those rare times when I actually felt too tired to paint, so I cleaned up and went to the blue sofa for a nap. Alias joined me, of course.

I could easily recognize Alice in my dream. She was still dressed in the cactus colored dress.

"I thought you would find me here," she said. "That's why I wore this dress when I visited you today. I know we met in a dream once before on the desert, but that was accidental."

"So you planned this?" Our voices sounded like we were in a huge empty room.

"Sort of, but I wasn't sure it would work. It's hard to pull you away from your work. I thought we could meet here in this cathedral."

I looked around and saw that we were inside a huge building, but the walls had been painted in life size desert scenes making it seem like we could see through the walls. The sky was painted halfway up the walls and on the ceiling. The ultramarine blue with colossal thunderheads above with warm browns and greens of desert scenes lower down the walls made it appear as though we were actually standing out in the desert, not indoors.

"You are gifted to be able to see this."

"I can see it. But I can't imagine how I could paint it."

"You will figure it out."

"I think I would have to buy a cathedral and paint it like this."

"I hope that someday you will get that opportunity."

"For now, I could make some sketches."

"Yes, that is a good idea."

"But why are we here?"

"To show you that we can meet like this."

"Where exactly is this place?"

"In your imagination."

"So we aren't really meeting some place, like when you come to my house?"

"No, this place is in your subconscious mind."

"My mind?"

"Yes, it is easy to access your subconscious mind just by relaxing and turning inward. Self-hypnosis, if you will. People do it all the time, but not many recognize they are doing it. In other words, they just don't call it that. They may call it daydreaming or spacing out or in. Mind wandering, etc."

"But, I'm asleep."

"Yes, but you just let both of us know that you are aware that you are asleep. Right now you are aware in your dream state."

"Can I be aware in my sleep all the time or is this a special occasion?"

"Good question. Maybe some people can do that, but I find it only happens with me occasionally when I don't try to make it happen. It's just a random event."

I suddenly woke up and it was an hour later and I could remember the dream. But it made me question how many times something like that happens and I don't remember it. It must be often because I know I have more dreams than I could possibly ever remember.

Interesting, I thought, as I sat up on the sofa looking around the room. I

257

was glad it was clean and tidy. It made me think of how grateful I was to have Leonardo in my life. I guess having another person around helps me keep myself more together. I let the beauty of the place sink in. I loved the tall windows and the endless view of the desert, the mountains and vast sky. The temperature inside was always perfect. Rainbows danced on the walls helping to make the energy of the place seem serene.

I thought of the time I was brought here in a van having been given a drug to keep me still. That was the first time I had experienced the feeling of everything in the Universe being energy. It seems like I often forget that, but somehow, sooner or later I remember.

That night when Alias and I were lying on the roof of the shed I noticed the sky was missing the moon. Stars were so close together I could hardly see solid black. Airplanes and satellites sailed by at different speeds. This time I didn't feel like yelling for someone to see me, and I was glad I wasn't flying somewhere. Knowing a frantic world out there couldn't touch me, I felt a stillness I'd never known before, and without a doubt I knew I was smaller than a molecule.

43: The Note

Absorbed in my work, I lost track of time, but after a few days I began to miss Leonardo. He hadn't been around in over a week. It was the longest he'd stayed away. I told myself that he was busy and I shouldn't worry, so I let a few more days pass before I headed out to his cabin.

I loved that time of year in the spring between the cold of winter and the scorching hot of summer. We'd had a gentle female rain the day before and everything felt fresh and looked green. The desert smelled like a huge flower garden. Out of the corner of my eye I saw a roadrunner trotting along side the trail. I was surprised both by how close it was to me and how big it was. I'd only seen a few from my window and in the distance I had not properly registered the size of it.

I looked forward to seeing my friend again and I hummed a song I'd heard on my iPod as I walked to his cabin. I couldn't remember the name of it – the song. Something about walking on the sunny side. I had tried to fix my hair by tying on a few feathers and some of Leonardo's beads. I wore the grey dress I'd had on when I was captured and my pair of gorgeous moccasins he had made for me. The dress, even though I hadn't worn it, looked like it too had merged with the desert.

When I came upon his cabin and didn't hear chickens, I stopped, listened, then approached the building at a slower pace. I could tell the animals were gone. I could feel my heart pounding in my chest. Breathing heavily, I hid behind a tree and watched the cabin for signs of life hoping someone hadn't come by, robbed him and left him hurt. I didn't want to rush in and get myself in trouble too, so I stood long enough to feel sure that nobody was around. Then I walked slowly to the door noticing there had been a lot of foot traffic in the sand. I pushed it open and softly called out his name.

Everything was gone except the rickety furniture. I could still smell animal skins, but none of his bags or moccasins were hanging on the wall. His work table was swept clean. I opened the drawers of his tiny dresser – nothing. No pots, pans or food products. Even the painting I had given him was no longer on the wall. Everything was gone except a note on the table held in place by a heart shaped rock.

With a shaking hand I picked up the note and took it out into the bright light of day, sat down on a bench by the front door and read.

My dear friend Laurence,
I apologize for leaving like this. My brother came to get me. He brought a u-haul with cages for the chickens and goats.
Sophia has pneumonia and is in the hospital. Abril contacted Alberto and sent him to get me. My daughter has been crying and asking for me, saying she wants to die if I don't come. They all thought she would recover faster if I came.
I didn't have time to go to your house to say good-bye. And I don't have time now to write a proper note to you either, or to tell you how much I appreciate our friendship.
I don't know if I will be able to come back or if I could ever find the place again. So I'm leaving you Alberto's phone number for when you get out. I know you will.

Call me: 520-202-0007,
Leonardo

This was not something I expected, but it made sense. I began to cry not only because I was sad he'd gone, but because I was happy he would be united with his daughter. I imagined him seeing her for the first time in four years. She would now be eight years old. I closed my eyes and visualized him healed and ready to be the father he was meant to be.

I looked at the note again. Interesting, the phone number ended in 0007, the same as the combination lock on my gate. I shook that information off as though it weren't important – a coincidence.

I had a light step walking home thinking of their reunion. My dad and I had been close. So I'd always felt some discomfort about Leonardo's separation from his daughter. I'd accepted it knowing he was taking this time to get well. Along the way I smiled at my saguaro friends. Suddenly I had a strong feeling that I was finally healing from the loss of my mom, knowing that one little girl's dreams were coming true.

Back at my place I sat on my sofa petting Alias. It was then the loss of my friend really began to hit me. I was alone again somewhere in the Sonoran desert. I told myself that I would feel sad for a few days, but then I'd be back cheerfully creating more paintings.

I wrote to Max:

Laurence: *Hi Max*
Max: *Hi Laurence*
L: *Sorry I haven't been writing much. I've been busy.*
M: *I know. These last paintings you've done are miraculous.*
L: *Thanks*
M: *Are you tired?*
L: *Yes*

I wanted badly to talk to him about Leonardo, but at that point words would not have helped how I was feeling.

M: *Maybe you should take a little break.*
L: *What would I do?*
M: *Nothing. Binge watch or read, or lay in your hammock and take long naps.*
L: *Maybe I will.*
M: *All artists need to take breaks from their work. That's how they come up with new ideas.*
L: *Okay, I'll take your advice. Over and out.*
M: *Good night, Laurence.*

Exhausted, I went to bed early. Leonardo walked through my dreams as if he had never left. I kept trying to grab hold of him, but when I reached out, my hands and arms just went through him. I repeatedly tried to call his brother, but I couldn't get the numbers right – which is what happens in dreams. I woke up in the morning as tired as I'd been when I went to bed.

I took a long shower trying to wake myself up, but it didn't work. I fell into the hammock and stayed there most of the day, and at sundown I went in, laid on the sofa and binged-watched a Netflix TV series. I woke up on the sofa in the middle of the night, got up and went to bed.

The next day I only felt a little better. I managed to do some laundry, make some food, and putter around in the garden. I didn't feel like going near my easel. I spent most of my time in the hammock and on the sofa with Alias who seemed to like the attention I now had time to give.

What was wrong with me?

44: The First Man

Pleasant days of spring dwindled, as the baking summer sun rose high in the sky to batter the desert once again. I went through each day tending the garden, reading, watching Netflix, and only making quick studies of desert plants and landscapes. Before Leonardo came into my life, I was used to being alone. But now I struggled with something I had never known before, the feeling of loneliness. There is a difference, you know, between loneliness and aloneness.

I was grateful for Alias. Alice and Romero only came occasionally and mostly in my own dreams now. I was totally out of the habit of conversing with Max who seemed to think I was buried in my work. At least I hope he did. Leonardo had been a real live person. And I was having a very hard time coming to terms with his absence. It was amazing how long it took me to actually accept that he was truly gone. At first I thought he would come back to get me. But I eventually gave up hope.

In spite of my resistance, I had to make myself get serious about painting again. From my roll of canvas I cut a piece 6 feet high and five feet wide. Grabbing my largest brushes I began to block in large shapes without first making plans or sketches. I painted from memory, working with burnt sienna, black, Indian red and yellow ochre. Using the flat black gesso, I painted the shape of the crack in the cliff that led to the cave. I didn't want a shiny surface.

I had taken photos of the rocks that surrounded the crack. But I was too impatient to find them, and I didn't want the photos to influence the composition. It didn't have to be a representation of the actual place. Also, I wanted this painting to be somewhat abstract – veering from my usual magical realism.

In the cabinets there were jars of acrylic products that I had found no use for until now – perfect for rock textures. Acrylic products have a shelf-life so I was surprised they still worked. I used a huge pallet knife and a spatula from the kitchen to apply textures layer by layer. I knew the drone would not be able to transport this heavy piece of art, but that didn't stop me. By now I had several large pieces that were rolled up and leaning in a corner. However this one could never be rolled, so I wasn't sure what I would do with it.

Although I wasn't feeling the level of creative joy I'd experienced before it felt right to be lost in the process of making a large painting. There was anger in the movements of my body and it showed in the work.

The texture took weeks to dry, so I kept busy working on smaller pieces in between. Rock-hard, angular and sharp edges began to appear in all my work, and I was encouraged to pull out some cadmium red and alizarin crimson which I spattered here and there to suggest blood on rocks. These were painful days.

Once again, I began to lose track of time. I worked late into the night and often slept in the day. Because of the heat I stopped going for walks on my trails; I ate, but I didn't have meals. I snatched raw food from the garden or grabbed something from the fridge and stuffed it in my mouth, only because I needed to refuel and continue working. I threw food in Alias' bowl, but showed him little attention. I began to spend less time chatting with Max. Months passed and when summer ended and a fall wind blew things around in the garden, I didn't attempt to tidy up.

One day the big painting was done. It was the longest time I'd ever spent on one painting, and I was relieved to realize I was satisfied with the results. There was a figure in the dark crevice between the rocks; Leonardo, naked, dirty, hairy and carrying a bow, like the first time I had seen him. This image of him reminded me of how disturbed I was when I first discovered the footprints he'd left in the sand. Then realized he was not a phantom, but a real human. This was a painting of the first man, and he appeared transparent and mystical. He had come and gone as easily as the dreamers.

The process of creating this painting made me realize how changes, even good ones, were hard for me. Before Leonardo came I thought I'd become used to my solitude, having only phantoms and a cat for friends. I had been prepared to live that way forever. Then there was one human being in my life and that had been a huge adjustment. But looking back on it now, I knew that before he came, I'd been growing restless with the way things were. I'd been reminiscing about Granger, George and even more about Manuel – the men in my life. Sometimes I thought of Apollo and Ana Sun. I had been secretly longing to go home. Funny how you can keep secrets from yourself, then have them leap out at you like a stalking cat.

Leonardo had been my perfect companion, never interrupting my workflow, teaching me things, sharing and trading. He had taken the place of my best friend, Granger, yet he was different. He wasn't gay and at the same time he never tried to have a romantic relationship with me. I think we both understood the dangers of that. Alone out here, surviving, we couldn't risk it. There were times when I felt attracted to him and I thought he might feel the same about me. But neither of us moved to act on it.

I began to think of Manuel which stirred intense feelings in my body and that drove me headlong into a powerful desire to go back to Phoenix. But not back to the life I had had before. I wanted something different. It was the first time in the three years since I came to live in the desert that I felt certain I wanted to return home. The ambivalence had vanished, but I had no idea how to go about leaving. When Leonardo was here, there had been a slim chance I could have made it out when his brother dropped off supplies, but I had never even bothered to ask about it. I had felt settled here, I had a friend and I had my work. Now my work wasn't enough. I missed Leonardo. I missed people and, I had to admit, I needed them.

Occasionally I felt stupid for not trying to send a message out with Leonardo's bags and moccasins. He mentioned something like that to me when we first met, but I guess I thought I had plenty of time. It never occurred to me that Leonardo would vanish in the night. I knew he would leave someday to go back to his family, but I thought he would offer to take me with him or he would tell someone where I was. There was still a chance he might be able to send someone or come back himself. But I was quickly losing hope. The big painting of him had taken almost six months to finish and at the same time I must have completed at least 12 smaller ones that were picked up by the drones.

When Leonardo had been around, I made sure I made contact with Max everyday, sometimes more than once. I didn't want him to turn on the cameras and find out they were covered. I removed the coverings when I decided to limit communication. I still wasn't sure if Max knew about my friend, nor was I sure that Leonardo wasn't one of *The Powers That Be*. The thought that they might kill me when they were done with me still crossed my mind from time to time.

I decided it was time to reach out more often.

Laurence: *Max, sorry I haven't been very responsive.*

Max: *It's okay, I turned on the cameras to see if you were okay. Are you okay?*

L: *Then you know I've finished that very large piece. How are you going to get it? I think the architect of this studio failed to provide enough wall space to store large paintings.*

M: *Don't worry about that. I know you will keep it safe from the elements.*

You can hang it out on the patio under the eaves. Cover it with plastic and canvas.

L: *Not a problem. I have lots of plastic and canvas.*

M: *It will give us time to think of a way to retrieve it.*

L: *Max, I think I miss my home.*

M: *You mean Phoenix?*

L: *Yes.*

M: *Tell me about that.*

L: *I don't know. Something just came over me and I can't think of anything else.*

M: *Why don't you give it a few days and let me know how you feel then.*

L: *Max, are you going to kill me when you are done with me?*

M: *Is that what you think?*

L: *Not really. Well, not all the time.*

M: *Nobody is going to kill you, Laurence. We love you! Why would we want to do that?*

L: *Why would you want to bring me here in the first place?*

M: *It won't be long now before you have most of your questions answered.*

L: *I hope you are not just saying that to get my hopes up, Max.*

M: *No, I'm not.*

L: *Thanks, I'll make contact again later.*

I studied the big painting for a while and assured myself that it was finished, so I grabbed the throw off of the sofa and collapsed in the hammock outside. The light breeze felt cool and refreshing. I thought about the fact that it was soon going to be November again making it exactly three years since I'd been brought here against my will. I fell asleep with the gentle rocking of the hammock and Alias purring beside me. I was dreaming of the painting and sitting in the cave with Leonardo, talking quietly in the dark. Then I wasn't sure if I was awake or not, but I heard a familiar voice that was not Leonardo's, but Romero's. I'm not sure if I opened my eyes, but somehow I was looking into his handsome face and comforting brown eyes. A sense of peacefulness came over me.

"My beautiful friend, Laurence," he said.

"Romero, where have you been?"

"You were painting and you were in a very dark mood. I thought it was best to let you work through whatever you needed to."

"You were right. I didn't miss you that much. I was living in a deep cave."

"Nothing wrong with that. I think when we have a strong connection with someone whether we are seeing them or not doesn't mean we are completely absent from one another. We are always in each other's dreams. Is that not so?"

"Maybe you are right. Now that I hear your voice, I'm thinking I missed you, but when you weren't here, I didn't think much about it. Maybe I will be able to do that with Leonardo. Romero, will I ever get to visit the place below the mountains where I can see you and Alice in real life?"

"I don't know. I suppose it is a possibility. You know there is a train that goes through there."

"I've heard that, Romero, but I don't know the name of the place."

"The name of the place doesn't matter," he said.

"Then how would I know what train to get on?"

"Don't worry. If you are to visit, someone will show you the way when the time is right."

A feeling of despair came over me when he said that. I couldn't imagine trying to get somewhere without first knowing the name of the place, and the way to get there. My mind was working over that quandary. I thought if he didn't tell me what I needed to know right now, he would disappear and I would never see him again. I wouldn't know how to find him. And yet at the same time I somehow knew I would.

All of the feelings about not missing him and the joy of knowing him suddenly made me vacillate between being uncomfortable and perfectly peaceful. I tried to reach out and grab him, so I could steady myself, but all the conflicting emotions and thoughts sent me whirling into a trance-like state, and I was suddenly transported back to the cave where I fell deeply asleep.

I woke in the night shivering from the cold. Both Romero and Alias were gone. Inside I found my cat in bed waiting for me. I wanted so badly to grab him and hug him tightly like a stuffed animal, but I knew he would hate that and jump off the bed and leave me alone. So I scratched under his chin and stroked his sleek body until I fell asleep and slept until morning.

Alice joined me for breakfast. For some reason I had not expected her. She sipped her tea from the dainty floral tea cup and smiled at me as though she were as happy to see me as I was to see her. I felt embarrassed by how messy the studio had become.

But I said to her, "I'm so glad you are here. I'm in need of a good therapist today."

"He was a good friend," she said looking at the giant painting I'd finally named *The First Man.*

"Yes, he was and I hope he comes back soon."

"I'm sure you do."

"He's not coming back, is he?"

"I don't know, Laurence. Because I appear to you to be magical doesn't make me capable of predicting what other people will do. I don't really know Leonardo or the circumstances of his life."

"Can you help me feel better about all this?"

"All this?" she asked.

"My life here in this house in the desert and him."

"Well, let me see. How about you remember something Leonardo told you."

I looked at the painting of him as if I could ask him to remind me, but it was just a painting. Then I remembered. "He taught me the Serenity Prayer."

"And that is?"

"God, grant me the serenity to accept the things I cannot change, courage to change the things I can, and the wisdom to know the difference."

"That sounds like a key to a door that would lead to a peaceful life," she said.

"What do you mean?" I asked.

"Let's take the first part. God grant me the serenity to accept the things I cannot change. That's almost like a Zen Buddhist statement. They might say it differently, like don't argue with the inevitable or accept everything as it is."

"That would be very hard to achieve," I said.

"It's not something one achieves. It is something one allows. But I'm not sure asking God for serenity is the right thing to do. I think we ask God for too many things. If we are going to ask God for anything it might be better to ask for the ability to accept everything as it is. Because when we don't accept things as they are we create more suffering. Serenity is something we might feel if we were to surrender to what is. I say might feel because being serene might not be what we are truly feeling. It's good to be calm and serene most of the time, but I don't think it is humanly possible to be serene in every instance. It would be dishonest.

Striving for serenity is just another way to avoid being with what is. If we feel angry, lonely, sad or whatever we would be better off being with the feelings until they passed. Serenity passes too, but we think we have to hold on to it and push away all other emotions, but all feelings slip away no matter how hard we try to hold on.

"I see," I said sadly. "I think I've been arguing with reality. I mean, I understand that he needed to leave. I was actually relieved that he went to be with his daughter. But I've been angry about having been left here alone. I know there is nothing I can do about his departure, but I keep hoping he will return. Then I feel disappointed each day when he doesn't show up."

Again she looked over my shoulder at the painting and said, "Hope is not always a good friend. There are times when giving up hope is the solution to ending suffering. Also, you don't need to fight with the feelings you are having. Of course, you are angry and sad. That is another part of what is. I think you have hit a bump in the road and you need to allow it to be there for now. You need to accept that he is gone and you also need to accept that you are not happy and you are not serene. You don't seem happy with much of anything in your life right now and you think you should be. Maybe you are happy with the success of that painting and you love your cat, but there are a lot of things going on that you keep trying to ignore. Can you accept that?

"What am I ignoring?

"There is the hidden emotion of anger. He left you. He didn't come back or send someone to get you. You are angry you didn't try to make contact with someone before he left too."

She sat her tea cup down on the table and began petting Bonita, who suddenly appeared in her lap. I had not seen her in a while and I remembered how the little dog always made me smile. She was looking at me as usual like she was agreeing with everything Alice said. That day I didn't smile. I started sobbing uncontrollably.

Alice could not touch me, because she really wasn't there in a body, but somehow I felt embraced. I cried so long I thought she would be gone when I managed to calm down. I grabbed a napkin on the table to wipe my eyes and nose.

"Well," she said, "that dam broke."

I wanted to say I was sorry, but realized I would be apologizing for the thing she was trying to get me to do.

"How do you always manage to do this to me?" I said that knowing she would understand that I was truly grateful for her skills.

Then she said, "The rest of the prayer is 'courage to change the things you can and the wisdom to know the difference.' You can't get to courage and wisdom until you have accepted what you can and can't change. He is gone. He didn't take you and he hasn't come back and you can't change that. But I know you have courage to get on with your life, and in time wisdom will come. This prayer came from someone who trusted in something more powerful than themselves. Can you find that something?"

269

"I don't know. I think I was just riding along on Leonardo's faith. I don't think I've been ready to find my own Higher Power," I told her. I said Higher Power like the words didn't quite fit me.

"Then, his leaving is a gift. Is it not?" she said.

Her words were not what I wanted hear. But I knew she was right. I took a deep breath and let it go. I could feel my shoulder muscles release. "Thanks," I said, still sniffling and wiping tears.

"You will be fine," she said as she started to fade. "Your Higher Power is the most obvious thing in your life. But the tricky part of understanding that is also learning that there isn't even a you who has a Higher Power." I could hear her devious laughter as she and the dog slowly vanished. I shook my head knowing that last statement was much too advanced for me.

When she was gone, I turned and looked at my painting and I was stunned at how good it was. Did I do that? I asked myself, or was it the hand of God working through me? I had a vivid sensation that God was everything. Its voice and energy flowed through me and made the art I called mine. I knew I could never totally understand the nature of God. But I was sure that God was an okay word for me to use for Higher Power.

What I did know, was by handing everything over to God I would be letting go of the illusion that I could, in any way, be in control. Painting here alone in this studio had taught me that even the hand that held the brush was not my own.

Leonardo had emphasized that one had to find the God of their understanding. For me that God was The Ineffable. What I think he was telling me was that all I needed to do is trust in something I could not explain. Just as the thought rose up in my mind I had a feeling that everything was happening all at once – that universal time was simultaneous. And now Alice tells me that there isn't even a "me" at all. That would mean there is only this oneness. I suddenly felt elated and I wanted to hang on to that feeling. But I realized there was no way I could do that. Because there wasn't an "I" to do it.

I sat quietly for a while, but then my mind started up again. I remembered that the reason Granger and I kept reading Valdez's books over and over again was because we had a hard time recalling what we had just read. His words changed us, but I could never put my finger on exactly how we had been evolving. We became different from my school mates. Granger didn't go to school, but I know if he had, the two of us would have been isolated from the others. Because he wasn't with me at school I was alone in a crowd and each day couldn't wait to get to the Sun's house where things felt normal for me – where the people around me understood the way I perceived the world.

I must have maintained that feeling of isolation long into my adulthood, making life more of a struggle at the university. If I've learned anything from Romero, Alice, and Leonardo, it is that there is no separation between me and others, no matter how they may be perceiving reality. Every human being sees the world in a different way and each person is on their own journey, but we are all a part of the same whole. We are all the same and different.

After clearing my emotions with Alice I felt light. I marveled at how my stuck feelings could make me feel like I weighed a ton. I began to go about my business as usual. I cleaned up the courtyard, turned the soil in the garden beds and covered them with some dried grasses that Leonardo had brought to me in bags. I also planted a few winter greens.

I tidied the studio, made a list of supplies I needed, cleaned the kitchen, and did laundry, taking note of clothing and food supplies that needed to be replaced. Even though winter was mild here on the desert, there were still things that I needed to do to make life more comfortable. I sent the lists to Max. He thanked me and said he would make sure I got everything.

Then I settled down to make sketches of my next series of paintings. I became engaged in art again. When I now thought of Leonardo, I visualized him united with his daughter, family and friends. I felt a sense of normalcy returning. I knew without a doubt that I was not supposed to have left with him. There was something else here for me to do.

45: New Light

While a lazy sun crossed the sky I sat outside of the patio in the clearing making quick sketches of moving plant shadows. I wasn't exactly waiting for the supplies I'd asked for, but I felt some concern since it was the first time it had taken so long for them to arrive. Max said not to worry. Everything was being handled and I had plenty of food. I thought maybe they had to do maintenance on the drones. So I went to my computer.

Laurence: *Max, Are the drones broken?*
Max: *We are gathering together the things you need.*
L: *It's so beautiful outside. I love fall. I think it is my favorite time of the year. I am remembering that it is close to the anniversary of my arrival here in the desert. I've forgotten so much about that event I sometimes feel like it never happened at all and that I've been here forever.*
M: *I'm glad you have made yourself comfortable and feel at home here. Do you feel like you have benefited from being here? If so how?*
L: *Wow! That is a big question Max. Let me see. Well, I would never have gotten this much art work done had I been so busy teaching. I never would have made this much contact with nature and for certain I would never have grown a garden. I probably would never have gotten a cat. That's a lot of nevers. And don't get me started about the dreaming and the dreamers.*

I still didn't mention Leonardo. It seemed like too big a subject to discuss with Max at this point. I was thinking that I might save that bit of information for another time. Or maybe I was still hoping that Leonardo would return to rescue me and I didn't want to give *The Powers That Be* the heads up.

M: *I'm happy to hear that your life in the desert has benefited you in many ways. I know you are an achiever and I'm glad you are having a chance to create the artwork you want to do without all those distractions you had in Phoenix. I am so proud of you.*

L: *I think about the school a lot. Being away from it gave me a chance to get more clear about teaching. You know, what works and what doesn't. I hope I have a chance to give it another try, however, I don't think the university setting is the place to do it. The teaching part was inspiring. It was all the other stuff that was thrown at me that kept me from exploring my own adventure into painting. How did they expect me to teach others to do something I hadn't quite developed myself? I was afraid to ask for a sabbatical since I was already on the edge of getting fired.*

M: *That was obviously not an inspiring situation.*

L: *I hate to think that I was so discouraged from not receiving more recognition from my employers. Maybe I just wanted to be more of a team player instead of working under a controlling hierarchy. It was so distressing having all those people above me trying to tell me how to teach art classes. Not any of these people had actually taken an art class or knew much of anything about it. None of them recognized the importance of art in the world. Nor were they in any way open to learning anything about it.*

M: *Maybe there are other schools that don't have that problem.*

L: *Probably. If I ever get out of here, that will be the first thing I do is check out other options.*

Max didn't answer.

L: *Max are you still there?*

Nothing

L: *Max?*

M: *Oh sorry, I got distracted.*

L: *You've never done that before.*

M: *As I've said before, I'm not perfect.*

L: *It's been three years since we first started communicating. You must get tired of it.*

M: *Laurence, you are my job. And it's a pretty easy job since you aren't demanding or mean or ever a bother. It's a pleasure working with you. We make a great team.*

L: *How much longer is this going on?*

M: *Okay I take back that, never a bother part. You never stop asking that. Do you really want to know?*

L: *I guess not. Thank you, Max, for everything. You are always here for me*

and you always say the right things, and you always send me what I need or want. Sometimes you make me laugh. I hope I get to meet you someday.
M: *Me too*
L: *Good night, Max.*

Later in the day, I started a small painting from the sketches. It was fun and I was feeling happy again. I finished it before bedtime and Alias and I snuggled in for a sound but dream-filled sleep. I don't remember the dreams, but when I woke up in the morning I felt like I'd been hanging out with Alice and Romero all night. I made a small breakfast of scrambled eggs and stir fried vegetables from the garden. Alias followed me to the table by the windows hoping for a nibble.

When I sat down, I noticed a different light in the room. There were the usual rainbows from the crystals, but there was also a bright white light glaring off the cabinet doors. I turned toward the windows to look for its source and was shocked to see a car parked beside the house. I could see its glimmering windshield and I froze in disbelief. I set my things down quietly and slipped outside to make sure the gate was securely locked. It was. When I came back in I closed the door and locked it. Then I grabbed my iPad and opaqued the front windows leaving only the top high ones opened. My heart was pounding and I was breathing hard, like I'd been running. I climbed on a chair and stared at the car from the top windows.

It flashed in my mind that maybe it was Leonardo who had come back or perhaps he had sent someone else. I saw no one inside the car. I thought they might be lurking around the property. Were they lost tourists, or criminals looking for a hide out? If it had been Leonardo or someone he had sent, they would have come straight to the gate.

I fired up the iMac and wrote to Max.

Laurence: *Max, there is a car in the clearing! Do you know about it?*

I waited ten minutes, and for the first time in three years Max did not answer. I thought the computer was down. First the drones, then the computer. What a scary time for things to break!

I made a protein drink thinking I would want to have more energy if I needed to run or fight. I sent another message to Max – no answer.

I tried to distract myself by squeezing some paint out on a pallet and starting another painting, but I was too shaky to do any work. Noon came and Max was still not answering. The car sat gleaming in the sun. Late afternoon, when I felt sure no one was out there, I cleared the windows so I could get a better look. It was a white SUV, something that could handle rough roads.

I tried contacting Max again.

L: *Max, are you there. What is happening? I'm starting to freak out!*

When I was convinced that no one was around, I ventured out to get a closer look at the car. I crept up to it slowly, checking the ground for footprints. There were none. It looked like someone had drug some branches around to cover their tracks. I walked down the road a short distance and saw the same scrapings, but I saw no footprints or tire tracks. It was like someone drove the car here, parked it, walked a ways dragging a branch, then vanished in thin air. I began to get the feeling they were gone.

Inside the car I saw a woman's purse lying on the driver's seat, which caused me to be concerned. Had a woman been chased here? Was she lost and wandering in the desert? But I would have seen footprints. There was also a stack of what looked like clothing. I opened the door and took out the purse, garments and a pair of shoes, and brought them into the house so I could examine them closer.

Inside the purse I found a wallet and a passport. It was my passport. Not my old one, but a new one. The wallet contained a driver's license, also with my name and photo on it. There was a car manual with a sticky note at the top that said, "This car is a hybrid so you must read this before driving it". It was signed, Max.

I could not believe what was happening. I went back out to the car and noticed that there was a pet carrier in the back seat with a note on it saying that there was a collar and leash inside of it. And it would be a good idea to put the leash on Alias in case I had to stop and let him out for a bit. I took all these things into the house and put them on the sofa. Both Alias and I investigated everything.

"Wow, Alias," I said. "Just like that, we can go?" He meowed as if in agreement. I picked up the manual and began reading. The car was called the Toyota Highlander Hybrid. It looked expensive. I had not driven in three years, but the car I had in Phoenix was a Prius, so I was familiar with hybrids. A handwritten note inside said the GPS was set to guide us out to the freeway close to Tubac. Wow. All this time I really didn't know if I was still in the US.

I leaned back onto the sofa fingering the new clothes and looking around the house that had been my home for the last three years. I wondered what I wanted to take with me. The huge painting of Leonardo covered some of the book shelves. Another large painting called *You are Invited* and a couple of other large ones, were still rolled up in the corner. The last painting I did sat on the easel. It was too wet to transport. Most of the books were the same ones I had in Phoenix. The only things I wanted were the bag and moccasins that Leonardo had given me, my journals and the iPad with photos of my paintings and some of the works on paper. I could also download all my desert photos onto it. I spent the rest of the day just hanging out in house and garden, taking pictures and making sure I didn't leave anything I might want to have.

I kept saying to Alias, "Can you believe it?" I was afraid if I waited until morning I might miss the opportunity to leave, but it was fast getting dark and I had a feeling the road might be a challenge even in the daytime. "We will leave in the morning," I announced with conviction to the cat. I could barely contain my anticipation.

I kept writing to Max and getting no response. So I pulled out a Valdez book and went to bed.. I opened the book to a passage that said: *The world is unfathomable. It has many facets. You can focus on the horrors or you can experience it's unimaginable beauty and magic.* That was all I needed to hear.

I lay there in the dark trying to sleep. Then gave up, put on warmer clothing and went out to the courtyard, climbed the ladder to the roof of the tool shed and lay there looking up at the stars. I would miss this when I got back to the city. I thought about Granger and how much I wanted to show all of this to him. Isn't that what a big sister is for?

I imagined owning this house and keeping it for a retreat. I thought about what it might be like being back in Phoenix and I vowed that I would work at George's cafe before I would go back to teaching at the university. I didn't know what I would do for money, but I didn't care right now. All I wanted was to see my family.

46: Rough Road

Early the next morning, I ate a hearty breakfast, tried again to contact Max, took a long shower and dressed in the skirt and top that I'd found in the car. I tried on the shoes, but they felt weird, so I put on my moccasins. I brushed my two-toned straggly hair and put on a little make-up. Then I washed it off because it was too light in color for my skin. I found the turquoise jewelry I had worn the day I was kidnapped, and put that on. I took the things out of the purse and put them into the rabbit skin bag and left the purse on the sofa.

When I managed to get the collar and leash on Alias he rolled around on the floor like a crazy thing. Then I had to wrestle him into the pet carrier. He immediately started screaming. "Oh boy, am I going to have to put up with you all the way home? It's okay, it's okay," I kept saying, trying to reassure him, but I felt like I was lying to him.

I collected some water, and made a couple of wraps, in case I needed to eat on my way out. I also grabbed Alias' bowls, and some food for him too.

I said my goodbyes to the house and garden and buckled the pet carrier into the passenger seat so Alias could see me and I could keep trying to sooth him. I looked at the studio where I had spent the last three years. I knew I would miss this place, out in the middle of nowhere. I found myself tearing up, and gave in to my feelings.

After a few minutes, I started the car, backed up, then headed out. I soon reached a fork in the road and remembered it from when I had walked out this far a year ago. The GPS said, "Turn left," so I did.

The dirt road was rough, but the SUV was handling it. It felt weird to be moving so fast and I could see the road stretched out in front of me for miles. As anxious as I was to get home I slowed the car down a bit so I could savor the beauty of the land I was leaving behind. The grey mountains in my rearview mirror began to look smaller and I thought for a second I wanted to turn around and go back. But then I remembered, no drones, no Max.

Everything seem way too easy until I reached an arroyo. The road seemed to completely disappear in front of me. I got out and looked over the edge to find an extremely rocky descent. I hadn't seen any tracks on the road coming in, but I assumed someone must have driven it in. I got back into car and started to move ever so slowly.

The arroyo was covered in rocks, some as small as gravel, others like boulders. I tried to pick a route where I wouldn't catch the bottom of the SUV on a rock, and be stuck. At one point, I heard a rock scraping the bottom so I stopped, got out again, and peered under the car. A large rock was right up against the bottom of where the engine was, and I knew that was not a good thing. I wondered if I should try backing up. Then I noticed there was a metal plate across the bottom and it already had a number of scrapes in it. Okay, this plate protects the engine, I thought, so I must be able to keep going.

I got back in and eased forward. The car screeched and stopped, the wheels slipping. Then we lurched forward with a jolt. I kept driving slowly, slower than I could ever remember going in a car. I had to concentrate so I could avoid getting caught on a rock again. I weaved along the dry creek bed. And finally, the road – if you could call it that – went up the other side of the arroyo. It was so steep I was worried about slipping backwards, but it turned out to not be a problem. Except for Alias screeching his heart out next to me. He really didn't like the sensation of being bounced around in his carrier.

I soon discovered there was a whole network of dirt roads in the desert. At every fork and turn off, I got out of the car and stacked rocks by the side of the road so I could find my way back if wanted to. I tried to make the rocks look inconspicuous so no one else could tell what they were. It was taking a lot of time to do this and I was feeling extremely impatient, but I didn't want to get lost and not know my way back.

The road was more than just rough. I kept coming to places where it was so rocky I was sure I would bottom out, but didn't. I was starting to feel terribly frightened that someone would be waiting on the road to catch me and take me back to the house or somewhere else. What if somebody was trying to rescue me and somebody else didn't want that to happen? What if Max had been arrested? I hated not knowing. I painstakingly drove slowly on that road for about three hours, with Alias complaining the whole way.

I was relieved to finally make it to a paved road. It was old and bumpy, but it was better than the rocky one. After another hour of driving we came to the top of a hill where I could see the Interstate, somewhere between Tubac and Nogales. I stopped and talked to Alias for a while, trying to explain our circumstances. Oh, how I wished he could understand. It was hard enough for me to fathom what was happening without having a freaked-out animal screaming in the car.

Having skimmed the car manual I knew which buttons to push to find the odometer. We had come a little over 21 miles. When I reached the highway, the traffic was whizzing by so fast I could only see streaks of color. That is when I noticed that I would have to turn right and head towards Mexico and find a place to turn back North. I sat there for a while sipping water and downing one of the wraps. Alias wasn't interested in food and water, but he did stop yelling for a while. I was gathering my courage for the plunge.

"Really?" I said to the whining cat. "You think you've got problems?" I pulled out onto the edge of the road and waited for a gap. It took longer than I expected, but when I saw an opportunity I took a deep breath, stepped on the gas pedal and joined the rush. Alias let out a long howl as we sped up.

About three miles up the highway there was an overpass and a way to turn around and head north. It was all coming back to me. I knew how to drive in traffic.

It seemed like it took much longer to drive the 52 miles to Manuel's house in Tucson than I would have thought. Or maybe I was just oriented to traveling no more than about 6 miles on my own two feet so I expected the car to go faster than it could. I asked Higher Power for patience. Now free, I wanted to be at my destination instantaneously.

I had no problem remembering the way. But I didn't know if he still lived there. When I saw his house my heart started leaping out of my chest and I began breathing as if I'd run a mile. I pulled up across the street and sat waiting. There were no cars in the driveway, and he used the garage for a studio space, so he always parked in the driveway. There was a sculpture in the yard that had been there the last time I was here. Did that mean he still lived here?

I took advantage of being parked to catch my breath, and calm myself. I let my head drop down onto the top of the steering wheel letting tears drop into my lap. I gave myself a time limit for how long I would wait before heading out to Phoenix. No longer than two hours, I thought. But I wasn't sure I could make myself sit there that long.

It must have been about forty-five minutes when he pulled up in his car, the same one he had before I left. Alias had fallen asleep so no one near could hear him if I opened the door. I wanted to jump out of the car and run to him, but just as my hand touched the handle a woman got out of the passenger side and the two of them went inside together. He looked happy. They were chatting playfully.

All day I'd been imagining that my friends and family were waiting for me as though they knew I was coming. Even though I'd wished for them to move on in their lives and let go of me, I'd been hoping for something different since this morning. I started the car and drove off without any feelings of disappointment. I no longer knew his life circumstances and I needed to prepare myself for changes in the people I once knew. If he was happy with someone else, then so be it. I just drove off heading for Phoenix. I was free and right now nothing else mattered. I felt astounded that all this time I'd actually been this close to home and yet so far away and isolated.

As I drove towards Phoenix, I thought about Manuel. I had replayed memories of the great times we had had together but I'd forgotten how we had drifted apart. There were days when thoughts of returning to him had kept me going, so I didn't let myself acknowledge that perhaps he had met someone else before I left. I knew now that my love for him had been pure fantasy. Even if it wasn't real, it had given me hope. Now I am free to start my life over again and who knows what that will be. All I could think about was seeing Granger and family.

Once I was in Phoenix the traffic thickened on I10. I'd never seen it quite so crowded. It took over an hour to reach the 52 and head north. It took another half hour to get to my neighborhood. Some things had changed – a new house here and there, an old one gone, but it essentially looked the same. I could hear my heart pounding over the low moaning of the cat. I wanted more than ever to drive up to my house, find the key under the rock where I left it, bring Alias inside and let him out to roam and make himself at home. I would lie down on my bed, take a long luxurious nap, then call Granger. But that house could now belong to strangers. There had been no house key inside the purse that I'd found in the car, and I wondered if calling it my house was accurate. I certainly had not been paying the mortgage for the past three years.

There were no cars in the driveway, but the garage doors were shut so I couldn't tell if someone was home. The yard was enchanting, just like I left it. I thought of my yard men, Carlos and Jesus. I gingerly walked up to the door and knocked lightly. No one came. Then I rang the doorbell. Nothing. My heart was close to popping out of my chest. I had chills. I stepped back and began to walk back to my car thinking I would drive to Scottsdale to see if George's coffee shop was still open. I was exhausted so the thought of driving away was disheartening.

Just as I touched the handle of the car door I heard the front door of the house open and turned to see Granger's form in the doorway. I stood frozen by the car looking at him. He was looking back at me like he was wondering what I wanted.

Then I said, "Granger, it's me...Laurence."

He didn't move. He rubbed his eyes like he needed to clear his vision. I started walking towards him and then he yelled loud enough for all the neighbors to hear, "Oh my God! Oh my God!" He was running towards me and quickly had a death grip on me, crying out, "Laurence, Laurence, Laurence!"

Just when I thought I had to take a breath he loosened his grip and held me at arm's length, staring into my face. George came running out the door and they both had me surrounded. Alias screamed in the car.

Granger ushered me into the house while George grabbed the pet carrier and brought it in behind us. It was November, and quite warm in Phoenix. I was surrounded by man sweat and the sound of a tortured animal. Everyone was crying. Once inside, George let Alias out and removed the leash so he could explore. I was afraid he needed to pee so I ask George to get the litter box out of the back of the car. He did that, just in time.

After a long crying jag we all settled in close while I told them the short version of where I'd been. But even without my telling everything the story sounded absurd.

Granger jumped up. "I have to call Mom and Apollo right now." He did. He could barely talk. I thought he might call Manuel but he didn't. I was wondering how he and George had ended up living in my house.

Finally off the phone Granger dragged over a chair from the dining table and sat close in front of me. "Laurence, are you okay? Do you want me to call a doctor?"

"I have a friend we can call," said George. "He makes house calls."

"No, no!" I said. "I'm healthier than I've ever been. I'm, well, I'm just shook up. It's hard for me to wrap my mind around being back here."

"Mom and Dad are on their way," Granger said, explaining to me that they had moved to Phoenix after I disappeared.

I realized that Granger and George were both every bit as disoriented as I was. Everything was beyond awkward.

I started to cry, and both men sat on each side of me holding on to me for dear life.

Granger kept saying, "Oh my God, Oh my God", like those were the only words he knew.

Soon we were all just wordless and were sitting there like that when the Suns, Apollo and her friend – disturbingly called Max – walked in the door. They were all over me then. I had no idea where Alias had disappeared to.

All I could say was, "I missed you all so much."

They all wanted to know everything at once. But I had no words except,

283

"It's going to take me a while to explain what happened, and yes I was kidnapped, but I was not hurt. I'm okay, really, I am."

They all wanted me to know how awful my disappearance had been for them and for some reason that made me feel guilty, as if it had been my fault. But I did understand and for the first time I felt like I was letting them love me. All I could do was cry, hold their hands and accept their hugs.

When things settled down, George prepared a huge meal and we all sat down for dinner. I felt like I was on a different planet. I must have had a totally dazed look on my face, and I realized they also looked like they were in shock.

Finally Granger said, "You would have been fired too." Then everyone laughed, because that just too trivial.

But somehow some normal talk seemed to be in store, so he kept on talking. "The art department is just a skeleton of what it used to be. Someone is teaching drawing and design and they offer a few craft classes for grade school teachers but that's it."

Then they all starting stumbling over each other trying to catch me up on everything that happened when I was gone. I'd missed their wedding.

George said, "Nobody ever believed you wouldn't come back. We didn't know what would happen to your house, so we tried to find out what we could do to hold it for you. We tried to take over the payments, but when we went to the bank they said the house was paid for and the only thing we had to do was take care of the taxes and pay the utilities. So we made a B&B out of my place in Scottsdale and moved in here. But each time we tried to pay taxes and bills we found out they had already been paid. We thought living here was the best thing to do because it would keep the place alive. And when Granger lost his job we needed the money."

"So what on earth did you do for three years in a house on the desert?" someone asked.

"Oh my, I could write a book about that," I told them.

Apollo and her friend Max were quiet, like observers. It was just too weird for me to be around someone named Max and I averted my eyes from him. Later I would learn that Apollo had met Max at work at her job in Los Alamos and they had started a new business that only extreme geeks would understand. They were now living in a mountain town near Tucson in a house Granger referred to as The Cave. It sounded suitable for an albino. They just happened to have been in Phoenix visiting Ana and Parker Sun.

When I finally asked about Manuel, Granger slapped his forehead then pulled out his cell and called him. There was no answer so he left a message saying. "You have to call me immediately!" But he didn't tell him why.

Slowly people trickled out and by nine o'clock I was exhausted. It had been too long since I'd been around so many people! Granger led me to the guest room which he explained had been waiting for me for years. They had moved my stuff from the master bedroom and bath into this smaller space. All my clothes hung in the closet and the bathroom articles were all there just like I'd never left. All I wanted to do was close the door and snuggle with my stressed out cat. I imagined waking up in the morning and driving back to my desert home so I could start a new painting. Seriously, I thought I would.

47: The Mail

No matter how hard I tried to distract myself, I couldn't make the voices in my head go away. Alias was also nervous and kept jumping out of bed searching the room and scratching in his litter box in the bathroom. He was used to going outside to do his business. I tried to soothe him, but I couldn't even soothe myself from that loud party going on in my head. When I lived in this house I thought I couldn't hear the traffic, but now I didn't just hear it, it roared outside my windows and I could feel the presence of Granger and George in the other room. Even people I loved seemed too close.

I must have slept some because when I woke up I couldn't remember where I was. I had finally escaped into my dreams which had taken me back into the desert house with my phantom friends, my studio, and my garden. The commotion here in Phoenix was both heavenly and terrible. The clock said 5:15 – too early for me be awake. I got up, threw on the clothes and moccasins, grabbed my rabbit skin bag and shuffled around the living room looking for the pet carrier. I could be gone before anyone else got up. I'd be back at my house in the desert by the afternoon. When I couldn't find the carrier, I decided to make a cup of tea instead and see if I could calm down.

From the kitchen I could see that someone was sleeping on the sofa. So this is how it's going to be, I thought. I searched the cabinets for my favorite teas and found them right where I usually kept them. I boiled water in a pan so as not to wake the couch surfer with the burbling of the electric water boiler.

When I sat down at the table and began to sip my tea, I noticed two certified envelopes addressed to me and postmarked two days ago. I was looking at them suspiciously when the body on the sofa began to stir. I turned my back on the person so I wouldn't wake him and have to meet someone new. I assumed he would go back to sleep. I assumed he was a he.

I kept staring at the official looking envelopes. It had been so long since I'd gotten any mail, it was an effort to make sense of it. When I looked up, Manuel was standing in front of me. He was wearing striped pajama bottoms and a sleeveless t-shirt, his hair was disheveled and he needed to shave. He said in a very quiet voice. "Laurence?" He knelt down in front of me looking into my face. Then he said, "I like your hair."

We both burst into laughter. Then he stood up, pulled me up and held me gently as though I were a wounded bird. "You don't have to say anything," he whispered. He gently lead me back into the guest room where we scooted the cat over and lay down together, my head on his chest. He stroked my hair and I felt his warm tears on my head. Alias purred.

We fell asleep like that and woke up around eleven to a quiet house. "They went to work," he said.

"Where do they work?"

"The Sanctuary."

"It's still there?"

"Still there and thriving."

"Granger works there too?"

"Part time, and he teaches at the Arts Center."

"What about you?"

"Still hanging in there at the university."

"Tucson didn't cut the art department?"

"A little, but nothing like what happened in Phoenix."

"I didn't miss the politics."

"You don't have to talk about things until you are ready. I thought you'd be skinny and poor, but you look like a mountain woman, all brown and muscular. I thought I'd have to take care of you. I don't think you are going to give me that opportunity."

"Desert woman, not mountain."

"Sorry. Whatever. I'm just glad you're back."

"I went straight to your house yesterday on the way back, but I saw you get out of the car with a woman. I didn't know what had happened when I was gone, so I just drove on."

"Cecilia, my assistant. Married with two kids. She's teaching my classes today. You would like her. She's very organized and keeps my studio and office like it should be. She's teaching me to be tidy."

"I love her already," I said.

We spent that entire day in the house alone. It was good because talking to only one other person made it easier. He listened intently, not interrupting, but I could tell by the expressions on his face that he wasn't sure what to believe. I was sure he was wondering if what I was saying was true or that I was crazy. And that was with my leaving out stories about Alice, Romero and the Queen. What he did understand was the drive to paint, and how I could have made myself at home in such a remote place. I told him about painting the image of him with the fish. It was because I'd hoped he or

288

someone would see it and recognize it was me doing the painting.

"It worked," he said. "It lead me on a wild goose chase, but it caused me never to give up on your coming back. I was sorry I had to quit trying to save you, but I never again thought you were dead. The police gave up long ago. We never saw any more of your paintings, but we knew you were somewhere painting."

"I had nothing else to do but paint and take care of a small garden. And when I finally met another person, he was a recluse like me, so we left each other alone to our work."

"I wish I could see the work," he said.

"I have photos." I showed them all to him on my iPad. And told him stories about the process of painting them.

"Wow, Laurence. These are great! You actually have no idea where they are?"

"Nope, but someone must have sold them, if you saw one in a gallery."

We were sitting at the dining table so I picked up the two envelopes addressed to me on the table. "Do you think I should open these?"

He held them looking them over carefully and said, "They look important."

"Not advertising?"

"No."

So I finally opened one of them. "It's from my bank," I said, groaning and not looking at it. I handed it to him. "You look at it, I'm scared."

He did, and his eyes went round. "Hmm. It's a bank statement. It says you have opened an account with eleven million dollars!"

"Right! You're kidding me. Tell me the truth." I slapped his knee.

"Look!" he said.

He showed me. "I don't have eleven million dollars! This is a joke. I'm probably in the hole for eleven million. They're probably charging me for rent, groceries, and art supplies too!"

"No look, it's right here," he pointed.

I looked and took the bank statement out of his hand. "Is this real? You know how they send those fake checks."

"Looks real to me. I use the same bank. It's their stationery. Open the other one."

This time I looked at the envelope myself. I studied it for a long time before opening it. "It says they are happy to handle my endowment for the The Castle School...what? Oh my God!"

Still holding the paper, I stood and walked over to the kitchen window and looked out into the yard that once was mine. Then glanced down at the document again, this time reading it through tears. It was definitely official.

"What's The Castle School?"

"Oh Manuel, it will take me a long time to explain."

"Well, I have a long time to listen." He was now standing beside me. He took the papers and looked them over. "What Castle School?"

"I think I need to go to the bank and find out what is going on." Snatching the papers out of his hand, I started walking towards the door without my purse or anything else.

"Good idea, Laurence, but it's Sunday. So you have the rest of the day to tell me all about this school.

"Oh," I said, stopping halfway. I turned and headed for the couch. He followed.

"Promise me you won't think I've gone crazy."

"I don't know. Tell me everything, then I'll decide."

Epilogue

A few days later, a financial adviser named Jason called, saying he worked for a company called Educational Investments. He told me he was being paid a handsome salary to help me with all the money I now had in my bank account, and the endowment and other investments that kept showing up. He had been hired by the CEO and didn't know who owned the company. He ended up becoming a good friend and an important part of The Castle School family.

I spent a few months with Granger and George while reorienting myself into the hectic world of what I call the 'habitat for extreme extraverts'. I spent a lot of days holed up in their guest bedroom, reading and drawing. I was the official owner of the house, but I quickly began to think of it as theirs.

I spent weekends with Manuel at his place in Tucson where we made plans for us and The Castle School. We both preferred to live in Tucson and build the school there, but we decided it needed to happen in the state capital where Queen Ellie had once lived. We found a place that reminded us of Tucson. The property had a huge house with two ballrooms that could be used for studios, and 10 acres of land with a huge pond that was fed by a natural spring. It was perfect for the kind of school we wanted to build.

It was easy to find Leonardo by calling his brother, Alberto, who turned out to be a famous poet. He came to see us right away bringing Sophia with him. His wife Abril had divorced her second husband and she and Leonardo were dating again. "Taking it slow," he said.

He still looked a bit like a wild man, but was wearing new clothes, a t-shirt with a coyote riding a bicycle, and some black jeans. Sophia was a beautiful and very bright little girl with a warm smile and a head of thick black curly hair. Leonardo told me that when he had used my computer in the desert he had done a lot of research about alternative schools, and had started teaching at one in Phoenix. He told me that he had wanted to go back to the desert to see if I was ready to leave, but Hernandez had paid him a visit in Phoenix and told him that it was best not to go back. Not just for his own sanity, but that he needed to leave me alone to complete my own healing process. He said it was very hard for him, but he made himself stay away. He had been ecstatic to hear from me. We would always share an understanding of how it was. Everyone else could only hear stories.

Leonardo's moccasins and handbags had become collectors' items. They sold for thousands of dollars all over the world, and were shown in museums. But most of all, he loved being a staff member of The Castle School.

Within five years the school was a full non-profit alternative school. We decided to use the Sudbury model of education, where students are solely responsible for their education, their learning methods, their evaluation, and their environment. We also embraced the Waldorf philosophy. We had staff members, not teachers. We believed that children were naturally responsible and motivated to learn, just as they had learned to walk and speak. We knew they would spend a lot of time socializing and that was the natural way for them to behave and learn. Staff members were always on hand to answer questions and help the students when they wanted it, but they did not tell them what to do. In our school there were no grade levels. There was no reason to separate the students by age. They socialized and learned from each other. Each week there were meetings run by the students where day-to-day issues were discussed and voted on. I won't go into more details about the school, but information about Sudbury and Waldorf schools is easy to find on the internet. I suggest you check it out.

Also, I cannot tell you the exact location of The Castle School. I can tell you that there are many alternative schools in the United States and if you are meant to find them, you will.

I never found out who kidnapped me or where the money came from. Occasionally Apollo would say something that led me to suspect that she and her partner Max were somehow involved. I also discovered that others had been kidnapped. Not just artists but scientists, writers, philosophers, and more. New schools were popping up in Phoenix and in other cities all over the country. Again, I cannot tell you where, but if you ask your Higher Power to guide you, you will certainly find them.

A lot of people ask me what happened to all those paintings? Well, they've been seen all over the world. Paintings done by the famous deceased artist, Mr. Laurence Donahue. There are even photos of him in his studio, news and magazine articles and several books about his life. He even shows up in college textbooks. Occasionally I would hear that one of his paintings would sell for as high as sixty million dollars. Does it matter to me that I don't get credit? Would it matter to you if you got what I got at the end of the ordeal? Probably not. I've never even tried to make any claims on the paintings. Who would believe my story anyway? It did make me wonder about the artists in history books. Who knows how many stories are made up and believed. Didn't we all use to believe that Christopher Columbus discovered America? We learned that in history books in public schools. So be it. Sometimes I ask myself if this is a moral issue, a big fat lie. But as I think things through I rationalize that everyone is happy, no one is actually getting hurt. And all that money is going to a really great cause. I question truth a lot and find that no story is ever really true. As Alice once said, "No words are ever true."

Manuel and I kept painting in our studios and sold our work in several galleries in Scottsdale and Phoenix. Once in a while someone would tell me my paintings reminded them of that famous guy. By then I was married to Manuel and had taken his last name. So most people never knew my last name was also the same as "the famous guy." The kids at the school called me Lorie. My name is now Lorie Martinez.

Manuel and I were staff members at the school only because the students continued to vote on having us. Granger and George ran the school cafeteria and people came to visit the school just to enjoy a healthy lunch with exceptional children. Carlos and Jesus, my former landscapers were on board to help the students grow a huge vegetable and flower garden. They and their families lived on the campus. All of us loved helping in the kitchen.

Alice and Romero lived somewhere in the back of my mind. I was able to remember their faces so I painted images of them and Queen Ellie and her astronaut king, and hung them in the school cafeteria. When the kids asked who those people were, I told them they were the founders of The Castle School. There will be more stories available in the future about Alice, Romero, Queen Ellie and her king.

Once, Manuel, Leonardo and I tried to find the house on the desert. The road that connected to the highway was easy to find, but all my markers were gone and we found ourselves in a maze. Leonardo also tried to find the way to his cabin, but also never reached his destination. He said he didn't try very hard because he didn't want to go to the place where he had once felt so down and out.

We think the arroyo may have taken out the road. I kept getting out of the car trying to find the view I had from the windows, but there were too many dirt roads heading off in every direction, so we gave up. I guess I could have tried harder, perhaps called Leonardo's brother, but I didn't want to bother him. Driving around on those roads seemed to help Manuel understand a little better about where I had been taken. He just kept saying, "And I went all the way to Hungary looking for you!"

As for me, I could not be more pleased with how things turned out. Manuel and I love having our studios in one building. We both encourage each other and support our individual painting styles.

I finally told Manuel about Romero and Alice. He wasn't as shocked by my story as I had feared he would be. He too had read and studied about Los Brujos on the Sonoran desert. Someday I hope to be taken by train to the place they live at the base of the mountains. If that happens I may tell you all about it.

I have to admit that, as weird as it all was, and as hard as it was, my experience in the desert shook me out of a dazed trance that I was living in, and awakened me to the true gift of life. I love living in a reality where my life's purpose is about providing an environment where children can grow up always knowing who they are. Never believing that someday they will grow up and become somebody. Because they already are somebody. People should not have to spend their lives trying to find out who they are. I visualize every day that The Castle School is inspiring others. And I'm eternally grateful that I've been given an opportunity to participate in a project that makes a difference in the world.

Many of the students of The Castle School are now entrepreneurs, artists, musicians, teachers, doctors, lawyers, architects, engineers and more. We have had no drug users, drop outs, or anything close to a suicide. The most important thing about our graduates is their ability to live peacefully in the world; all of them finding ways to contribute to society in healthy and helpful ways.

The years I spent teaching at the university were valuable, because it gave me an opportunity to see what didn't quite work. I still encourage education of any kind, but not all people learn the same way, and too many worthy and bright people fall through the cracks. It's important that parents and educators learn to meet each child on their own terms and not force them to fit into a regime that can cause damage. Some people are fine with ordinary educational systems. So those schools deserve and need to exist. I say let's be sure we choose what works for each individual. A world with educated people will be a better world.

Granger and George adopted four children which made Ana and Parker happy grandparents. We sold the house in Phoenix and the two men built a house on the school grounds, so they and the children could be a part of the community. Apollo and Max were married and continued living in their cave in the desert. I love talking to Max. It's like we've known each other for a long time. I've never asked either of them outright if they had anything to do

294

with the kidnapping. I guess I just don't want to know.

Alias lived to be fifteen years old and died a peaceful death. His grave is on The Castle School campus and Granger made a giant cat sculpture for his monument. The younger kids like to climb on it. We have other pets now who live on campus for the students to enjoy and learn to care for.

Looking back on my life, I am grateful for my crazy time spent on the desert. Without it, I don't think I would be where I am now – living in a utopia – which, by the way, is only a made up story and a prayer for a healthier, happier planet.

When Javalina Learn to Fly

Made in the USA
Columbia, SC
27 July 2018